Death Without Dignity

Joseph Meigs

authorHOUSE®

AuthorHouse™
1663 Liberty Drive
Bloomington, IN 47403
www.authorhouse.com
Phone: 1-800-839-8640

First published by AuthorHouse   3/26/2010

ISBN: 978-1-4490-9715-8 (e)
ISBN: 978-1-4490-9713-4 (sc)
ISBN: 978-1-4490-9714-1 (hc)

Library of Congress Control Number: 2010923949

Printed in the United States of America
Bloomington, Indiana

This book is printed on acid-free paper.

Chapter 1

I lived thirty-four years before coming upon someone freshly murdered. In fact, up until September 3, 2009, I was never the first person to come upon ANYONE that had just died—from any cause.

The closest I came to being first on the scene occurred the day Aunt Gertrude died of a stroke, when I was eleven, but I was at least the fifth or sixth person to get to her after she fell flat on the kitchen floor, while making a rhubarb pie. My cousins and my uncle and my mother all beat me to the discovery by at least fifteen minutes. Mother even had to drive eight miles from the Set-and-Go Beauty Salon, where she was getting a perm when her sister's stroke hit, while I was just two doors away from Aunt Gertie's place, playing house (or was it playing doctor?) with Betty Sue Worthington. The only people I preceded at the scene were the ambulance crew. It was just as well that Gertie never finished making the pie. I never liked rhubarb.

Now that I'm an adult, I must admit that I've occasionally speculated about being first to discover a body. I thought about it one day when I was in the deep rough on the Burnt Tree Golf Course, over in the nearby town of Raysville, Georgia, forty or fifty yards off the fairway in a thick growth of pines. Something made me half expect to find a corpse, not necessarily a golfer's. Such morbid thoughts were probably prompted by the dire nature of my golf game at the time.

I got a similar premonition when I was jogging on an isolated trail a couple of miles from my house, suddenly fearing that I might trip over a body that had been dumped there, partially covered with leaves and pine straw, more morbid thoughts, this time, maybe caused by a lack of oxygen to my out-of-shape lungs.

I certainly did not expect to find a corpse on a college campus—in an academic building, in a bathroom stall, at 9:15 in the morning. But there lay one of my colleagues, Hugh Disner, Associate Professor of English, Assistant Dean of the College of Arts and Sciences, at Northwest Georgia University—father of four? five? six? children—husband of a beleaguered wife—and driver of an ugly van.

Finding him there both horrified and surprised me, since I had heard him—alive—no more than five minutes earlier, when I first attempted to visit the men's room on the top floor of the McAddle English Building, where my office is located.

I had postponed my visit because I could hear Disner singing inside—something from HMS PINAFORE, I think, with lots of "no never's" thrown in. Hearing his singing was made easier by the fact that the door was still propped open, with a wooden stob, inserted there by the cleaning crew the night before, who, no doubt, hoped to facilitate the drying process of the mopped floor. Disner had not bothered to kick out the stob, I guess because he did not mind that his singing and even the noises from doing his "business" could be heard by a hall audience, particularly those pausing long enough to sip from the drinking fountain to the left of the door, or those waiting for the elevator five feet from this same door to the right.

I had returned a few minutes later to find the door closed and no sounds emanating from Disner, so I figured the coast—or maybe the air—was clear, though I knew from past experiences that he sometimes graded papers while sitting on the john. After making sure that a man drinking at the fountain was not going into the toilet (I value my privacy), I pushed open the door.

I did not actually discover Disner until I entered the last stall, the fourth one, not paying attention to the first three, but once I was in number four, I could not miss him. His right leg and wingtip-shoed foot invaded my stall by a good eighteen inches, the left leg and foot appearing directly under the wall between our stalls, the two legs joined by his green trousers and a pair of yellow jockey shorts, both of which were stretched between his ankles.

My first reaction was a sense of territoriality. *Why the hell are you sticking your leg in my stall, you idiot? Isn't your stall big enough? Just like a professor who has become a partial administrator!*

But territoriality gave way to alarm, and I left my stall and pushed open his already ajar door. He was slumped forward in front and slightly to the side of the toilet, as if he had slid off it. His left arm was splayed out

2

on the tile floor, his hand curled around a wad of tissue paper. His bent right arm lay in the bowl, his hand hooked over the front of it. His face was slightly turned toward the bowl as if he were about to throw up in it. His mouth was frozen in the shape of one who had just said, "Okay?" but it could also have been "Oh, no!" or "Oh, Hell!" I'm not an expert on visual linguistics.

The only positive note was that his shirt draped over his private parts.

What made me think that he had been murdered and was not simply the victim of a stroke, a heart attack, an aneurysm, or the like? Just above his right eyebrow, maybe two inches from the top of his nose, gaped a brownish-red hole about the circumference of a pencil. It had leaked— before his heart actually stopped pumping, I guess— a stream of blood, which had curled down his cheek, forming—the wound and the trail of blood—the shape of a semicolon. The trail of blood had dripped off his chin onto his yellow dress shirt, skirting along besides his chest pocket, in which a pen rested precariously, ready to topple out. The blood had eventually found its way down onto his green pants, circling around his pocket, from which his wallet protruded. I thought that if it were not for the blood, Disner would be a loyal representative of the University on School Colors Day, since yellow and green are the school's colors. As it was, with the addition of the blood, he reminded me of a Bolivian flag.

But I had taken for granted that Disner was dead. What if, despite the hole in his head, he was still alive?

Nah—one look at his eyes proved otherwise, for they were fixed wide open and staring at nothing, the kind of position that bystanders in movies always correct by shutting the lids with a gentle downward tug using the thumb and middle finger. I figured I'd better not touch them, in case, like in the movie MANHUNTER, there might be fingerprints on the lids from the killer. I did not care to look too long at his open eyes. I did push his pen down into his shirt pocket to keep it from falling on the tile floor, and I shoved his wallet farther into his back pocket.

Figuring it was time to act like a rational and responsible citizen, I ran to my office and called Campus Security. I left it up to them to bring in the Emergency Medical Team and members of the County Sheriff's Patrol. I then rushed back to the men's room—a crime scene now, though it certainly should have been off limits for a murder—being better suited for some kind of safe zone, like home base in a kid's game. Disner was just as I had left him, except that some of the blood on his polyester pants had slid down onto the blue tile floor, the price one pays, I suppose, when wearing material with no capacity for absorption. I thought about the cleanup crew and how they probably would not like having to deal with bloodstained grout.

While I waited for the police and emergency people, I pondered the nature of death. There certainly was no dignity in death here, what with the commode and toilet paper and Disner akimbo. Even Elvis could not have looked noble when found dead in the john.

And I wondered about the cliches and archetypes associated with death. Did Disner see his life flash before him as he died? Did he whip through Elizabeth Kubla-Ross's five stages of death at the last moment—anger, denial, bargaining, fear, and acceptance? Did he feel as if he were traveling down a long tunnel with a light at the end? Did he see a psychopomp coming for his soul—the Grim Reaper, an angel of death, Gabriel, Michael, a pale horse, a crow, a sparrow, a loon, or the wind? Given the cramped quarters in the john, I'd opt for the wind. Besides, if the Grim Reaper had shown up, he might have contradicted his own name and snickered at Disner. The wind would definitely be more objective in such matters.

And what had the killer said, "Eat lead, Professor," or "Take that, Disner," or "How do you like them apples, Hugh?" Or did he shoot Disner without saying a word?

And who the hell would have killed Disner and why? Was it a spur of the moment slayer, driven to madness by Disner's singing or his occupying a stall too long, or for not kicking out the stob and shutting the door to the hall? Had the killer knocked at Disner's stall door or had Disner left that door open as he did the main door? Was it a former or present student of Disner's, who had heard Disner finish one too many declarative sentences in a lecture with his interrogative "Okay?" Had Disner made a colleague jealous because he had been appointed Assistant Dean of Arts and Sciences, a position that meant a reduced teaching load? Was it a prospect for a teaching job that Disner had picked up from the airport, as he had me when I first came to interview at NGU, and who had sworn revenge, while riding in the car, for Disner's slow driving or for his incessant gibberish about group discussions, holistic grading, textbook selection, heuristics, or hermeneutics? Was it his wife, who wanted revenge for his keeping her pregnant for all those years and making her drive that ugly van?

Wouldn't I be a prime suspect? I'm Tyler Davidson, assistant professor of English, in his fifth year, and I have never liked Disner. As a matter of fact, I have often added to my "Cask of Amontillado" list of a "thousand injuries of Fortunato [i.e., Disner] I had borne as I best could," beginning the moment he picked me up at the airport, right on through to the ordeals of getting trapped with him in the men's room, while he tried to engage me in topics germane to our field—while he was whizzing—on to his tediousness in every committee meeting or workshop we had both attended and his pomposity as an administrator (manifested by his thumping on the cushioned armrests on his administrative chair whenever he spoke, as if he were the king on his throne), all culminating in his seeming resistance to my receiving tenure. I had a disdain for him that everyone—except maybe Disner himself, and perhaps one or two of the teachers in physical education— was aware of, since I tended to grimace conspicuously whenever I saw him.

Should I alter anything to make myself look less suspicious? No, I would not want to interfere with legitimate police work, and, besides, what could I possibly do to make myself seem less guilty? Remove the toilet paper from Disner's left hand? Shove his legs and feet more into his own stall? Wipe my fingerprints from the door of his stall?

It would all be pointless. I'd just have to take my chances. After all, I was only guilty—up to that point—of a lack of displaying proper sorrow. I think I can be excused if I have difficulty showing pity for the death of someone named Disner. I would have the same problem if the President of NGU, Altoona Popson, had died, or the head of the English Department, Torrance Bwanger. With names like those, you need to stay alive.

I was tempted to look through Disner's wallet—reenact the scene in ALL QUIET ON THE WESTERN FRONT, in which a German soldier goes through the belongings of a dying/dead Frenchman, looking at his family pictures and developing a degree of empathy for his enemy—but I decided against such a move.

Exactly what should I be doing until the police arrive? Watch over the body, as in a wake, but how does one do that? Straddle and hold onto it? But why? Disner certainly was not going anywhere. Should I just guard the stall, in case someone came in to use the facilities, saying to him, "I'm sorry but you'll have to go somewhere else; there's a dead man in here"? Or should I stand guard at the entrance to the entire men's room, maybe find, in the maintenance storage closet, one of those sandwich boards placed in the doorway by the clean-up crew, warning about a wet floor, and set it outside the main door with a note attached: "Closed due to a corpse"?

However, before I had time to act, as I stood holding open the stall door, a student entered the room and strode in my direction, but stopped when he saw me. I studied his most salient features, in case the police asked me about him—medium height and build, baggy jeans, t-shirt under a plaid long sleeved shirt, spiked brown hair, a cheek tattoo that looked like a wound caused by briars, an earring in his left ear, and a tongue pearl that I would bet made him lisp—a description that fit approximately ninety percent of the males on campus and about fifty percent of the females. He was not carrying books, but that was par for the course with the students I knew. I was relieved by the fact that he did not brandish a gun.

I must have appeared to be holding the door open just for him, in fact, inviting him to join me in the stall, for he slowly began retracing his steps, eyeing me all the while, until, like Hamlet in the scene where he leaves Ophelia and exits the room without ever looking at the door, he made his escape, having never gotten close enough to the stall to see Disner. I wanted to explain to him what was going on, but figured maybe it might be best that he went away with the impression that I was a bathroom pervert.

But then a disturbing thought—what if the killer should come back to check on his work, to finish off Disner in case he were still alive, maybe, upon seeing me in there, pretending to need to use a stall, or wash his hands, or comb his hair, so that he could catch me off guard? What would I do if he pulled a gun, the same one used to snuff Disner? Would I divert his attention by pointing behind him, as if someone else had just come in, and then wrestle away the gun when he turned, jamming my fingers into his eyes and karate chopping him in the throat, as I had in my hero fantasies? Would I pretend I had not even seen Disner, casually wash and dry my hands, while whistling, and then saunter out, hoping I wouldn't get a pencil-sized hole in my head too?

What if, in fact, the student who had just entered and left was that killer and he was now standing in the hall, ready to take me out?

Dummy, the killer is long gone and now there is yet another student wondering about the weirdness of the faculty at NGU. I knew I was being paranoid. Time to guard the main door.

But first I took one more peek at Disner, and it was then that the horror of his murder finally hit. Here was a man who had entered the toilet, with no thoughts of violence, but now was dead, fragile as five year old, sun-baked masking tape. I gazed at him for approximately a minute, thinking that by concentrating on him I could make him come back to life (as I had attempted to do with a dog I once owned, who got run over by a car), but the longer I stared, the more upsetting the scene became. I found myself getting sick. It was only seconds before I was barfing in the first stall.

Chapter 2

After I recovered from throwing up, I did take up a position guarding the main door, dropping the idea about the sandwich board, instead leaning up against the door with my legs and arms spread, imitating Leonardo DaVinci's proportionate man spread-eagle in the circle.

It was now 9:45. I soon had to turn away two professors from the English Department—Gaylord Cherry and Glenn Glick—neither of whom I considered to be particularly suspicious, though I suppose I could report their attempts to enter the men's room with some slight incriminations. Cherry seemed nervous when I told him to use the facilities on the next floor, rubbing his forehead as if he were trying to smooth out the furrows. I figured he most likely was upset about having to hold his pee all the way down the steps to another men's room. Glick asked, "Why, is there a dead body in there?" but then cheerily marched off down the hall, never asking for an explanation. Realistically, they both probably figured someone had written graffiti on the walls, or smeared the floor with stercoraceous matter.

What was keeping the police and emergency team? Was this one of several murders the same day on campus and Disner and I would have to dutifully wait our turn, as if we were in long line at the First Commercial Bank on payday?

Finally, a wave of people showed up, a mixture of deputies from the sheriff's office, campus police, and members of the Emergency Medical Team, most exiting from the elevator, although two campus policemen actually came up the five flights of stairs. I motioned superfluously into the men's room and mumbled "third stall," knowing that no one could miss Disner. A sheriff's deputy stayed in the hall and asked me, "You the one

7

that called this in?" He talked as if his had peanut butter in his mouth, the healthful kind with less oil.

"Yes, I'm the one."

"Who's the victim?"

"He's Doctor Hugh Disner."

"A teacher here?"

"Yes, in the English Department."

"And you are . . . .?"

"I'm Tyler Davidson. I teach here too."

"Well, Professor Davidson, don't go anywhere. We'll need to get a lot more information." With that, he joined the rest of the crew inside the men's room.

While the main bunch of investigators and medical staff tended to Disner and the crime scene, a campus cop, who appeared to be as young as most of the students on campus, first propped the door open with the stob, then stretched yellow police tape from the drinking fountain on one side to the elevator on the other. Why he did not wait for the investigation to be completed before doing this, I was not sure, but everyone entering or exiting had to climb over the tape, which hung at crotch height for the average man, forcing the short-legged people to stretch on tiptoes to climb over it, a ritual that was repeated numerous times while I waited. No one ever balked and tore down the tape. I guessed that when it comes to doors of men's rooms, once any piece of equipment has been officially placed by someone in authority—whether it be a stob or police tape—it becomes sacrosanct, like tags on pillows and mattresses that remain attached because people fear flouting the manufacturer's dictum not to remove them, under penalty of law.

At about 10:10, after a flurry of activity inside, including, most likely, an official confirmation that Disner was indeed dead, a man dressed in a light brown suit stepped off the elevator. He looked to be someone who never told a joke nor laughed at anyone else's. His face made me think of Dick Tracy—not the Warren Beatty version, but rather the angular-jawed cartoon. Speaking with a bass voice deeper than Darth Vader's, he asked, to no one in particular, "What have we got here?"

The campus cop who had taped off the crime scene stepped forward and said, "Who are you?"

"I'm Detective John Smockley, from the county sheriff's office."

"Oh, sorry, Detective, I'm new with the campus police department. It appears that a man's been murdered."

"I assume the victim is in here," Smockley said, gesturing toward the men's room.

"Yes, he is. Go right in. He hasn't moved, if you know what I mean." The campus cop snickered, but then clammed up quickly, biting off the last syllable of his "wa-ha-ha," as Smockley glared at him without the first hint of a smile.

"There's nothing funny about a murder, Officer . . ., Officer . . ., I didn't get your name."

"That's Dunceton, sir. Officer Dunceton. And, of course you're right. There is nothing funny about this."

Smockley wheeled and climbed over the police tape. After he had disappeared inside, Dunceton shrugged to everyone standing about him and said, "Didn't anyone think it was just a bit funny, that guy getting snuffed while sitting on the toilet?" I wanted to agree, but thought it unwise. When none of us responded, he slunk to the drinking fountain, where he masked his chagrin by slurping enough water to fill a gallon jug.

After ten minutes or so, Smockley reappeared, stepping over the police tape, this time snagging it with his trailing foot so that it bowed out almost to the breaking point. Dunceton, who had been leaning against the wall by the drinking fountain, tried to stifle a laugh, but failed. I was glad he did, since I myself came close to chuckling too.

Smockley turned and again glared at him. "You find something else funny, Officer Dunceton?" he asked.

"Uh, no Sir. Sorry." He returned to the drinking fountain and began another round of slurps, keeping his back to Smockley.

Smockley stared at him before turning to me. "I'm Detective John Smockley. You're Professor Davidson, and you're the one who found Professor Disner dead, right?" He took out a small spiral notebook like those I'd seen selling for ninety-nine cents in a five-and-dime store.

"Yes, that's right."

"What time did you discover Professor Disner?"

"About a quarter after nine."

"Did you move anything or touch him?"

"No."

"We'll be checking, you know, for fingerprints and other evidence."

"I realize that. I did push open his already opened stall."

"What prompted you to do that?"

"I felt the need to check on him. I had just seen his legs sticking into the next stall. I thought maybe he had received an injury while sitting on the john too long."

"Obviously he received more than an injury. How'd you know he was dead?"

"Oh, come on. You've seen him yourself. He's got a bullet hole in his forehead."

"Did you hear anything?"

"No—well—yes, earlier."

"What do you mean?"

"About fifteen minutes before I found him dead, I heard him singing."

"What was he singing?"

"Something from HMS PINAFORE, I believe."

"What's that?"

"A musical."

"What does it sound like?"

"Why do you need to know that?"

"I need to collect all the evidence I can, Professor. One never knows what will be useful down the road. Now, what did it sound like?"

I hesitated, conscious of the other cops and medical personnel filling up the hall, several of whom, including the kid campus cop, were now staring at Smockley and me. "Well, Professor?" Smockley asked.

"Oh, all right, if you insist." I sang a couple of lines with "No, nevers" in them, though without Disner's bravado.

Smockley seemed to warm up a bit. "I don't care much for musicals, but I do recognize the tune. Why do you suppose he was singing that particular selection? Did it have some special meaning for folks around here?"

"Beats me."

Smockley started to write a note on his pad, but then paused and asked, "What courses do you teach?"

"English—literature—Shakespeare and the like."

"Did Professor Disner teach the same ones as you?"

"Not exactly. He covered mostly literature from a different century than I do." I thought about telling Smockley that Disner taught courses in Victorian literature while I specialized in the Renaissance, but I didn't think Smockley would know the difference.

"Then you weren't rivals for the same courses?"

"Nope—ours were almost completely different. The only courses we usually taught in common were the freshman writing courses, and neither of us particularly wanted to teach them." I did not mention that Disner and I were sometimes in competition for Honors students.

Smockley jotted down a couple of lines in his book and then asked, "Do you have any ideas about who might have been responsible for this?"

"I imagine the head of the department was. He was the one who assigned us our courses."

"No, I mean, do you have any idea who might have wanted to kill Professor Disner?"

"Oh, sorry, I thought we were still talking about schedules. I can't think of anyone who would do such a thing to Disner . . . I mean Hugh." I did not think it necessary to run through the catalogue of suspects I had thought of earlier.

"Did you see anyone in or near the men's room besides Professor Disner?"

"Oh, yes, I saw a student and then Professors Glick and Cherry." I then described the student for him.

"In your opinion would either Glick or Cherry have any reason to kill Professor Disner?"

"None that I know of. You'll have to talk with them." I took some comfort in spreading my discomfort around the department.

He asked a few more questions, which I continued to answer, without indicating my own feelings about Disner. I did mention throwing up.

It was not long, however, before I began to feel a bit edgy about being interrogated in the hall. How could any passer-by determine if I was a suspect or simply a witness? Knowing that people assume the worst, I could imagine rumors spreading that, since I was at the scene, I was somehow involved in the death of Disner. This was the year I was supposed to go up for promotion from assistant professor to associate, and it certainly would not help my case to be connected with the murder of a colleague. I could imagine a member of the promotion committee, Glick for instance, saying, "Granted, Professor Davidson has a good teaching record and has just published a new book, but wasn't he mixed up in the homicide of Hugh Disner?" I asked Officer Smockley if we could continue our questions and answers in my office.

"You feel nervous about being near the dead man, do you, Mr. Davidson?" Smockley tilted his head up and to the side after he asked this and swished what sounded like an excess of saliva around in his mouth.

He seemed to be a person I would dislike intensely—if I really got to know him, which I hoped never happened.

"Actually, yes," I answered. "Dead people give me the creeps, and, besides, I'd as soon not be seen here by the killer—if he hasn't already seen me."

"How'd you know it was a he?"

"I don't. I assumed only a male would come into a men's bathroom to do a killing. Make it SHE, if you want, or IT, or THEY. I'm not trying to be technical here. Now can we go to my office?"

"You seem agitated. Is there a reason you're agitated, Mr. Davidson?"

"No, of course not. I've just discovered a colleague dead—murdered no less, unless a stray bullet from a hunter outside the building nailed him—in a bathroom stall, in MY building, places people are supposed to be safe in, and now I'm being asked lots of questions in front of everyone who comes down the hall. Why would I possibly be agitated?"

"Okay, Mr. Davidson, calm down. I don't need to go to your office. I have no further questions at this time. But keep yourself available. I'll need more information from you after I confer with the other investigators, particularly the fingerprinting expert." He flipped shut his notebook and slid it into his shirt pocket, all the while smiling with a frozen grin, like the mannequin in the movie MAGIC.

As he climbed back over the police tape, he spoke to me one last time. "Oh, Professor, you sing pretty good." He then disappeared into the men's room, preventing me from correcting his grammar. I looked about, discovering the other hall members nodding in agreement with Smockley's comment. I hurried to my office. It was now 10:45 and I had a class at 11. I still had not peed as I had intended an hour and a half before. Damn Disner—and Smockley—and whoever killed Disner.

Chapter 3

Back in my office I scraped together some class notes for my American lit survey, realizing that I would not have time to type out the quiz for Poe's "The Tell-Tale Heart," as I had intended. I figured I could make up some questions once I arrived at the class and give them verbally. I closed my door just as the bell tower began clanging out, in largo time—or is it adagio? Which is slower?—the notes of "For the Beauty of the Earth," indicating that it was five until the hour. At the pace it was playing, the tower would be hard pressed to finish the tune before the hour came.

When I arrived at class, I debated with myself whether I should tell the students about Disner's death, but was reluctant to provide information that I knew would disrupt the session completely. I often thought that teaching was half akin to being a standup comic. Announcing a murder would certainly kill the humor. I figured if anyone brought up the murder, I would cover the subject as succinctly as I could.

No one did.

However, frequently during the quiz and the ensuing discussion of "The Tell-Tale Heart," I had visions of a dead Disner sprawled in the stall. I saw his arms and legs as I discussed the part in the story where the deranged servant/killer sawed off the old man's limbs. I recalled Disner's blood—and the toilet— while pointing out Poe's description of the killer's use of a tub while cleaning up the old man's blood. And I was reminded repeatedly of Disner's eyes with Poe's descriptions of the old man's cataracts. I saw myself being grilled by Smockley, as I covered the parts in the story with the investigators sitting in the bedroom with the killer, parts which made me identify with the narrator's nervousness, though I had nothing to hide—certainly not a man's body I had just buried under the floorboards, or toilet tiles, or whatever.

Was it my imagination or were the students in the class beginning to look at me as if I were a killer, or at least a mad man. Even though I had not mentioned the incident, I still felt as if they knew something, even suspected me of foul play. Was I gesticulating wildly like the narrator in the story? Was I pacing the floor with heavy strides like he did? Was my voice getting louder—louder—LOUDER? Could they hear the beating of my heart? I found myself imitating, first, what I imagined to be the killer's voice in the story, but also Disner's voice, even throwing in a couple of "okay's" at the end of irrefutable, declarative sentences. I stopped short of singing "no never."

And I made a couple of other tell-tale errors. "Do you think Disner—I mean the old man—knew what was coming?" I asked at one point. "The men's room should not be where someone dies," I declared later, prompting a lot of strange looks from the class and a comment from Callie Umpton, "Don't you mean the bedroom?"

I began thinking think about the possibility that the killer could be in this very room. How about Stanley Stopman? He had the look of a killer—particularly when I gave quizzes, scowling at me and pulling at his fingers until the knuckles popped. How about Simon Fitzwater, who was always edgy, glancing away quickly when I looked at him, darting his eyes to the ceiling, then the blackboard, then to the floor, back to me again, as I sensed, only when I had shifted my gaze to someone else.

Reading through Poe's story did eventually help me become partially optimistic. If the killer were in the classroom, maybe he would blurt out a confession, like guilty characters seemed to always do in the courtroom at the end of Perry Mason episodes, maybe even while answering a question I directed at him, along the lines of, "Yes, Professor Davidson, I did think that the title was ironic, when we consider what's going on in the narrator's mind, and . . . [pause] . . . and, I just murdered Professor Disner." Maybe emphasizing the ending of Poe's story, when the killer does suddenly confess, could induce the blurting out, but I would settle for simply a Freudian slip from the killer, who might say, for instance, "I'm a bit hot. Could we open the stall door, I mean the HALL door?"

But then paranoia rushed back. What if Disner's were only the first murder perpetrated by a serial killer, playing an academic version of DEATHRACE 2002 with some buddies and scoring higher or lower points depending on the ranking of the victim—with administrators like Disner receiving more points? Or worse, someone was on a revenge spree, eradicating professors, and I was on the list. I started thinking—in between questions and answers about Poe's story—why anyone sitting in front of me (or standing, as in the case of Buford Cluttle, who got cramps easily when he sat for very long) would want to kill me. Was there a ultra-conservative—maybe even a religious zealot— in the group who was offended by one of my selections, such as Walt Whitman's "Song of Myself," in which the narrator sexually describes the sea as if it is his lover, or offended by my cavalier attitude toward Jonathan Edward's piece, "Sinners in the Hands of an Angry God." Maybe Buford Cluttle blamed me for his cramps. Maybe stilted Glenda Duffledorf thought I had been checking out her legs when she wore a short skirt to class, or maybe Sally Sirenus was ticked because I DIDN'T look at her legs when she suggestively crossed them ala Sharon Stone in BASIC INSTINCT.

When class finally ended, I hustled to the men's room down the hall from the classroom and made a long overdue visit to pee—after first leaning down to check under the stalls, fortunately finding no dead body this time. While there, I mulled over the fact that I had started this term— as I am sure most professors do at the beginning of each semester—with the same optimism that an overweight person begins a new diet. But, now, in addition to the usual deflators of having lots of badly written papers to grade, obligations to attend a plethora of useless committee meetings, and continuing publication pressures, I was somehow involved in the murder of a member of the faculty—one that was a half administrator to boot.

After I finished—once more checking under the stalls—I climbed the stairs to the main office of the English Department, to talk with the head, Bwanger, figuring that if I did not find him, he would be looking for me. He was there, all right, along with several other faculty members, engaged in a worried discussion of Disner's murder.

"Oh, Tyler, just the man we wanted to see. Tell us about what you saw. The police told me—us—that you discovered the body." He was wringing his hands as if he were washing up for surgery, while he quizzed me with his face. The rest of the group—except my friend Ben Sturgeon—fell in behind him as if to physically support Bwanger should he fall backwards when I answered. Sturgeon simply sat down with an amused expression.

I was not exactly keen on drawing even more attention to myself, but relayed to them essentially what I'd seen, leaving out, this time, the fact that I had thrown up. After I finished, a process delayed by interjections, questions, and reactions, various members offered their opinions on the identity of the perpetrator.

Bwanger was sure that it was a disgruntled student and warned us to lock our office doors and be careful about being alone in any bathroom with a student. Zelda Huzlet, gesturing as if she were doing the macarena, was certain that someone from another department had killed Disner, so that his administrative post could be filled by someone outside the English Department. She warned us to keep an eye out for anyone from another department using our toilet facilities. Gertrude Lonzer opted for a thief, while Glenn Glick (after berating me for not informing him of Disner's death when he and Cherry visited the men's room while I was standing guard) opined that the killer could be an outside agitator, though he could not come up with any issues that had brought in agitators. Ben Sturgeon simply snorted, "Probably was the administration; they like to kill people just to improve accretion rates."

While the secretary of the department, Yvonda Dunkirk, vociferously defended the notion that someone from our rival university, Southwestern Georgia University, had done the deed, I slipped out and headed for my office, making sure I detoured the crime scene. Once I rested safely behind my locked door, I read my e-mail, beginning with one sent out by Bwanger, notifying the department about Disner's murder. I was sadly unmoved by the message, I suppose because I had already seen the real body, but also because e-mail has a way of depersonalizing any message, even one about death. Plus, it was from Bwanger, who had never been, in my thinking, a great purveyor of sadness. How much pathos can a person generate, who usually sends out notices about no pay raises and mishaps with the coffee pot. To top it all off, the notice was about Disner—making me realize that I have a pecking order of sympathy and Disner ranked down there with people I read about who died while drag racing in heavy traffic.

Chapter 4

After finishing my last class for the day, I felt the need to escape. Being confined to my office made me feel as if I were a live version of the old man with the bad eyes in Poe's story, trapped under the planks in his bedroom. But walking in the halls was not much better, since I kept half expecting to stumble upon another body. I didn't dare visit a men's room.

I had a strange need to be engulfed by people, but not the ones associated with the University, so I drove to the Walmart in Raysville. Before I climbed out of my car, I looked in the rearview mirror for a moment. Did I have the appearance of a killer? I tried to envision the typical face of one portrayed in movies—carbuncular face, scars from a childhood disease, beady eyes, big eyebrows, small, arty eyeglasses like those worn by Karl Marx (or maybe horn-rimmed ones like Buddy Holly wore), stringy hair, scruffy beard. I didn't have any of those features, except my hair needed washing and almost looked stringy.

Inside the store I shopped for items I did not really need, filling my cart with an eclectic assortment of inexpensive items—batteries, gift wrapping, a small picture frame, a bottle of aspirin, a box of saltine crackers. I roamed the aisles for more than an hour, letting Walmart work an odd sort of therapeutic magic.

Finally, my disdain for the crowds and noisy public announcements grew stronger than the mixture of feelings resulting from discovering a dead Disner—anger, anxiety, and repulsion. I checked out and drove home, where I fixed dinner, careful to avoid foods with colors that reminded me of the scene in the toilet stall earlier—red, yellow, and green—thus eliminating about three-fourths of my usual diet. I opted for foods with neutral tones, slapping together a turkey sandwich on whole wheat bread, holding the tomatoes, lettuce, cheese, and mustard.

As I ate, even with the absence of the colors of death, I still thought about Disner, particularly the hole in his forehead. Having recently taught John Donne's "Meditation Number 17," I wondered if Disner's death truly diminished me, and I wondered if the bell tower were tolling a bell for Disner right then over on campus, and if it were, was it also tolling for me, since Disner and I were not islands, but part of the same continent, the same "main," and all that.

I doubted it.

But I did think about what I was doing at the exact moment Disner was shot. Was I marking a comma splice on a badly written paper? Did I experience a tell-tale reaction, such as an eye twitch, a brief tinge of a headache—or, more appropriately, a forehead ache?

I also thought about the detective who had grilled me, Smockley, if that really was his name. Maybe I had heard his name wrong and it was actually Sprockley or Shockley or even Dockery. Whatever his name was, he obviously did not trust me. I wondered why.

I got a strong urge to call Laura Allworth, whose voice I had not heard for almost two months. Laura is the woman I love, or at least the one I did love.

She was a graduate student at NGU when I met her—at an auto repair class— working on her master's degree in the Psychology Department. She and I lived together for almost a year while she finished her thesis and taught part-time in her department. It seemed to be a perfect match—we both liked Faulkner and Flannery O'Connor, our co-favorite movie was HAROLD AND MAUDE, we both liked to hike, we were good in bed together, we laughed at the same jokes, we both liked the house to be cool, even cold, and I loved her dog Clovis.

The seeds of discord came from the disparity in our academic degrees. I already had my Ph.D. She wanted to earn hers, too. It made for competition that diluted our affection. Invariably, she would end any argument with the snide comment, "I can't win in this debate; you're the one with the doctorate." And she would frequently say, "You should have ended up with that Paradit snob; she's more on your level." Susan Paradit, associate professor of Economics, was the woman I was semi-dating when I first met Laura. I severed the relationship with Susan as soon as Laura and I became serious. I have not talked with Susan in over a year.

After receiving her master's degree, Laura began applying for acceptance into doctoral programs. Unfortunately for me, the University of California at Berkeley, nearly three thousand miles away from NGU, offered her the best package.

After she took up residence on the West Coast, I flew out to spend a whole week with her—twice. I even applied for a job at nearby San Jose State, after reading about the opening in the CHRONCLE OF HIGHER EDUCATION, but never even reached the interview stage. The visits with Laura were pleasant, if not exactly torrid.

I tried calling her a few times after the visits, but repeatedly got no answer. It was one of the few times in my life I regretted the absence of an answering machine. Her e-mail responses to my numerous messages were usually written in the style of a minimalist novelist.

I even wrote a poem for her, in a moment of acute bleakness. It went like this:

I wonder if you ever think of me
        of times of stolen glory
        and rushing ecstasy
        of moments of eyes mirroring eyes
        and hours of wordless oneness.
I wonder if you recall our days
        under the skies
        on the trails of green
        in the sun and rain and snow.

I wonder if you ever have a nagging hint
of something lost,
a longing for days
when all was found.
Now, do you think of coffee spoons
        and research tasks
        other glories, other ecstasies, other eyes,
        no thought of me at all?

A couple of weeks after I e-mailed it to her, she responded with a comment about the absence of rhyme and how overly sentimental it was. I guess she thought I wanted her to critique it for me. I wondered what grade she would have given it.

I speculated why she was drifting farther from me. I never believed that there was another person involved. She basically was a very private person who enjoyed her solitude—or being accompanied only by Clovis—so I imagined that she felt stifled by my continued interest in her, even though I was a country's breadth away from her.

Ultimately, I came to the conclusion that she simply did not love me enough to sustain our relationship, maybe not even liking me, causing me to lose much of my self-confidence, to the point that I lost all interest in women and dating for the whole year.

Little did I know that the year of apathy would soon end, due to Disner's death. In the meantime, I tried to call Laura, hearing only continuous ringing, with no answer or message—at all.

Chapter 5

Disner's obituary appeared in the Raysville Ruralite the next Tuesday—no sooner than this since the paper came out only once a week. The paper couldn't be faulted for not issuing a special edition just because one college professor got shot.

Even if I had not known Disner personally, I could have guessed that he was employed at the University—or at least was a county VIP—due to the length and language of the notice. It consisted of typical obituary information—done large.

It stated that Disner had passed away (with no mention of murder or toilet stalls) the previous Thursday and was survived by his wife, Breda, and their five children, William Shakespeare Disner, aged seventeen, Horace Walpole Disner, aged twelve, Jane Eyre Disner, aged eight, Emily Dickinson Disner, aged five, and Samuel Johnson Disner, aged four. The obit writer must have done a thorough computer search, for the names of the immediate family were followed by a plethora of surviving relatives, father, mother, father and mother-in-law, grandparents, aunts, uncles, nieces, nephews, cousins, cousins of cousins, cousins of cousins of cousins. The list had more entries than an epic cataloguing of heroes before a big battle. I even thought about those tedious passages in the Bible where so and so begat so and so, ad infinitum, except the Disner list didn't include the word "begat."

The piece also included a long listing of Disner's accomplishments, mostly focusing upon his becoming the Associate Dean of Arts and Sciences. There was also a listing of what I considered to be acceptable or at least tolerable affiliations and memberships, such as the Boy Scouts, the Bird Watchers Club, and the Lions Club, but there were others that prompted in me either a groan or puzzlement. The former group included the Big Panther Club (the rah-rah athletic boosters, which he annoyingly touted by always wearing the school colors or by donning team jerseys), various come-on honorary groups, including one called Outstanding Methodist Educators of America (for which, as I knew, Disner had paid a healthy membership fee); the University's TGIF Poker Club (a listing that seemed hardly appropriate in an obituary), and participation in his church's annual amateur Christmas pageant (in which, as I had once witnessed, Disner hammed it up as he played several parts, including Joseph). Among the perplexing memberships was one in a group called Outdoor Adventurers (a strange entry—maybe even a lie—since Disner never seemed to be the outdoors type), and one in the NRA (troublesome since I could never imagine Disner toting a gun). There was also mention of his being a blood donor, but I knew I wouldn't be keen on receiving blood from him, being afraid that it might bring with it some of Disner's personality, causing me, for example, to begin saying "okay" at the end of sentences.

At the end of the column came a twist on a rather standard line in obituaries: "The Disner family requests that in lieu of flowers, donations be made to Hugh's favorite cause, the County Aid to Unwed Mothers." I was perplexed as to why Disner would have anything to do with that service. Was there something I didn't know about his extracurricular activities?

Accompanying the column was a picture of Disner, which must have been taken at least twenty years previously, with him sporting more hair, which was not as stringy as is was at the time of his death, appearing in the photo to be even a bit curly. And he had a more vibrant countenance, perhaps because the photo pre-dated marriage and five children. The one constant was that the leisure suit he wore in the picture matched some that he still often donned, colored, I would bet anyone, either light green or yellow (though of course I couldn't prove it since the picture was in black and white). I suppose no reader requires a completely up-to-date photo of the deceased, since of course it would be taken in the mortuary with the subject laid out on a slab.

To the left of Disner's obituary was a birthday greeting from a widower named Glogman to his deceased wife, a variation on the "Lordy, lordy, Barbara turned forty" style, here being a note saying, "Trixy, Trixy, you would have been sixty." To the right of the column about Disner was printed a "letter" from a widow to her deceased husband—on the tenth anniversary of his death—begging him to give a "sign"—any sign that he was still present in the neighborhood. I momentarily wondered what the widow writing the letter would interpret as a sign—a squirrel running across the road in front of the car, a traffic signal changing to red, a storm coming in, an ache in the knee?

What about Breda Disner? What would she see as a sign that Disner was still watching over her and the kids? Anything colored yellow and/or green? That would come easily, since half the faculty and students wore those colors, particularly on Fridays, which President Popson had declared to be "School Spirit Day." How about noises from the men's room, either singing or the sounds of flatulence, or ugly white vans excessively covered with stickers stating personal preferences, or any large group of children? I know I'd think twice myself if I were to hear someone say "okay?"

I came to realize that reading an obituary could actually be entertaining—as long as it wasn't your own. I never was one to give assignments in class for students to write their own obits. It just seemed too morbid to me. I chose instead to have them write up self-descriptions for a personal ad for soliciting dates. Maybe the ads were not all that different from obituaries.

Chapter 6

Though I've never been keen on going to funerals—they give me the same uneasiness that I get on airplanes when the landing gear clunks down or the engines change cadence—I attended Disner's funeral—or at least three-fourths of it, the last part being a private family ceremony at the graveside, during which Disner was "laid to rest," or "put six feet under," or "planted"—whichever euphemism fits. The parts I attended took place approximately five miles away from the murder site in the stall at NGU, at the First Methodist Church of Raysville, whose very name made it more prestigious than the Second Methodist Church or any of the ones named after roads.

According to the five-by-seven program handed to me by a tall usher at the door, the initial part was a pre-service viewing of Disner's body in an open casket; then came a service that would include comments by both a Reverend Robert Philhuster and Disner's supporters, followed by a reception in the basement of the church (ironically, the Recreation Room), during which the attending crowd was invited to offer condolences to Disner's family. The program was printed on yellow paper with fancy green printing—Rage Italic, I think. The line on the front cover read, "In Memory of Hugh Disner, a man who loved God, the University, and his family." I wondered if that was the correct order.

By a slight miscalculation of the time, I had arrived relatively early and enjoyed the dubious luxury of being among the first to view Disner. He was lying on a slight incline in a mahogany coffin, one that seemed in the right price range for a college professor/half administrator, complete with a red velvet lining, and large gold colored handles. A silver tag with "Permaseal" was fastened to the middle front. Behind the coffin stood a man—I suppose from the funeral home—whose face looked like a wrecked car that had been repaired by a rank amateur unskilled in Bondo techniques. He seemingly was guarding Disner, I suppose potentially to prevent a scene like the one in HAMLET, when Hamlet loses control and leaps in Ophelia's grave site—something I couldn't possibly imagine happening with Disner. Or maybe the guard was a micro version of the people who carry on a wake, keeping vigil over the body of the dead, since the Disners had not chosen to have one. I was comforted by the fact that I was seeing Disner in a coffin, in a church, not stretched out on the dining room table like the sheriff in the movie PLACES IN THE HEART.

Disner himself looked both better and worse than he had when I last saw him crumpled in front of the toilet. His eyes were now shut, as was his mouth (though he still looked as if he had just said "okay"). The mortician had earned his pay by repairing the wound in Disner's forehead with makeup (probably a kind of putty akin to Bondo), even leaving Disner with a slightly furrowed brow, giving him the appearance of someone troubled by what had happened to him—or cool, like someone trying to pick up a date at a single's bar. Disner wore an unsullied green suit, with a yellow vest, taking with him into eternity the school colors.

What troubled me the most was the waxy appearance the makeup gave Disner, making him look like a lacquered mannequin. I've always been under the impression that the ideal is to make a dead person look as if he is about to spring back into life, or, at worst, to appear to be sleeping. A line from Browning's "My Last Duchess" popped into my head ("That's my last Duchess painted on the wall / Looking as if she were alive.") Disner just looked dead, like a toy doll whose batteries had run down. Of course, lying in a coffin didn't do much to improve his appearance, even with the velvet lining.

After giving Disner one last close-up viewing—during which I got a whiff of an odor that reminded me of the green liquid soap contained in the dispenser in the men's room—I sat down in the fifth row of pews and watched the other viewers. Mostly, they were mourners, though I did spot a few who seemed to be simply curious onlookers and a couple of ghoulish types who appeared to enjoy going to funerals, like the title characters in HAROLD AND MAUDE. Others acted as if they were in a haunted house—or in a church for the first time in their lives. One couple looked as if they were standing in line just for the sake of standing in a line and could have just as easily been waiting outside a theater or Ripley's Believe-

It-Or-Not Museum. One person in line got a call on his cell phone while he was waiting, a call that he answered in hushed tones.

The procession included people I recognized—President Popson, for instance, appearing to be faux dapper in a dark three-piece suit, having lost some weight since I had seen him last (perhaps prodded into an administrative diet by an image-conscious board of trustees), now appearing less in the shape of a pear; Bwanger, who walked to the casket as if he had on ski boots; Glenn Glick, who twitched a lot, as if he were being given small taser shocks, accompanied by his daughter, Deidre, who seemed to be weeping more than anyone else; and Detective Smockley, who scanned the crowd as if he were a Secret Service agent, assigned to protect the President. When he spotted me, he stopped moving and gazed at me intently, turning away only when he realized that he had fallen three or four yards behind the next person in line.

After the procession of mourners had finished viewing and everyone was seated, Disner's wife and the rest of the family—including Disner's five children—made their entry. It was the first time I had ever seen the youngest of the Disner children subdued, for, from what I had observed, he usually was wilder than Faulkner's spotted horses. Mrs. Disner—Breda—appeared sullen. I wondered if she were angry at God for prematurely "calling home" one of the family, angry at the killer for murdering her husband Disner, angry at Disner himself for leaving her with five kids, or angry over a skimpy death benefit from the insurance company. She sat next to the oldest child, William, who encircled his mother's shoulders with his left arm and tilted his head toward her, a posture he would maintain through the entire service. Of all the children, he was the one that looked the most like Breda. The other children all had Disner's bovine appearance.

After everyone was seated, a man in a black robe, Reverend Philhuster, stood up and took a position right behind the casket. Speaking with such commanding bombast that I found myself straightening up in the pew, he praised Disner's virtues as a husband, father, churchgoer, contributor to the local society, teacher, administrator, and "dynamic personality." He did not mention any of Disner's obnoxious habits, such as driving at a maddeningly slow pace or his constantly saying "Okay?"

Bwanger was the first lay testifier to Disner's worth: "Hugh Disner was a wonderful asset to the English Department. He would take on any task I assigned, offering valuable service to the department and university as a whole, including picking up prospects from the airport, going on recruiting trips, participating in phonathons, sharing his opinions in brown-bag luncheon discussions, always showing up for the campus Hullabaloo game day—you name it, he did it."

A former student of Disner's named Gene Twosser, speaking with an aspirated voice that made me think of a faucet that had been turned on with no water supply, praised Disner as an inspiring teacher: "He always made us feel good in class by having us form a large circle, and he allowed us to visit his office anytime he was there. He loved to talk, okay?"

My god, I thought, *Disner developed a disciple before he died, or at least a conversational plagiarist. Either that or Disner was giving a sign that his spiritual presence was hovering closeby.*

Twosser was followed by Glenn Glick from my department, who spoke in a stream-of-consciousness, leaving me mostly in the dark about his feelings concerning Disner (and concerned about his abilities as a teacher). A few words and phrases did register with me, such as "the minute you're born, you're dying," and "Death, where is thy sting?" and "insufficiently bloomed flower." I thought about this latter phrase, in reference to Disner. True, he would no longer develop as a half administrator, never blossom into a full fledged dean, nor have the opportunity to dazzle others with his lengthy comments in committee meetings. And, of course, he would not be able to father any more children and thus fall short of qualifying as the head of a Maytag family.

Next came a few songs, some of Disner's favorites. I was disappointed that I did not hear a BIG CHILL version of "Jeremiah Was a Bullfrog," but I was treated to an organ rendition of selections from HMS PINAFORE, which sounded considerably better than Disner's own offering sung in the men's room (and my version for Detective Smockley). There was also an organ version of the University's alma mater—Disner being such a zealous advocate of this institution—played at dirge pace befitting the occasion, accompanied by the voices of many of the mourners, none of whom seemed to know the whole song—most of them having learned it only piecemeal at graduation ceremonies, a line here, a line there, such that there was near silence on some phrases but then a surging of voices on certain easily remembered words, such as "hail," "sons" (not "daughters"), "thee," and of course "alma mater." As soon as this ended, one of Disner's own children, Horace Walpole, sang a piping version of "Evergreen," made popular by Barbra Streisand, but the poor child forgot some of the lines, actually some of the similes, but filled in gamely, producing lines that included "Love, soft as an easy girl."

The reception afterwards—no, I couldn't call it a reception. Receptions in my mind have refreshments—little sandwiches, mixed nuts, mint candies, cookies, punch, guests holding cups with their pinkies extended. There was none of that to be had here. No, this was strictly a condolence session—a giving and taking of grief.

I stood in line waiting to offer my own condolences to the Disner family—the five kids, Breda, a couple of older people who, as I learned shortly, were Breda's mother and Hugh's father. Breda was the only one seated. In between the various pats on her head, low toned whispers, and hugs—the latter action made difficult by the fact that she was seated—she posed rigidly, her legs crossed, with the crossing leg spasmodically jerking up, as if a physician had bonked her just below the kneecap with a rubber percussion hammer. As was the case in the previous service, she did not seem grief-stricken so much as angry.

As I waited, I listened to the comments and conversations of those about me. "I haven't kept much contact with him since he became the assistant dean." "I was so shocked, since I had seen him just the day before he died." "He was so young; what was he, forty? I'm fifty two and it just makes a person think." "Hugh had so many children. I wonder what will become of them." "Did he leave Breda anything?" "I'm missing my afternoon nap." "Who's going to fill his position as assistant dean?" My own thoughts centered on the fact that I was still alive and Disner was the one who had died and on the fact that Smockley never seemed to take his eyes off me.

When I finally stood before Breda, she studied me the same way as Smockley. Did she believe I had finished off her husband? Did she wish that I had? I couldn't think what to say to her, so I borrowed a phrase from Tolstoy's "The Death of Ivan Ilyich" (the translated version obviously) and intoned, "Believe me." When she did not respond, except with more glaring, I said it again. "Believe me." She sighed heavily and turned away, as if I had interrupted her with advice on a dessert at a business luncheon at a posh restaurant. I moved on before I had to say "Believe me" again.

Feeling an intense desire to get out of there, I headed for the nearest exit, but Smockley intercepted me, latching on to my tricep with his thumb and forefinger. "Leaving so soon, Professor? What's your hurry?"

"I've got to teach a class." I pulled my arm loose.

"Class more important than paying respects to your colleague, is it?"

"I did pay my respects."

"Maybe so, but so far I haven't noticed a whole lot of reaction to Professor Disner's death on your part. Most people respond to the death of an acquaintance with grief, horror, some show of strong emotion. You seem to take it completely in stride. How come?"

"I don't know. I guess I really didn't know him all that well. I'll probably react more strongly after I've had time to absorb it all. Now, I'd like to go."

"All right then, but don't go far. I still have some unfinished business with you."

"Can I go as far as my building or should I have the class join me here?"

"Don't get smart with me, Professor."

"I wouldn't dream of it. Now, if you'll excuse me." I didn't wait for a response, but rather exited the recreation room/condolence parlor/anger room as fast as I could without actually running.

Chapter 7

After leaving Smockley, Breda, and a dead Disner, I thought about swinging by the department before heading home, but I did not feel up to talking with Bwanger, who surely would be there directly, and the rest of the departmental cast, so I changed into my running clothes in the gym and headed out for the road along the river near campus. I did not actually have a class, as I had told Smockley, but Smockley didn't need to know that, though I could imagine a grilling, stichomythic conversation with him later:

"Did you murder Hugh Disner?"

"No, of course not."

"I think you're lying."

"Why would you think that?"

"You've lied to me before."

"Excuse me?"

"You've lied to me before."

"When?"

"You told me at Disner's funeral that you had to get to a class."

"So?"

"You didn't have a class. I checked."

"I was mistaken."

"You lied."

"All right, I lied. I actually went running."

"Why? Were you feeling guilty?

"No, I simply like to run."

"When?"

"Mostly after committee meetings, funerals, and conversations like this one."

"I suggest you never lie to me again."

"All right, but running doesn't make me a killer."

"We'll see."

The air along the river was refreshing in the late afternoon, especially because it contrasted so sharply the smell of death at the funeral. I had run a good two miles before I could no longer sense an odor like green detergent in my nostrils. While I ran, thoughts of the ignominy of Disner's death ran though my head. When Donne wrote, "Death, be not proud," meaning that Death is not the ultimate victor when someone dies, he certainly was not anticipating Disner's death in the toilet stall. Death could indeed be quite proud by the way it demeaned Disner. I hoped that when it came for me, it would not catch me in a toilet stall—or even at the basins in the men's room.

No, I wanted to be doing something I enjoy or at least something constructive—more than just taking a dump. I could envision dying at the end of a dynamic lecture. It would certainly startle into consciousness some of the class sluggards—give them something to remember long after lines from Shakespeare had faded in their heads. It would be particularly satisfying if I died in class right after uttering a complaint, such as, "Your last set of papers just killed me." I actually would not mind dying right after playing tennis or a little one-on-one basketball with my grandson or granddaughter, who was going off to college on a tennis or basketball scholarship.

I really hoped I would not end up getting murdered like Disner, at least not on Smockley's watch. I wouldn't want him poking and probing me, measuring the angle of bullet holes or the depth of knife wounds. Can a dead person feel violated? I was feeling anticipatory violation just thinking about it. He would probably interview my dead body and insinuate that I had done it, the bastard. Maybe I could put it in my will that Smockley was forbidden to touch me, but there would probably be no reading of the will until after he had already laid his hands on me.

These and other morbid thoughts made me tired. Despite the cool breeze, which should have completely invigorated me, I began to feel as if I were running with sandbags attached, like the dancer in Vonnegut's "Harrison Bergeron." I was considering stopping my run and walking back to campus when a movement in the river caught my attention. I turned just in time to see a little blue heron taking off from its perch on a stump in the middle of the flow, though I would not have been surprised to spot a body floating down the river. The bird seemed to be misnamed, for it was gray rather than blue, and huge, a wing span of five or six feet. It flapped in powerful but graceful strokes, each of which propelled it yards and yards, its legs flowing beneath it like ribbons. As I watched the flight, I truly understood why William Cullen Bryant wrote so passionately about a waterfowl, as I watched this magnificent bird pursue its own "solitary way" in flight, seeking a "marge of river wide."

I started running again, trying to match the heron's easy glide with my strides, once again feeling the cool air, which I imagined was generated by the movement of the bird's wings. Smockley probably would have shot it and caused the breeze to stop, like Coleridge's ancient mariner did.

After the run, before heading home for dinner, I stopped at Blethens Groceries in Raysville, picking up some essentials—beer, wine, salad fixings, and a large t-bone.

As I walked from the checkout register toward the exit, I looked out through the tinted glass and spotted Smockley standing outside on the sidewalk, leaning on the top of a plastic trash can container, the kind that has two side holes for depositing waste. He must have changed from his funeral-going garb, now dressed in Dickey's work pants and a red and gray flannel shirt. On his feet were low-rise boots and white socks. At least he wasn't wearing the University's colors—yellow and green. In his hand was a cigarette. He smoked tough.

My first reaction was that he had seen my car in the parking lot and was waiting for me, maybe even having followed me to the store. He did not see me at first, since he was studying the cars and people in the parking lot, honing in on a couple standing behind their car, seemingly arguing, with the man flinging his arms upwards as if to indicate repeated touchdowns, the woman jabbing him in the left shoulder with her index finger. What was running through Smockley's mind? Was he hoping they would turn violent so he could step in, flash a badge, read them their rights, and haul them away? Did he get his jollies from witnessing conflict—like most guys would get worked up over seeing a shapely woman in a mini skirt?

I realized as I observed Smockley that I had not really looked at him in detail before, no doubt because I always felt uncomfortable around him, since he in fact believed me to be Disner's killer. It was as if I could make him disappear if I avoided setting eyes on him. He appeared to be about thirty-five to forty years old, maybe five-ten, weight around one eighty, salt and pepper hair, nearly a crew cut, receding slightly in the front. His hips were wide, as were his shoulders. I could picture him as a middleweight boxer, maybe even a light heavyweight, the aggressor in the ring, stalking his opponent, hoping to deliver one or two solid blows, while ignoring a flurry of jabs delivered by his opponent, even when they drew blood from him. If Smockley were a dog, he'd probably chase cars. As a human, he looked like a cross between the obsessed captain of the Orca, played by Robert Shaw in JAWS, and the gunfighter named Wilson, played by Jack Palance in SHANE. I could imagine him in the middle of an interrogation, tossing a gun on the floor and saying, "Pick it up."

And what was he like outside of investigating crimes? Was he a local, born and raised in the county, now living a hundred yards from his parents in a double-wide on a farm? Was his house surrounded by yard ornaments—fake deer, rabbits, cast off car parts? Was he religious? I could picture him sitting stiffly in a pew of a protestant church, listening attentively to the sermon, but not participating in the singing, dressed in his Sunday suit, arms folded across his chest. Did he have pets? No cats, for sure, but I could picture him sitting on his back porch watching a pit bull or a rottweiler devour meat scraps. Was he married? From where I stood I could not detect a ring on his finger. If he were married, did he have children, and if so, were they treated like Bull Meecham's kids in THE GREAT SANTINI? Had, in fact, Smockley himself been in the military, a zealous soldier who took orders and did "the job" with tight-lipped stoicism and rigidity, never shying away from danger, never complaining about long marches or tedious assignments, or even army chow? And what kind of food did he eat, and did he ever eat out? I could imagine him at a Ryan's buffet, selecting steak and potatoes while ignoring anything remotely unusual or exotic—like ethnic food. Did he drink a lot? If so, what was it—Colt 45 Malt Liquor? Bourbon? Could he hold his liquor? I bet he could, with the best of them.

As I deliberated whether to escape from the store by using the other exit and then try to sneak past him, or simply to go out the door in front of me and confront him, he suddenly straightened up and mashed out his cigarette on the top of the trash container and took three or four steps toward a similarly aged woman that passed by me carrying two plastic shopping bags. As the automatic doors swung open, I could hear her calling out to him with a pleasant voice, "I'm finished. We can leave if you'd like." I assumed this must be Mrs. Smockley, though, contrasting his rough demeanor, she appeared genteel, refined, kind. I could envision her setting out fine china for company, serving Waldorf salad and English tea, collecting souvenir spoons which she kept in a spoon rack, playing bridge, and sending thank you notes promptly. She was dressed neatly in a light blue, full-length skirt and a white blouse.

Smockley looked my way through the still opened doors. After nodding at me, he quickly turned to take—in one hand— the packages she was carrying. Using his free hand he guided her toward an SUV in the parking lot. He did not look at me again. I waited until the two of them had driven off before I exited the store, wondering all the while if Mrs. Smockley—if indeed the woman joining him was truly his wife—had saved me from another grilling, but also wondering if Smockley had even known, as he stood on the sidewalk waiting, that I was in the store to begin with.

Chapter 8

Two days after Disner's funeral, I was on my way to campus to attend a meeting of the Teacher Evaluation Committee (TEC, for those into acronyms). I had managed to avoid contact with just about everyone in my department—mainly by going directly to and from my classes, while bypassing the departmental office and the faculty lounge, leaving my mail to collect in the process. I simply wanted to avoid discussing Disner's death. I also cancelled my open-door office hours, electing instead to meet students only by appointment—usually with the door closed. This was motivated by pure paranoia about vulnerability, a Wild Bill Hickok syndrome, wherein I did not want to chance being caught with my back exposed—or was it a Wyatt Earp syndrome? a Jesse James one? one of those guys who did not want to get caught with his back to the saloon door. I hate being an unreliable narrator. I did make a couple of visits to Ben Sturgeon's office, where I could take refuge. He did not mind closing his door. In exchange, I told him essentially all the details about my bad day—or rather Disner's—at the Okay Corral/men's room.

The ordeal of getting to this meeting intensified my paranoia. Even under the best of circumstances, I am not keen on being held up in traffic, but ever since Disner's murder, I had been even more sensitive to traffic and people around me, feeling particularly vulnerable when out in my car. After leaving my house in Raysville, I was forced to creep through the Raysville strip—a microcosm of every ugly succession of business establishments in America, with no order nor ordinances—a conglomeration of stop lights, fast food establishments, slow food businesses—including steak houses, Chinese and Mexican restaurants, and pizza places—banks, gas stations, the new Walmart, acres of asphalt parking lots, and a glut of signs, both commercial ones and road indicators—with very few trees and bushes. One of the signs read, "Raysville—God's country," but surrounding the sign and trailing along most of the route was an alarming collection of litter. I began to think that if this is God's country, I would hate to see what Satan's country looks like—probably not much different from Raysville. Getting murdered along here would be as undignified as getting snuffed in a toilet stall.

On this same highway, I got trapped in the left lane behind a laboring car that appeared to be driven by the headrest, the actual driver of which was determined to stay even with the car in the right lane—both motoring along at least ten miles an hour below the speed limit. The driver must have been one of Disner's children or a clone of Disner himself, who always drove as if he had an open bottle of shock-sensitive nitroglycerin on the seat. The back bumper of the car bore a sticker that read, "I brake for nobody," but the driver braked for everyone and everything, including unseen wind currents and, of course, every slowing of the car next to his. In the back window was a NGU student parking decal. I kept thinking that if this guy is not bright enough to stay to the right, how in the world is he going to handle comma splices in his writing course or the Krebs cycle in a biology class.

Once I arrived at the intersection that served as the main entry into the University, I was forced to sit through a light that was supposed to be one of the new "smart lights," which has sensors that control the light in such a way that no one has to sit more than thirty seconds or so for the change. This light must have been in the Highway Department's inventory of "stupid lights," as it refused to change to a left directional arrow, to allow motorists to turn into the campus. After what seemed to be five minutes of waiting, as I observed the free passage of car after car proceeding straight ahead, all the while wondering if I was in someone's gunsights, I took matters in my own hand and made an illegal left turn into campus, absolutely sure that I would get caught by someone like Smockley—or maybe Smockley himself, who, I would not have been surprised to find, doubled as a traffic cop.

"You broke the law," he would probably sneer.

"I was forced to since the light wasn't working."

"What other laws have you broken lately?"

"None than I can think of."

"How about murder?"

"Excuse me?"

"Murder—you know, when you kill someone."

"I know what murder is, and it's a lot different from running a light that does not work correctly."

"I've discovered that people who are willing to break one law or also willing to go the distance—break others, ones much more serious."

"That's not the case here."

"I don't believe you. I'm going to have to run you in."

Fortunately, no cop stopped me, and I made it to the parking lot next to my building with only the nuisance of another student driver, who stopped his car in front of me on Campus Drive to allow his one passenger to climb out, a procedure that could have been completed with more speed by an entire troupe of circus clowns exiting an old Volkswagen.

Once in the lot, despite my apprehensions about vulnerability, I was tempted to sit in my car and delay arriving at the meeting until the usual ten-minute, preliminary period had transpired, during which, as I had witnessed far too many times, members talked about the weather, pedagogical matters, and personal tragedies—in no particular order. It would be followed by about ten minutes or so of real meeting content, which would then in turn be followed by twenty minutes of digression, and then twenty minutes of repetition. I figured I needed to get there just for that second ten minutes.

But I knew that even those few minutes would be too much to bear. After all, it was still a COMMITTEE MEETING. If a person knew that he had only one day to live, would he spend it in a committee meeting? Disner probably would have, even if he knew that he might die during the meeting itself. For me, dying in a committee meeting would be on a par with dying in the men's room. Can a person register as a conscientious objector to attending meetings?

I stayed in my car long enough to hear the end of the Beatles singing "Nowhere Man," before climbing out, already feeling as sapped of energy as if I had given a pint of blood.

The bell tower was at that moment trying its best to muddle through "Chariots of Fire," but, because of the slowness of pace, generating absolutely no image of championship, Olympic British runners in the surf, only visions of out-of-shape chuffs, slogging through quick sand. It sounded as if the entire tower were dying, making me think that it might at any moment begin to sob and then sway back and forth before crashing down in front of the University Center. Maybe the song was too difficult for it. I wondered how it would have handled "In-a-gadda-da-vida." It probably should always stick with a tune more appropriate to its speed, like Bach's "Sheep May Graze."

To make matters worse, the clocks on the tower—at least the two I could see without going around to the opposite side—were all ten minutes slower than the time just announced on the radio station, which was consistent with the time that showed on my own watch. I had noticed this discrepancy before. It was as if the University were in a different time zone from the rest of the county. I wondered if the meeting would begin according to Eastern Standard Time or Bell Tower Time.

As the tower segued into a version of "Rock Around the Clock"—or a dirge for Disner (it was hard to tell the difference since it was played at a pace as if time were no object)—I made my way from the lot to the walkway to the main entrance of the building, but was blocked by a threesome intent on walking side-by-side, in time with the phlegmatic rendition coming from the clock tower, forcing me to pass in the grass, just as one of the three, a young man who looked like Mickey from the Monkeys, announced to the other two, "I've decided I'm never going to her class again. Doctor Smith's so unfair. She calls on me all the time when I haven't read the assignment." His comments caused me to notice the crumbling terrazzo surface of the walkway, exposing ugly cement, as if a bad case of sidewalk psoriasis had set in, an ironic sight in view of the administration's multi-million dollar efforts to beautify the campus by upgrading the appearance of the bell tower and a couple of remote academic buildings, but failing to correct several of the most glaring faults in the middle of the campus. I would not want to get murdered here either.

Once inside my building, but before joining the group in the meeting, I detoured to the men's room—the one on the fourth floor, not the murder site on the top floor where Disner had met his finisher. I certainly did not want to run the risk of meeting Smockley, who I figured was re-dusting there for MY fingerprints or searching for specks of MY saliva. Besides, for all I knew, Disner's student/disciple who had delivered the stirring tribute to Disner at the funeral might have by now made the men's room into a shrine for Disner, emblazoning the door or one of the walls inside with the word "Okay." In fact, I had been plagued with reservations about using any of the men's rooms for the last few days, even briefly entertaining the notion on a couple of occasions of using the women's room—though I certainly would have knocked first.

Knowing how long the meeting probably would run, I braved the men's room this time. No one was inside, though there was the usual evidence of recent visitors—unflushed toilets and urinals. I felt edgy the whole time I was there, even though I had checked under the stall doors upon first entering—partly from fear of Disner's killer showing up, partly from fear that Smockley might suddenly step out of a stall and accuse me of lurking in men's rooms to attack other victims.

Chapter 9

When I entered the conference room, where the meeting was to take place, Bwanger half stood and pointed to an empty chair to his right, between Cherry and Glick, as if he were choreographing the meeting. "Tyler, I was beginning to think you were not coming." To Bwanger's left sat Sturgeon and Rainwater. I wondered if the placements were intentional and represented Bwanger's estimation of political stances. I hoped he did not lump me with those next to me, two of the most conservative members of the Department. Bwanger remained hovering above his chair in a half crouch so long after I had found my seat that I imagined he had hemorrhoids that would flare up if he sat down. Either that or he was going to offer a prayer before beginning, maybe to the god of meetings.

On the conference table rested a framed picture of Disner, sitting in a plush roll-around chair in an administrative pose, forearms resting on the padded arms of the chair, his brow knitted both horizontally and vertically, such that his eyebrows seemed to make one continuous line and the distance between his forehead and chin was reduced by a fourth. Beneath the picture a mailing label was attached, on which was printed, "Hugh Disner, In Memorium."

"What have I missed?"

"A lot, actually," Bwanger answered. "Professor Glick was just telling us about his wife's breaking her ankle at a bowling alley, and Professor Cherry was filling us in on a report out of your old stomping grounds, the University of Michigan, about a group of students who were taken out into the wilderness and taught the same subjects that a control group was taught back in conventional classrooms. The outdoor people didn't have any electronic equipment to work with, cell phones, televisions, or computers. The assumption was that they would fare poorly."

"What happened?"

"Well, it seems that she stepped into the gutter on the right side of the alley while watching her ball roll . . . ."

"No, I meant what happened to the students in the Michigan experiment?"

"Apparently they did better on standardized tests than the control group."

"What was the conclusion?"

"They, the administrators, believed that the fresh air and better eating made the outdoor group feel better. Plus they didn't stay up late hours and as a result were more rested and alert."

"Does this mean that we're going to try teaching our students outside here at NGU?" I actually had visions of teaching Shakespeare in our own Forest of Arden or Thoreau by the campus pond.

"Good gracious, no!" Bwanger finally sat back down as he said this. "It would make the two new academic buildings we're getting—and all the other fine facilities—superfluous. We can't have that."

Ben Sturgeon leaned forward. "You know, Tyler, sort of like the military's needing to use all the bombs and other technology they've developed, to fight a war, so that all that governmental equipment doesn't go to waste."

"Well, not exactly like that, Ben." Bwanger twisted his neck and head as if trying to ease a kink. "We simply need to make use of what's available. And besides, we don't want to get the reputation as a university that we're off traipsing through the woods. It's bad enough that the Rainbow People camp out in the woods near here every other year."

"Yes, and don't forget all those motorcycle people that come through here on the way to Tennessee and North Carolina every year," Glick added. Glick looked like both his name and his opinions. He had slick hair, combed straight back on the sides, making him appear to have small wings on his head. He spoke with a slushiness that made me think of slimy avocados or canned asparagus. He seemed to love attending meetings, so much so that I vowed to look up information on his college degrees. I would bet that somewhere in there was a major in committee work.

"Dr. Bwanger, is this something that we need to decide on in this meeting?" I asked, actually puzzled.

"No, no, it just seemed interesting."

"Maybe we better get on to the business at hand then," Sturgeon said, before winking at me and leaning back in his chair.

"Yes, I guess we must." Bwanger straightened his tie and shuffled some papers. He looked disappointed that we were not going to pursue the topic any more right then. I got the feeling that if he ever attended a concert or a boxing match, he would be content to watch indefinitely the warm-up group or the preliminary bout, but I doubted if he ever went out. However, despite his indication the meeting would begin, he still was not finished with pre-meeting chatting. "One last thing before we begin. Tyler, why don't you tell us more about Hugh Disner's murder. We've being dying—uh, I guess that's an inappropriate word—eager to know more about it."

"Well, actually, I wasn't there for the murder."

"Yes, of course. What I meant to ask was what he looked like when you found him."

"Dead—he looked dead."

"Did you try to resuscitate him, you know, give him mouth-to-mouth?"

"No."

Glick joined in. "I think I would have. I've done it before, you know, when my cousin almost drowned in the swimming pool."

Cherry came to life. "I once did a Heimlich maneuver on a person in a restaurant—a guy choking on a chicken bone." Cherry was the kind of guy who was always two or three seconds late dimming his bright lights to oncoming traffic. He had the appearance of someone who had been in academia too long. His teeth looked like pieces of worn chalk and his face resembled the pages of old paperback novels. I figured if he had actually tried to perform a Heimlich, he would have gotten it all wrong—maybe hugged the guy from the front. In any case I couldn't imagine him having enough strength to make an obstruction pop out of anybody.

"But where exactly was he?" Bwanger insisted. I noticed Sturgeon rolling his eyes.

"In the toilet stall."

"Oh, my! Where in the toilet stall?"

"On the floor in front of the toilet. Look," I lied, "Detective Smockley told me not to discuss what I saw." I figured I could put Smockley to use somehow, even if it were to simply get Bwanger off my back, though I worried that Smockley would find out what I said and use it against me somehow—probably help him make a case that I was a chronic liar.

"Of course, I understand. Maybe I shouldn't be telling you this," Bwanger said, sotto voce, leaning toward me as if he intended to butt me from five feet away, "but Detective Smockley asked me several questions about you and your relationship with Disner. Does he think you did it?"

"Did what?"

"Murder, er, kill Disner."

"I certainly hope not." I noticed Glick staring at me, mouth agape, like a tetra in a fish tank. Cherry looked uncomfortable as he played touching-finger-tips. Sturgeon gave a muffled laugh, while Rainwater glared at Bwanger.

"I did have to inform him of your cutting remarks about Hugh in that last meeting you and I both attended."

"Which meeting?"

"The General Education Monitoring Committee meeting. You made a comment that having Hugh Disner take charge administratively was roughly akin to having the slowest truck lead a convoy."

"I really didn't mean to slur Disner personally. I was actually offering my assessment of most administrators."

Sturgeon laughed louder, but then stopped and came to my rescue. "Torrance, it's getting late. Let's really do get on with the main business."

Bwanger looked disappointed for the second time in the last three or four minutes, but actually got the prescribed meeting going, one that dragged on at the pace of the songs issuing forth from the bell tower, through a discussion of a departmental evaluation form (which Glick called an "instrument," a word which inspired in me images of something metallic, shiny, solid, maybe hinged or revolving, like the gun that killed Disner, most definitely not a piece of paper).

I drifted in and out of the discussion, slowly developing a headache. About the time that it had developed into the shape of a dark monster that shook violently back and forth, Sturgeon spoke to me.

"Tyler, are you all right?" he asked.

"I'm fine. I just have a headache." What I should have said was that sitting in this meeting was roughly equal to sitting in a dentist's chair, attending a funeral, like Disner's, and being interviewed by Smockley, all in the same time frame.

"Well, we'll be finished here soon," Bwanger announced. "Now, Tyler, what's your opinion on organization?"

I tried to ignore the headache to offer an opinion, but escaped completely answering the question by redirecting it to Sturgeon, who responded by saying, "Thanks a lot, Tyler; you owe me one." Finally, Bwanger, hearing the clock tower chiming out the hour (after just finishing a gluey rendition of "When the Saints Go Marching In"), brought the meeting to a close, with a parting comment about lots of unfinished business to be addressed at a subsequent meeting.

Chapter 10

As soon as Bwanger ended the meeting, I hurried from the room, but as I was coming out of the door into the hall I nearly crashed into none other than Detective Smockley, who must have been standing exactly in the door frame and who, being just as surprised as I, jumped back a step or two and put up his hands, palms toward me, as if he were a mime feeling an imaginary glass wall. "Whoa there cowboy! What's the hurry?"

"Sorry, I didn't expect anyone to be in the doorway. My only hurry is getting out of a headache-producing meeting."

"Headache, huh? Having lots of them since Professor Disner's death, are you? And were you hurrying because you thought I might be here and you could avoid me?"

"No, of course not. How could I have known you'd be here?"

Just then, Glick and Rainwater appeared behind me, jockeying for room to squeeze by Smockley and me. Glick cast a furtive look my way. As they started down the hall, I could hear him mutter what sounded like "I knew he did it," though it could have been "I need to diet." He then breathed out what sounded like "tut." I thought, at least you could make a natural sound of disdain, you asshole, and not go for some phony onomatopoeic version. I truly believed that Glick was genetically unhappy. He certainly could serve as a foil to anyone who was happy.

I turned my attention back to Smockley, who had lowered his arms, but now held them in a tough-man position, straight down, the backs of his hands facing me. "I need some information," he asserted.

"Now?"

"What's wrong with now?" He reached into his coat pocket and pulled out a small writing pad.

"I just came from a committee meeting. That ought to buy at least twenty-four hours of respite from answering questions in any circumstances."

"Are you afraid to talk with me?" His voice was beginning to sound like my car does when a branch gets caught beneath it.

"No, of course not. What is it you want?"

"How long would you say it was between when you first went to the men's room and didn't enter, as you claim, and when you went back and found Professor Disner in the stall?"

"I don't know, five, maybe ten minutes."

"And you didn't hang around outside waiting after you first tried to go in?"

"No, I went back to my office."

"Did anyone see you in your office?"

"No, I was in there with my door closed."

"That's very interesting, Professor."

"Why?"

"I'll let you know later after you've recovered from your committee meeting." He entered some more notes on the pad and then, after backing away two or three steps, crammed it back in his shirt pocket. After wheeling to his left, he strode off down the hall with the robotic pace of Yul Brynner's character in WESTWORLD, leaving me completely puzzled. Smockley was the kind of guy who in the past would have crumpled beer cans on his head—back when the cans weren't so flimsy.

Just as Smockley disappeared around the corner, Bwanger suddenly appeared. "Is there anything you want to talk about with me, Tyler? Maybe I can be of assistance." Bwanger was such a striking contrast to Smockley that I almost laughed. Smockley's Dick Tracy face was all angles. Bwanger's face looked like a cross between those of a cherub and Shakespeare's Falstaff (at least the illustration in my Shakespeare textbook). I was not sure if Bwanger was pudgy, plump, rotund, or chunky. He was not really obese, but not burly or stout either—maybe just portly. I doubted if he could keep pace with Smockley walking across campus or even down the hall.

"No, thank you though. There's not much to talk about other than I recently discovered a dead man in a toilet stall in the building in which I teach Shakepeare and Thoreau. As I said in the meeting, I've been told not to talk about it."

"Of course, I understand. I was just wondering if, on the day of Disner's murder, you happened to see anyone else around." He fidgeted and swayed, reminding me of a child that needed to pee badly.

"No, I didn't."

"Did you hear anybody else's voice from the men's room?"

"No, I only heard Disner singing."

"Well, they say that you were there twice, and I was wondering . . . ."

"Who's they?"

"Which they?"

"You just said THEY knew I had been there twice. I wanted to know who gave you the information."

"Oh, that THEY. It's just that I overheard you talking to that detective a few minutes ago, and I was just curious about . . . ."

"So, this detective guy, Smockley, has become a THEY? I didn't think he was that big."

"He is the law, you realize."

"Please, give me a break. But why are you asking me these questions? Were you there too?"

"Oh, no, of course not." He looked even more uncomfortable, as if I had just asked him about bruises on his wife or close similarities between his writing and an earlier author's. He straightened each of his sleeves with the opposite hand and then said, "I just want to keep abreast of anything going on in our department."

"I'll try to keep you informed of any developments I'm allowed to talk about. Now, if you'll excuse me, I've got to get to the parking lot."

"Okay, maybe we can talk again later in the week," he said, waving goodbye to me as if I were leaving on a plane.

I hurried to the staircase, fortunately not coming upon Smockley, but still feeling edgy as I descended the steps and even as I crossed the parking lot outside, where I heard the bell tower playing "How Great Thou Art"—with less bombast than George Beverly Shea usually gave it.

Chapter 11

Almost two months before Disner had made the throne in the men's room his seat in eternity, I had committed myself to a signing in Atlanta at a Thoreaubooks store for my novel DAVIDSON'S HELL. It was a parody of Dante's "Inferno" in THE DIVINE COMEDY, in which I assigned social and political transgressors to appropriate levels of hell and corresponding punishments, leaving out for the most part perpetrators of crimes that normally get people sent to prison in our judicial system, such as murder, rape, and theft. For instance, drivers who habitually block the left lane on an interstate are made to drink a gallon of liquid and then forced to poke along in slow traffic while their bladders scream at them. I also devised a punishment for people who talk too long and loudly, particularly in public toilets, spending eternity in a small crowded room with political pundits and evangelical fanatics. Ironically, Disner would more likely make it into my hell than his killer.

It was only three days since Disner had been laid to rest, and I remembered that Detective Smockley had cautioned me to remain available for questioning at any time, but I figured I did not have to apprize him of my every move, so I left for my signing in the east part of Atlanta without informing him that I was leaving town. Finding a dead colleague, attending his funeral, being under suspicion by a Sheriff's Department detective, and worrying about who might be the killer's next victim were enough to make the journey south seem like a vacation escape.

The drive from NGU to the All-Georgia Mall took a little over an hour and a half, leaving me about forty minutes to find the Thoreaubooks store and set up for the signing.

The mall itself was approximately the size of the Pentagon, surrounded by a parking lot as large as all the combined runways at a major airport, dotted by islands in which were planted an impressive array of trees, shrubs, and flowers.

It qualified as slightly upscale, boasting high ceilings, fountains, lots of glass, music emanating from almost every stationary fixture, and containing most of the well known department stores, including Macy/Rich's, Sears, Belks, Dillards, and Saks Fifth Avenue.

Unfortunately, I parked on the side farthest from the Thoreaubooks. My miscalculation, as I discovered immediately upon looking at one of the upright directories/maps inside, necessitated a hike for what seemed to be a distance equal to that of eight football fields, or maybe even eight soccer fields, if someone wanted to quibble. I passed through the food court, consisting of small-scale versions of seemingly every fast food and ethnic food restaurant in America. Then weaving my way around a dazzling array of midstream kiosks, I cut down the Lerner Shops-Star Electronics-World Health Food-Pro Sports Footwear-Solar Sun Glasses-Big John's Tie Wear-Eddie Bauer-Sears corridor, finally locating, in yet another wing, Thoreaubooks, opposite to Victoria's Secret. I had only fifteen minutes to spare.

As if to justify the name of the place, everyone in Georgia seemed to be shopping there when I arrived, most of them cruising the corridors with cell phones glued to their ears, probably talking with each other in the mall since there could not possibly be anyone left at home.

Bad omen—no signs announcing my appearance, no chair, no table. I entered the store and introduced myself to the woman at the cash register, one Betty Slidehurst, who informed me that the manager would be back from her break at any time.

Some fifteen minutes later, a woman with "lazy" written all over her, wearing a silver name tag and a red apron with Thoreaubooks emblazoned on it, sauntered in, moving as aimlessly as a goldfish. Betty pointed toward her and said, "That's our manager, Patty Dewdrane." I wondered if Betty had ever entertained the notion of offing Patty while Patty occupied the ladies' room.

After I introduced myself to Ms. Dewdrane and reminded her why I was there, she immediately offered an apology for not having set up before I arrived. "The store has been incredibly busy this morning, "she complained, though at that moment I could see only one customer in the whole establishment. "My goodness, I need to get you a table and chair," she exclaimed, as if the idea had just come to her, "and a table cloth and some easels." With that, she scurried off, returning ten minutes later with a folding card table, which she set up just inside the front opening of the store. Another trip, after she refused to let me help, produced a metal folding chair, a red Christmasy tablecloth, and two small easels. "There, that ought to do it," she proclaimed with a triumphant smile.

"What about copies of my novel?" I asked, unable to hide the alarm in my voice.

"Weren't you supposed to bring them?"

"No, you indicated several weeks ago, when we last talked on the phone, that you had ordered them?"

"I did?"

"Yep."

"I'll check." She whisked away, leaving me to imagine that I would spend the next few hours with nothing better to do than hand out the descriptive flyers I had brought.

In a few minutes she came back, carrying a box. "Here they are. They were in the processing room. Sorry."

I looked in the box, only to discover that it was filled with copies of a book entitled DEFENDING YOUR LIFE AGAINST SPAM. "These aren't mine," I told her.

"Oh, dear! Tell me again the name of your book."

"It's called DAVIDSON'S HELL." Images of Ms. Dewdrane residing in my fictional hell raced through my head, with her sitting atop the spinning orb I devised for people who have lived their lives in a disorganized daze.

"I'll be right back." She gathered up the box she had brought and hurried away, absent for several minutes, during which I paced in agitation, giving serious thought to writing a sequel to my book, totally devoted to sending to Hell all managerial types who were too stupid to be hired for even the most menial jobs.

She finally returned, this time with fifteen copies of my book. "I found them," she declared with a broad smile, as if she were the winner of a treasure hunt." They were right where they should have been. Well, I'll leave them for you to do with as you wish. Let me know if I can help." She whirled away, whereupon I began arranging my display.

Once the table was set up, with two of my books standing upright on the easels, the others in two neat piles, I borrowed some scotch tape from Betty at the register to hang on the front and side of the table a couple of computer printouts I had brought, which read, "Meet the Author of

DAVIDSON'S HELL." I also strategically placed the flyers so that anyone who came within eyeshot of the table could see them.

As soon as I sat down, I discovered another problem—the front edge of the table was even with the opening of the store, making it impossible for me to see people coming down the corridor until they essentially were right in front of me. I thus began a series of maneuvers for creeping outward, lifting the table and pushing it a few inches, then humping the chair out, until eventually the table rested completely outside the opening and I could see both ways down the corridor. My only concern during this process, besides worrying that I might be violating some mall policy or one imposed by manager Patty Dewdrane, was a gamy front leg on the card table, which tried its best to collapse each time I inched forward the table, twice dipping dangerously down and to the side, almost spilling my books out into the corridor. It made me recall the image of Disner slumped in front of the toilet.

Finally comfortable with my aggressive position relative to the passers-by, with optimism that would rival that of Leibniz or Voltaire's Pangloss, I began the task of selling copies of my book. However, this optimism began to fade when I realized that in the first thirty minutes or so, no one passing by or coming into the store even looked at me or my display, and that it took almost forty-five minutes before someone actually stopped and asked about the book and took a flyer. I began to think that even though I was a hundred miles from campus and Disner's death site, the people in the mall knew about Disner's murder and were avoiding me because they suspected that I had more to do with the killing than just discovering a dead body. I eventually added a handwritten sign to the front of the table, asking, "Need some humor?" though I was tempted to erect a sign that read, "I didn't do it."

The dearth of readers interested in my book did give me time to watch the parade of shoppers in the mall, many of whom reminded me of the zombies roaming the otherwise deserted mall in the movie THE DAWN OF THE DEAD, whole squads of them moving as if on autopilot, sleepwalking or actually dead. I began thinking that there was not all that much difference between the live shoppers and a dead Disner.

I did see a few power walkers striding by, reappearing two, three, or even four times while I sat there, seemingly trying to walk off what would never come off. Occasionally what appeared to be an entire street gang—judging by a similarity of logos and icons—would pass, carrying shopping bags instead of the weapons I half expected. There were lots of older men, trying to look young by sucking in their stomachs and by wearing baggy, low-slung pants and expensive looking running shoes, one guy even stepping frequently on the cuffs with his Nikes. One man was pulling a Jack Nicholson in AS GOOD AS IT GETS, carefully stepping over and around all the lines in the terrazzo floor. Another walker studied that same floor as if it held the answers to most of life's mysteries. The couple from the painting AMERICAN GOTHIC stiffly strode by, the man carrying a long paper tube instead of the pitchfork.

Lots of people drifted by while eating or drinking something they bought in the food court—iced cappuccinos, ice cream cones, cookies, tacos, etc.—consuming enough calories on the move—just in my purview— to feed a small country. Some were sucking on straws from drinking cups that appeared to be empty, judging by the lightness of movement, as if the cups were now simply props (reminding me of all those empty looking cans actors pretend to drink from in movies). It appeared to me that shopping was just one more opportunity to eat unhealthful food.

The eaters all made me think about Disner, who had constantly snacked on junk food. I tried to remember if there had been any food on the floor in the toilet stall where he lay dead. I would not have been surprised on that fatal day to spot a Little Debbie wrapper or a bag from Dunkin Donuts. Had he been putting something in while something else was coming out of him?

Occasionally some passers-by would look my way, even reading the signs I had taped on, mouthing the words "Davidson's Hell," with a puzzled expression, but they would quickly look away and hurry on down the corridor, making me seriously doubt the efficacy of my title.

After almost an hour, I started getting actual visits, with a variety of reactions. One picked up a copy of my book from the pile and held it aloft as if weighing it to see if it had sufficient heft to merit the price on it. Another touched one of the copies on an easel and then quickly drew back her hand as if the book were radioactive—or had the numbers 666 emblazoned on it. A woman who looked like Dana Carvey's Church Lady asked, "Is this a religious book?" and then added, "I don't buy a book unless it's religious. Is this one a warning about Hell for all of us?" I answered that, in a way, it was and then tried to explain my purpose. I lost her when I carelessly threw in the word "academic."

She was soon followed by a twenty-something year-old, who also wanted to know what the book was about. Carefully avoiding the word "academic" this time, I told her that it was a satire aimed at people who should do better but don't, including administrators, and a fictional hell I designed for them. She drew back and, after jamming her fists into the tops of her hips, exclaimed, "My grandmother's been an administrator for thirty years—a school principal—and I don't think you should make fun of her—or plan a place in hell for her." I told her that Granny would probably enjoy it, but granddaughter would have nothing more to do with it.

A woman in a rabbit coat and high heels asked me, "Is this available on audiotape with you reading it? I like only a book that I can listen to with the real writer reading it. Otherwise, how am I supposed to interpret certain lines?" I thought about suggesting using a modicum of imagination, but told her that the printed version was all I had to offer. She turned in a huff and exclaimed, "Never mind, then!" She was immediately followed by a man dressed in a green Sunday suit and yellow tie (Disner's favorite combo), who asked me, "Is this book free?"

A guy who reminded me of Dr. Strangelove, without the wheelchair, but with a seemingly undisciplined arm, asked me if there would be copies of my book in the store after I left. I told him yes. "I'll come back then and read it. I don't ever buy books. I'd rather just read 'em in the store."

"Does the book still look new when you've finished it?" I asked.

"Nope, I'm pretty rough on 'em. I've cracked a couple open so the pages started coming loose. But that's the bookstore's problem, or the publisher's, not mine."

The most annoying visitor was a man named Dwight Biggers, a former repo man who laughed at every comment he himself made, punctuating the humor and sagacity of his comments by good-naturedly—or was it ill-naturedly—punching me with his fist. I received several periods on the arms, a couple of exclamation marks on my chest, a semicolon and colon on my back—when I happened to turn away from him while he was describing to me how ruthless he had been in reclaiming an auto, even as the funeral of its owner was taking place. And, of course, no other customers dared approach me with Biggers at my table, hooting and punching. I eventually made up an excuse to find the manager at the back of the store, but not before Biggers dotted my rib cage with a whole string of ellipses marks.

As he was leaving, he asked me, "Which mall are you gonna be in next, in this area? I'd like to bring you some of my writing, particularly the story I wrote about a man whose son had just died in the car I showed up to repossess—of course with me not knowing before I got there that it'd been wrecked. The father wanted to pay off the loan on the car so that he could keep it—said he wanted to bury the entire car next to his son's grave, since some parts of the kid were still in it—you know, smashed into the dash and all."

In my present state of paranoia, I began to wonder if Biggers could be a killer, maybe the father of a disgruntled student I had offended, who was after me now, punching me to soften me up for the kill, like a cat playing with mouse. I told him I had no plans for other signings.

I was relieved when he was gone, but he made me think about Detective Smockley. I wondered what he would say if he were to drop by.

"What kind of book is this?" he would ask.

"It's a satirical work, inspired by Dante's "Inferno.""

"Who's Dante?"

"He was a fourteenth century Italian writer."

"I don't read Italian."

"His work appears in translation, and my book is written in English."

"What in the hell is an inferno?"

"What you just said."

"I don't get it."

"Hell—Dante's inferno is a version of hell. So is my book. It's a humorous look at people going to hell for what they've done in their lifetimes."

"What's so funny about going to hell?'

"It's the way I wrote the book—you know, make people swim in shit it they talked shit all their lives."

"I still don't see why that's funny."

"No, I guess you wouldn't."

"Does this apply to you?"

"What do you mean?"

"Do you think you're going to hell?"

"No, I don't believe in hell."

"No conscience, huh?"

"That's not what I meant."

"So you could kill someone without worrying about going to hell."

"I don't plan to kill anyone."

"But you might have already killed someone, and aren't sorry about it, isn't that right?"

"No, stop twisting my words."

"I don't twist words. I'm just a cop. You're the professor. You're the one that makes a career out of playing with words."

At one point I caught a glimpse of someone who looked just like Smockley, darting into Victoria's Secret. I kept my eye on the store for quite some time, first imagining that Smockley was spying on me from behind a teddy-clad mannequin, then becoming convinced that he was the mannequin, until a man who came to inquire about my book jerked me back to reality by asking, "See anything over there that turns you on?"

I did have some pleasant visitors. One woman picked up a copy and held it to her breast as if it were a sacred text, saying, "I love to get books from the authors themselves. It's like fresh literature." A father of two boys came over to let them meet a "real author" and see that books are not simply spit out by machines. My favorite of the day was a college-aged girl, who looked at my name and declared to her gruff-looking male companion, "Tyler Davidson, honey, I've read all of his books. Let's get one signed." I dared not disabuse her of the misconception about how many I had written, which, in reality, was only one.

I tried to keep smiling at everybody with whom I made eye contact, even cheerily saying "hello" to dozens of them, but about half way through the three hour signing, I began to lose some of my charm. I began to feel somewhat like a combination of a flight attendant speaking to passengers exiting a plane, the bell-ringer for the Salvation Army outside a store, a man at a flea market selling corn stalk dolls, and a barker on Bourbon Street trying to entice people to take in a strip show. Once or twice I was tempted to stand farther out in the corridor and shout, "Step right up, folks, get DAVIDSON'S HELL while it's hot."

I did manage to hand out at least half of the flyers I had brought, learning after an hour or so that I needed to practically force them on shoppers who came into the store, particularly if they halfway encouraged me by looking my way.

At the end of my stint—made lengthier by the fact that the store never provided me with even a cup of water—I contacted Manager Dewdrane, whom I had seen, after our initial contact, only the one time when I was escaping from Biggers. To her credit, she did have me sign five unsold copies, a practice that my publisher encouraged, since signed copies were less likely to be returned to the distributor and ultimately the publisher.

Right after leaving Thoreaubooks, I paid a visit to Victoria's Secret, first inspecting the mannequin I thought was Smockley, then honing in on a man who, with his back to me, looked a lot like Smockley, who turned out to be, when I accosted him, much older and more frail than Smockley, a guy who was making his way to the cashier to purchase for the woman in his life—or maybe for himself—a black bra and panty set and who acted when facing me as if it really was for himself. Castigating myself for my paranoia, I exited the store in such a hurry I almost knocked over a rack of silky slips.

I then attempted to retrace my steps when finding Thoreaubooks, only I took a left turn at one intersection instead of properly forging straight ahead and ended up in the Kay Jewelry-Sharper Image-Nature Outdoor Clothing-Godiva's Candies-Big Sound System-Dillards corridor. To my relief, when I finally reached the parking lot, Smockley wasn't waiting at my car to admonish me for leaving town without reporting to him.

As I drove the hundred miles back to campus, I reflected on some of the people I had met—or at least observed that day. I realized that most people did not come to a mall to meet an author, nor even to buy a book. And if they did come for a book, it usually was not for themselves. And if it were, it would most likely be something from the gardening, self-improvement, pet care, inspirational, or children's sections. I decided that my next book should have a title covering all those categories—maybe "Timmy and His Dog Peppy Find Happiness While Planting Daisies in the Billy Graham Memorial Garden."

I concluded that I would never want to be murdered in a mall.

I also concluded that on any given day I could be a murderer myself— gladly removing from the aisle of America's malls any number of obnoxious shoppers. But at least I had escaped the murder scene at my university for a while.

Chapter 12

I left my office at five before three to attend the meeting of the Teachers' Awards Committee (not to be confused with the Teaching Evaluation Committee), to which Bwanger assigned me as a reward/punishment for winning the Outstanding Teacher Award at the end of my third year. Does success always lead to amplified duties? Is this somehow related to the Peter Principle, except instead of rising to one's level of incompetence, one simply rises to a level of success and then gets screwed? I think I should call it the Dick Principle since someone—me—is still getting screwed here.

My one consolation was that at least, for a couple of hours, I would not have to meet with Smockley, who had called me that morning, announcing that he wanted to ask me some questions that afternoon. "Sorry, Detective," I said, "but I'll be tied up in a meeting until five, or maybe even later. Can we try for tomorrow?" This had to be one of the few times in my life that I wished for a long meeting. I just hoped he would not decide to make me sweat by showing up at the meeting and staring at me the whole time, while jotting down notes on that ever-present pad he keeps in his shirt pocket.

As I skipped down the stairs from the top floor to the fourth, I could hear the clock tower clanging out "The Battle Hymn of the Republic," though a more appropriate title here would be "The Battle Dirge of the Republic." Was it my imagination or was the music even slower than before? The music was enough to dampen any positive feelings I might have about avoiding Smockley, but then my spirits were temporarily lifted again by the smell of popcorn or maybe quesadillas. Was someone fixing snacks for the meeting? Judging from the names of the members of the committee listed on the memo announcing the meeting—Huzlet, Corincher, Cherry, and Johnson, along with Bwanger—I doubted it, but then again I could be wrong, and the next two hours might actually be bearable.

Nope, no snacks at the meeting, at least not for the whole group. Gladys Corincher was testing with her right index finger the temperature of a burrito that lay in a microwave tray. So much for making the time bearable, but thankfully Smockley was not there.

Bwanger began the meeting with the usual committee foreplay—ironically, in view of Corincher's burrito—with comments about his own self-diagnosed gastric problems: "I woke up three or four times last night with a burning sensation in my stomach. I'm sure it's a peptic ulcer."

"Are you sure it wasn't just acid reflux?" Cherry asked, with the authority of one who had been there, felt that.

Before Bwanger could answer, Huzlet jumped in. "How can you tell the difference between an ulcer and reflux? Are they the same?" she quizzed.

"No, they're quite different," Bwanger averred. "You see . . . ."

While Bwanger explained, I tried my best to slip into a temporary coma, but failed, so I did the next best thing and began doodling, drawing a miniature caricature of Bwanger, with a television screen replacing his abdomen, on which was playing a scene of a bubbling caldron.

As he complained, Bwanger made me think about the Renaissance concept of the doctrine of correspondence, which holds that one's interior being is written all over his exterior appearance. I began to wonder if Disner's killer actually looked like a killer, whatever that might be. Of those at the meeting right then, Bwanger looked most like a hostile alien, if not a bona fide criminal. He had a pinched face, which seemed to match his turbulent stomach, which rumbled with the sound of a muffler-less pickup truck almost every time there was a caesura in his medical lesson. Still, it was difficult for me to imagine him as a killer.

Of the rest, Glick seemed the least guilty. With his ashen complexion and fretful seriousness, he was just too bland to qualify as a killer.

"Well, enough about me. Let's get down to brass tacks," Bwanger finally asserted. The main business of the meeting in fact was not about brass tacks at all but rather a consideration of a proposal to have some new Departmental awards for teaching and/or research. I thought I might lightening the mood of the meeting by offering a couple of bogus suggestions about recognizing good teaching—including giving medals or medallions to deserving teachers, like bronze or silver stars given by the military, even a purple heart for anyone injured on the job (with the proposal that Disner be given an academic medal of honor for dying in our building during class hours) or have a band show up in the classroom to "hail" a teacher receiving a teaching award. The only problem was that Bwanger took my suggestions seriously and praised me profusely.

While Gladys Corincher, now finished with her burrito, offered the notion of inviting appropriate administrators, such as the Dean or the Vice President for Academic Affairs, to sit in the classes of the award winners, I let my mind run over existing so-called "rewards" the faculty got for high achievement in teaching and research.

They did not amount to much.

The "reward" for success as an assistant professor usually was promotion to associate professor (with a whopping five hundred dollar raise) and success there garnered a promotion to the rank of professor (and another five hundred added). It seemed to me that the titles ought to at least sound better, if they represented a climb up the academic ladder. "Assistant" and "Associate" just didn't cut it for positions normally requiring a Ph.D., and after climbing to the top of the ladder, a teacher merely received the title of "Professor," which is what any uninformed freshman—or Smockley—called every teacher anyway, including part-time instructors with only a master's degree. One does not get a noble sounding title until he retires and becomes a "Professor Emeritus" (though the term SOUNDS more imposing than its real meaning, which refers to having served one's time, which, of course, could be in prison too).

Administrators, on the other hand, get nifty titles like "Chancellor," "Bursar," "Comptroller" (or "Controller," which sounds equally imposing), and expanded names like "Director of Matching Funds" or "Dean of Research and Graduate Studies."

Even people outside the University get better titles than most of the teachers. Smockley was referred to usually as "Detective Smockley." I thought about suggesting to the committee that we bestow heroic epithets or Anglo-Saxon kennings on a teacher who accomplished anything worthy, names like "the Great," "the Magnificent," "the Learned," or, appropriately in a couple of cases, "the Slayer" or "the Butcher." Most of the people I knew in the University would have distinctly unheroic epithets. Bwanger would likely be called "The Bumbler" (Alliteration goes a long way with epithets). Glick surely would be "The Geek." Disner would be "The Drone." President Popson would be—well, he wouldn't need anything extra, since his name made him sound like a clown anyway.

Realistically, I did wonder if Disner's acquiring a title had anything to do with his murder. Did getting tabbed "Associate Dean" bring on his doom? Did his sudden, though small, fame make someone jealous? After all, his picture did appear in the RAYSVILLE RURALITE as well as the University's own FACULTY NEWSLETTER, with his title underscoring the picture. Of course his picture and title also appeared with his obituary, but I doubted if his detractor would get jealous over that.

This topic was hammered into flat foil for the next half hour, as various committee members opined what activity should be rewarded and what those rewards should be. I lost track of many of the suggestions, but I did hear a case made for rewarding anyone who supplied cookies and donuts for the Department (usually brought my members who wanted an excuse to eat these items themselves) or for arranging socials for the Department. A case was even made for rewarding someone who sang at a high school class reunion.

I began wondering what kind of rewards the police received for their work and what they had to do to get the rewards. For example, what did Smockley do to get promoted from regular policeman to the rank of Detective—nail a serial killer or was it something much more minor, such as hauling in a kid for skateboarding on sidewalks? Or did he have to go back to school and earn a higher degree? Or did the promotion come automatically because he served for some specified number of years? Was the reward more than a $500 raise? Did he also receive a bigger locker, a more convenient parking spot? Would he get some fat bonus for bringing to justice Disner's killer? Would it be an even bigger bonus if the killer was an administrator or a full professor, but lesser if the guilty one were lower in rank, maybe just an assistant professor, like me? Would he get any accolades at all if the killer came from outside the University?

The meeting stretched until ten minutes before five (with Bwanger ending it with false altruism, "I know you have lots to do, so I'm not going to keep you all the way to five"). As I left the building, I again heard the tower slowly playing "The Battle Hymn of the Republic." I wondered if there was a defect in the tower such that it repeated songs or, worse, it had taken two hours to get through the rendition I heard when first heading to the meeting.

Chapter 13

As I exited the building, I breathed a sigh of relief that Smockley had not been waiting for me again in the hall or staircase. But then—trouble ahead. Up against my car, waiting for me, leaned Smockley—or rather DETECTIVE Smockley—wearing sunglasses, holding a toothpick between his compressed lips, his hands stuffed into his front pants' pockets, his legs crossed, his back against the passenger-side floor. He looked like a man leaning against a bar in a singles' nightclub, waiting to pick up a girl who might be attracted to a motorcycle stud, except Smockley was wearing a suit, with his note pad poking out the top pocket of his coat. The suit made me wonder if detectives wore them to be more intimidating. If I recollect correctly, Clint Eastwood and Charles Bronson's characters wore them—or at least sport coats and ties.

"Do all your meetings take that long?" he asked, talking around the toothpick.

"Usually—or even longer. Why did you need to see me again?

He removed the toothpick and held it between us, pointing upward. After a dramatic pause, he answered, "We need to talk."

"Oh, no. If we're going to talk, we first need to set the rules."

"Rules? We don't need to do anything new."

"Well, if there aren't any rules, then someone count to ten!"

"What in the world are you talking about?"

"You know, like in BUTCH CASSIDY AND THE SUNDANCE KID. Sundance counts to ten, and then I kick you in the groin."

"Try that, Buster and I'll arrest you."

"Well, all right then. What do you need to talk about?"

"I've been hearing some pretty incriminating evidence against you, and . . . ."

"Regarding what?"

"What do you think?"

"I don't know—about doing terrible things to cats with forks? What have you been told and by whom?"

"Oh, 'whom' is it. You professors sound so proper."

"Never mind that! What have I been accused of?"

"Things." He stuck the toothpick back between his lips. "About how you didn't like Professor Disner. How you made fun of him, even in your classes—without actually saying his name of course. You're too sly for that."

"If I never used his name, how did anyone know I was referring to him?

"Did you in fact talk about him—in class, or anywhere else for that matter?"

"No, not exactly. I often made jokes about people with annoying habits, and I did throw in a few gratuitous 'okay's' like he often did, but I didn't have to be necessarily talking about him."

"But you admit you did make fun of him, or someone just like him?" Smockley wiggled the toothpick up and down, rapidly. I had the feeling that behind his sunglasses his eyes were dancing.

"Who told you all this?"

"Students, your colleagues, your own department head. Seems like lots of people knew of your dislike for him."

"Even if all that were true, that wouldn't make me a murderer."

"But it does provide a motive." He removed the toothpick and pointed it at me.

"Yeah, for me and about two thousand other people who knew him. He was a sap, you know, and I wasn't the only one who thought so."

"Sounds like sour grapes to me." In went the toothpick.

"About what?"

"He was moving up the university ladder, wasn't he, faster than you? He had been made an administrator—or at least a part-time administrator."

"Yes, so what?"

"Didn't that bother you—him getting ahead of you like that—particularly since you thought he was a sap, as you called him?" Out came the toothpick.

"I don't consider his becoming an administrator getting ahead of me—as you phrase it. In fact, I see it as a step down."

"You're telling me that you'd never want to be an administrator—have a reduced teaching load and make more money than you do now?"

"You've got it, unless I could fill a new administrative position, like Controller of Absurdity, Director of University Comedy, maybe Dean of Derision."

"But . . . ."—at this point he pulled out his note pad from his coat pocket and began flipping through it, stopping midway.—"you were a part-time administrator here at the University—in your third year, I believe. What do you have to say to that?"

I started to say that I would like to know what his eyes looked like behind those Ray Bans—narrowed into slits or wide open, with his pupils dilated—but I answered,"Yeah, I helped organize some silly English honors program."

"As an administrator, right?"

"I suppose. But I quit after just one year."

"Why?" In went the toothpick.

"Because I didn't like being an administrator—and because most of the so-called honors students weren't qualified to be honors students—just a bunch of average students who liked to play video games and make out on the couches in the Honors Room."

"What's to keep me from thinking that you're really still in the market for being an administrator? One bad experience doesn't rule out your wanting to do something else to grab more pay."

"Look, doesn't my quitting after one year tell you something about my attitude toward it all?"

"Why'd you take the job in the first place—if you're so opposed to being an administrator?"

"Because Bwanger, my department head, asked me to, with the implication it would help me get tenure."

"Meaning what?"

"Meaning that I can't get fired unless I do something really egregious, I mean very bad."

"Like what? And by the way, I may not be a college professor, but I know what 'egregious' means." Out came the toothpick.

"Sorry, but in answer to your question, doing something like mooning the crowd at graduation."

"Or committing murder?"

"Well, sure, I guess that would pretty much cancel out my tenure, if and when I ever did such a thing."

"Seems to me that you've already admitted that you're willing to do undesirable tasks to make it up the ladder—call it tenure or promotion or getting a more prestigious job—like the one Disner had."

"I'm not admitting anything of the sort."

"What's your next level of success? What are you gunning for now."

"I choose to ignore your choice of words there, but I am trying to get promoted to associate professor."

He scribbled a note in his pad. "I thought you were a professor."

"I am a professor, but not in rank."

"I don't get it. Are you messing with me?" In went the toothpick.

"No, it's just that we use the term 'professor' to equal the term 'teacher,' while the rank of full professor, or simply professor, comes after about ten years or more. I'm an assistant professor in rank now, hoping to rise to associate, then professor eventually."

Smockley frowned at me as if I had just explained the different meanings of the word 'sodomy' and then wrote another note in his pad. "The point is that it would help you to have an administrative job on your resume, right—a job like the one Professor Disner had?"

"I suppose it would for some people. Administrators seem to like rewarding other administrators, but I'd rather earn my promotion with teaching awards, publications, service work, et cetera. I never wanted the position Disner held."

"Why not?"

"Well, for one thing, I'd have to get a briefcase or attache case, preferably in leather, and I'd have to dress like you—wear a suit, or at least a coat and tie, maybe even carry around a pad of paper like you do. I probably couldn't do the toothpick thing though. Most administrators aren't seen with toothpicks in their mouths."

Smockley removed the toothpick and held it up at eye level, inspecting it as if it were a piece of evidence in the murder case. He then put it back in his mouth. "What's wrong with my suit?"

"Nothing specifically, but it's still a suit. Disner wore one too."

"Why did Professor Disner's choice of clothing disturb you? Were you jealous that he looked more professional than you?"

"No, it was because of the colors he wore."

"What do you mean?"

"He wore combinations of the school's colors most of the time—you know, yellow and green—a green suit and a yellow shirt, or in the summer, a yellow suit and a green shirt." I got an image of Disner dead in the toilet stall with the blood dripping onto his yellow and green clothes. I could not help but smile.

"What's so funny, Professor?"

"Nothing. I just don't like yellow and green, I guess."

Smockley removed the toothpick and tapped me on my shoulder with it, and though its point had been softened by Smockley's chewing, it still stuck me with sufficient force through my knit shirt to make me feel as if I had been stung by a bee. "Do you mind!" I exclaimed, backing a step away. "I hope you don't have a communicable disease."

He stared at me several seconds, but then said in an even tone, "All right, Professor, that's enough for now. I've got you at the scene of the murder, and, despite your lame protestations about not wanting to be an administrator, I'm beginning to detect a motive, based upon your past duties with that honors business, that plus the fact that you didn't like Professor Disner. I've just got to discover the weapon you used. I'll be seeing you again—often, in fact. You probably ought to think about getting yourself an attorney."

He jammed the toothpick into his shirt pocket. I started to ask him if they were in short supply, but I didn't want to prolong the conversation. Accompanied by the chimes—once again playing "The Battle Hymn of the Republic"—I drove quickly from the parking lot, so quickly in fact that I cut off Smockley as he tried to exit in his SUV.

Chapter 14

But I didn't go home immediately. Earlier, upon learning that I was going to attend the awards committee meeting, Ben Sturgeon had invited me to his house for a beer when it was over. As I drove there, I thought about Smockley's grilling and wondered if his aggressiveness with me indicated his suspicion of me or something else. Could making me feel defensive be his way of shaking out loose details I was hiding from even myself?

When I arrived at Sturgeon's house, I was met by his wife Kim, who greeted me at the door with a bottle of Heineken's in her hand. "Hi, Tyler. Here, take this. Ben said you'd probably need it immediately."

"Yes," I answered, "right now's a good time, though at the beginning of the meeting I just came from—with refills during the meeting—would have been better, and maybe something stronger right after the meeting in the parking lot."

"Why's that?" Ben asked, having joined Kim and me in the foyer.

"I'll tell you after I've finished at least this bottle." We all drifted into the den, where Ben offered me some veggies and dip. With the Heineken's in one hand and a carrot in the other, I began describing the meeting, including the suggestions for awards that I had facetiously offered and those that other members had seriously considered.

"You should have suggested that the award winner be given one of the administrator's designated parking places for a week or maybe a month," Ben offered.

Kim responded, "That'd be great for the award winner, but can you imagine any administrator who would give up one of his most prized possessions, with his or her name painted on the curb?"

"Maybe," I added, "the administrators could choose one of their own—the person who has done the worst job for the preceding month—as a kind of punishment. Make him find his own place, as the faculty and other staff members do everyday."

"Get serious, Tyler!" Sturgeon snorted. "Do you think any of the administrators would admit that one of their own ever did a poor job? And, besides, how can one judge poor performance among administrators, anyway? So much of what they do is meaningless or shrouded in mystery, there's really no way to tell if a job's done badly. No, I guess we'll have to find another way to reward our honorees. I actually like all that about having a band strike up in class, or at least give a drum accent for clever remarks. But tell me about what went on in the parking lot."

"Oh, it's just that Detective Smockley was waiting for me at my car and raked me over me—again—about Disner's murder."

"Does he think you had anything to do with it?"

"I guess. He said that he's gotten lots of reports—even from Bwanger—that I bad-mouthed Disner all the time."

Well, Hell, I've done that myself."

"That's right, you have. Maybe you're the one that murdered him. Maybe I ought to get Smockley on your case for a change."

"Bring him on! I'd like to be accused of something exciting. As it stands, all I ever get accused of is for taking too long to return exams and essays and for favoritism in my grading, giving A's to only the students who actually earn them."

Kim joined in. "I know that Ben thought Disner was an ambitious ladder climber and a sneaky little turd. What made you dislike him so much, Tyler?"

"Well, for those same reasons and for a bunch of petty trivialities."

"Such as?" Kim offered me another carrot.

"Among other reasons, he was always camped out in the men's room—you know that he graded papers while sitting on the john, don't you—and he always wanted to talk pedagogy with me in there. I couldn't even whiz without him spouting off about learning communities, holistic grading, or recruitment techniques. Many a time I wanted to pee on him. I thought it poetic justice that he was murdered in the john. And he became especially annoying when he became the assistant dean of Arts and Sciences, talking as if he were being filmed—which he might have been, for all I know. I hear he demanded a new executive chair with extra padding in the arms, to thump on with his forearms, I guess, and a heavy-duty swivel mechanism.

Anyway, lots of things like that, plus I'm convinced he tried to prevent my getting tenure."

"Does Smockley know about that last thing, with your tenure business?" Kim asked.

"He didn't mention it, but he does think I had some motive—over and beyond simply not liking Disner. He believes—are you ready for this?—that I was jealous of Disner for getting that administrative post as assistant dean and that I wanted the position myself."

"Why would he think that?"

"He thinks I'd want the so-called perks that go with the job—the extra pay and a reduced teaching load—and the prestige. Plus he knew about my having dabbled in administrative work before—with the Honor's Program. I guess he figures it's in my blood and that I'm willing to spill somebody else's to get such a position."

Sturgeon began laughing. "Why, I can see how the detective would think that. After all, you just LOVED doing that Honor's business, didn't you?"

"Sure, Ben, about as much as I LOVED going to personnel meetings and putting together my tenure documents. I'm quite sure I'd still be doing the Honors' job right now, except for a couple of incidentals—like the idiocy and lack of qualified students."

Kim spoke up. "You can joke about it all you want, but I'd be careful with this detective, Smockley, if I were you. I've lived in this area long enough to have heard lots about him. He grew up here and has worked his way up in the ranks, starting as a city cop and getting just enough education to become an inspector. He's always been suspicious of people connected with the University, maybe with a chip on his shoulder about more educated people, and he's suspicious of Northerners, and that of course includes you since you're from Michigan. If he thinks he's right about something, he won't let up. If he believes you're guilty, he can make life difficult for you even if you're completely innocent."

"I see your point. He comes across like a bull terrier, but don't worry, I'll be careful. Actually, right now, he's not my main concern. There's someone lurking out there that murdered Disner, someone who knows that I was in the vicinity when the murder took place and therefore knows that I could possibly provide a clue to his—or her—identity."

After another hour's worth of conversation, more beer, and lots of carrots, along with broccoli, and celery, all serving as alcohol absorbers, I drove home, half way expecting Smockley to be waiting at a traffic light for me—or in my driveway, if for no other reason than to administer a breathalyzer test to me.

Chapter 15

I had only a few minutes before the monthly English Department faculty meeting was to begin at 8 am. I was already on edge from having slept only a couple of hours the night before and from an incident at my office soon after I arrived. As a result, I was not looking forward to a meeting in which Disner's murder would undoubtedly—again— be discussed, with me as the go-to person for first hand reporting. If only I were one of the faculty members who had an 8 o'clock class and could skip the meeting.

I had arrived at my office well before 7 am to prepare for my 10 am class in American Lit, one in which we would be discussing two of Poe's works, "Ligeia" and "The Raven." I had figured I was alone in the building and, with my door closed, would not be disturbed, at least until closer to 8. As I slumped in my roll-around chair, rereading the opening lines from the poem, I heard my own version of a rustling noise outside in the hall and then a bump against the door—not a distinct rapping or tapping, as in the poem, but a softer sound as if someone were leaning on it. I wasn't completely sure—it could be from a lack of sleep— but next I thought I heard the doorknob being slowly turned, as if someone were checking if it was locked. I straightened up quickly, feeling a bit of the "fantastic terror" that Poe describes, and looked at the center of the doorknob to make sure that the locking mechanism was horizontal, indicating that the door was indeed locked.

I waited for what seemed like a half an hour for the noise to reoccur, but heard no sound other than the whisper of the air conditioning overhead. Half of me wanted boldly to fling open the door and confront whoever was there. The other half (maybe a bigger fraction—maybe even three-fourths) decided to sit quietly and pretend nothing had occurred. Needless to say I did little preparing for teaching either of Poe's works, as I sat watching the door handle and listening for sounds, even half expecting a willowy voice to pronounce the name "Lenore" or "Disner" or "Tyler."

Thoughts of a dead Disner in front of the toilet in the men's room raced through my head. Then visions arose of ME slumped on the floor of my office—with a bullet hole in my forehead—but I took some comfort in the fact that when someone discovered my body—maybe the cleaning staff—my arm would not be in the toilet bowl, as Disner's had, and my pants and underwear would not be down around my ankles and I wouldn't be dressed in the same blood-stained yellow and green clothes Disner wore when he died. I'd be on my beige carpet dressed in dark blue pants and a light blue, long-sleeved shirt, with the sleeves rolled up, and no tie. And I wouldn't look as if I'd just said/asked "Okay?" like Disner.

As I had done in the men's room the day I discovered Disner's body, I began to fantasize about overwhelming the killer, this time by opening the door so quickly he could not react in time to prevent my grabbing his gun and karate chopping him in the throat or ramming my knuckles into his solar plexus. Maybe I dodged a bullet in the process. Then the fantasy took the shape of a scenario in which I got wounded, but still managed to disarm him, whereupon I pinned him to the wall—with one hand—while I used the other to dial 911—or Smockley directly.

"Detective Smockley, you can stop interrogating me. I've got your man."

"Where?"

"Here in my office. He tried to kill me, just like he did Disner."

"Is he dead?"

"No, I've got him pinned against the wall. Could you just get over her and arrest him?"

"Maybe he's just someone trying to get back at you because YOU killed Disner.'

"Are you crazy?"

"No, just determined to bring you to justice."

I got so absorbed in my fantasies, I failed to notice the absence of any more sounds of bumping or rustling or door handle turning.

Finally, I could stand it no longer. I "opened wide the door," but was greeted with, not Poe's "darkness there and nothing more," but rather an empty hall, though there lay on the floor the announcement for the morning's faculty meeting, which had appeared in all of our mail boxes the day before. I felt like a ninny, but I was relieved that no one was out

71

there, and I was also relieved there was not a big black bird in my office squawking "Nevermore." I did wonder why someone else's meeting notice was outside my door.

Now, at five till eight, still unprepared for my class, I locked my office door and headed for the English Department office, where Bwanger said the meeting would take place. I almost stopped at the men's room on my floor, but was simply not up to a real or imagined confrontation with a potential killer. I could remember the time when the worst thing about the men's room was unflushed toilets. Now it reminded me of death, Disner, funerals, and Smockley. I decided to visit the one on the fourth floor, though I did give thought to waiting until I got home some seven hours later.

As I neared the English Office, I could hear the bell tower chiming out a miserable rendition of "Yankee Doodle," played in such a way to emphasize casualties of war. It was only one of several patriotic songs bonging out from the tower almost every day lately—along with "The Battle Hymn of the Republic," "She's a Grand Old Flag," "America the Beautiful," "God Bless America," and the national anthem." A few of these had replaced such non-patriotic regulars as the "Whiffenpoof Song" and the ironically appropriate "Send in the Clowns." Due to the tension I was experiencing over Disner's murder, I was not feeling particularly patriotic and the bell tower's lugubrious renditions did little to perk me up.

Chapter 16

The faculty meeting took up nearly the entire two hours from 8 to 10, leaving me only a few minutes to further prepare for my class on Poe. Fortunately, Bwanger took time during the meeting to read, in their entirety, as if they were sacred scripture, the minutes from the Department Heads Meeting (even though all faculty members had already received them on campus e-mail), thus providing me with a few moments to sneak in peaks at my text book, though I had to be careful since Bwanger, standing at the lectern in front of the group, had direct line of sight to me.

When I wasn't reading and marking lines in "Ligeia" or "The Raven" or listening to Bwanger, I was thinking about the noises outside my office that morning—and about the memo someone had dropped. Whoever it was, if indeed someone had actually even been there, it probably was not Smockley. How could he have received a copy of the memo for the meeting? It had to be someone in this room. And why would they hang around in the hall and try my door handle, without knocking or calling out to me? I tried to see who didn't have the memo on their desks, but it was a difficult task since many members had multiple sheets of paper, any or none of which, from my vantage point, could have been the memo. Cherry, Glick, and Huzlet had no paper in front of them., but I knew that didn't really prove anything. Even Bwanger didn't have a copy of the agenda, but he seemed to have memorized it anyway. The line from Buffalo Springfield's "For What It's Worth" kept running through my head, "Paranoia strikes deep."

I didn't have time at the end of the meeting to do a person-by-person search of who was missing the memo, since I had less than ten minutes to get to class, but such a check would not have been particularly desirable anyway. I could imagine asking each person, as he or she was leaving the room, for the memo, making up some phony reason, "Hey, Clark, I lost my memo. Can I check yours just a second. I have a question for Dr. Bwanger." I imagined how awkward that would get after asking about three or four people still within earshot of each other. Why couldn't the person who dropped it at least have had the decency to write something on it to help in the identification process?

As I was heading out the door, Bwanger caught up with me. "Tyler, can you come by my office for a minute? I want to touch base further with you about recent events."

Running around an infield with Bwanger was not exactly my ideal for the rest of the morning, but I knew I'd have to talk with him again, having been so short with him in the hall previously.

"Not right now. I have a class. But I'll come after it's over."

I rushed to my office to pick up a set of quizzes I planned to return to the students. Then I hurried down the stairs to the second floor, hearing as I did the bell tower repeating the miserable rendition of "Yankee Doodle" I had heard earlier.

Chapter 17

With no quiz made up, still feeling testy due to rising early and then enduring knuckle-whitening time in my office, followed by Bwanger's superfluous two-hour meeting, I entered the classroom just as the bell tower labored through the last notes of "America the Beautiful," followed by ten widely spaced bongs for the hour. The class was sitting in near darkness, the room illuminated only by the minimal sunlight that crept around the edges of the closed blinds. I marveled, as I often had before, that no one would take the initiative to turn on the lights when entering. Maybe they thought of the switched off light in the same way they did the stob holding open the men's room door—as high-tech equipment not to be touched except by trained authorities. At any rate, switching on the lights gave me an opportunity to be dramatically symbolic—dispelling darkness, bringing enlightenment, et cetera, except my actions were greeted by a round of groans and a comment, "It was nice with the lights off."

The first order of business was to return the set of papers I had corrected over the last four days—when I wasn't thinking about who killed Disner and fretting about the pressure Smockley kept applying. The first paper went to Karen Klogman, who apparently skipped my numerous marginal comments and charged straight through to the last page, where, instead of giving a score, I had written a comment to the effect that I was withholding it—for her benefit—until she revised the paper, clearing up several egregious errors in grammar and syntax. I had added that it was not a passable paper as it then stood.

I was just about to hand Daniel Duffman his paper when I heard an insistent voice summoning me."Excuse me, Professor!" It was Ms. Klogman.

"Yes, Karen, is there a problem?"

"You didn't put a grade on my paper!"

"Did you read my comment?"

"Which one? There are comments all over the paper."

"The one on the last page."

"No, I just noticed that there isn't a grade."

"Well, read that one. It explains why there's no grade."

"I don't understand."

"You will, after you read that last comment." I continued passing out other papers, several to the "have's" in the class, one with an A- to Susan Montagne, an A+ to Walter Herbert, an A- to Jennifer Harrison, then some turned in by the "semi-have's," with B's on them, a few average performances with C's on them, such as the one turned in by Cletus Troutfinger, with no shred of originality, and a couple turned in by definite "have-not's," marked with near-failure D's. I was in the process of giving one of the latter to Tina Truff, when I again heard Ms. Klogman.

"It's not fair!"

"What do you mean, Karen?"

"I've been looking at the papers other people are receiving, and they all have grades on them." She waved her hand around, palm upward, gesturing toward those sitting closest to her, as if they were her support group. "I spent a long time on this paper and I think I deserve a grade as much as anyone else!"

I briefly entertained the prospect of snatching up her paper and slashing on a large scale F and proclaiming—loudly so the rest of the class could hear—"There, you have a grade! Are you happy now?" But still worrying about alienating any of my students—or potential killers, as I now thought of them—I answered as politely as I could, "Why don't you see me after class and I'll explain further why there is no grade yet." I could not help but wonder if Disner had returned a set of papers immediately before ending up on the toilet stall floor with a bullet in his head.

"Oh, all right, but I still don't think it's fair." Her exaggerated sigh that followed reminded me of the hissing noise I heard a monitor lizard make during an episode of ANIMAL PLANET.

After giving the rest of the class their papers, I began lecturing on—discussing, or was it "facilitating the learning process for"—Poe's "The Raven" and "Ligeia." It is amazing to me how a little fear and suspicion can make one more hostile toward others, but at the same time more tolerant. I did not sigh, roll my eyes, huff, look askance—do anything to show displeasure—during the entire class period—even when Buffy Bridgetower came in late, allowing the door to slam shut after her, and crossed right in front of me, squeezing between the lectern and the front row of desks rather than walking behind me. I did not go into a rage when Dirkson Slidgendorf, who, I suspected, had difficulty pronouncing his own name, particularly when he was drunk, fell asleep, not even waking up when his supporting arm collapsed and his head slumped to the top of the desk. I did nothing to quieten Heather Roach and Donald Roundson, who carried on an animated and flirtatious conversation while I was explaining how losing someone we love—like Poe's Lenore—can mess up our heads so that we might even interpret a bird's squawking as the word "nevermore."

I withheld derision when, after I had been discussing "The Raven" for almost fifteen minutes, I called on Rodney Bacon, an ectomorph with hair like broken guitar strings, to comment on the passage in "The Raven" that includes the line "Nothing farther then he uttered—not a feather then he fluttered," for only then did he laborious pull his back pack from under his desk, take out his textbook, and open it to "The Raven," reminding me of the phlegmatic people in the checkout line at the grocery store, who wait until their goods are completely totaled and the cashier is standing by the cash register filing her fingernails before they, the customers, even begin looking for their purses and/or wallets to settle the bill. I also patiently listened to Wanda Biggerstaff speaking in dangling modifiers, and with cool aplomb I answered Bonita Cluff, who, in response to my giving a definition of Gothicism, asked," Is this going to be on the exam?" I did not grimace when I spotted Thomas Muffler, someone who appeared to be at war with his own genetic coding, in the seeming covertness of the back row cram his index finger in his nose—up to the second joint. I did not try to calm down the annoying exuberance of Polly Peckingham, who I suspected was one of those customers at Red Lobster that would join the wait staff in singing "Happy Birthday" to a total stranger.

The closest I came to being negative occurred when Billy Coggins responded to a question directed to him about the ninth stanza of "The Raven," which begins with "Much I marveled this ungainly fowl to hear discourse so plainly, / Though its answer little meaning—little relevancy bore." I asked him if Poe made us believe that there really was a bird in the narrator's presence. He first removed his cap and patted down his hair, as if this ritual might help him find an answer, and then mumbled something that sounded like "er . . . flute . . . bummer . . . gland . . . joystick." Instead of having him repeat his mumbling response (and suspecting that a more audible answer might actually make less sense than the mumbling), I simply said "Yes, of course," and then moved on.

Through all this, thoughts of Disner kept entering my head; after all, part of the lesson was a discussion of "Ligeia," which is about a dead person coming back to life by interfusing the body of someone else—a woman named Rowena—who has just recently died but whose body is still perfectly usable. Help! What if Disner's spirit took over someone else's body. It would probably be easy to figure out if Disner took over a faculty member's body, but more difficult if he claimed an administrator's body, since so many of them resembled Disner in personality to begin with. I guess I'd have to listen for the tell tale Disner give-aways, an "Okay?" at the end of every declarative sentence or singing while standing at the urinal in the men's room.

I also thought about Smockley. If he had been sitting in my class that day and observing me, would he interpret my seeming apathy toward idiocy and my failure to commend the good students as signs of my being distracted, or being out and out guilty? And speaking of guilt, how about the students? Did they feel guilty—even the good ones who had read the assignment—when I put them on the spot, like I did when Smockley questioned me.

I was unbelievably tired by the end of class, but that wasn't the end of my labor, for I still had the problem of explaining, with only partial success, I suspected, to Karen Klogman why it was to her benefit that I had not marked a grade on her paper and why, if I had gone ahead and put down a grade, it would have been an F.

"Didn't you like my paper?" Her voice had become monotonic.

"It's not a matter of liking or disliking your paper. I'm simply a grader. I try to be as objective as possible."

"Did you have something against it because it's hand-written?"

"No, I actually like receiving papers that way, as I mentioned in class at the start of the term. I think hand written ones have more personality." I did not go on to explain what personality her loopy, ornate style, with hearts for periods, made me suspect that I was dealing with. I did come close to asking about how much time she spent in a tanning booth, my guess being four or five times a week, but I remained consistent in my "let's-not-offend-anyone-today" mode. After finishing with her, I staggered out of the room, hoping Smockley wouldn't be in the hall waiting for me, for I knew that on this day I was almost weak enough to confess to any crime he might accuse me of.

Chapter 18

Finding no trace of Smockley in the hall, I hurried to the English office to see Bwanger, but before meeting with him, I checked my mailbox.

I half expected a threatening note, where someone had pasted—onto a crumpled piece of paper—irregularly sized letters cut out from newspaper headlines, stating "Confess you killer!" or "I know you killed Disner!" or, worse, "You're next, Professor!" Fortunately, there was nothing that exciting, only a flyer from a publisher listing several new—and no doubt superfluous—rhetorics and grammar books and the newest FACULTY NEWSLETTER, on the front page of which was a picture of President Popson smiling at the camera. He was flanked by a man on his right and a woman on his left, who, according to the caption, had just donated 1,000 acres of inherited property to the University—actually, farm land thirty miles south in a place more remote than the campus of NGU itself. The three people were arranged for the picture such that Popson seemed to be the center of attention, he facing the camera, the other two turned toward him in sycophantic poses.

The photograph reminded me of the numerous other pictures I had seen in newspapers and flyers over the last year, with Popson as the centerpiece, though the other picturees were usually the raison d'etre for the photograph. He had appeared (with exactly the same smile each time) paired with graduation speakers, alumni honorees, honor graduates, new faculty members, retiring faculty members, people receiving promotions, award winners, high achieving campus athletes (with Popson wearing a football jersey), visiting authors (but not poets, who merited only a vice president or dean), the governor, new members of the Board of Trustees, someone who had donated a commemorative tree (with Popson in a suit, holding a shovel), the new manager of the University Center's food court (with Popson holding up a chicken leg), and the people who spent a whole Saturday cleaning up the Altoona River near the University (with Popson holding a bag of litter, sporting the same tee shirt the actual river cleaners were wearing). If the myth is correct that photographs steal a person's soul, Popson surely by now must be picked clean of his animus.

All the pictures with Popson in them also made me think about the ones he would never appear in. I doubted if I'd ever see him posed with drunken fraternity boys, carousing at the grand opening of a new frat house, or with a visiting rock singer, participants in minor sports and intramurals, part-time faculty members meeting with him to plead their case for benefits and higher pay, or any assistant professor who had just been denied tenure. And he certainly would not be pictured with anyone from the University who had been arrested. That meant of course that if I did get hauled in for Disner's murder, I would not be joined in a picture by Popson. And obviously, no one could expect to see him in a picture accompanying a dead person, like Disner, even if the picture had been taken when both people in the picture were still alive.

Popson would be in the eighth circle of DAVIDSON'S HELL, along with all of those who had taken credit for accomplishments they had demonstrated no part in, all of whom faced eternity struggling to reach the end of a road, but are thwarted by huge, amorphous blobs like Jabba the Hut, who block the transgressors' way.

In the Newsletter there was also a eulogy/obituary for Disner, more succinct than the one appearing in the Raysville newspaper, written in the same depersonalized, desensitized language as administrative notices about impending power outages, lapses in the phone service, or increases in healthcare premiums. It made me think of the scene in MONTE PYTHON'S THE MEANING OF LIFE, in which the headmaster at a boy's prep school perfunctorily informs one student of his father's demise, amidst notices about classes, sports, and the dining schedule. The piece in the newsletter barely mentioned Disner's history as a student or teacher, mainly focusing on the fact that he had been a halftime administrator, though he had held his post for barely over a year. I thought about what Marc Antony said in his impassioned speech at Caesar's funeral, that a person's good is often interred with his bones. In Disner's case, his sappiness was buried with his bones, and he came off looking better in death than he ever did in life.

There was a small photo of Disner in a graduation robe, smiling, with a hint of having just said "Okay." I would have liked it better if the editor had managed to find an old photo of Disner accompanied by Popson or somehow interposed Popson's image in the picture through some kind of editing wizardry, but of course Popson wouldn't allow that if he got wind of it. There was no mention of the cause of Disner's death, or where he died, maybe because the editor had a difficult time coming up with the least offensive word for the murder site—the toilet, john, head, water closet, latrine, throne, crapper, privy, shitter, etc. He could at least have used the word "facility."

I found Bwanger in his office, sitting in his roll-around chair, staring out the window that overlooked the bell tower, his elbows on the armrests of his chair, his face resting in both hands. When I knocked on his doorjamb, he sighed heavily and then wheeled around to face me. "What's up?" I asked.

"Oh, I just want to get a handle on what's happening in the Department . . . get a feel for your thoughts on all this bad business that has taken place. We didn't get to finish the other day."

"What exactly do you want to know? I thought I made it clear the other day that I couldn't really talk about much having to do with the case."

"I understand, but is that detective, Smockley, still asking you questions? Someone told me that he saw the two of you talking in the parking lot."

I wondered who would have reported this information to Bwanger—probably Glick. "Yes, he's asked me more questions about what I discovered on the day Disner was murdered. Why are you asking?"

"Well, I just don't want people to get the wrong idea about us. It's bad enough that one of us in the Departmental family got murdered. I don't want outsiders suspicious that a faculty member here was the perpetrator."

"I'm sorry if I've caused a stink because I needed to use the john just when Disner was lying dead on the floor in the stall next to mine."

"You don't need to be sarcastic. It's just that we have an image to keep up."

"An image?" I asked.

"Yes, we're teachers of literature. People expect us to have higher ethical standards. Even a hint of malfeasance can besmirch our reputation."

"Yes, I see what you mean. We teachers of literature don't want to be equated with mathematicians or lawyers, who routinely murder people as part of their vocation. Stop worrying. Smockley's just doing his job. After he gets all the information he needs, he'll move on."

"I certainly hope so. I don't want him hanging around our building any longer than necessary. By the way, has he mentioned me?'

I was taken off guard by Bwanger's question, as I had been previously in the hall when he asked about my seeing someone in the men's room. "No, should he have?"

"No, no, of course not. It's just that I don't want to be dragged into this mess. I represent the English Department, okay?"

Good old Bwanger, I thought, acting like he's concerned about the Department when in fact he's simply trying to keep up a spotless image for himself. It's never been a secret that he has ambitions beyond being Department chairman. I wondered if he had been at all jealous of Disner for moving up the corporate ladder. Does an associate dean, who is actually only a half-time administrator, but one who has that magical word "dean" in his title, rank as high or even higher than a department head, who in fact is also only a half time administrator, being still a half time teacher, but one who has the equally magical word "head" in his title. I wondered who would get the prime perks—a key to the executive wash room or an assigned parking place—if suddenly there were a shortage and only one of the two administrators could be given them. I suppose I could check the most recent BD-190 salary report and find out which of the two received the bigger salary, but I didn't really care at that point. In my thinking they both were overpaid.

But was there more to his concern about Smockley's questions than simply keeping up an image? Did he have something to hide? His fretting made me begin to worry that he might try to shift more focus on me, just to keep himself out of the picture.

And what was the deal with that "Okay"? More verbal plagiarism? Just what was the connection between Bwanger and Disner? Could I depend on Bwanger? Probably not. Damn, now I had two people to think about—Bwanger and Disner—not to mention Smockley.

Chapter 19

The next morning I felt hostile, pessimistic, not in the mood to teach, plus I felt bloated, my pants too tight, and my ankles still hurt from a hike I'd taken over the previous weekend on rough and rocky terrain up near the Tennessee border, at times hurting enough to give me images of James Caan in MISERY—after Kathy Bates has taken the sledge hammer to his ankles to hobble him. But I made my way to my eleven o'clock class—Shakespeare, usually my favorite—where my first task, after rearranging the desks from the previous class, which inexplicably were in the shape of a figure eight, was to collect a set of papers due that day. I did not want to wait until the end of class to receive them, since I had experienced far too many moments in which students did their final editing during class discussion.

As I gathered them, I thought how ridiculous it was that I had willingly forced them to write something I did not want to read. "Fool," said I to myself. "Isn't there a way to test their comprehension of the plays without assigning papers?" One answer would of course be to require only exams, with no assigned essays, but I would still have to grade the exams. How about depending on their class responses? A difficult means of assessment, since I'd constantly be writing reminders of their performance during the classroom discussions, plus many good students, with keen awareness of the subject matter, rarely say anything in class, being either shy or defiant.

As a last recourse, I could use the badly named—or misspelled—technique of holistic grading, having no marks except a final comment, but I always needed my own marginalia—both positive and negative— as a guide to what grade to assign the essay. In any event, I knew I'd end up grading first those that I predicted to be superior, leaving a period—a few hours—of utter hell during which I'd be marking the dregs. Maybe Ben Sturgeon had the best ideas—demand a surcharge if a paper took more than fifteen minutes to grade. I could cathartically write on the paper, with total honesty, whatever comment comes to mind—including "This is incredibly boring" or "This is crap"; or I could require that bad writers serve time in stocks outside on the lawn in front of the University Center.

Thinking about completing the grading process by the next class period, for the set I was collecting—as I had promised—made me grow weary. I lurched a couple of times in the narrow aisles between rows of desks, and I know I must have sighed loudly when I picked up the paper typed by Dwight Proofton, a religious zealot who wrote every paper with a religious theme. His previous one had been about how Shakespeare provides—in the main character in THE TAMING OF THE SHREW, Petruchio—a model for Southern Baptist men, since Petruchio's main purpose in the play is to correct a forward woman named Kate and make her acknowledge his superiority. I wondered what direction his latest submission would take, titled as it was, "Richard II as Jesus." I considered going to the front of the room and lying down on the desk for a couple of minutes to recover before starting on ROMEO AND JULIET, a discussion that would no doubt prompt Proofton to write about the Capulets as the Pharisees or Romeo as John the Baptist.

The only good thing that day was that two students—Donald Dunloof and Peggy Rumstinger—were absent, having not sent their papers with someone in attendance, and two more—Betty Depresdieu and Billy Bottingham—told me they did not have their papers ready and asked if they could bring them to the next scheduled class. I had to make a grand show of displeasure—for the sake of those who had their papers ready that day— saying loudly that I would have to penalize them, but actually I welcomed the news since their tardiness meant I could spread out the grading process over more days, with four fewer papers that I was required to finish by the next class period. At this point, I did not want to give my students extra reasons to be hostile toward me.

Approximately half way through the class, I gave the students a few minutes to discuss in small groups some of the topics I had raised earlier. As they worked, I thought more about someone's motives for killing Disner. I'm convinced that Disner never even dreamed that someone was out to murder him, mainly because, I'm almost sure, he never did anything controversial enough to elicit such extreme measures. I know that he was tedious and boring, sappy and trite most of the time, but these are personality traits that make others want to avoid him, not put a hole in his head. He probably had a picture in his high school annual, in the "Superlatives" section, with the caption, "Least likely to be murdered." This all made me think that if Disner got zapped by a killer, any of us at NGU could—including me.

Who would want me dead? Which people have I offended over the last few years, and what's the statue of limitations on grudges? If I went back to my first year at NGU, I had a fairly sizeable list of potential revengers.

Let's see, which students? How about that sneaky little shit Gully Hatterson, who looked like the Pillsbury Doughboy, who was a member of the English Honor's Program, until he received a D in my World Lit class—mainly because he failed two of the major exams, having almost never come to class, opting instead to lie around the Honors Room on an ugly petunia-patterned couch with his girlfriend, Claraline Cuneteri, on top of him. This was the same Claraline who, herself, received a grade of incomplete in my American Lit class, for which she never made up the work, thus eventually receiving an F. Or how about Pitt Fallows, the class fop, whom I privately chastized for showing off in front of his classmates by quoting from French symbolists—in French—no matter what the topic was being discussed—while snapping his fingers above his head. Or could it be Disner's old protégée, Bryan Twincher, whom, I must confess, I partially ignored simply because Disner constantly hounded me about his progress—even while I stood at a urinal in the men's room—which now qualifies as a murder scene.

How about other faculty members? Glick might be harboring a grudge, dating all the way back to when we rode together to SALAM (the South Atlantic Literary/Arts Meeting) and I refused to listen to a preliminary reading of his paper on humor in Milton's PARADISE LOST in the car as I drove and then failed to laugh at any point during the official reading at the conference. Gladys Corrincher could be pissed at me for never coming to any of her supposedly casual, but, actually, carefully orchestrated brown-bag luncheons to discuss matters concerning freshman English, including such hot topics as effective essay prompts, collaborative learning, classroom activators and ice breaking stimulators, learning communities, and holistic grading.

Gertrude Lonzer might have overheard me talking with Ben Sturgeon, making fun of her dreadful poetry and morose reading of it. Or maybe Cherry across the hall has been stewing about my request that he not shout across comments about conversations I was having with students and my subsequent practice of shutting my door to maintain some privacy, mainly from him. Could Clark Bisson could have it in for me—Bisson, the hacking, cheating golfer with whom I played once and then for evermore avoided? Then again, I sometimes wonder about Susan Paradit, Associate Professor of Economics and the woman I dated for almost two years, mainly because I felt pressure from Bwanger to keep my love life "in-house" or rather "in-university." She might still feel resentment toward me for choosing Laura Allworth, over her. That, and the fact that I scoffed at her new oversized and overpriced SUV.

There could be any number of administrators willing to take me out, too. I'm sure Macon Dwiddler, from the amorphous Student Services, probably heard me making fun of his fruity efforts to drum up interest in NGU at recruitment sessions in Atlanta, by giving away NGU tee-shirts and the like for silly reasons such as being the first to arrive on the night of the recruitment or the one coming from farthest away. Maybe Devlin Peterkin had it in for me, since I did not demonstrate proper deference to him as an administrative superior and instead beat him repeatedly in tennis. I wondered if Bwanger disliked me because I didn't exactly show much enthusiasm for some of his favorite University activities, like the game day/barbecue called the Hullabaloo, held for faculty member every fall just before classes begin, or the various overly hyped retreats he sent me on supposedly to improve teaching. He'd also probably like to kill me for not living up to my billing as the son of Professor Walter Davidson, whose illustrious career at the University of Illinois and the University of Chicago helped me secure the job at NGU in the first place and then later get tenure. Maybe even President Popson might remember an episode early in my stint at NGU, when I didn't receive my first paycheck and Popson thought I sicced the Union on him and the Bursar.

Of course, the one person who no doubt would have the most reasons to kill me is now dead himself—Disner, whom, as almost anyone on campus knew, I made fun of constantly and showed the most antipathy to. Maybe I should watch out for his family members—particularly his wife Breda, who glared at me as intently as Smockley did, at Disner's funeral, or even one of his children, who, with young people's gift for perception, might have sensed by antipathy toward their father.

After a few minutes of deep thinking on these issues, I noticed that all of the groups had ceased discussing and were now staring at me. I wondered if my thoughts showed on my face. Did I look disturbed?

It was an easy matter to divert their attention away from me by having each group report on their conclusions. My timing was perfect. The last group finished as the bell tower began playing "My Foolish Heart," indicating the class period had come to an end at ten of the hour.

Chapter 20

The next day, as the bell tower clanged out a languid rendition of "The Yellow Rose of Texas," I entered the classroom on the third floor to observe and evaluate Glick's class in World Literature, as one of my assignments for the Teacher Evaluation Committee. I had been momentarily delayed in getting to the room by a string trio of music majors, including a cellist and a bass player, who were using one of the landings in the staircase to practice a baroque piece, and by students sitting or lying on the hall floor, waiting for class, creating a gauntlet of legs that I had to negotiate as if I were a football player in training, running through a set of tires.

Glick seemed to be nervous the entire period, losing his train of thought in key moments of a discussion of Voltaire's CANDIDE, vigorously rubbing the sides of his face with both hands and sweating profusely, such that his forehead gleamed as if he had slathered it on K-Y jelly. I wondered if he simply felt uncomfortable being evaluated by a colleague, under pressure to perform well in order to secure a positive rating—and a possible salary increase—or if he was somehow involved in Disner's murder and felt ill at ease because the very person who had discovered Disner's body was now sitting in his class. For sure, his nervousness did not translate into positive energy; he was still as dull during the class as he had been when reading the humorless paper on Miltonic humor at the SALAM conference. He was also vague, rambling, and totally uncreative. If anyone should have called upon the muse of teaching for inspiration, it was Glick.

His class proceeded at the rate of the songs played on the bell tower, as he lectured (not discussed) from prepared notes in a halting voice, seemingly having just taken them off the internet or received them from a dial-a-lecture service and had not looked at them before coming to class, all with no originality whatsoever. I kept getting images of drivers who follow all the rules of safety, taking no chances, dutifully signaling well in advance of turning, keeping their speed at or below the posted speed limit, and approaching any green light with the brakes partially on, as if hoping the light will change to yellow so they can stop.

And he repeated himself so much that I got images of those repetitious, swirling weather flow graphics demonstrating storms moving through the area, broadcast on the nightly news. This was done with a voice like the one that an answering machine defaults to after the electricity has gone off.

His most distinctive style was a kind of pedagogical syncope, wherein he would often begin a sentence, with a perfectly good subject, then interject so many modifying phrases before he got to his verb that he would have to pause, trying to remember where the sentence was going, staring at the ceiling as if he were listening to the music of the spheres, before repeating the subject, still without a verb in sight. Obviously, it was difficult to follow his train of thought, a problem aggravated by his penchant to use words that he must have gleaned from BEOWULF, words such as "faldor," "dryhten," "frofor," and "geweald." I kept waiting for a student to raise a hand and ask, "Professor Glick, what do those words mean and what is your point?" but no one did.

He made me think about the parable of the talents, in which one person is given five talents, another three, and the most hapless but one talent, which he promptly buries so that he won't lose it, failing to do anything whatsoever with it. Glick for certain was given only one talent, and it was not in teaching. And if it were in teaching, it was now buried under mounds of dirt, or, if I can get away with mixed parables, under the bushel basket. On the other hand, I wondered if the Peter Principle was at work, with Glick having risen to his level of incompetence, a position he would occupy for the rest of his life, unless he managed to snag Disner's vacant position as Associate Dean of Arts and Sciences. He had made it known even before Disner had gotten the job that he, Glick, wanted it. Had he snuffed Disner so he could take over? What a waste, if he had. He would be even more incompetent there than he was as a teacher, but that's the point of the Peter Principle, isn't it, to keep advancing until you're in your LOWEST level of competency.

My problem was that, using the guidelines endorsed by the Teacher Evaluation Committee and, subsequently, by the whole English Department, I had to rate Glick on his teaching ability. I noticed that all the entries were worded positively, something Glick himself was responsible for, such that the rater, using a scale of one to five (five being the most positive), was asked to answer such questions as, "Was the teacher enthusiastic?" I wondered if it would be worse to be low on the scale of enthusiasm or high on the scale of dullness.

The upshot was that Glick was simply a bad teacher. I wondered if he knew it himself, or was he a modern example of the humanistic philosophy of the Renaissance and Neoclassical periods that suggested that people commit evil deeds only out of ignorance, actually believing that what they do, no matter how bad, is good. If he thought he was a good teacher, would he be upset, offended, even vindictive, if I bed-panned his pedagogy? Is that what happened to Disner? Did he give Glick a negative review and Glick got even—toilet job for toilet job—for the injury? Did Glick's phlegmatic nature belie an undercurrent of hostile rage? Should I tell Smockley of my concerns? I secretly hoped that Glick would turn out to be Disner's killer. A long stint in prison for murder would at least prevent him from continuing to murder the art of teaching and, in the bargain, keep him from ever filling Disner's former position.

I found myself hating the whole process, eventually dispensing with the individual questions on the check sheet (thus negating the committee's work to form such a list), instead giving an overall assessment that I hoped would not offend Glick—nor get him a raise —"Professor Glick seemed to be prepared for the class and covered the material that was listed on the syllabus, which was Voltaire's CANDIDE." I hoped Bwanger, as department head, would not pay much attention to the review anyway. If he did read it and interpreted it in a positive light, I might have to douse myself in gasoline and light a match.

Chapter 21

After a night that offered a headache-producing mélange of threatening sounds, red herrings, and sleepless hours, I hurried from the remote faculty lot where I was forced to park, due to the fact that the one next to my building was closed. I was on my way to the office, where I'd promised my students I would be at 8 am for the hour preceding the class period in which I was administering an exam—just so I could answer any last minute questions and/or re-provide information on Poe and Hawthorne (which I had already given in the regular class periods).

I did not mind the hike itself, but I was running late (made obvious by the silence of the bell tower, which had already completed its cycle of patriotic music and eight bongs). Attempting to park in my usual lot and then driving to the second lot had required an extra five minutes, and the walk to my building from there would take another three or four minutes. In addition, during the drive from my house to campus, I once again had been delayed by a left and right brace of lane blockers, who seemed to be in a conspiracy to frustrate all drivers who desired to get someplace in a reasonable time.

I had tried to park in my regular lot, but was prevented from doing so by a wooden barrier, guarded by a student traffic-control trainee.

"Why can't I get into my lot?" I asked.

"They're keeping it closed."

"Who's 'they'?"

"Campus Security."

"Why?"

"To keep cars from parking here."

"I can see that, but for what purpose?" I was beginning to feel as if I were in another stichomythic conversation with Smockley.

"They're having an alumni fundraiser here tomorrow."

"Why does that keep me from parking in it?"

"They're going to set up tables all over the lot."

"When?"

"Tomorrow."

"What time tomorrow?"

"At noon."

"So why is the lot blocked today?"

"So that they can make sure that no cars are here tomorrow."

"Couldn't you—or THEY, as you call them—simply block it off tomorrow morning?"

"They're afraid that people will park today and leave them overnight."

"What's wrong with that?"

"People might not move them in time."

"But who would be leaving them all night anyway?"

"Oh, students, who visit the dorms all night—you know, to stay with a girlfriend or boyfriend."

"Can they do that? I thought this was a lot for faculty parking only."

"Yes, it's perfectly legal for students to use the lot at night. They just have to remove their cars by seven the next morning."

"So, then, what's the problem?"

"Sometimes they leave their cars all the next day."

"I see. Do they ever get towed?"

"Yes"

"Then couldn't you just tow them tomorrow if they're still here after seven?"

"Yes, but there's also the problem of faculty members who stay all night to work, keeping their cars here right into the next day."

"Good God, surely there aren't many who do that!"

"I can't say. You probably know better than I."

"Let me get this straight. You're telling me I can't use my lot TODAY because students might not vacate the premises TOMORROW—several hours before this recruitment business—and certain zealous faculty members might be holed up in the building from tonight all the way through late tomorrow afternoon?"

"Yes. The lot needs to be kept open."

Seeing that I was caught in the makings of a Pirandello/absurdist drama, I headed for the next lot, which necessitated a hike to my building along a foot path through a section of woods, which consisted of a dense collection of white pines, red oaks, maples, and poplars, though there was just enough light to nourish a thick undergrowth along the sides of the path. The trail had been named after a former administrator of NGU, one Jonathan Wakeless, who was either an outdoor enthusiast or a minor functionary who was not important enough to have a building honoring him. His name was emblazoned on a wooden sign at the head of the trail near the parking lot. It made me think about the administration's penchant for naming everything in the locale after one of their own. I wondered if Disner's murder site would become the Hugh Disner Memorial Men's Room.

This morning there was a semi-dense fog shrouding the path, which at that time of the day should have been populated by students tardy for class, or other professors, but which was strangely deserted—except for a lone, hooded figure coming toward me from approximately half way through the woods, hands in the jacket's pockets. The hood stood out forwards from the person's head, such that the face seemed to be deeply recessed, making whoever it was look like the Grim Reaper.

I slowed to almost an ogre-like shuffle, shifting the copies of the exam I was carrying from my side to my chest, keeping my eyes on both the faceless cavern of the hood and the pockets with the hands in them. I began contemplating turning around and retreating to my car, as if I had forgotten a book or some other papers, but I suddenly did not like the prospect of walking with my back to this person. Maybe I could go sideways into the woods through the underbrush—which no doubt was filled with poison ivy or oak—but that would bring me to a creek that runs parallel to the path, with no recourse but to wade through or face my potential attacker. Plus, I would look pretty damned silly if the person were just a chilled student heading back to his dorm after spending the night with his lover.

What was in those pockets? What expression did he wear hidden in the hood? What would I do if he pulled a gun?

He came nearer, maybe thirty yards away. I began walking even more slowly, eventually stopping altogether on the right side of the pathway. What would happen with my class and the exam if this person shot me? Would I look as ugly in death as Disner did slumped in front of the toilet?

Would this killer drag me over the creek and dump me? Who would ever find me? Did he just pull something out of his pocket?

I realized that even with all my education—getting through the public school system and then through undergraduate and graduate schools, with courses such as Old English and Faulkner's novels—I had never enrolled in a course on evasive actions, teaching you how to prevent someone from killing you. The closest I came was participating in a couple of forced boxing matches in P.E. classes, but that was done to amuse a couple of blood-thirsty gym teachers, not really to instruct me on self defense. Reading BEOWULF wouldn't help unless I wanted to rip out my attacker's arm or bite off his head.

He came closer, closer. I continued standing, having stepped completely off the path, immobilized by fear, wondering what I would see first, his face or the gun he must be carrying in one of his pockets. Now, though he was only three or four yards away, I still could not see his face, but he was definitely pulling something from his right pocket. I partially covered my head with the set of exams, and I even contemplated calling for help—"Mama"? "Smockley"?

As he strode past me, he pulled out—what was it? a gun, a knife—no, a handkerchief, into which he forcibly blew his nose. I never saw his face, partly due to the hood, partly due to the handkerchief, and partly due to the exam copies in front of my own face.

I stood and watched him amble down the pathway I had just traversed, eyeing him until he faded into the fog. He never looked back. I was relieved, but not totally. Had he intended to kill me, knowing somehow that I would be using this path, this morning, but suddenly changed his mind, figuring it was too public a place? Had he covered his nose with the handkerchief just so I wouldn't get a good view of him? Would he be waiting at my car later in the day?

Embarrassment, even shame, replaced my semi-relief. I realized that my paranoia was growing daily and was diversifying, or, more technically, "generalizing." Ever since finding Disner dead in the toilet stall, I had been experiencing claustrophobia each time I was forced to use a similar stall anywhere on campus, particularly in my own building. This claustrophobia had extended to confinement in just about any small enclosure, including the shower, where I got visions of Marion Crane in Hitchcock's PSYCHO (I had taken to using baby shampoo so I could keep my eyes open while I washed my hair) and even my office, which, I discovered upon measuring it, is only four times the area of Disner's stall. This morning's episode on the trail, combined with slow trips on the highway from my house to the University, during which I inexplicably felt vulnerable, helped add agoraphobia to my list of maladies. It seemed that I also had xenophobia, a very broad kind in which everyone, my students and colleagues included, was a feared foreigner. I figured I would also develop a case of acrophobia, since the murder took place on the top floor of our building.

Things did not improve significantly when I reached my office, as I sat with my door open, sweating out each set of footsteps coming near my office door, the most troublesome being those made by someone stopping nearby and lingering, out of sight. Again, where was Smockley? Why wasn't he there harassing me, asking me questions, like he'd been doing ever since Disner was murdered?

The only comic relief arose when I received a call from one of my students in the upcoming class, who, without first identifying himself, asked, in a quavering voice, "Doctor Davidson, are we still going to have the exam today?"

"Yes, of course," I answered, "who is this?"

"Uh, it's Larry Hinslinger."

"Why would you think that we weren't going to have the exam?" I was momentarily alarmed that he might have believed that I'd be dead by then and he wouldn't in fact have to take the exam.

"Well, I just heard on the weather report that there's a cold front coming through today and that there's a fifty percent chance that we'll get some icy rain."

"What difference does that make?"

"It could be dangerous, you know."

"For whom? Aren't you on campus, where you can simply walk to your classes?"

"No, sir, I live in Raysville and have to drive about three miles. I don't want to have a wreck." Judging by his record of missing classes and quizzes and his recurring requests to turn in papers late, I knew that in actuality he simply did not want to wreck the impending exam.

"When is this cold front supposed to come through here?" I had visions of half the class showing up in hooded jackets.

"About noon, they said." I thought about the episode at the blocked parking lot—more info from the ubiquitous "they," I guess.

"Our exam is at nine this morning. Don't you think that you could take it and then get back home if you need to?"

"I suppose I could. But, like I said, I don't want to wreck the car. It's my parents', you know."

"You won't. See you at nine." I hung up before he could offer other versions of his fears, then turned my attention back to my own alarm. Was Hinslinger in fact calling to check if I was still alive? After giving the matter some thought, I realized that I was interpreting everything in terms of my own paranoia about murder. It was time to take the lesser of two miracles, the more believable story being that Hinslinger was worried about failing an exam.

However, despite my newfound rationality about Hinslinger, I did think about taping a large note on my door, which read,"I know nothing. I saw nothing, so go away," or "Come in only if you mean me no harm." I also thought about closing my door, then opening it only after people knocked and identified themselves, but I realized this plan would do me no good if I didn't know who the killer was. So, until nearly nine o'clock, I sat and worried about hooded figures appearing at my door, shooting me, closing my door, and leaving my body for the maintenance staff to find when they came to collect my trash and recyclable paper, another ignominious way to die.

Chapter 22

At five before nine, as the bell tower hammered out "Supercalifragilistic-expialodocious"—at the pace of an arthritic blacksmith banging on a horseshoe—I made my way down the stairs to my classroom on the third floor. I felt none of the usual charge I got before an exam, wondering how the students would respond to a particular question I had spent extra time composing or how they would perform on the exam overall. I could recall on past occasions wishing I had a recording of Wagner's "The Ride of the Valkyries" to play like Robert Duvall's charging character did in APOCALYPSE NOW, as I swooped into the room—sans helicopter and bombs, of course—loaded with exam copies, claiming that I loved the smell of toner in the morning, though I knew toner didn't have much of an odor.

Today I trudged to the awaiting class, feeling like a wounded carrier pigeon, delivering an unwanted message. I was at least thankful that I was surrounded by a stampede of students going to or leaving classes, though I was alarmed twice by mysterious figures wearing hooded jackets, both of whom seemed to pause and look my way. I could hear outside the building the bell tower sounding out the line that contains the words, "Um diddle diddle diddle, um diddle diddle ay."

Waiting outside the door of my classroom stood Betty Twonder, clasping her hands as if she had been praying. "Doctor Davidson, can I talk with you a minute before you go in?"

"Yes, what's up?" I asked, betting, based on her previous slipshod performance in the class, that she would answer either with "I'm too sick to take the exam and I need to go back to bed" or "My grandmother called this morning to tell us that grandpa is on his death bed and I need to go home."

It was neither. Instead, she complained, "I woke up this morning and realized that I didn't tell you at the last class that I can't come to the exam today because I need to meet with the Homecoming Queen Committee."

"Why do you have to do that?" I asked, realizing that the main reason she had not given me this information at the previous class was because she had skipped that session (along with several classes previously).

"Well, you see, I'm in the running for Homecoming queen, and I need to be there for the meeting."

"Why on earth did they schedule the meeting during prime class time hours? Shouldn't this sort of thing be done at five or six in the afternoon?"

"I don't know. They just told me to be there. It's supposed to last an hour."

"Did you tell them you had an exam?"

"No. I figured you'd let me take it tomorrow. Can I?"

I suspected that she wanted a whole day to study for the exam—of course after consulting with someone taking the exam this morning. "I'd rather you take it right now," I said with as level a voice as I could manage.

"I really have to go to the meeting." Her voice took on the whine of a small engine car at about 7500 rpms. "It might hurt my chances to be queen if I'm not there."

"Then come immediately after the meeting and take it—at ten this morning."

"But I have other things to do then. Oh, hi, Jeanette." She was speaking to an acquaintance passing by in the hall. "I'll meet you at twelve for lunch at Biggers Cafeteria. Now, where were we?" she asked, after re-facing me.

"I was giving you an option for taking the exam, at ten o'clock." After the events of the morning, I found myself becoming less and less tolerant. "I'll leave it up to you. You're the one who has to decide which is more important, the exam or your other activities. Now, I've got to get the exam started. Let me know what you decide." I could hear the bell tower busy knocking out nine bongs, though none of the sounds matched, making it all sound as if a three-year old were randomly picking out notes on a xylophone.

She sighed loudly and then, with a frown, announced, "Oh, never mind. I'll just take it now, even though I haven't studied for it, thinking I'd be going to my meeting. It will be your fault if I fail it."

"The good news is that it's an open book and open notes exam," I responded. "If you've read your assignments and listened in class, you should do all right," but I was certain that she had done neither.

Inside the room, I distributed the exam copies while reminding the students that they were allowed to use their notes and the textbook but also cautioning them not to spend all their time (fifty minutes) looking through them. "Just be brilliant," I added.

Those who were fully prepared put on their best test faces (game faces?) and began writing answers immediately. Those who were less prepared, including weather worrier Larry Hinslinger, flashed faces riddled with angst, as they took time to search through their notes and the textbook before writing answers. Those who were totally unprepared, including Homecoming queen aspirant, Betty Twonder, took on the appearance of lost souls heading for hell, as they spent almost the entire period searching for answers they would never find. I could not quite figure out how to describe and classify those who did not seem to do anything, neither looking for answers nor writing words on their answer page.

As they worked, I tried to grade papers from another class, but soon discovered that I was forced to serve as a monitor/proctor, prodded into this role by Cletis Drackles, whose eyes were fixed upon me almost every time I looked up from grading papers. My first concern was that he was a potential killer, sizing me up—in fact, maybe he was the hooded figure on the Wakeless Memorial Trail, though he was not wearing a jacket nor was there one at his desk. However, by pretending to be looking down at my papers, but actually watching him with peripheral vision, I quickly ascertained that he was peeking across the aisle to his left at Susannah Singstress's answers whenever he thought I was not looking at him.

Eventually he happened to glance at me, right after an extended period of harvesting answers from Susannah, and discovered that I was staring straight at him. I shifted my eyes from him to her and then back to him, then shook my head no. From then on he seemed to work all on his own, but I made a note to compare their answers. It would be a dead give away if both answer sheets contained some bizarre, wrong answers, which could be possible since Susannah was an even weaker student than he was. If he were going to cheat better than some rank amateur, he should at least pony off Robert Warner to his right—and try not to be so damned obvious.

To her credit, Betty Twonder did not appear to cheat, though she sighed frequently, even more loudly than she had in the hall.

Drackle's cheating made me wonder if he had cheated all his life—maybe even as a kid when completing the puzzles and contests on restaurant placemats. And is there some connection between cheating and other criminal activity? Do cheaters turn into felons, murderers? Did the person that killed Disner cheat? Had Disner caught the killer cheating and failed him or her for the exam or maybe even the course?

Associating cheaters and criminals led me to return to the notion of correspondences between evil and ugliness and also between evil and stupidity (or, more properly, a lack of Reason with a capital R, our supposed guide to morality). If ugliness did indeed reveal a potential killer, as it did with such characters as Shakespeare's evil Richard III, who claimed that dogs barked at him because of his appearance, I would lay money on Drackle, who looked about as unpleasant as his name sounded—with hair that made it appear as if he had just come from working under his car on a dripping oil pan, eyes that seemingly were inherited from some kind of lupine ancestry, lips that were forever locked in a smirk that begged for someone to forcefully wipe it off, and fat and scarred ankles, connected to sockless feet, which were crammed into Birkenstocks.

My rambling thoughts were interrupted by Belvis Broadstory, who magically appeared beside me—just outside the peripheral vision that had served me so well moments before in observing Drackle's cheating. I do not know how long he stood there, but eventually he cleared his throat to catch my attention. "Dr. Davidson?"

"Yes, Mr. Broadstory?" I answered, turning to his scrunched up face.

"I can't answer number three or number eight."

"Why not?"

"Number three asks for symbols of evil in Hawthorne's 'Young Goodman Brown.'"

"Yes, what's the problem?"

"I don't believe in studying evil. I'm afraid it might make me evil to think about evil."

"You don't think it might have something to do with the fact that you were absent the whole week when we were studying 'Young Goodman Brown,' do you?"

"Oh, no sir. I just didn't want to study evil. My mama told me that knowing is doing."

"Okay, but what about number eight?"

"It asks for examples of techniques to create 'veri'. . . ., how do you pronounce that word?"

"Verisimilitude."

"Whatever. Anyway, I can't find it anywhere in my notes or the textbook."

"That's because it's a term that I introduced in class."

"I must not have been there when you explained it."

"Why didn't you ask someone for the notes from that class?"

"I don't know anyone in class."

"Well, look closely at the two parts of the word, 'veri' and 'similitude,' and see if you can figure out its meaning."

"Does it have anything to do with the military?"

"Nope, think about it some more."

After he returned to his seat, he gazed at the blackboard as if he thought the word and its meaning might still be there, having escaped complete erasure. He then began studying the floor beneath his desk, as if the answer might be magically revealed in the patterns of the vinyl tiles.

As he finally began writing, I thought about the difference between my first impression of him and the current one. On the first day of class, as I called the roll, I wrote the words "sharp features, alert eyes." Now, I'm afraid I would have to write "blockish and boorish." It still was not as radical a reassessment as the one I had for Trudy Summerstile, who had transformed in my estimation from my first description of her as Elizabeth Taylor in "Cleopatra" to Elizabeth Taylor in "Who's Afraid of Virginia Woolfe," who stridently protested whenever I announced an upcoming quiz, exam, or paper to write. At that very moment she was glaring at me with blatant ill will, I suppose for simply giving the exam, though it could be for something more specific, like having to explain and illustrate "verisimilitude."

The first person to turn in the exam was Flora Hartzcross, the end of whose nose glistened as if a snail had crawled across it, leaving a trail of slime. She had coughed and sneezed during much of the exam, twice leaving the room, ostensibly to blow her nose out in the hall or in the women's room. She laid the exam and her answers on the desk, with a muffled apology, and exited the room, leaving me with the dilemma of how to pick up her paper without handling all her germs. I wished that I had brought a pair of gloves or some tongs or tweezers. I solved the problem by sliding sheets of paper I found in the desk drawer under and over hers, hoping I would remember not to touch the infected pages when it came time to grade the exam. Knowing how tainted her pages were made me vow to always guard against smearing all the students' papers with my own germs when I became sick, but then I wondered, why start now.

Close behind her came Wanda Gloaming, whose answer pages appeared to have lots of white spaces between her written answers, as if she had left room to go back and fill in more information, but could not think of anything else. She was an English major, whose spelling was atrocious and whose diction remained at about a sixth grade level. She had confessed to me that she didn't like to read, causing me to ask, "Why on earth did you choose to be an English major then?"

"My parents have been on my case since I was a little girl to read more. I was hoping that majoring in literature would help me do that, but I still have a hard time concentrating on anything over a page or two." It made me wonder if a similar problem occurs in other disciplines. I could not fathom a student majoring in math who hated numbers, figuring, calculating. But Wanda could be like someone with loads of psychological problems who wanted to major in psychology, hoping the experience would cure her paranoia, schizophrenia, or just general neuroses.

After about five more minutes, following a minor wave of students turning in their completed exams, I began reading some of the answers. I immediately felt like calling the whole thing off. Trudy Blitherspoon's definition of the phrase "willing suspension of disbelief" was the exact wording Cletis Drackles had offered in class when I called on him two weeks prior to the exam, having said, "I think it means a magical way to support the main structure—like bridges." Because I was mindful of Disner's death and a bit on edge about offending anyone, I was probably too diplomatically ambiguous in correcting Drackles (saying, as I recall, something like, "That's close, with some of the right words, but let's pin it down more precisely). In any event, Trudy assumed that Drackles had been correct. I wondered how many more answers would be duplicates of wrong answers in class, dutifully recorded in notebooks now in use for the exam.

My spirits took a further dip when I discovered that I had erred in my numbering of the questions, such that the last six were "15, 16, 17, 15, 16, 17." I figured it would not be a major problem until I looked at the pages submitted by Belvis Broadstory, who omitted the second series of 15, 16, and 17. I dreaded the confrontation I would have with him, which would begin with his complaining that I had marked him down for omitting the last three questions. He would say, "I figured the second group and the first group were the same."

"But did you actually read the second group and see that they were different questions from the first set?"

"No, I just figured I didn't have to do them."

I quickly informed the remaining examinees to renumber the last three to make them 18, 19, and 20 and then sat mulling over the possibility that Disner had made an equally trivial mistake which might have set some on-the-verge-of-losing-it student to follow him to the men's room. I wanted this exam over so that I could hide in my office with the door locked. I would have even settled for a grilling by Smockley.

Chapter 23

I hid in my office for most of the afternoon, skipping lunch. Fear is a better diet plan than any of the popular ones—Atkins, Grapefruit, Scarsdale, even the Russian Air Force scheme. Maybe someone ought to market it—making people feel as if they're potential murder victims. The only trouble is that fear also speeds up one's metabolism, increasing the need to pee, a definite problem with me since I was paranoid about using the men's room, in fact hitting it only during the breaks between classes, when I knew there were several people using it.

At three o'clock I attended a meeting of the Mabel Tretorn Memorial Scholarship Committee, during which I paid only cursory attention to the proceedings, wishing I had worn a sleep mask and inserted earplugs, especially when Bwanger was speaking with too much phlegm in his throat, making me want to scream at him to clear it. Does an abundance of phlegm indicate a phlegmatic humor? I couldn't picture Bwanger active, for example, on the ski slopes or in a rugby scrum. Who was I to talk, though. This session was making me feel as if I had Elmer's glue in my arteries.

As soon as the meeting finished just before five, I hurried to my office, where I donned my running gear before leaving the building, accompanied by the bell tower butchering the "Largo" ("Going Home") section from the Second Movement of Dvorak's NEW WORLD SYMPHONY, normally my favorite piece, but not when it sounds as if were being played on a xylophone. I did not want to return to campus that evening, so I drove my car to a turn out on River Road, where I sat for almost an hour, enjoying the late October colors and invigorating, low fifties air—with only a couple of thoughts about being followed by someone.

After locking the car and leaving my keys under the right front fender on top of the tire, I spent a few moments loosening up, leaning against the car at an angle with my hands on its side, my legs stretched out with tension on my calves, such that I must have appeared to be attempting to roll the car over. I then took off down River Road, turning left after about a quarter of a mile onto a dirt and gravel side road called Raccoon Run Lane, which I knew ran for approximately three miles before coming to a dead end and which was populated by no more than six—maybe eight—houses, only a couple of which had dogs to contend with.

By the time I was heading back toward River Road and my parked car, the sun had set, but there was still sufficient light to see the road and the houses. When I was about a mile from River Road, I slowed my pace; then with about a half mile to go, I began walking, so that I could relax my muscles gradually before driving home.

As I approached the residence closest to River Road, a trailer that looked like an oversized breadbox, I spotted in the driveway a familiar looking van, a white one, plastered with lots of bumper stickers. It had to be Disner's, unless there happened to be another one in the county as ugly as his. I wondered who had driven it there. Had Breda sold it the week of Disner's funeral? I was pretty certain Disner himself had not driven it there.

About the time I reached the other side of the property, now past the trailer and the driveway, the porch light came on and the front door opened. I was partially hidden by a row of shrubbery, but I could still see the figure that stepped out into the full light and then turned to speak to someone who remained in the shadows of the doorway. I could hear her say, "You're useless" and "I knew I couldn't depend on you," but I did not quite make out what her male interlocutor—judging by the deepness of his voice—said in response. The woman standing in the light was Breda Disner.

I picked up my pace, almost to jogging speed again, hoping I would reach my car and be gone before Breda drove down the road.

No such luck.

I was still a couple of hundred yards from River Road when I heard a vehicle approaching from behind me. I contemplated taking refuge in the brush and trees off to the side, but the vehicle came so quickly I didn't have time to act that defensively, so I chose to keep moving, facing straight ahead, though I was strongly tempted to look back at the rushing car—or van—to make sure it was not about to run me down, but in the process giving up my anonymity.

Within seconds, a white van, assumedly with Breda at the helm, roared past, the noises coming from its engine and from the tires on gravel almost drowned out by the rap music blasting from the speakers inside. It had been steered straight down the middle of the road, the driver having made no attempt to move to the far side. Fortunately I had ample clearance due to the size of the road, which was wide enough for two cars to pass each other, but I still felt as if I was in the backwash of air created by a semi, with lots of dust and flying gravel.

In three or four more minutes I was back at my car. I did not bother to stretch, as I usually did after a run, but left almost immediately. I figured if I tightened up from the run, well, then, I'd just have to tighten up. It would probably go with my state of mind better anyway.

On the way home, I stopped at Blethens Groceries in Raysville, picking up a few items for healthy eating—a bunch of bananas, red grapes, carrots, broccoli, a pineapple, and the perfect complement to all the foregoing, some rocky road ice cream.

I was looking forward to getting home, even if it meant starting in on grading the exams from my nine o'clock class, but as I approached my house I was struck with alarm. Parked in front was the white van that had just recently whisked by me on the gravel road. The odds that it was NOT Disner's van seemed as low as the odds of my making full professor that year. I paused, letting my car idle, unsure whether I should pull into my driveway or drive away.

What was Breda doing here? I seriously doubted that she had picked out this street randomly. If she were here to see me, I wondered how she knew where I lived. As far as I could remember, none of the Disners had ever been to my house.

I finally edged up beside the van to speak to Breda or whoever was in there, but I couldn't see anyone in the driver's seat. Maybe she's visiting one on my neighbors, I speculated, here on some kind of mission for the church, delivering food for the needy, one of whom could have been the man out on the gravel road. But on the other hand, was it possible that she and that man had driven here and were at this very moment getting it on in the back of the van? I didn't hear any squeaking or see the van rocking so I discarded the notion. Besides, why wouldn't they have simply stayed at his house?

After deliberating for a couple more minutes—feeling sweat collecting in my armpits that did not come from jogging—I pulled my car into my driveway all the way to the rear so I could enter via the back porch, which would be illuminated by a motion sensitive light the second the car pulled up.

After unloading my groceries, unlocking my back door, and reaching in to snap on the kitchen light, I entered and set my purchases on the counter. Something told me that I needed to check the rest of the house, but I felt vulnerable. I figured it wouldn't hurt to be armed, but with what? Most of my grocery items would be useless. I opened the drawer in which I kept silverware and knives, briefly considering a six-inch slicer I kept there, but I began thinking how ridiculous I'd appear if Breda showed up at the door asking for directions and I met her with a knife that made me look like Norman Bates/ his mother. I opted to carry the pineapple with me. It had a bit of heft and its spiky skin gave good purchase—and it probably would not frighten away any harmless visitors.

I headed into the living room, but immediately cringed in terror, as I caught the distinct odor of cigarettes. Before I could turn on a light, I caught the glow of one roughly in the spot where my couch rested. My first instinct was to heave the pineapple at that spot, but I was afraid I might miss and instead simply antagonize the intruder. "Who's there?" I demanded, as I fumbled for the light switch.

"It's just me," came the voice I recognized as that of Breda Disner, just before I finally managed to turn on the overhead light. She was sitting on the couch with her legs crossed, her right hand cupping her left elbow, her left hand holding a cigarette up near her ear. I, in contrast, was poised like a quarterback, armed cocked to throw a pass, except I had a pineapple in my hand.

"Hello, Tyler," she said. She was less tense—certainly less surly—than she had been when I saw her at Disner's funeral.

"How the hell did you get in?" I asked, trying to control my anger and remaining fear. I tried to hide the pineapple behind me, but I could feel one of its spines poking me in the back.

"Your door was partially open. I hollered for you, but got no answer, so I took the liberty of coming in to wait for you. I was feeling a bit of a chill sitting in the van. I hope you don't mind." I almost believed her, though I was certain that I had locked the door that morning. "What are you holding behind you?" she added.

"Oh, just this," I stammered, producing the pineapple.

"Why are you carrying it around?"

"I was just about . . .," I paused, "to cut it up for dinner." I set it on the table and then, to divert attention from it, changed the topic. "I didn't know you smoked."

"There's a lot you don't know about me, Dear. Hugh didn't like for me to smoke in public—said it was a bad witness, whatever that means." She took a long drag and then held the smoke for what seemed longer than I could hold my breath under water, finally blowing it upward, her head tilted like that of a model for earrings. She flicked the ashes into an empty bowl on the table, in which I usually kept a supply of M & M's.

"Why are you here?"

"I need help." Yeah, I thought, help to keep secret her tryst with Mr. Gravel Road.

"Why me?"

"Because Hugh talked about you all the time."

"Me? What for?

"I think he was jealous of you. He frequently said that you didn't care what people thought about you, that you probably didn't even care if you got tenure when that came up a couple of years ago. And it bothered him you still got tenure without doing all the things that people usually do."

I wasn't sure if she was complimenting me or not. "But that doesn't answer my question. Why do YOU want my help?"

"Because I feel as if I can trust you. You don't play up to the authorities or curry public opinion. I like that."

"You know, don't you, that there are some that think I'm the one who killed your husband?"

"Like who?"

"That detective that's been on the case, Smockley."

"Nonsense. He doesn't believe that, and neither do I."

"What makes you so sure?"

"I just know, trust me." Her tone made me think that she herself could know who the killer was.

"Okay, but back to your earlier comment. What is it you want me to help you with?"

"I need for you to find something in Hugh's office."

"Why don't you just go get it yourself?"

"I can't. The police have his office sealed—as part of the investigation. Besides I never had a key. Hugh's was in his pocket when he was murdered."

"I don't have a key to his office either."

"But you can get one."

"How? By marching into the Dean's office and announcing to the secretary, 'I've come for the key to Disner's sealed office. I want to rummage around in there for an hour or so, looking for evidence that might implicate me or Mrs. Disner'?"

She gazed at me for several seconds with a disturbing detachment; then she took another long drag on her cigarette. I thought about asking her if she'd mind not smoking in my house, but realized the timing wasn't right, since I'd already allowed her to finish most of the cigarette. Finally, she answered. "Tyler, don't be an idiot. I'm talking about the master key that the secretary of the English Department keeps. Hugh had to borrow it all the time, since he was quite forgetful, always leaving his keys at home or locking them in the car, necessitating calling me to come open his car for him, but that's another story. Haven't you ever done that?"

"What? Locked my keys in the car?"

"No," she sighed, "borrowed the key from the secretary?"

"Well, actually I have."

"Good, so you've set a precedent."

"All right, so I get the master key. What then?"

"You choose an appropriate moment, preferably when the police aren't sniffing around, and find something for me."

My mind raced with possibilities about this "something," the dominant one being pictures of Breda with her lover that a blackmailer had sent Disner. "What exactly is it you want me to find?"

"Some letters."

Aha, the blackmailer sent letters, not pictures, to Disner, describing Breda's sordid little affair.

"To and from whom?" I asked.

"They're to Hugh. I don't want to divulge the name of the person who sent them."

Yep, I'm on to something. "How will I recognize them, assuming I do get into his office and assuming I have lots of time to search without Smockley showing up?"

"I imagine they're fairly torrid. You see"—here she hesitated—"Hugh was having an affair."

Taken totally by surprise, I found myself stifling a guffaw. "Excuse me for resorting to a cliché, but 'Surely you jest.'"

"No, I'm not jesting. I would never jest about something so tawdry."

"But who? When?" I stammered.

"I'll tell you when it becomes necessary. For the time being you'll just have to go along and trust me." Suddenly, she stood up. "Before I continue, can I use your restroom?"

"Of course, it's down the hall to the left." As soon as she left the room, I began worrying about how presentable the bathroom was, but then a more serious concern arose. I hoped no one was in there—some person who had entered my front door before Breda arrived. It would be more than I could handle if two Disners got murdered in the pair of bathrooms I frequented the most. My god, I thought, wouldn't Smockley have a field day if I were the discoverer of another Disner demise in a bathroom.

Chapter 24

While Breda was gone, I carried the pineapple to the kitchen and placed it on the counter. Then I returned to the living room, where I thought about her revelation concerning Disner's affair. He was probably the last person I could imagine involved it something so hush-hush. It was hard enough fathoming his persuading Breda to marry him, let alone having sufficient sex with her to produce five children, and now I was supposed to imagine him having sex with a lover. I could almost imagine zombies like my students from that morning class, Larry Hunslinger and Cletis Drackles, having sex before I could picture Disner in the throes of passion. I wondered if he spouted, while doing the dirty deed, any of his usual Disnerisms, along the lines of "Your breasts turn me on, okay?" (I couldn't for the life of me imagine him using a word with more sexual zip, like "tits"). I wondered also if he sang to his lover, something from HMS PINAFORE perhaps, figuring it would turn her on. Did he keep on his tie? Did he wear yellow or green condoms, thus remaining loyal to the university while bonking his lover? Did he have to consult a manual, a special one issued for administrators? Did he prepare a script to follow, like lecture notes for class?

Breda reappeared, sans cigarette, and sat down again on the couch, wiggling back into the cushions as if she planned on staying a while. It was as if I were actually seeing her for the first time. She wore a pair of slim-cut black jeans, which accentuated her slim legs, a gray long-sleeve blouse, and a mauve sleeveless sweater. On her feet were Brooks running shoes. Her almost shoulder-length hair was still dark and full, complementing an almost perfectly proportioned face that just about any Renaissance painter would have dreamed of.

She looked pretty good.

I'd even say "damned good," except I was prejudiced by the fact that she had been married to Disner. I asked, "Would you like something to drink, some wine, maybe?"

"Yes, that would be nice. Do you have anything red?"

"Yes, I think I do." I located a bottle of merlot that was half empty (or was it half full? After this day it was definitely half empty), a California offering that I had selected from a shopping cart full of bargains at Walmart. I poured some into the closest thing I had to a wine glass—a clear tumbler. Before leaving the kitchen, I ran my hands over my stomach and then pinched the flesh on my sides. Not bad, particularly if I sucked in a bit.

Back in the living room, as I handed the wine to her, I caught a whiff of a distinctive, but unidentifiable perfume, something like lilacs. Had she been wearing it when she first arrived? Had she just applied it? Exactly for whom was she wearing it? Must have been for the guy she had just visited, but wouldn't I have sensed it at least faintly when I first discovered her in my living room? I knew I was standing too long in front of her after giving her the wine, so I backed up a few steps and sat in an upright wooden chair I had rescued from a dumpster soon after I moved in. I ventured to say, "Nice perfume," though I wasn't totally sincere, since perfume generally gave me a headache.

"Thank you, I guess. Hugh gave it to me for an anniversary present, but I was a bit ambivalent about ever wearing it since I suspected he gave the same present to a lover.

"How'd you determine that?"

"Sometimes I could smell it on him when he came home late and when I hadn't been wearing it myself."

"Oh," was all that I could respond with. I wanted to change the subject—again—so I asked,"Are you sure the police haven't already found the letters? Smockley's pretty shrewd, you know."

"He's not mentioned them to me. I think that he would have, if he had found them." She held the wine tumbler with two hands, like a three-year old drinking milk. I was tempted to offer her a straw.

"How often do you talk to him?"

"All the time. Even though he treats me politely, he makes me feel extremely uncomfortable, as if I'm a suspect in Hugh's death. I feel as if a pit bull is poised in front of me, baring his teeth and growling, while wagging his tail."

"I know what you mean," I said, feeling a temporary glow of relief that I wasn't the only suspect.

"Why do you suppose the police haven't found the letters yet?"

"They're somewhere no one would think to look."

"How do you know this?"

"Come on, Tyler. I was married to Hugh for almost twenty years. He hid stuff from me all the time at home."

"Like what?"

"Porno pictures, among other things."

This time I couldn't help but laugh out loud. "Porno pictures! Disner? I mean Hugh?"

"Yes, I discovered them one time when I came home early from a trip to my parents' house. He was in the shower and didn't hear me come in. The pictures were spread out all over the bed. I really didn't want to know what he had been doing with them or what he was doing at that moment in the shower, but I did make him tell me where he had been hiding them. He confessed that he kept them in between pages of an article he was working on at his desk about graveyard imagery in English poetry, all contained in a file with big rubber bands wrapped around it. I hoped he hadn't used the rubber bands in some perverted way. If you want more details, I'll paint them for you. Take your pick—oils, acrylics, watercolors, pastels."

"No thanks. I've got the picture. Now, are you're absolutely sure that there actually are such letters?"

"Yes, I've seen one of them."

"How and when?"

"Like I said before when we talked about the keys, Hugh is . . . was . . . very forgetful. He got careless not too long ago with one of the letters—left it mixed in with a syllabus and a couple of memos he had printed out from e-mail. I was looking at the syllabus to see when he'd be off for a vacation when I discovered the letter. She writes well."

"What'd you do with it?"

"Nothing—just stuck it back in the middle of the pile and started fixing beef stroganoff for dinner. In my rage I over chopped the beef, leaving it almost like hamburger. We ended up with something more like shepherd's pie for dinner. Next morning the letter was gone. At any rate, by the tone and by a couple of references, I figured there must be more." She gently swirled her wine glass, controlling her motions so that not a drop spilled.

"Why not just let the police find them, or better still tell Smockley about them? They could have some bearing on the murder."

"Oh, come on, Tyler. It would give Detective Smockley a concrete reason for me to do away with Hugh."

"Well, did you?" I thought about the man living in the house off River Road.

"No, I didn't kill him. I just don't want his sordid little liaisons to get around. It's bad enough that I'm now the widow of a murdered man. I don't want the stigma of being the female version of a cuckold, added."

Again, I almost believed her, but her story about my supposedly unlocked door made me uneasy, as did the incident on the front porch out on the gravel road. She had spoken then with the tone that a person uses only with an error-prone business partner, a cohort in crime who did not complete his part of the deal, or a lover that one feels superior to. Could the man on the porch be all three? Why had she called him "useless"? I wanted desperately to ask her what was going on out there, but figured it would be more appropriate—and revealing—if I waited for her to volunteer information about the encounter.

"Well, are you going to help me?" she asked, breaking my train of thought.

"I'll have to think about it."

"Try not to think about it too long. The longer we wait ['*we?*' I thought. *Is this a tool of persuasion to include me already in the plan?*], the more likely Detective Smockley or one of his assistants will find the letters. According to what he told me, they've been carefully reading all Hugh's e-mail, but I don't think they've found anything terribly helpful. They're bound to sift through every scrap of paper in the office, sooner or later."

I half expected her to pull a gun out, point it at me, and then, reminiscent of a scene from CASABLANCA (or was it PLAY IT AGAIN, SAM), demand letters of transit, but instead she got up, set her wine tumbler on the table next to the M & M bowl she had used as an ashtray and moved toward the front door. I felt awkward as I joined her there. Does one shake hands in such circumstances? Hug? She swayed ever so slightly toward me as if the latter were about to take place, close enough for me to catch another whiff of her perfume, but then she retreated through the door, saying as she left, "Goodbye, Tyler, call me as soon as you've made up your mind."

As soon as she was gone, I tested the door to make sure that it did actually completely shut and stay locked, thus ruling out the possibility that it could have been open on its own accord when Breda arrived earlier. It worked fine, but I still had to admit that I could have simply left it ajar myself that morning. I really did not want to face the possibility that someone besides Breda or myself had opened it.

It was already after 7:30 pm and I needed to get started on the exam answers I had brought home from the 9 am class. But first I prepared some dinner—skipping the pineapple for the time being. An item of food loses some of its culinary appeal when it has just functioned as a potential weapon. As I ate, I thought about what it would take to help me make up my mind whether to help Breda. On the one hand, she sounded convincing—again, almost. On the other hand, if I helped her, would I be getting swept up in some scheme in which I was a patsy? Scenes from the movie BODY HEAT raced through my mind. I even imagined I heard wind chimes clinking on the front porch.

After grading as many exams as I possibly could (only eight), I decided to go to bed, but first I propped a chair against the front door, while promising myself that I would purchase a dead bolt for it and the back door the next day.

As I lay in bed, a flood of thoughts rushed through my mind about Disner's murder, Breda, and the man out on the gravel road. I found her to be attractive—in a dangerous sort of way. Before I helped her, however, I'd like some answers to a few nagging questions. Why hadn't she told me about that guy, and why was she admonishing him? Had she not seen who I was as she passed me on the road? And should I believe her excuse for not going to Smockley with information about the letters—that she truly had so much pride that she didn't want people to know about Disner's affair?

Smockley! Thinking of him set off a whole new train of thought. I wondered what kind of questions he asked Breda. Did he already know about her dusk-time trysts? Should I tell him? Should I let him know about the letters?

Sleep came reluctantly, and when it did it was suffused with nightmares that involved the principal characters I had been thinking of, mixed into the plot of Shakespeare's HAMLET. In the dream, two members of the clean-up crew in my building came to my office and informed me that they had both seen Disner's ghost, with a grizzled beard and eyes that fixed upon them, floating around the top floor of the English Building, speaking my name. I vowed to them that I would speak to it "though Hell itself should gape and bid me hold my peace." Then it showed up, actually looking more like my conception of the Ghost from Christmas Past than

Disner, and I asked it, "Why the sepulcher had opened its ponderous and marble jaws to cast him up again," whereupon, despite the objections of the two janitors, it led me up to the open roof of the building, stopping near the ledge overlooking the bell tower, which at that moment was gonging out the song "Midnight Blues."

It spoke (or should I be calling it "he"? Pronoun usage is a bit fuzzy when it comes to ghosts). "Mark me. I am Disner's spirit, doomed to walk the night until this crime is purged away. I need someone to revenge my most foul and unnatural murder." It sounded like someone speaking through reverb equipment.

I first offered it some white wine that I happened to have in my backpack (white seeming to me a better choice for something dead), but it refused, maybe because ghosts can't tolerate alcohol. Then I asked it what had happened. It answered, "I was grading papers in the toilet stall and began to doze, but was awakened by a sting [which I interpreted as the gunshot to his head] from a serpent who now wears my crown" [which I interpreted to be the guy out of the gravel road]. It then went into detail about lust and lewdness, people sating themselves on a celestial bed, and other matters, but much of what he told me was a bit obscure. I don't think ghosts are particularly remarkable for clarity. When the bell tower began clanging out an aubade that I recognized, celebrating the coming of the dawn, the spirit panicked and vanished, cautioning me to leave his widow "to Heaven and to those thorns that in her bosom lodge to prick and sting her," or something like that.

Chapter 25

When I awoke the next morning, my legs ached, as if I had been climbing a steep mountain during the night, and I felt decidedly unrested. After I dressed, I drove to the University, where I was again forced to park in a different parking lot from the one next to my building, only this time I chose one which necessitated a longer hike than I had taken the previous day, but one which allowed me to stay on the main roads through campus as I hurried to my building. I never did see anyone walking towards me with a face obscured by a hooded jacket.

As I approached my building, I could hear the bell tower chiming out the notes to "Chim Chim Cheree." I really wasn't in the mood for a MARY POPPINS week, but the pace of the notes negated the potential cherriness of the tune, thus making the rendition come closer to fitting my foul mood.

Arriving at the mail boxes to check my mail, I discovered that the fourth thing on a list of what I did not want to happen that day was about to become a reality—having to talk with Bwanger—the first one being getting murdered, the second being finding someone else murdered, and the third being having to talk with Smockley. I began to hope that some of the good luck I knew to be the subject of the song coming from the tower would rub off on me.

As I could have predicted, the meeting with Bwanger was another question/non-answer session, with Bwanger asking the questions and me avoiding providing any information relevant to the Disner case. "You need to tell me everything, Tyler. I'm a friend and a colleague. I'm entitled to as much information as you can provide."

"I promise, Dr. Bwanger, I've told you everything I could think of."

After leaving Bwanger, I returned to my office, locked the door and pretended I was not there. In fact, except for the two hours I spent teaching classes, I stayed hidden for the whole day, spending most of my time thinking about Breda Disner and why she had visited me.

Just before six, with the bell tower chiming out a song I could not recognize, I walked to my car, following the same very public route I had traversed that morning. It was growing dark.

From campus, I drove out to River Road again, where I stopped at the same turnout I had chosen the night before. I sat in my car for a while, pondering my next move. I hoped that I would see either Breda or her tryst mate come by, but I realized that I would not recognize him or his vehicle, since I had not been afforded a good look at his car parked in the shadows—maybe a Jeep or a pickup truck—or him as he stood partially hidden from the light in his doorway talking with Breda.

After sitting for about a half an hour with no Jeep or pickup at all matching the shape I thought I saw the night before, or Breda's van, I decided to drive out to the gravel road—still with no real plan in mind. I glided past the house Breda had visited, wondering if Breda were there. Her van wasn't, but there was a four-door sedan parked out front—a Japanese model maybe, but I couldn't be sure—definitely not a Jeep or a pickup.

After turning around at a spot down the road, I parked my car within sight of the house, the distance of a good nine iron shot, near a section of woods, which seemed to deepen the darkness. If I had been Robert Frost in a carriage, my horse would have given his harness bells a shake to ask if there were some mistake, this night seeming to be the darkest one of the year. But I didn't mind the darkness since it provided better cover for me.

I still wasn't sure what I hoped to accomplish—maybe see Breda drive up, see her and her acquaintance embrace, kiss, carry on in the front yard, or maybe simply see the man himself, who might get in his car, drive to some public place like Blethens Groceries—with me following him at a discrete distance—where I could eventually sidle up beside him, perhaps in the produce aisle, and engage him in conversation, maybe comment on the ripeness of a melon he happened to be holding—and in the process get a good look at him.

But what if Breda had told him about me? What if he knew who I was already? Probably everyone knew I was the person who had found Disner dead in the toilet stall. So what would I do if I did meet this guy? What then?

After a short while, I began to feel conspicuous despite the darkness. I thought about parking farther away from the house, but it wouldn't be as easy to see anyone coming or going. I considered returning to the turnout on River Road, parking there, and then jogging back along the gravel road, but there was a problem. I was dressed in the clothes I had worn to class—dress pants, a long sleeved dress shirt, a sport coat, and leather dress shoes. I'd have to scrounge up—from the mess in my car—some running gear, at least some running shoes.

But then there was the possibility—if I should jog on the gravel road—that Breda would roar past me again, and I doubted if she would fail to recognize me. What if she tried to run me over with that ugly van of hers? I'd die as ignominiously as Disner had. But then again, why would she do that, after coming to my house the previous night asking me to retrieve letters from Disner's office.

I was beginning to feel tension in my neck, a sure precursor to a debilitating headache. Even though it was in the fifties outside, my car began to feel stuffy to me. I rolled down the driver's side window and breathed in the cool air as I considered what to do.

As I squinted at the house, I was suddenly aware of a pair of hands gripping the doorsill. I jerked away in alarm with a gasp that I hoped was not as loud in actuality as if was in my head. "Can I help you?" a deep voice demanded from the darkness.

"What?" I stammered.

"Can I help you?" I briefly contemplating correcting the speaker's grammar by asking, "Don't you mean, 'May I help you?'" but I didn't think a grammar lesson was in order right then. Instead I blurted out, "Why did you sneak up on me like that? You could give a person a heart attack, you know."

"I live here. I want to know what you're up to, just sitting out here." He pulled himself in closer to me, but not close enough for me to see a face, only a hooded jacket. This was the second time in a couple of days that I felt like I was dealing with synecdoches, hooded jackets and now some hands.

"Nothing. I was just thinking about jogging—yeah, jogging—but I was procrastinating, you know, trying to decide if I had enough energy today."

"Why are you still wearing street clothes if you're planning to jog?"

"Oh, that—these!" I pulled at one of the buttons on my shirt, creating a miniature tent. "I was going to change. See!" I groped in the darkness for a tee shirt or shorts I was sure were somewhere on the passenger seat or floor, but all I could feel were text books and papers—probably the batch I needed to grade that night. "Damn, they're here somewhere. I just need to turn on the light."

"Don't bother!" he snapped. "It doesn't matter."

"Say, who are you?" I asked.

"I'm Brad Crawford. Why do you need to know?"

"Oh, no reason, other than I just like to know whom I'm talking with in the dark." I was slowly regaining my composure, enough to use the proper form of "who/whom." but I still felt the need to find evidence that I was equipped to jog, as I now searched the contents of my back seat, while trying to see the face outside my car.

"I suggest you park somewhere else."

"Yeah! Why's that?"

"Because this road is narrow and people driving down it don't usually expect a car to be sitting on it in the dark. You might get hurt, if you know what I mean." He withdrew his hands from the doorsill, making it impossible for me to see any evidence that anyone was actually still there.

"Okay," I said, immediately realizing that I sounded like Disner." Maybe you're right. Watch yourself. I'm going to pull out now." Since there was no reply, I felt like I was speaking to just the darkness. After several seconds of silence, I cranked up and left, hoping that my taillights would help reveal the physical identity of the mysterious Crawford. They didn't.

As I drove by Crawford's house, I spotted Breda's van parked in the illuminated driveway, seemingly with no attempt on her part to conceal it. She must have arrived while I was talking with Crawford, my attention diverted by his hands on my doorsill. I always thought that fear made one's senses more acute, but obviously acuteness can be quite focused since I noticed a scar just above his left hand on his wrist, but missed seeing a van pull in that was as big as a storage garage.

What was she doing here now? What was her relationship with this guy named Crawford? Who was tending her kids while she was out gallivanting on gravel roads? In answer to the latter question, I supposed with as many children as she had, one was bound to be mature enough to take care of the others, but why was I even thinking about Disner offspring? Why was I strangely attracted to Breda? She definitely was rising in my estimation, the more she seemed to be independent of Disner. She definitely was no longer just Disner's widow in my mind.

No matter what I thought of her, I still was relieved that she did not know of some secret shortcut to my house and beat me to my house, parking her van in front. I still exercised caution as I pulled in my driveway, surveying the front door to see if it looked open, checking for lights inside (including a glow from a cigarette). After parking in the rear, I entered the back door as I had the night before, reaching in to turn on the kitchen light, then proceeding through the rest of the house, switching on the other lights before entering the rooms. I also checked the front door to make sure it was as I had left it that morning. I even checked the closets.

After I ate a tuna sandwich and some chicken soup, I settled into the one activity—grading papers—that could drain away almost every ounce of excess adrenalin that had been produced by Breda, with her surreptitious perambulations, and Crawford, with his hands on my door and his deep voice. I started to cull out the dregs—those that I suspected would be most difficult to read or requiring the most deductions of points—for later marking. I usually did this with a pile of papers, hoping that while I was grading the sensible, coherent, developed ones, some academic fairy might grade the others for me, particularly the tedious, verbose ones that reminded me of long messages left on answering machines. This night, I decided to take them in the order they were turned in, theorizing that the worse the reading, the more I would be distracted from the intrigue associated with the Disners. Plus every poorly written one would serve as a foil to make the good ones appear even more stellar. I started with the last exam submitted, Horace Glogg's.

Reading his answers was roughly equivalent to reading random graffiti on the wall in a bus depot men's room, with few sentences cohering, all written with varying slants and styles, with the added complication that Glogg's words made me think I was reading Chaucer in the original. The only truly readable part came when he decided to carry on a written dialogue with himself, in response to a question about Poe's use of the grotesque, first asking, "Do I knowe this anser?" then following with, "Yes, I think I doe, but I'll hav to think aboot it. Is their meaning to live? Will I find my pourpose? Did Poe kno the secrete to undestanding God? What is the grootesque?" I got images of the ad that shows eggs sizzling in a fry pan with the caption saying that this is your brain on drugs.

Seeing Glogg as a foil to all the other students in the class made me realize that I might have felt worse about Disner's death if someone I disliked more than Disner had just died. The trouble arose in that there was no one I disliked more than Disner.

After Glogg's answers, I proceeded to those submitted by Daniel Duggon, whose first answer, in response to the question concerning the dream sequence in Ambrose Bierce's "An Occurrence at Owl Creek Bridge," made a case that Bierce was influenced by Freud (since the years of their lives overlapped) and that he intended for us to interpret the planks on the bridge as phallic symbols, the noose around Peyton Farquhar's neck as an umbilicus, and the river into which he drops as amniotic fluid, indicating a desire to return to the womb. At least Duggon had read the assignment, which was more than I could say for Glogg.

The only truly disturbing note came at the end of Duggon's answer sheet, where he had written, "Give me an A or DIE!" I wondered should I be alarmed. Was this Duggon's way of being chummy and cute? Chummy I could do without. Cute I could do without. Would I have been upset with this remark if Disner had not been murdered? Probably not, but I vowed to call Smockley the next day and report the incident. What really pissed me off was that even grading papers was not a diversion from thinking about Disner.

I began thinking what I would like to do if I were not a teacher. In which profession would I not have to grade papers—or do paper work at all—a job that would get me outside, away from crowds? Be a forest ranger maybe? Nope, the government probably makes them do all sorts of paper work. How about being a painter of houses. They probably don't have to do much paper work, but could I put up with people changing their minds on colors at the last minute, standing under the ladder telling me I missed a spot? Maybe not.

I waded through another six or seven exams, reminded at various junctures of the chaos theory, maybe the butterfly effect—wherein one event conditions all subsequent actions, in a random zigzag of cause and effect. I could see evidence of a student's mishearing a term in my discussion, for instance, writing down as the definition for "verisimilitude" not what I actually said, which was "authenticity," but rather "audio equipment," thus leading to other concepts that took the student farther and farther from the actual meaning, resulting in a line in the exam answers stating that "Hawthorne's use of verisimilitude probably demonstrated early music lessons, maybe with an electric guitar."

This made me again think about Disner, wondering if his death came as a result of random cause and effect, wherein a student or faculty member on the way to the university, carelessly forgot that he had a gun in his backpack, got cut off by a driver weaving in and out of traffic, swore revenge, followed the offender to campus, mistook Disner for him because Disner came from a car that looked like the speeder's, tailed Disner to the men's room, and then shot him with the gun he never intended to bring to school in the first place.

Of course not all of the test answers were incoherent and chaotic. Several made the grading process almost a pleasure. The variety of answers prompted me to think about the diversity of students in any given class. There were a few flashy sport car types, a Mazda RX8 maybe, who looked attractive and handled all the curves of the course with ease. And there were some ponderous Buicks, some overbearing SUV's, some squatty vans, some NASCAR-type Chevys and Fords, a couple of exotic foreign touring sedans, and a couple of beat-up clunkers, that moved at the speed of a bushhog in deep weeds.

I was just beginning on the answers submitted by one of the Ford Escorts in class, Cloris Frampton, when I heard a real vehicle pull up out front.

Chapter 26

I went to the bedroom window, where, with the light off, I peered out between two slats of my Venetian blinds. Sitting in front was Breda's van, but I could not see anyone in or around the vehicle. I released the slat I had bent down, jumping back when it made a "ping" that sounded to my ears like a gunshot, and then stood waiting in the darkness, until I heard a knock on the front door. I debated whether to stay in the bedroom, pretending that I was not home, go to the door and tell Breda and/or Crawford (who could be with Breda or by himself, using her van, for all I knew) to go away so that I could grade my papers (which suddenly took on an appeal that they did not have just moments earlier), or open the door and confront whoever was waiting there.

I chose to open the door. It was Breda—alone.

"Can I come in?" she asked.

I started to tell her she was guilty of the same grammatical error as Crawford, but I opted for another line of sarcasm. "Well, this is a switch."

"What do you mean?"

"You actually knocked at my door this time and waited until I let you in."

"I explained last night why I came on in. Now, if you don't mind, I'd like to step inside."

"Sure," I said, trying to act as if I were merely letting in the cleaning help to scrub the tile in my bathroom, though in reality I was glad to see her.

"Thank you," she said. As I held the door open, she entered, emitting a faint odor of the same perfume she had worn the previous night. She was wearing a dark blue cardigan, which she held together at the top with one hand. With her other hand, as she passed me, she reached out and patted me on my chest, sending a wave of excitement through me that I could feel all the way down to my insteps.

After I closed the door, she sat down on the couch next to the pile of papers I had just been grading. I remained standing, just inside the front door. She immediately removed her sweater, revealing a light blue blouse unbuttoned one button more than my libido could tolerate. She made matters worse by leaning forward and tying the sweater around her waist. I tried not to stare at her cleavage, but it was difficult. "Have you thought about what I asked you to do?" I was surprised by how quickly she got to the point.

"Yes, I've thought about it, but to tell you the truth, I'm having a few problems," I answered, as I moved into the room a couple of strides.

"Such as?" she asked.

"Well, for one thing, as you no doubt are aware, I've seen you out visiting this guy named Crawford—twice, in fact, in just the last two days."

"And?"

"And what?"

"What's your problem?"

"I just want to know how he fits into all this, who he is, why you're seeing him, et cetera."

"I don't have any obligation to tell you about him."

"And I don't have any obligation to go foraging around in your dead husband's office, either."

"That's true, but why do you need to know about Brad—that's his first name."

"Yes, I know. We've met, or at least I've met his hands and his hooded jacket—more than once if I'm not mistaken. Look, I'd be more willing to help if I knew what was going on here."

"What do you want to know about him?"

"For starters, how'd you get to know him?" I tried to hide my jealousy by straightening a pile of books resting on top of my bookshelf to my right.

"He painted our house. Hugh thought we needed to spruce it up a bit when he became the associate dean. I think he envisioned giving big parties, maybe to rival the one given every Christmas by the Dean of Arts and Sciences, Fred Hacklett."

"At the same time as Hacklett's?"

"No, he wasn't that bold. He thought about giving a New Year's party or maybe a spring fling or something—around Easter. I told him he ought to offer up a Maypole ceremony—make it really pagan and dissolute. I didn't think he would go for it, but who knows, he probably had something equally entertaining going on in the bedroom of his girlfriend. Anyway, he hired Brad, who was one of his more mature students at the time, to paint for us. I think Brad developed a thing for me during the process."

"Does he still have this 'thing' for you?"

"Yeah, at least he tells me he does."

"And you?"

"What do you mean?"

"How do you feel about him?" I again tried not to let my jealousy show, this time by checking out imaginary cobwebs at the top of my wall.

"I simply see him as someone who is useful to me—or at least I did until about twenty-four hours ago."

"Meaning?"

"Meaning that when I went to his house last night, I tried to persuade him to get Hugh's letters for me. I even offered to pay him."

"What happened?"

"He refused, saying that there's no way he could get into Hugh's office without drawing all kinds of attention to himself. He made me angry enough to shout at him."

"Yeah, I heard you."

"I was afraid of that, when I saw you on the road, but there you have it, so you don't need to fret about him. He doesn't mean anything to me."

"So why were you back out there tonight?" I still was not sure if I believed her, but her partially unbuttoned blouse made her argument seem more convincing.

"I wanted him to swear that he wouldn't tell anyone that I asked him to help me get the letters."

"Did he?"

"Sort of, but I'm not sure I can trust him." She suddenly stood up. "Listen, can we change the subject here; I'm sick of thinking about him. I know, is there any wine left in that bottle you had open last night?"

"I think so, but if there isn't, I've got another bottle, a merlot, but a different brand from the one I served last night."

"It doesn't matter. Pick one. After today, I could drink everything you've got, but if I did, I'd have to sleep here. I couldn't afford to get stuck with a DUI. It's not seemly for a grieving widow to be careening around county roads drunk, though I guess I could use the excuse that I WAS a grieving widow."

She sat back down, tucked her legs up beneath her, and tilted over on the armrest, causing her blouse to gape open even more than it had previously. That and her comment about spending the night almost made me forget that I was supposed to fetch some wine. I had a momentary fantasy of lying in bed with her, but the image was negated in large measure by a vision of her in bed with Disner and by another image of her in bed with mystery man Brad Crawford and, for a fleeting moment, by an even more disturbing image of her in bed with Disner AND Crawford. I went for the wine.

After I had poured two glasses, finishing the bottle from the previous night and opening a new bottle, each of which cost me under five dollars, I delivered a glass to her. She pushed my papers to the far end of the couch and then patted the space next to her. "Have a seat," she said, but then added, "Oops, I think that's supposed to be your line, since you're the host." I took a seat, pushing the papers completely off the couch onto the floor. Seeing them made me realize how far I had distanced myself from Glogg, Duggon, Frampton, and the rest of my students, while Breda lolled on the armrest. "Well, did you make a decision?" she asked.

"Yes, I poured you some wine from the new bottle. I'm drinking what was left from last night's bottle."

"No, silly, I mean about helping me get Hugh's letters." I realized that it was the second time she had called me silly, but the word sounded sexy coming from her.

"I haven't decided about that yet. I mean, I don't want to sound selfish, but why should I risk getting in even more trouble with Detective Smockley" (I had forgotten about Glogg et al, but, for sure, not Smockley),"maybe getting caught in the office. Besides, what's in it for me? Why should I do this?"

I had my own answer, but Breda said it for me. "Because I interest you."

"How do you know?"

"Please, Tyler. I'm a woman. Give me some credit."

"But you know I didn't like Hugh. He totally annoyed me. I doubt if that was any secret."

"That's him; this is me." She reached over and patted me on my thigh, sending even more of a charge through me than her pectoral pat earlier, a feeling that came only once or twice a year—usually involving a long stay in the shower. "And I'm really flattered," she added.

I wanted to believe her, but images of Crawford kept nagging at me. I decided to use her boldness to ask the most pertinent question I could think of. "Who do you think killed your husband?"

She removed her hand and used it to pull her blouse together at the top. She stared at the floor for several seconds." Do you not want to talk about it?" I asked.

"No, I don't mind discussing it with you. It's just that I don't really have an idea who killed him. Detective Smockley thinks I did it." I couldn't help but laugh. "What's so funny?" she asked.

"Like I said before, I thought I was the prime suspect. But why does he think that you did it?" I was hoping she would punctuate her answer with another thigh pat.

"Hugh—we—I—there were differences between us. You weren't the only person he annoyed, you know. I lived with him all the time. Take whatever he did to annoy you and multiply that by hundreds, thousands if you want, and you've got my feelings. Somehow, Detective Smockley knows this."

"How'd he find out?"

"Acquaintances, I guess. Like you, I didn't always hide my feelings—my frustration and antipathy. I think I rolled my eyes too often in front of others when he told corny jokes and then laughed at them himself—by himself."

"That sounds pretty petty," I responded, while realizing that Disner's minor infractions were my own main causes for disliking him.

"You're right of course, and I shouldn't be denigrating the dead, but there were some major issues. I particularly got disturbed after he became an administrator. He was practically never around to help with the kids—all of whom were his idea, by the way—and when he was, he still acted as an administrator. He started making the kids keep a schedule of events, submit strategic plans, write up summaries of their activities, supposedly because he couldn't actually spend as much time with them, but mainly because he couldn't stop being a damned administrator, which showed in the fact that he always wore a tie and carried around a gigantic set of keys that he easily could have left at the office

"I noticed that you seemed angry at the world when you were at the funeral. What gave?"

"Oh, I was just reminded of all the crap that came with his being associated with the University—stuff that he bought into, like that tiresome notion that we're all a part of a University family. The irony is that he wanted a big family of his own—something he got in spades with all the children, at my expense of course—but then he wanted to remain a part of the academic family. It all made me sick. I just wanted to get away from constant crowds, sometimes even my children, and have a chance to pursue my own career."

"In what?"

"Writing. Before I married Hugh, I was a journalism major and I wrote poetry. I also painted in oils and pastels. I gave up what I wanted to do to stay home and take care of the family Hugh wanted."

"Have you thought about pursuing your interests now, since Hugh's not around anymore—maybe meet someone who would encourage a pursuit of your career?"

"Come on, Tyler. What are the odds of a thirty-eight year old widow, with five kids, being able to pursue a career in writing AND finding 'true love'? I'm out of practice with my writing, and I wouldn't exactly be what you call the prime choice on any of those dating programs. I'd be the first one eliminated."

"Oh, that's not true. I think you're extremely attractive."

"How can you say that, Tyler? You've never even noticed me before." She let go of her blouse and folded her hands on her laps.

"Maybe, but that's because you were always with Hugh. It was difficult disassociating you from him. Besides, I'm not in the habit of hitting on married women, particularly the wives of my colleagues, especially those with children."

"My point exactly—at least the part about the children."

"That's not what I meant. Look, they'll eventually grow up and move on. But you'll continue to be attractive—and" (here I was afraid I might be going too far) "desirable. I certainly find you that way."

"Thank you for lying." She rested her hand on my thigh again. This time I laid my hand on top of hers. The five-dollar stuff we were drinking began to taste more like fifteen-dollar wine—maybe twenty.

When we finished the bottle, remembering what she said about getting drunk and having to stay the night, I offered to run out for more wine, but she stood and said, "I really need to get home, while I'm still sober enough to drive."

"Well, you're certainly welcomed to stay here if you want to, with no strings attached," I replied.

"I better not do that. I'm just not sure how I feel about being here—with you." She moved to the front door. "I hope you understand."

"Of course," I said. "And about the letters, I'll get them for you tomorrow. I'll call you after I've done the deed."

"Fine, I'll talk to you then." After kissing me on the cheek, she was gone, leaving me to wonder what the hell I had gotten myself into.

Still I had promised I would get the letters for her, and I would.

Chapter 27

At 4:45 the next afternoon I was standing in the English Office, shifting my weight from leg to leg, asking the Departmental secretary, Yvonda Dunkirk, for the master key. "Where's yours?" she asked with a husky rasp. She reminded me of Bond's foe, Rosa Klebb, in the movie version of FROM RUSSIA WITH LOVE, with her flat, straight hair, colorless attire, and expressionless face.

"I left them in my car," I answered, raising my arms and spreading my palms upward, hoping to affect a classic "I screwed up" pose.

"Why can't you just go back and get them?"

"Well, you see, my car is way across campus. I couldn't park in the lot because . . . because it was full." I wondered if I would be going through all this if I were actually locked out of my own office. Probably so.

"Did you lock your car?"

"Yes, I always do."

"Then, how are you going to get into it, if your keys are locked inside?"

"Oh, I . . . I carry a spare key in my wallet, just for the car." Why is it, I thought, that people who are totally phlegmatic and apathetic ninety-nine percent of the time become so incredibly logical and prying when I'm up to no good. I felt like screaming, "Just give me the damned key, you mephitic bitch," but I simply asked once more, "May I get the key?"

"Here, take them, but don't spend too long up there. I'm leaving in just a few minutes." She opened her desk drawer and then handed me a metal loop as big as a hitching post ring seen as a prop in Westerns. On it was the lone master key, so labeled. I was tempted to ask why the excess, but I was afraid that her answer might cut into my foraging time.

As I exited the English Office, she uttered one last command: "Make sure you don't open any other doors but your own." I speculated about what she envisioned me doing. Did she think I might raid other professor's offices, robbing them of their copies of British lit texts, maybe grabbing a couple of rhetorics and grammars for good measure? Perhaps she thought I might dart straight to the maintenance supply closet and swipe some of the industrial strength toilet paper we're forced to wipe with or some of that green liquid hand soap used to fill the dispensers in the men's room (and I guess the women's room, unless they are stuck with the other school color, yellow). She might even suspect that I'd detour to the departmental supply closet, where she kept, locked up, manila folders, chalk, erasers, and notebook pads. I wondered what she would do if she actually caught me in the act of searching Disner's office. Probably call Smockley.

And speaking of Smockley! I had forgotten to call him about Duggon's threat on his exam answers. Oh, well, it'd just have to wait.

On the way up the stairs and down the hall, I thought about Breda's visit the previous night. I was still struggling with a conflict between my reason and my emotions, feeling as if I were becoming an actor in an academic version of PEYTON PLACE. I could sympathize with Breda's chagrin at discovering that her husband had been popping someone other than her, and I could understand why she wanted to save face by avoiding the scandal that would be revealed by the contents of the letters to Disner. But I was also aware that this all gave her strong motives to seek revenge on Disner herself. Plus, stealing the letters might actually impede Smockley in his efforts to discover the real killer.

So why was I on my way to Disner's office to help her out? I had to admit that she excited me, even though she could have been Disner's murderer and even though she had participated in sex with Disner at least five times, judging by the five children. I rationalized this latter fact by entertaining the possibility that, in Disner's absence, approximately nine months before each birth, in no particular order, she had hopped on the refrigerator repair man, the next door neighbor who dropped over at midday to borrow a screwdriver, the bagboy at Kroger loading groceries in her van, her priest, who suddenly discovered his libido while privately praying with Breda, and maybe one of her kid's soccer coaches—either that or she and Disner practiced artificial insemination to the tune of $15,000 a child, highly unlikely given his professor's salary at the time.

The possibility that she murdered Disner was more difficult for me to dismiss, but after she touched me three times—once on the chest, twice on the thigh—I would have agreed to do almost anything for her—short of firkling the bursar.

I had purposely chosen 4:45 pm as the breaking and entering time (well, maybe just the entering time, since I had the key), figuring that most of the faculty would have cleared out, leaving only those who were still bonding with their computers. My plan was to secure the key from Yvonda, go to Disner's office, quietly unlock the door, reach in and twist the locking mechanism on the inside door handle, close the door, return the key to Yvonda, and then return to Disner's office, where I could search for the letters at my leisure, or at least until six or so, at which time Doris McGuire, a member of the housekeeping staff, usually made her rounds to empty waste cans and collect recyclable paper. I had not calculated that one of the computer bonders would be Glick, whose office adjoined Disner's. At that moment, he was sitting with his door wide open, at his computer, his fingers jabbing at the keys in frantic staccato as he mouthed the words he was typing. I wondered if he ever wore himself out listening to his own voice.

As soon as I walked past his door, he stopped typing and looked up. "Helloooo, Tyler," he said, drawing out his o's like a vocal showoff, sustaining a final note in a camp song. "What are YOU doing here so late in the day?" he asked. "Aren't you usually out of here as soon as your class is finished right after lunch?" I had never noticed it before, but, due to an ultra-conservative haircut, his ears stuck out like small satellite dishes. He probably would have heard me even if I had tried sneaking into Disner's office from the other direction.

"Yes, usually I am," I answered, surprised that he would even notice me amidst his fervor at the keyboard and also surprised that he knew my routine. "I'm up here to work on an exam for tomorrow," I lied.

"I thought you gave one yesterday—in your American Lit survey. One of my students was complaining about how tough it was."

"That's good to hear, but I'm giving a different one tomorrow."

"In what?" He stood up abruptly, holding his hands as if he were about to conduct an orchestra.

"In what, you ask? In my Shakespeare class."

"Seems to me like you're about to get yourself into trouble."

"How's that? What do you mean?" I was seized by a momentary panic that Glick knew what I intended to do.

"Messing with all those letters," he answered.

My god, he does know! How could he possibly have figured it all out?

134

"Letters?" I queried.

"Yes, the exam answers you're getting. I like to call them letters—you know, love letters from our students to us. It makes them seem not so difficult to grade, except when you get two sets in two days, like you're doing."

"Oh, letters! I see! Ha, ha, ha!" I laughed loudly, like Disner used to do before he was murdered and like Bwanger still does, as if volume might reinforce sincerity. "Well, I better get busy."

I moved on down the hall, pausing at Disner's door. I knew that if I tried to open it right then, Glick would hear me with those big ears, whereupon he would step out from his office and question my motives. I knew I had to think fast since Yvonda would be waiting for the key. I decided after just a moment of thought to take the initiative with Glick. I opened Disner's door, making lots of noise. Sure enough Glick came out, but before he could ask what I was doing, I volunteered an explanation. "Hugh had one of my textbooks, with some of my notes written in it, notes which I need for an upcoming class on KING LEAR. I was told to use the master key and look in his office."

Glick cocked his head and replied, "I don't think anyone is allowed in there. The police have pretty much kept it off limits for everyone while they complete their investigation." He eyed me with the intensity of a guard dog, as I opened the door.

"I know, but I just need to look in this one book. I don't even need to remove it." I hoped this explanation would stave off any suspicion Glick might have, all the while thinking that Glick was a perfect candidate for the sixth circle in DAVIDSON'S HELL, in which nosy busybodies spend eternity with extraordinarily long noses that poke through open doors—doors that abruptly slam shut, pinching the noses.

While Glick stood firm in Disner's doorway, I pretended to search the shelves for my book, knowing of course that it at that moment it rested on my own desk next to my computer. After what I considered to be sufficient futile hunting, I said, "Well, it's not here. That's too bad, because I really need those notes. Maybe Hugh loaned my book out to a student."

"Yes," Glick responded, "Hugh was always giving students books and material. He was very generous that way." He seemed satisfied that my visit to Disner's office was legitimate, so he backed away from the door. As I closed it, I pulled the key from the front knob with my left hand, while I twisted the locking mechanism on the inside to the unlocked position, with my right hand. Glick seemed not to notice, as he gazed down the hall. It all made me think that failure also makes one seem more convincing.

Chapter 28

Convinced that Glick suspected nothing amiss, I returned the masterkey megaloop to Yvonda, who met me at the door of the English Office. "What took you so long?" she crackled. "I was just about to come hunt you down!" I would not have been at all surprised if she suddenly started jabbing at me with a switchblade jutting out of the toe of her shoe, while shrieking Russian epithets.

I handed her the key ring. "Thanks, keep the change," I said, before turning away and hurrying back upstairs.

I slowed to a halt as I came around the corner of Disner's hall. Glick's door was still open. Not wanting Glick to see me again so soon, I stood for a moment, assessing the situation. I could horseshoe around the halls and enter this one from the other end and make my way to Disner's door, but what then? Could I open it without alerting Glick to my machinations? It was now a minute or two after five.

I strode to my office, where, after unlocking my door from the outside with my key, I reached in and turned the inside locking mechanism to the unlocked position, as I had just done at Disner's office, then closed the door. I tried to open the door without a sound, but was greeting by a loud "clack." I tried several more times, even attempting to muffle the sound by crowding up close to the door, all without success. I knew Disner's door would be just as loud, drawing Glick out of his office immediately. I needed a new plan.

Entering my office, I hit upon an alternative, which entailed a phone call. I dialed up Glick, who answered immediately. "Professor Gluck?" I asked, disguising by voice so that, in my mind anyway, I sounded like Andy Griffith in Mayberry.

"Do you mean 'Glick'?"

"Oh, yes, of course, 'Glick.' Are you him?"

"Yes, this is HE. What can I do for you?"

"Sir, this is Officer . . . Officer Clydesdale, with Campus Security. There's been a small accident involving your car."

"What kind of accident?"

"Someone has gone and smacked right into it—crumpled up your rear bumper."

"But how can that be? I backed into the space and left the car pointing outward."

"Yes . . . . Ah, now I see the report," I said, rustling some of the papers on my desk. "It was your front bumper that got bashed."

"Are you sure you have the right car, or rather the right owner?"

"Absolutely. You drive a . . . " (Here I had to make an informed guess, being approximately seventy percent sure about what Glick drove) . . . a blue Toyota Camry don't you?"

"No, I have a Buick Regal, a white one."

"Oh, wait, yes, of course, a Buick Regal. Sorry, but we've had several accidents lately and I got confused. At any rate, we'd like for you to come down and sign the report form." I suddenly realized that my voice had transformed into that of Don Knotts, a pitch or so above that of Andy Griffith's, but Glick didn't seem to notice.

"Now?"

"Yes, as soon as possible. We need to remove the car that hit yours."

"Oh, all right. By the way, who hit my car?"

"Uh, a student, one who was illegally parked in your faculty parking lot, I might add."

"That figures. The dirty bastards are all the time stealing my spots."

"Well, we're working on the problem. Now, can you come soon?"

"I need to finish one item of business on my computer, and then I'll be there."

"We'll be waiting."

As soon as I hung up, I hurried down my hall to where it intersected Glick's hall and peaked toward Glick's office. His door was still open. I figured he had not had time to leave, and, if he had, he would have closed his door, so I waited . . . and waited . . . and waited some more, five, then ten minutes. It was now 5:15. What was taking him so long? Had he managed to leave his office in the few seconds it took me to run from my office to here?

I waited another five minutes and then decided I could take it no longer. I walked down his hall, past his open door. He was working frantically at his keyboard, eyes glued to the screen, such that he failed to notice my passing. I backed up and said, "Still at it, Glenn?"

"Yes . . . , I . . . ., just . . . . , damn. I was trying to finish this report, but I need to go outside."

"Why's that?"

"Someone hit my car."

"Oh, my. When?"

"I'm not sure. The officer in charge just called me."

"Gosh, I'd be there in a heartbeat if I were you. People leave the scene, you know, forcing you to have to get them on the phone later, to clear up insurance matters and other stuff." Seeing that this did not move Glick to immediate action, I groped for one more incentive. "Plus, there's always the possibility somebody might have even been injured."

Glick cocked his head as if he were listening to a distant siren. After a long pause, he said, "Perhaps you're right. I guess I better go. I can finish this when I get back." He slid his chair back from the computer and stood up.

Now, for me, ideally, he would have closed up shop for the day, gone to look at his car, found it unscathed, searched for Officer Clydesdale, puzzled for a few moments over the odd phone call, finally figured it was a prank perpetrated by one of his students, and then gone home. Instead of this latter step, however, he would be returning to his office, thus complicating matters for me. I would have to work extremely fast, likely within a six or eight-minute window of opportunity, maybe ten tops.

I walked with him as far as the elevator, where he punched the down button and waited. I excused myself and ducked into the adjoining men's room, the very one in which Disner had been murdered. After making sure no one was in there, I stood by the door and waited, hoping Glick would not suddenly feel the call of nature and find me lurking just inside. As soon as I heard the elevator doors close and the motor begin its whine, I hurried back to Disner's office, which I immediately entered, locking the door from the inside once I was in. I was fairly certain no one had seen me.

Chapter 29

As soon as I had closed the door, I began searching the top of the desk, one of the locations that Breda had identified as a possible hiding spot for the DISNER LETTERS, as I decided to call them. It was Breda's theory that Disner may have hidden the letters in a way similar to Marion Crane, again in PSYCHO, who hid the $40,000 that she had stolen earlier, by wrapping the money in the current edition of the newspaper and leaving it out on the nightstand in plain view. I suspected that Smockley would be a bit more thorough than a panicky Norman Bates, who never looked inside the paper, but rather simply threw it in the trunk of Marion Crane's car, as he tried to clean up his Oedipal mess.

Still, I did as Breda had asked and rifled through the most conspicuous items sitting on the top of his desk: both the local and the campus telephone books, a couple of tall tomes (the Norton facsimile edition of THE FIRST FOLIO OF SHAKESPEARE and an oversized edition of ART AND ARTISTS), the University's Student Handbook, the dictionary issued by the English Department, and a daily calendar with apothegms written by Roman Catholic bishops. For the most part, I ignored several folders piled there, since they clearly had already been investigated by Smockley, who had encircled each with a rubber band and then written on a memo-sized piece of paper both the words "Checked for evidence" and his initials, JSS.

I also ignored the rest of the memorabilia and artifice cluttering the desktop—a small breadboard on which were inscribed the Ten Commandments, a blade for a circular saw, on which was painted a quaint farm house, and a ceramic duck on which was affixed a small gold-colored plate, stating, "Presented to Dr. Hugh Disner by the North Georgia Poetry

Club." I figured it would be difficult to hide sheets of paper in any of these items, unless Disner had transcribed the letters onto microfiche, a move I highly doubted he would consider. I wondered what Smockley had been thinking as he surveyed all this. Did the possibility that someone killed Disner for questionable aesthetics ever enter Smockley's mind, in which case he might have worried about his own safety, in view of the blocky suits he wore?

I next turned my attention to the walls, the second location Breda had suggested that I check, on the off chance that Disner had hidden the letters behind one of the pieces hanging there. They were not behind the six-year old Norman Rockwell calendar, made of bamboo, suspended, just inside the door, from a nail that, when driven in, had broken pieces of the plaster loose. They were not behind his diplomas, one from the University of Texas and one from Florida State University. Nor were they behind two framed reprints of paintings by Joshua Reynolds, THE INFANT HERCULES STRANGLING THE SERPENTS and CUPID UNTYING THE ZONE OF VENUS, situated on the far wall of the office, or behind an amateurish oil painting of lilacs in bloom in a dooryard, done by someone with initials I did not recognize, D.G. I also failed to find them behind the photos plastered about, several of the Disner children, individually and as a group, one of an elderly couple I took to be Disner's parents, side-by-side pictures of the Pope and George W. Bush, and a couple of Disner himself, one in a graduation robe, holding what looked to be a program, the other of him in fishing gear. It struck me as strange that there were no pictures of Breda.

Seeing all this made me again think about the doctrine of correspondence. If one's character can be determined by physical appearance, as in the case of Shakespeare's Richard III, can one's character also be determined by what he or she keeps in the office, on the desk, on the walls, wherever? I began to wonder what people might conclude about me if they rummaged through my office, as I was doing right then in Disner's. What would they make of the items on my desk—the framed picture of Edith Sitwell, which I had placed there as a reminder of one of the many faces Jim Dixon put on, in Amis' LUCKY JIM; my metal statue of Shakespeare, with one arm missing so that old Will looked like Venus de Milo; my unused, indeed, still wrapped, daily calendar, supplied by the English Department; my personal lamp sitting on top of the desk (which I purchased for three dollars at a yard sale and brought in so as to avoid turning on the annoying, oftentimes buzzing, overhead fluorescent lights—an idea I got from watching the film JOE VS THE VOLCANO); or the piles of final exams from several previous terms. What would they make of the paintings decorating my walls—three of my own watercolors I had painted while viewing rural landscapes a few miles from the campus?

My daydreaming was suddenly interrupted by muttering coming from next door. Glick must be back in his office! I wondered how many times he had rechecked his bumper to see if it was actually damaged and how many timed he had walked around the parking lot looking for the imaginary Officer Clydesdale. And I wondered if he suspected that I'm the one that called him. I shot him a bird that I hoped would register in his brain.

It was now 5:40. I had already spent more time in Disner's office than I had planned. I realized I had to pick up the pace, so, as quietly as I could, I turned my attention to the third area Breda had suggested, the file cabinet that indicated—notably by a card taped on the front—that the material inside was at least ten years old. Breda had figured that Smockley would concentrate on anything dated within the last couple of years. I couldn't be sure, but I looked anyway, a task made easier by Disner's careful labeling of each file. Several were marked by the names of various committees Disner must have served on, such as the Dean's Advisory Committee (probably early on sparking Disner's interest in the position of Dean, after of course serving as Assistant Dean); the Athletic Advisory Committee (It never hurts a potential administrator to be in good with the coaches); and the Graduate Admissions Committee (since I suppose it makes a member sound discriminating).

I had no luck searching these and other committee files, so I turned my attention to some of the folders for courses he had taught at least ten years previously. I figured if he did hide the letters in one of them, it would be one for a course in an appropriate subject, like romantic fiction or cavalier poets. I would have suggested that he hide them in the files for satiric comedy or the mystery novel, but of course he never asked for my advice.

All I could find in each folder was a collection of neatly typed lecture notes and photocopies of critical articles supposedly germane to each course, published in scholarly journals like PMLA and ENGLISH LANGUAGE, with titles such as "Love and Anarchy in Keats' Odes" and "The Rapture of the Forbidden." There were a couple of articles for which I could not ascertain in what journal or magazine they had been published, one entitled "Porn as Pop Culture," another called "Breasts in Montage."

Even though I was feeling more and more rushed, I could not help but look through a few of his lecture notes, discovering that Disner had written himself instructions for gestures, pauses, even laughter. I was amazed to find, for instance, that he had jotted a "ha-ha" besides his line about the narrator's seeing the sea beasts in the water in "The Rime of the Ancient Mariner." I could only imagine the reaction of his students in class when Disner heartily roared at what I considered to be one of the more serious junctures in the whole poem.

It was 5:50, and I kept hearing noises, grousing from Glick's office and the faint sound of doors successively opening and shutting, as Doris McGuire began her clean-up ritual of moving from office to office, beginning on the far end of the hall horseshoe where my office was located. I was beginning to picture myself as Grace Kelly in REAR WINDOW, frantically searching for a dead woman's wedding ring taken from her by her killer husband, as Raymond Burr, with his penetrating eyes, made his way up the stairs to his apartment in which Kelly was now trapped.

I still had one area to check—one that even Breda had forgotten to suggest—the books on Disner's shelves. I wondered if I would have time before Doris got to Disner's office, but the thought suddenly struck me—why would she bother opening the door of a dead man's office? Surely, since his murder, she had discovered that there was no accumulation of trash. Was she such a creature of habit that she checked anyway?

On the other hand, maybe someone did fill up the can—perhaps Smockley, but with what? Files he had checked and discarded? I didn't think he would do that, in view of the folders on the desk. How about refuse from fast food restaurants? I could in fact picture Smockley with his feet propped up on Disner's desk, holding a Big Mac with one hand as he leafed through Disner's files with his other, then tossing the bag and wrappers in the trash. If he did, I wondered what Doris was thinking.

I took the precaution of moving Disner's trash can, which in fact did contain the remains of a visit to Subway, just inside the door, hoping that Doris, if she did check, could pick up and empty the can without actually entering the office proper.

I then turned my attention to the shelves, starting with Disner's collection of the HARVARD CLASSICS, figuring that if Smockley had elected to search through Disner's books, he might have left this set until the end, out of a sense of anti-intellectualism or because they appeared to be undisturbed. I could hear the bell tower beginning a rendition of "Somewhere Over the Rainbow," meaning it was 5:55. It played the song at the rate of molasses oozing out of a mason jar on a cold morning, just at a time when I needed something played allegro to encourage quick searching.

I found nothing in Volume I containing Ben Franklin's "His Autobiography," or Volume II, containing Plato's "The Apology." Nor did I find anything in Volumes III through XVII, each of which I held upside down and shook, hoping a letter would drop out. I could hear Doris getting nearer, now on Disner and Glick's hall, and I was getting nowhere.

But then, when I shook Volume XVIII, containing Sheridan's "School for Scandal," I hit pay dirt! A letter dropped to the floor! I knew I should immediately begin searching for other letters, but I had to scan the contents, discovering that it was a complaint about Disner's being far too concerned about his reputation and afraid that together he and the letter writer would cause a scandal in his own school. It was signed with the same initials I had seen on the oil painting, D.G. I figured Breda would be pleased with me.

The letter made me wonder if others were filed by subject matter in corresponding literary pieces, but I realized that even if they were, I'd still have to search through all the volumes. The process suddenly became easier, however, when I looked closely at the rest of the volumes, noticing for the first time that a few were not exactly even with the others—jutting out almost imperceptibly or recessed a quarter of an inch or so, a major oversight for someone as punctilious as Disner. I concentrated on these, discovering that each did in fact contain a letter. And again, even knowing that speed was crucial, I could not help but read samples from a few.

The letter in Volume XIX, containing Marlowe's "Dr. Faustus," expressed D.G.'s feelings of guilt and a conviction that the two of them were going to hell as a result of their relationship. In Volume XXII, "The Odyssey," tucked into the pages where Odysseus complains to Calypso that seven years was long enough to spend with her and he wants to return to Penelope, there was a letter in which D.G. apparently was responding to Disner's declaration that he needed to end the relationship and return to his home and his wife. The one in Volume XXXIV, inserted into Descartes' logical piece "Discourse on Method," was a complaint about Disner's being too rational, stating, "You need to loosen up. Remember that song by Rod Stewart called 'Passion' that I played for you? It says that even the President—and by extension, that could include an administrator like you—needs more passion."

I found other letters in Volume XLI next to Coleridge's "Dejection: An Ode," Volume XLII next to Byron's "Youth and Age," Volume XLVI in the pages of Shakespeare's "The Tempest," and Volume XXXVIII, containing the works of various medical practitioners on the subject of diseases, all of which I suspected indicated D.G.'s state of mind and concerns, but I did not have time to read the contents, since I could hear Doris banging about in the office next door. I carefully folded all the letters I had collected and shoved them inside my shirt so that they lay against my stomach.

I was faced with a choice—take what I had found and exit right then, hoping Doris would still be inside the adjoining office and not see me, or hide in Disner's office while she emptied the can I had placed near the door—in which case I would have to stand behind the door and pray that she did not peek around and see me, or crouch behind—or even under—the desk, a position that would be, I knew, very difficult to explain if she actually found me there.

My decision was suddenly made for me. I could hear her inserting her key in the lock. I was nearer to the door than to the desk, so I squeezed tightly up against the hinges in the corner. As soon as the door opened, I could hear a mild gasp of surprise, coming no doubt as Doris discovered the trashcan in an unusual place. Then an arm appeared and pulled the can outward, both disappearing, accompanied by Doris's voice, "How did it get . . . ?" and "Oh, well."

After a brief moment of sounds of paper dumped on paper, the arm reappeared with the empty can, and then the door closed. I breathed a sigh of relief—a quiet one—figuring I could then take my time and search for other letters—at least until I had to deal with Glick, if he were still in his office when I wanted to leave.

I had just returned to my task, having removed and added to my stomach one last letter from the remaining volume that looked slightly out of place, number XXIX, containing Darwin's "Voyage of the Beagle" when again I heard the sound of a key in the door. Before I could make it to my former hiding place or behind the desk, the door swung completely open, revealing a surprised Doris, who suddenly raised her hands straight up, as if I had just commanded her to "stick'em up."

"Oh, Professor Davidson! What are you doing in Professor Disner's office?

Chapter 30

For several seconds, Doris continued to hold her hands above her head, reminding me of a religious zealot singing hymns in a revival. I tried to shush her by extending my own hands and pushing down, as if I were patting two large dogs at once. I was not bothered so much by her discovering me in Disner's office as I was by the likelihood Glick would hear us.

He did.

He appeared in no more time than it took to push back from his computer, leap from his seat, and hustle over one office's worth of hall, taking up a position behind Doris, peering over her right shoulder until she shifted to her right, forcing him to sway to his left. They repeated this shift a couple more times, making me think I was watching the goddess Isis in an Egyptian dance.

After a few seconds, Glick reached out with both arms and pushed Doris to the side, then stood facing me, his arms extended still, as if he thought I were a surgical assistant ready to slide latex gloves on him, all the while staring at me with the intensity of a Doberman. I noticed he was wearing one of the green and yellow watches presented to donors who contributed at least a thousand dollars to the bell tower fund, making him partially responsible for the dirge version of "Somewhere over the Rainbow," played just minutes before.

For a moment I did not speak, though Glick's face seemed to be shaped like a question mark, demanding a plausible explanation, something I could not immediately offer. I wondered what he was thinking. Was it, "So you did kill Disner and now you're trying to destroy incriminating evidence" or, "You're a thief and you're raiding his office for valuable books you can sell on E-Bay, like that expensive Facsimile Edition of Shakespeare's First Folio"; or maybe even, "You've found evidence that I had something to do with Disner's murder and you're going straight to the cops with it and I'll do whatever it takes to stop you"?

Since Doris was still standing next to Glick, I was not sure which one I should address and how. I finally sputtered to them both, "You're probably wondering what a nice guy like me is doing in a place like this." Neither one smiled or answered, so I quipped, "Tough audience," and then added, mainly for Glick's benefit, "When I returned to my office, I realized that I had looked for the wrong text. I should have checked the Norton edition of Shakespeare, not the Bevington, the one I mistakenly checked earlier, so I got the key again and . . . . ." My voiced tailed off. I was almost sure that the letters were making a crinkling noise from under my shirt.

"From whom?" Glick demanded. He had lowered his arms and was now alternately curling his fingers into fists and straightening them.

"From? you ask. From Yvonda Dunkirk, of course."

Glick cocked his head and tilted it back. "But I saw her out in the parking lot—leaving for the day."

"Well I guess I got them from her, opened the door, and then returned the key before you saw her. See, no key." I held my hands up and rotated them, as if I were a magician assuring an audience that I didn't have an ace velcroed to the back of my wrist, then pulled at my pockets, stopping short of turning them inside out. "You must have been too busy to hear me. In fact, I thought I heard you on the phone when I was here opening the door." I figured this should cover me for the fake phone call I had made and provide a reason why he would not have heard me.

Glick said nothing, but rather studied me as if he knew I was lying— which, of course, I was—and was trying to figure out how to expose me. While he ruminated, I considered what it was about him that made me dislike him more than I had disliked Disner, which is saying a lot—and why, in fact, it was not difficult for me to imagine Glick slumped in front of the toilet with a hole in his head, instead of Disner.

Part of the answer to these questions came because I distrusted anyone who was rah-rah gungho in his loyalty to a particular group, cause, country, religion, or institution, in Glick's case, the University, a fact that Glick flaunted by wearing the bell tower watch and, by once, in a Homecoming parade, riding in a 60's vintage white Cadillac, with antlers mounted on its hood and the letters NGU painted on its sides—I assumed with nonpermanent watercolors, unless he were even more rabid in his support of the University than I first thought.

The other reason I disliked him was that he was so incredibly ponderous. Whenever he talked, I could envision his words leaving his mouth and then sinking to the floor under their own weight, looking like the melting clocks sliding down in a Salvador Dali painting.

Facing Glick at that particular moment, I could not help asking why I was on this mission. I've never been one to take these kinds of risks. Why now? Was getting into Breda's favor (or was it her pants) really that important? Why didn't I urge her to do her own sneaking into Disner's office or finagle gravel-road Brad into helping her, so that I wouldn't be the one caught in awkward moments like this one, mano-a-mano with Glick.

And speaking of Breda, I wondered what Glick would say if he knew I was on this adventure on her behalf. Would he reveal some latent chauvinism and say, "Yeah, that's just like a woman—paranoid about her public image." I wondered what his current wife was like. I remembered he had previously gone through a messy divorce with a woman named Agnes, a divorce which he had announced to all of his colleagues via e-mail and one which, as best I could remember, involved another man, though it was unclear exactly how this third party figured in the mix. My head screamed to the point that I had visions of squiggly lightning bolts emanating from it.

"Can I check the recycle box?" Doris! I had almost forgotten her.

"Excuse me?" I responded.

"The recyclable paper—that's what I came back to check on. I forgot it a few minutes ago when I emptied the trash."

"Oh, sure." I stepped out of the way, letting her walk behind Disner's desk and look in the leg well underneath. *Thank God I had not tried to hide there.*

Finding nothing in the receptacle, she left. As soon as she was out the door, Glick spoke up again. "You wouldn't happen to know anything about a person named Clyde Dale, or maybe Clydesdale, would you?"

"Nope. Is he someone pictured on a milk carton?" When Glick did not respond, except to stare at me, I glanced at my watch—which did not come from any donations to the bell tower fund—and then added, "Oh, look at the time. I better be going too. I've got places to go, people to see, papers to grade, preparations to make."

"What about the Norton?" Glick demanded.

"Norton?" I queried.

"Yes, the Norton Shakespeare you claimed you were searching for." He went heavy on the word "claimed." His stare had evolved into a glare—like that of a stern priest who believed I should be the subject of an exorcism. Was he looking at my stomach? I self-consciously folded my hands over it.

"Oh, the Norton. I couldn't find it, so I figured it must be at his house. I'll have to give Bre . . . uh, Mrs. Disner . . . a call and see." I paused since Glick had stopped staring at me and was now eyeing the shelves.

"What's that blue volume there on the third shelf? he asked. "Isn't that a Norton Shakespeare?" He brushed past me and pulled out the book he had spotted, then opened it to the inside title page. "Yes, it is a Norton, but it's got Hugh's name in it. Why would he want to borrow yours if he had his own copy?"

"Gee, I don't know, but you're right; it's not mine. Mine's . . . ," I hesitated. "Mine's black, as I recall. I guess that's why I missed seeing that one on the shelf. At any rate, mine's not here. It's . . . somewhere else. I better go try to find it. Be sure to lock up when you leave." I hurried out, leaving a scowling Glick still holding Disner's Norton. I figured I'd be pushing it to remind him to replace the book where he had found it.

Chapter 31

As soon as I arrived at my car, I removed the letters from under my shirt and laid them on the passenger seat. Then I drove to my house, where I was supposed to meet Breda. She had asked that we meet there instead of her own house since she wanted to avoid explaining to her children what we were doing. I hoped she would be waiting in my driveway, but I suspected she would go on inside and make herself feel at home, as she had two nights before.

She wasn't there.

Just where the hell was she? She knew I was going to sneak in Disner's office some time close to 5 pm and then bring the letters to her. It was now almost 6:30. Maybe, I thought, an emergency had arisen with one of her children, or she had wrecked her van. On a more positive note, maybe she had stopped for groceries, intending to fix dinner for me as a reward for my efforts. Or, even better, maybe she had stopped off at the ABC store to pick up some potables to help us celebrate our joint success in espionage.

Most likely, I thought, she was out with Brad Crawford giving absolutely no thought to any kind of reward for me.

I went in the house and paced back and forth for fifteen minutes or so before heading out to River Road, turning off onto the gravel of Raccoon Run Lane, sure that I would find Breda's van in Crawford's driveway.

Crawford's car was there, but the van wasn't. That still did not rule out the possibility that Breda was there, so I parked my car in the driveway and approached the front door, over which shone an outdoor flood light. I intended to confront the two of them together then and there and get them to admit their relationship, or—in the event she was not there—at least confront Crawford about why he had been reluctant to help Breda retrieve the Disner letters.

In my two previous visits, I had not paid much attention to Crawford's house—which in reality was a mildew-stained, burnt umber, singlewide trailer, one manufactured by a company called Elmwood Homes, as a rusting placard to the side of the door proclaimed. The front yard with its packed dirt and absence of grass (except for a few tufts that looked like widely spaced implants on a bald man who has opted for the economy plan) gave the appearance that a horde of children played on it daily— either that or a herd of sheep grazed there. A row of semi-dead azaleas stretched the length of the house across the front. Propped against the house were several used tires, partially filled with water, a perfect breeding grounds for mosquitoes. A couple of the window screens were broken out, now hanging limply by strands down one side of each, as if someone or maybe a dog had plunged through them from the inside.

When I stepped onto the front porch, the same spot where I had first seen Breda and Crawford together, I discovered the door to be partially open. Holding the handle with one hand, I knocked loudly with the other, but got no response. I had visions of the two of them humping in the back bedroom, where they couldn't hear me, so I hollered, first, Crawford's name, then Breda's, adding, "Are you here? It's me, Tyler."

I again got no response, so I opened the door wider and looked into a space that served as both the living room and kitchen, illuminated by a multi-coned lamp. The walls were a cheap-looking walnut paneling, into which several holes had been punched, seemingly with a fist. The living room furniture consisted of a triple couch, covered in a material that looked like mattress ticking, and a large television, over which was draped a sweatshirt and a bra. The entire floor area looked as if county residents had mistaken it for a cardboard and newspaper recycle bin. The kitchen counter was covered by a confusion of clutter, including opened cans—mostly for refried beans and Spanish rice—their crinkled-edged lids pointing straight up; boxes of crackers (Hi-Ho's) and cereal (Fruit Loops and Cheerios) lying on their sides, the inner cellophane bags ripped open, allowing the goods to spill out; a carton of milk; an opened jar of Cheese Whiz with a knife stuck in it; lots of dirty dishes stacked like wrecked cars in a space-strapped junk yard; and enough empty beer bottles—a mixture of Old Milwaukee and Budweiser—to create an art deco wall. There were also a microwave oven, liberally covered with duct tape, and a refrigerator, covered by magnets that pictured naked women.

The whole place smelled like a fraternity house on Monday morning, right after Homecoming weekend. Why, I wondered, would Breda be involved with the biggest slob in north Georgia?

I called out again. "Crawford, are you here? I need to talk with you."

No answer. I hesitated for a moment, trying to decide whether I should leave or press the issue. I felt nervous about being there, but I was determined to have it out with one or both of them. I headed down the dimly lit hall leading away from the living room and looked in what had to be Crawford's bedroom, illuminated by a small lamp, topped by a shade decorated with satyrs dancing around a maypole, painted on with glitter paint. The room was messier than the living room or kitchen, with clothes stacked in disorganized piles, MOTORTREND magazines lying about, and still more beer bottles—mixed with beer cans that appeared to have been crumpled, I suspected, on someone's forehead.

I moved on down the hall to what I figured to be a second bedroom, but what turned out to be a small office, surprisingly neat, with orderly book shelves—filled with technical magazines and guides—and a desk, on which sat a stylish lamp and a computer, along with a cup full of pencils and pens and a box containing a stack of paper that appeared to be the manuscript for a book. Off to the side rested a slender vase filled with red and white carnations.

The only thing that did not appear to be neat was the figure slumped in the expensive looking roll-around chair in front of the desk. He was wearing a work shirt with his name printed on it.

It was Brad Crawford!

His legs were splayed out, his arms dangling almost to the floor, his chin resting on his left shoulder, his eyes seemingly focused on a point about twenty feet beyond the wall, outside the trailer. In the back of his shaven skull was a neat but obviously lethal bullet hole. He looked deader than Disner had when I saw him in the toilet stall—if there can be such a thing as "deader."

The first thing I thought was—Smockley's not going to like this. The second thing I thought of was—the killer could still be somewhere close by. The second thing became the primary thought and I bolted from the room, running through the mess of the living room/kitchen—nearly slipping on a Wheaties box—to my car, which I cranked up and drove away as fast as I could, leaving a trail of dust in the air on the gravel road. I had not bothered to close the front door.

I sped to the turn off next to the river where I usually stretched before running, and then I cut the engine and sat for a while, considering my options. My mind was racing. Had I left clues to my presence at Crawford's house, fingerprints, tire prints, saliva? Should I call the police? Should I call Smockley directly? Should I drive to Breda's house with the hope of finding her home and report to her what I had just discovered and then call from there? Should I go back and call from Crawford's trailer? I could at least answer this latter question right off. Hell no! I already felt lucky just to get out of there without meeting up with the killer.

I knew I had to call someone, but I didn't want to use my own cell phone, which I figured could be traced—if it in fact even worked out there in the hinterlands— so I drove back to campus, stopping at the first pay phone I came to and called the number for the county sheriff, for the second time in one day disguising my voice so that I sounded like Andy Griffith. After hearing the voice of the dispatcher, I whanged, "Uh, yes, this is Clyde Dale; I want to report a death, a possible murder, at the first house on the right on Raccoon Run Lane, the gravel road off River Road. Please hurry." Before the dispatcher could respond, I hung up, hoping that my call would not be dismissed as a prank.

I was not sure where I wanted to go then. I thought about going home, but what if the killer were waiting for me there? How about my office? Would I be safe there or would I feel trapped, once inside.

I started driving, mulling over the events of the last couple of hours. What part did Breda play in all this? She was, in fact, the only person I could think of that had ties to both Disner and Crawford. And she had not been at my house when she said she would be. Had she been delayed because she was out murdering Crawford? Had she shot Crawford for failing to clean up his trailer?

What would Smockley ask me, and how would I answer?

"What were you doing at Crawford's house?"

"I was out that way jogging and needed a drink of water and stopped at Crawford's and saw the light on and the door open and went in and . . . ?

"I don't believe you!"

"That's your prerogative."

"Don't hide behind big words, Professor."

"Oh, I forgot. You're not exactly a sesquipedalian, are you, Smockley?"

"What?"

"Forget it."

Maybe I shouldn't even tell him about my visit, but I knew eventually he'd find my fingerprints on the doorknob. Then where would I be?

I looked at the passenger seat, where Disner's letters lay. What to do with them, I wondered. I knew I should simply take them to Smockley, but there were two problems with that plan. One, Smockley would be all over me for breaking into Disner's office, and, two, giving them to him would pretty much shoot the hell out of any chance I might have of making an impression on Breda.

Chapter 32

Before deciding to whom I should give the letters, I read through the four whose contents I had not scanned in Disner's office. The one that had been inserted next to Coleridge's "Dejection an Ode" revealed that the writer was in a sorry funk: "How do you think I felt tonight during intermission at the Chamber Orchestra concert and you spent the whole time jawing with Dr. Bwanger, especially since I had just told you I wanted to make love—right then, somewhere, anywhere?"

I paused for a moment, thinking that this was way more information than I wanted to read, but then I went on.

"What were you arguing about? Me? You were so animated I thought you were going to have a stroke—or kill him. At any rate, the night was one of the worst times I've had to endure. It didn't even help to see your wife eyeing Dr. Davidson. You probably didn't even notice that, did you?"

I tried to remember if I had even noticed Breda that night. I had for sure seen Disner and Bwanger talking, but had not considered that they might be arguing, mainly because Disner had always been animated when he talked. In fact, on that very same night he had collared me and raved, arms flying sideways and above his head, about some new teaching technique he had been trying out on his students, in which he would exit the room for five minutes, leaving them free to discuss a question he had posed or sit in dead silence. His enthusiasm while describing it all to me could just have easily been mistaken for anger, I figured, to anyone watching us. I wondered how Smockley would respond to the letter writer's comment about me.

The letter in the volume on medical treatises made no reference to me, but was still interesting. "You really are an insensitive asshole sometimes. How dare you ask me if I was having unprotected sex with other lovers!"

The letter hidden in "The Tempest" also contained no reference to me, but was noteworthy in its passion: "Sometimes I wish I could kill you, or me, or both of us." Smockley would definitely be interested in this one.

The letter I had found next to Byron's "Youth and Age" did contain another reference to me. "You seem to take great delight in putting me down, treating me like I'm a child, because I'm only 21. Maybe I'd be better off with someone younger than you. Since your wife seemed to be interested in Dr. Davidson at the concert, maybe I too would find him more appealing than you. Wouldn't that be a real sexual twist?"

I puzzled over this last line for several moments, then turned my thoughts back to the problem I was considering earlier—whom to give the letters to. It was a problem that seemed more complicated now that I knew I was mentioned in the letters.

I considered a compromise. I would photocopy the letters, then maybe give the originals to Breda and send Smockley the duplicates. But no, he'd know I'd given him copies and would want the originals so he could check them for fingerprints. All right, then, I could give the photocopies to Breda, but they'd have to be pretty damn good copies or she would figure out as easily as Smockley that they were not the originals. Maybe, I thought, I could antique them a bit, rough them up, make them look like originals, though I wasn't exactly sure how to do this. Still, this seemed like the best plan, so I headed for the photocopy room in my building on campus.

My decision in itself caused another dilemma—having to enter my building. It was bad enough during daylight hours, with lots of people around. Now, it was after seven, with most students and faculty in long night classes or already gone, along with the staff, no doubt out doing something I should have been doing—going to a movie, drinking with friends, eating dinner, getting laid. Why is it that a crowd of university people only show up when I'm in a hurry and feel no danger—clogging the staircases or lying prone on the hall floors so that I have to step over them?

The photocopy room was on the fifth floor, leaving me with the option of taking the elevator—and risking confinement for about thirty seconds in what I considered to be, even on a good day, a moving coffin, wondering if the killer would suddenly join me—or climbing the steps—and risking a confrontation on one of the landings. I opted for the stairs, figuring that if I did meet the killer, I would at least have a chance to run away—either up or down or through a door.

I started up. It did not improve my state of mind to recall how many horror movies I had watched in which a staircase became the locus of a murder, the danger zone, on a par with dark alleys, cemeteries, and boiler rooms of abandoned high schools. I feared hearing "ink-ink-ink" PSYCHO noises accompanied by a figure in a wig and a blockish dress rushing out and stabbing me in the face.

I made it to the third floor landing without incident; however as I climbed the first half of the flight from the third floor to the fourth, I heard the door above me open, but could detect no one coming on down the other half of steps. I paused, waiting to see who it was, but the person never advanced. After a few seconds the door closed, softly, as if someone were guiding it to prevent it from slamming. Was it by chance Doris, the clean-up lady, still working her shift, or could it be someone fresh off a visit to Raccoon Run Lane?

I waited for about ten seconds and then retraced my steps down the half flight and entered the door to the third floor. After passing through the hall, I took the staircase on the other side of the building to the fifth floor, carefully opening the door into the hall and listening for movement—even breathing noises—from anyone, before heading to the copier room.

There I tried to duplicate the letters as quickly as I could, but was slowed by the machine, which acted as if it were an accomplice for the murderer. First, it ran out of paper—forcing me to find a new pack in the supply closet and refilling the drawer in the copier. Somehow, in the process I managed to hit the on/off switch, shutting it all down, necessitating an automatic five-minute restart period, a fact that was flashed in maddening detail by a timer spelling out the minutes remaining. When it did finally come back on, it allowed me to copy two letters, "The School for Scandal" complaint and the "Dr. Faustus" lament. But when I started copying the third letter, the "Odyssey" parallel about Disner's attempt to return to his wife, the machine jammed. I was stooped over, pulling out the offending sheet located at C1 when I sensed someone's presence in the doorway.

It was Glick.

Chapter 33

"Glenn, you still here? I thought you'd be long gone by now."

Glick didn't say a word for several seconds, remaining stationary in the doorway, holding a small bundle of paper, frowning with most of his body. Was it my imagination or did he look like he wanted to ask me about the fake phone call and Clyde Dale again?

He finally spoke: "I have an article I've written that needs to be copied." His tone suggested that I should step aside and let him take over the copier, something I was not about to let happen. At least, I thought with some relief, he probably was not Crawford's killer, since he seemingly had been in his office the whole afternoon, except of course when he went to the parking lot to check on his car—hardly time to drive out to Raccoon Run Lane and snuff Crawford.

But, then again, there was no way for me to tell how long Crawford had been dead. In my haste to get out of the trailer, I had not conducted any kind of forensic analysis, as if I were capable anyway. Glick could have been a visitor just about anytime to Crawford's trailer. Still, I had difficulty picturing him as a killer.

However, I could picture him as a meddling asshole, a role he reprised by walking over towards the copier and peering at the letters I had stacked on the top edge. "What are you copying there?" he asked.

I positioned myself so as to block his view of the letters and then answered, "Just some papers my students turned in. I want to keep copies of some of them for a course file."

"They look like letters," he responded. "You DO know the rule forbidding using the machine for personal matters, don't you?"

"Yes, of course I do." If I had not felt guilty because I was copying the letters I had stolen from Disner's office, I would have told Glick to buzz off. Instead, I said, "They are in fact letters, business letters I had my students write persuading someone to hire them."

"Can I read one?" he asked. He shifted to his left and then to his right, trying to see them, as I swayed in tune with his movements to prevent that very thing. I was beginning to think that Glick did a lot of swaying, this time without the cleanup lady, Doris, in front of him.

"I don't think that would be a good idea. It would be a violation of some kind of rule governing confidentiality, if I'm not mistaken."

"Oh, all right then, but how long will you be? I need to leave as soon as I've finished copying these." He held his papers up for me to see as if he needed to validate his remarks.

"Just another minute or two. I don't have too much more to do." I quickly loaded in the letter about Disner's Cartesian lack of passion as Glick backed up a few steps and leaned on the counter. After finishing it, I proceeded to copy the letters about the writer's dejection, concern over age difference, the parallel to Shakespeare's TEMPEST, and outrage over comments about other lovers. All the while, Glick continued to stare, as if he were trying to read the letters from six feet away. I continued to do my best to block his vision, still with my torso but also with my hands, as I continually folded or smoothed out the letters.

As I was finishing, I again thought about why I disliked Glick so much, maybe even more than I disliked golfing fans who shout "You-da-man!" before Tiger Woods has even completed his follow through. For one thing, Glick was not one to ever compromise a habit. He could not stop himself from prying into other people's business. Plus he was genetically unhappy and then probably further misshapen by parents who never taught him to lighten up. Even at that moment, Friday evening, getting near 8 pm, he was still here at the building, doing schoolwork—administrative work, in fact—dressed like an administrator, in his dark gray suit and red tie, as if he had just read Malloy's DRESS FOR SUCCESS. I tried to picture him in sweat pants and a tee shirt—without success. The nearest I came was picturing him in an IZOD golfing shirt and slacks. I could not extend the image enough to picture him on a golf course, though I could see him on a patio with campus VIP's, holding a glass of scotch, swirling the glass so that the ice clinked.

Right then he was tugging at his trousers with one hand as if he were trying to neaten up his overall image, while with his other hand he was patting the breast pocket of his suit coat, as if he had a weapon in a shoulder holster.

After I finished copying the letters, I started to leave, but then became conscious of the possibility that I might meet Disner/Crawford's killer. Remembering Glick's comment about leaving as soon as he completed his task with the copy machine, I decided to hang around and leave when he did. Glick might actually prove to be useful. The only problem was that I needed a reason for my stalling. Talking with Glick about academe was not one of them.

A survey of the room offered me the solution. Someone had left on the counter a carton originally containing a dozen donuts from Dunkin Donut—probably Dorothy Cloaninger, who simultaneously controlled her weight problem and her penchant for donuts by buying them, eating a few herself, and then leaving the rest in the copier room for others to share. There remained a whole glazed donut and a half of another, both having become so dried out that the sugar coating looked like large flakes of dandruff. After saying, "Oh, good, someone left a few goodies," I selected the whole one—to prolong my stalling— and ate it while Glick worked. I subdued a fleeting thought that someone may have predicted that I would be unable to resist eating a donut and had tainted it with some kind of poison, but how would they have predicted I would even be in this room, I asked myself.

Glick finally finished his copying. As he was collecting his pages, I brushed sugar from my hands with exaggerated sweeping motions that I was sure made me appear to be playing cymbals and then said, "Heading home are you, Glenn?"

"Yes, I've got a late dinner engagement with the new Vice Chancellor for Environmental Control, Dowell McDimmons. Do you know him?"

I started to question both the name and the title, but let it ride. "Nope, don't think so. Well, I'm going too. I'll follow you out—stairs or elevator?"

"I always take the elevator."

I started to say, "Of course you do," but I simply added, "Sounds good to me," though I couldn't imagine why Glick couldn't walk DOWN the steps.

After we both had stepped into the elevator, Glick pushed the button for the first floor, but just before the door closed completely, a hand suddenly appeared on the upper leading edge, causing the door to jerk back open. A man stepped in, about six feet tall, medium build, unshaven, hard looking. He wore a black, hooded sweat jacket. He positioned himself between Glick and me and then said, "You're going down, I assume."

As we rode down, I was thinking, Why me? Just a few weeks ago, at a little after nine in the morning, I was minding my own business—or rather I was on the way to the men's room to do my business—when I found Disner dead. I did not ask to find him dead. I was not a sensationalist who went around hoping to discover a dead person so I would be sought out by the police and the media, given the spotlight, my fifteen minutes of fame. But, now, here I was riding an elevator because I was afraid to be alone on the staircase in my own building, accompanied by a guy I disliked immensely—and who probably disliked me as much—joined by a guy who at any minute might whip out a gun and shoot me—witness be damned. And I was worrying that the donut I had just eaten could be laced with something deadly like Ricin and I was worrying about what lay ahead for me at my house, which I would be afraid to enter, and worrying about what to do with the damned Disner letters and what to tell Breda and how I would respond to a grilling from Smockley. How the hell did things get so complicated?

The elevator reached the first floor without anyone killing me. The door opened. Smockley was standing there. "Well Professor Davidson. I was just coming to find you. Seems like we've got lots to talk about."

Chapter 34

I waited as Glick and the stranger in the hooded jacket stepped from the elevator, but Glick prolonged my wait as he stood in the hall gazing at Smockley, then me. I wondered what he was thinking. But for reasons I cannot explain, I also wondered what sign he was—probably a Leo, with dark side tendencies to be pompous, patronizing, bossy, dogmatic, and interfering. Smockley was probably a Capricorn, practical, prudent, disciplined, and careful, or maybe a Taurus, with a penchant for goring people.

After a few seconds of what seemed to be a hall standoff, I figured that I needed to give Glick a hint to leave. Not having a cattle prod, I said, "See you later, Glenn." He hitched up his shoulders as if he were trying on an ill-fitting suit coat and then wheeled about and left, but not before sighing loudly and looking at me as if I reeked of body odor (which I might in fact have been doing, given my apprehensions arising during the last couple of hours). I halfway hoped that the hooded guy would be waiting for Glick and do him harm.

As soon as Glick was gone, Smockley spoke. "I wouldn't have predicted you'd use the elevator."

"I usually don't." As I answered I shifted the letters I was carrying slightly behind me, hoping Smockley wouldn't notice them.

"Why now?" He held the same small pad of papers I had seen before, only this time he toyed with it, as if it were a deck of cards and he was going to do a one-handed shuffle. I wondered if he ever did shell games. At least he did not sport a toothpick this time.

"Well, Glick wanted to, and I . . .uh." I paused, not really wanting to explain to Smockley that I had been nervous about taking the stair case, that I had been afraid that someone might be lurking for me, that Glick had offered an odd kind of security.

Smockley saved me the trouble of answering. "Never mind, it's not important. Want to tell me about Brad Crawford?"

"I think he's dead."

"He is for sure. That's why I'm here. Are you the one that called it in?"

I paused. There was no sense lying. "Yes."

"I thought so. I listened to the tape of the call and recognized your voice. Did you kill him?"

"You don't waste any time do you? No, I simply found him dead, or at least he looked dead."

"Seems like you're finding lots of dead people lately. Any other DEAD PEOPLE you haven't told me about?"

"No, just Disner and Crawford."

"JUST Disner and Crawford? How many do you consider a significant number?"

"Well, if you really need more, there were those six the police in Michigan dug up in my back yard when I was in grad school—seems the neighbor's dog got curious about the odor and raised everyone's suspicions by scratching up mounds of dirt—Let's see, there was an ex-girl friend, who I had caught reading COSMOPOLITAN, when I surprised her by coming home from a cancelled Milton seminar."

"Enough, already!"

"And then there was a shoe salesman who convinced me that I should buy the fourteen mediums when I knew that thirteen wides would . . . ."

"Stop!"

"All right, but you knew what I meant about there being only two." Trying to make Smockley lighten up was like convincing a corpse to practice carpe diem.

"I'm not sure I do. But let's change the subject. What were you doing snooping around in other people's territory?"

"Do you mean Crawford's?" I was alarmed that Smockley might have already discovered that I had been in Disner's office.

"Of course Crawford's. What else could we be talking about?"

"Nothing, nothing. I just wanted to be sure. Anyway it's a long story."

"I've got plenty of time."

I wondered just how clean I should come. Should I tell him about finding Disner's letters, my feelings for Breda, or stay with just the discovery of a dead Crawford? I knew I was not particularly good at lying. I almost admired people who were. I bet Glick could lie with the best of them. Disner was probably the state champion. Smockley, on the other hand, impressed me as someone who did not often lie.

"Well," Smockley asked, "why were you out at Crawford's house?"

"I was curious."

"About what?" Smockley seemed impatient.

"About Crawford. He introduced himself when I was out running on his road."

"Did the two of you run together?"

"No, actually we met just a day or so ago, when I was sitting in my car near his house, contemplating whether I wanted to run. He came up to check on why I was parked there."

"You had never met him before that?"

"No."

Smockley pulled out a pen and wrote something on his pad and then frowned at me. "Let me get this straight. I'm supposed to believe that after one meeting with a guy you had never met before that you'd just drop by his house to chat with him. You must be one social son of a bitch, Professor. Want to try again?"

"All right then, the truth is that I thought he was seeing Breda . . ., uh, Mrs. Disner."

"Why should that concern you?"

"I felt some obligation to her."

"Why?"

"Well, as you know, I'm the one who found her husband dead. I felt a need to protect her, maybe to fill in for her dead husband, sort of in the tradition of ancient tribes.

"Don't go mythic on me, Professor."

"I can't quite explain it, but I did."

"What exactly did you feel you were protecting her from?"

"I don't know, I guess this Crawford guy. I didn't particularly like him."

"What'd he do to you, kick your car, spit on you?"

"No, he just seemed to be a threat."

"Why would he be a threat?"

164

"I can't say for sure, maybe because he wore a hooded jacket. It seems that I've seen lots of people in them lately, at times when I was feeling a bit paranoid anyway, like the guy who got off the elevator with us a few minutes ago."

Smockley put the pad in his pocket and responded, "You didn't need to worry about him. He's a police officer."

"A police officer!"

"Yes, I sent him upstairs to see if you were in the building, while I waited down here. We spotted your car outside and didn't want to miss you. But back to Crawford. You must have gone all the way into his house. You couldn't have seen him from the front door, even if it was open. We found him dead in a back room."

"I hollered at the front door, but got no answer. I thought maybe he was in the back somewhere and couldn't hear me."

"I see. You feel that you have the right to barge into people's houses if they don't come to the door."

"No, but . . . ."

I was on the verge of telling him about Breda and the letters, but Smockley spoke up again. "Professor, I've got to be straight with you. This looks bad. You admit you had something against Crawford, and you admit going in his house, with all of this coming on top of your seeming involvement with Disner and for all I know with his wife. I want you to come down to the county office tomorrow morning to answer more questions. As we speak, I have a team headed to your house to conduct a search. I'll join them shortly. I suspect we'll have lots more to talk about after we finish."

"Don't you need a warrant to do that? I've seen episodes of LA LAW."

"It's already been done. I filled out the affidavit and got it singed by the magistrate, before I drove here."

"What did you write down on the affidavit that you'd be searching for?"

"Primarily, a gun, the murder weapon, in fact."

"But I don't even OWN a gun!" I decided against telling him of my inquiries at a local pawn shop regarding the purchase of one.

"We'll see. Plus, based upon our preliminary search of your car, we'll be looking for any letters or notes Professor Disner might have sent to you that would incriminate you, what's called probable cause."

"What did you mean by a preliminary search of my car? Didn't you need a warrant for that too?

"I got one before the search although I probably didn't need it. Since cars can be moved from one place to another too quickly, they fall in a different category than houses. Plus, you mainly give up a right to privacy with them since they're out and about in public anyway. It's the same with your trash, for which you have forfeited privacy by placing it outside on the street. In your case, there were some interesting pieces of evidence left in plain view on the seat."

"What are you talking about?"

"I'm talking about some drawings you did, on a note pad that you must have kept for some time in your car—doodles of Disner, with an arrow through his heart and a knife stuck in his ear."

"What makes you think Disner is the person in the sketches?"

"For one thing, you've got him sitting at a desk with his name written on an oversized nameplate."

"Oh, but they were just jokes—from a long time ago."

"I'd hate to see your drawings when you're serious. The one part that puzzled me was the picture had a conversation bubble coming out of his mouth with the word 'okay' written in it. What did that mean?"

"Oh, nothing. I guess I was pretending that he approved of the joke."

"Sounds sort of sick to me, Professor. At any rate, it gives us reason to search even further for evidence."

"Like what?"

"Oh, for example, a letter in which he responds to some kind of threat you might have made to him sometime in the past. You've been so vocal complaining about him over the years, we'd like to see if there is any written evidence that you took your disdain to a higher level, something that would justify our search."

"Are those the only items you can look for, a gun and a letter?" I had visions of Smockley finding the rocks I had stolen from national parks.

"Actually no. Since the gun and letter could be hidden anywhere in the house, we have the right to look at just about everything, and if we happen to find anything else incriminating along the way, we can use it. If the only item listed on the affidavit were large, like a stolen television, we couldn't look for small incidentals, no matter how incriminating they might turn out to be. They would fall under the prohibition against searching for what is called an 'elephant in a matchbox.' And of course we can seize anything that is out in the open—like a potted marijuana plant. Do you have anything like that around?"

"No, of course not, but does this mean you can tear my place up like the cops do in movies, rip up my bedding, slit open my couch, empty my pantry, strew files and stuff all over, making no attempt to clean up afterwards?"

"We don't operate that way, at least not me." His appearance supported that contention. "At any rate, if we do find something in your house—or garbage—or car—the next step is to get a warrant for your arrest."

"Just how many kinds of warrants are there?"

"Several, the worst being a death warrant, but we won't talk about that unless you get charged, convicted, and sentenced to die. I suggest you talk all this over with your attorney."

"I will. And when you get to my house, don't kick down the door or anything. Take my key."

"All right, give it to me." He waited while I removed it from my key ring and then said, "By the way, what are you carrying there?" He leaned to one side in an attempt to see the letters, which I had by now shifted far enough around behind me that they could almost have been a fanny pack.

"Oh, these! Just papers I've got to grade." I waved them back and forth in front of me as if were fanning myself and then folded them across my chest, my two arms mostly covering them. "When I'm not being interrogated by the police, I actually have to earn a living."

"You won't be making jokes like that if we find anything at your house. I'll see you tomorrow." He turned and marched away. I was certain he had missed his calling as a mortician.

Chapter 35

I stood for a minute or so trying to decide what to do next. I did not want to rush home and give Smockley the impression that I was trying to beat him to some incriminating evidence, hidden, for instance, under a geranium or in the jar containing artificial sweeteners. I guess the joke was on him. If only he had known that important pieces of evidence had been right in front of him! Fortunately, he was thinking in terms of a single letter, not a batch of them.

Hearing a door shut somewhere above me on another floor, I suddenly realized that I did not want to stay in the building any longer, particularly now that Smockley, his cohort, and even Glick were gone. Holding on tightly to the letters, I hurried out, jogging to my car, figuring that I'd be a harder target to hit on the move than Disner had been sitting on the toilet or Crawford perched at a computer.

Once I was on the road in my car, I returned to my thoughts about what to do. I briefly entertained the notion of leaving town for a while. Why hadn't I lined up another book signing in some distant city? What should I do about the letters? Why hadn't I just gone ahead and given them to Smockley?

I knew why. He would want to know the reason I did not inform him about them earlier and let him search for them. Well screw him. He had his chance. It wasn't my fault if he didn't have my analytical mind—or was it Breda's. I had lost track of how I came up with the location of the letters.

Should I go ahead and contact Breda and make some arrangements for her to see the letters? I knew that it was a dumb thing to do, but I wanted her to be on my side, or me be on her side—I was not sure which and why. But I decided not to give her the originals. They might be the only real evidence I could offer to show that someone besides me had a reason to kill Disner. But I would have to make Breda think I was giving her the originals, so before I did anything else, I followed through on my earlier plan and antiqued them a bit, first by sitting on them for a few minutes. Then, after placing them on the passenger seat, I spit on my hand and rubbed it across some of the pages. As I studied the crinkled and semi-smeared pages, I became convinced that, despite the admittedly amateur job I had performed, they could pass for the originals, particularly if the reader were focused on the contents, as Breda most surely would be. I'd just have to let them dry a bit before Breda saw them.

I pulled off at a gas station and, for the second time that night, used a pay phone, again avoiding a record of my calling Breda on my cell phone. I was nervous about talking with Breda. Should I start by telling her about Crawford, someone she herself might have killed? Would her voice give away her attitude, hint at what she had done that day? Would she be tense, relaxed, cavalier, deadly? As the phone rang, I gripped the receiver so tightly that my index finger started to cramp.

After about six rings, someone picked up the receiver but did not answer for several seconds. I started to hang up, but then a small voice piped up, as if the speaker were participating in a playground game. "Who is this?" the voice asked.

Given the choice that it was one of the Disner children on the line—probably the youngest—or else Breda, who had been breathing helium, I asked, "Is your mother there?" All I got in response was an even more playful "Who is this?"

I tried a variation."I'm a friend of your mommie's. Is she there?" Again, all I got was "Who is this?" this time with the laughter that only a three-year old can make. I figured it might help if I used Disner's own favorite sentence follow-up, so I said, "Go get your mommie, okay!" Sure enough, I heard the phone clunk on something hard, as a receding voice yelled, "Mommie, there's a phone man."

About thirty seconds later I heard scuffling noise and then a muffled voice, as if there were a hand over the phone, saying, I think, "Take Boo to your bed and I'll be there soon," but it could just as easily have been "Make boodles of eggs and I'll beat the moon," then a more distinct and assertive, "Breda Disner here."

I decided not to mention Crawford right off, so I said, "Breda, it's Tyler. It sounds like it's not a good time for you, but I have the letters. What do you want me to do with them?"

"Actually, I'd like for you to give them to me." There was no hint in her voice that she was rattled, alarmed, on edge—no indication that she knew about Crawford.

"What then?"

"I'm going to burn them. You can help me."

"Do you plan to read them?"

"I haven't decided. I'm almost afraid that if I do, I might want to dig up Hugh and kill him all over again. Have you read any of them?"

Trying to ignore the ambiguity of her comment about re-killing Disner, I lied, "I only checked them to see if they were in fact from Disner's—Hugh's—." I paused while I searched for the right word.

"His whore," Breda filled in.

Disregarding her choice of terms, I asked, "Do you still want to meet tonight?"

"The sooner the better. I'm sorry I didn't meet you earlier, but I had a bit of a crisis with my son William."

"Should I come to your house?"

"No, I don't want the kids in on this. I'll come to yours."

"I don't think that would be a good idea right now."

"Why, are you 'entertaining' someone tonight?" Her voice took on a new coldness.

"Sort of. Smockley's there, or will be soon. I'm at a gas station. He's gotten a warrant to search my house."

"Oh, really? Why now?"

"I'll tell you when we meet. Can you drive to the turn out on River Road near Raccoon Run Lane?" I purposefully did not mention Crawford or his house.

Without any surprise in her voice, she responded, "Give me thirty minutes. I've got to get Amy to bed. The older children can tend to her while I'm gone."

Chapter 36

Figuring I had given Smockley et al sufficient time to begin their search, I drove to my house. I always felt that the host ought to be there when a party was at his own place. I did not want to be rude.

On the way, knowing that Smockley had already searched my car, I hid the Disner letters under the seats, the originals on the passenger side, the photocopies on the driver's side.

When I arrived, Smockley's cohort in the hooded jacket, with whom I had shared the elevator, was carrying out a plastic tub, like one I bought for $4, in which I keep my woolen sweaters. He was heading toward a SUV with "Sheriff's Department" written on it in yellow and green letters. It appeared that the Department hired the same color coordinator as the University. It was parked next to the brown SUV I had seen Smockley driving. "What exactly are you carting away there, Detective?" I asked.

"All the papers I found lying around your house." He was so stern that I wondered if he were related to the genetically unhappy Glick.

"Does that include all the essays from my Shakespeare students I'm supposed to be grading?"

"I don't know. I just took whatever was there."

"Well, then, feel free to grade them for me. I was going to give them back in a couple of days."

"Oh, all right then, show me which ones they are and you can have them. But don't take anything other than those papers."

I carefully sifted out the essays, holding each one up in front of his face. "Satisfied, Detective?" I asked after retrieving the last of the lot. He did not answer, but put the bin with the remaining papers on the seat of the SUV.

I walked to the back of the house and entered the kitchen, where I found Smockley, wearing latex gloves, looking in my refrigerator. "Looking for evidence, Detective, or are you just hungry? I'm afraid I don't have much to offer."

"You'd be surprised what we find in a person's refrigerator—drugs, murder weapons, even body parts."

I glanced at the contents—a few aged vegetables, left over pasta, some salad dressing, an open can of olives. "You might want to check out that old cucumber. It might have some embedded hair follicles from when I bludgeoned someone with it. And you might check the freezer. There could still be some uneaten appendages I cut off from my victims—you know, a finger or two, a nose, stuff to snack on down the road. I'm a real fan of THE TEXAS CHAINSAW MASSACRE."

Smockley slammed the door shut and glared at me. "I'm going to enjoy putting you away," he said. He then turned and walked into the living room, going straight to the ashtray next to the couch, which contained the remains of Breda's cigarette. Right then I wished I had cleaned up after her. Smockley pulled out some tweezers from his shirt pocket and lifted the butt to his nose. After sniffing at it three or four times, he placed it in a small baggie. I figured he would have been overjoyed if it had been a joint. "Smoke, do you, Professor?"

"No," I said.

"Then, whose cigarette butt is this?"

"I can't remember. I have so many friends drop by that it's hard to keep up with them all. Some smoke, some don't."

"Never mind. People leave tell-tale evidence on their cigarettes, you know, like traces of lipstick and, of course, DNA."

"You speak as if the person who left the cigarette is guilty of something."

"Not necessarily. Actually, I'm under the opinion that it's someone who can tell us more about what you have been up to." He raised his voice on the word YOU, as if he wanted his colleague out by the SUV to hear him.

Just then another detective came from my bedroom carrying a pile of clothes that had been lying on my floor in need of washing. "Are you planning to do my laundry?" I asked, as he went out the front door.

Smockley answered for him. "We'll be checking your clothes for evidence—maybe some blood stains."

"My god, don't you think that if I had murdered someone I would clean up my clothes?"

"Some killers get careless—or cocky. Maybe you're one of them."

Smockley and his crew spent about twenty more minutes checking under cushions, mattresses, pillows, and lamps and through clothes in my chest of drawer and books on my shelves, as I kept looking at my watch, conscious that Breda was waiting for me out on River Road. Smockley even discovered a watch that I thought I had lost, which had fallen behind my chest of drawers. Finally, after giving me back my key, they left.

I waited two full minutes and then hurried out of my driveway in my Subaru to meet Breda, but I quickly discovered that I was hurrying too fast, as, within a couple of miles of my house, I found myself on the bumper of the green and yellow lettered SUV, which apparently was taking exactly the same route as I was, no doubt heading for Brad Crawford's house on Raccoon Run Lane. It was trailing Smockley's vehicle. I slowed until I was a good five hundred yards behind them, hoping that, in the dark, Smockley and the rest had not noticed that it was my car trailing them.

After they turned off River Road onto Crawford's road, I pulled into the clearing where I could see Breda's van sitting. As soon as my car was beside hers, I rolled down my passenger side window and said, "Let's go somewhere else."

"All right, but didn't I just see a vehicle from the Sheriff's Department go by? What's going on?" Her voice gave no hint that she knew about Crawford.

"I'll tell you later. Just follow me." As I drove toward the University, I pulled out the photocopies of Disner's letters and set them on the seat next to me, figuring that my cramming them under the seat might have helped age them even more than my earlier efforts. I was almost fooled into thinking I had a plan.

But as I rested my hand on the letters, I could not help but think about the chaos theory. I knew that no matter how carefully I planned a course of action, something could mess it all up, and that presupposed that I knew what the hell I was doing, but I really didn't. I did not know, for that matter, what anyone else was doing. I envisioned a bee (or should it be the traditional butterfly) fluttering by on the way to a particular flower, with one of the three people in my post-Disner life—Smockley, Breda, or the killer—stepping in and swatting at the insect, changing its direction and causing me to have a different destiny. Why hadn't I chosen another, simpler, career than teaching, maybe in oceanography or with the National Park Service, but then I realized that the field I had chosen—college teaching—was supposed to be simple and safe—at least murder-free.

After reaching the campus, I found a spot for our cars in a remote commuter parking lot, which at that time of the evening was for the most part deserted. As I pulled in, I could hear the bell tower chiming out what I thought was "Kumbaya," but it could have just as easily been a slowed down version of "Honky Tonk Women."

Chapter 37

Before I could get my seatbelt unhooked or move the photocopies of the letters off the passenger seat, Breda had exited her van and opened the right side door to my car. She climbed in, sitting on top of the letters, apparently not seeing them. I did not mind as I figured her body weight would help age them some more. "Can you tell me now what was happening back there on River Road?"

I paused before I answered. It was a technique I had used in class to make myself sound more professorial—as if I were giving the questioner a chance to figure out the answer for herself. I half expected Breda to cut into the pause with, "Oh, I know. They were returning to the scene of the crime where I shot Brad Crawford." Instead, she suddenly changed the subject and asked me a different question. "Where are the letters?"

"You're sitting on them."

"Hell," she said. "I didn't see them." She shifted her torso toward the door and raised her hips, as she reached under herself. "Do you mind if I go ahead and look at them right now?"

"Sure," I said, "let me turn on the overhead."

"No," she nearly shouted, grabbing my hand. "I'll use this." She reached in her purse and produced a small flashlight. "No sense in drawing attention to us, is there?"

"I guess not," I responded, though I was doubtful that a flashlight in a parked car would be less suspicious than my car's dome light.

As she read through the letters, she emitted an assortment of reactions—including "hmmm," "that son-o-bitch," "I see," "that asshole," "wow," "crap,"and "I wondered about that." At one point she exploded with "I'm going to kill him for this," a statement which further complicated

175

my belief that she had already killed her husband. When she was about halfway through the stack, she turned to me and asked, "Did you tell me that you looked at these carefully?"

"No," I lied again. "As I said on the phone, I just scanned them enough to know they were what you were after."

"Are there any other copies?" she asked.

"No," I answered, reacting a bit like I do when I think I am about to be hit in the groin, in this case spasmodically jerking my feet from the pedals and pulling the backs of my calves up quickly against the front of my seat, under which rested the original Disner letters.

"Are you all right?" she asked.

"Of course. What makes you think I'm not?"

"You're acting a bit strangely—like you're on edge."

"Maybe I am. I did have to break in your husband's office to get the letters; I did have to put up with Glick next door, and let's not forget the clean up lady, who opened the door while I was in Hugh's office; and I did have to endure a Smockley search of my house—all in one night. That's probably enough to put anyone on edge." As I said this, I was thinking that she should have been the one on edge—if, in fact, she had murdered Brad Crawford that afternoon and Disner a few short weeks before. But she seemed to be completely at ease. She was, in my thinking, either an innocent widow or the coolest killer in all of Georgia. I was confused.

And to confuse me further, right after she was finished reading the last of the letters, she said, "I'm glad he's dead." She then turned off the flashlight and sat in silence for a few moments. I chose not to interrupt her thinking.

Finally, she said, "I feel sorry for Hugh's lover. Hugh sounds as if he was a bigger shit with whoever wrote these letters than he ever was with me. Thanks for retrieving them. I certainly would not want them out and about. I can just picture people sitting at their breakfast room tables—or at the newspaper table at the public library—lapping up the sordid details of Hugh's divertissements. You've been a big help." She leaned over and kissed me on the cheek, then patted my shoulder. I got mildly excited, but kept my legs tight up against the seat.

"Are you still planning to burn them, like you said on the phone?" I asked.

"Yes, as soon as possible."

"Well, let's not do it here," I said, having visions of a contingency from the University community showing up in the parking lot, the firemen

176

to put out the fire, campus police to investigate, and a few students who figured that the Housing Department was conducting an unscheduled cookout.

"Of course not," she said. "I meant somewhere a bit more private. Why don't you leave your car here and ride with me. I think I know a good place."

I figured this was a good chance to broach the subject of Crawford's murder. "You don't mean out at Brad's house, do you?"

"Actually, I did. Even if he's there, he won't mind."

"What do you mean by that?"

"He already knows about the letters, and besides, I figure that at this very moment he's dead to the world."

"You mean really dead, don't you?"

"Dead to the world, really dead, whatever."

I looked at her profile, but in the darkness, I could not read her face. I suspected that she looked like Barbara Stanwyck in her role in DOUBLE INDEMNITY. "How can you be so cavalier about him?" I asked.

"Because he's basically a nothing. Surely you could see that." When I sighed loudly, she asked, "What's your problem concerning Brad anyway?"

"I just don't think you ought to talk like that about a man who's dead," I answered.

There was a five second delay before she said, "Dead? Did I just hear you say 'dead'? What are you talking about?"

Again I was faced with the problem of deciding if she was innocent or guilty. "He's dead—shot like your husband was. I'm the one who called it in—after of course finding him with a bullet in his head."

"When? Where?"

"This evening, out at his house."

"What were you doing out there?"

"I sort of needed to know what was going on between the two of you. When you didn't show up to meet me, I thought you might be there."

"How could you be sure he was dead?"

"I'm not an expert, but now having discovered the bodies of two people shot, I think I can give an educated assessment. Believe me he was dead."

"I guess that explains why the Sheriff's vehicle was on the way out there. Why didn't you tell me right away?"

"I would have, but you wanted to get right to the letters. And besides . . . ."

"Besides what?"

"I don't quite know how to say this, but I thought you might be the one who did it."

"Me! How could you possibly think that! Are you crazy?"

"Well, I did see you out there at Crawford's house."

"Not today, you didn't. Plus I've already explained to you what my connection with Brad was." She went silent for several seconds and then asked, "Does this also mean that you think I murdered my husband?"

"I must admit that the thought crossed my mind."

"But you were still willing to help me with the letters, right? Wouldn't that make you an accomplice?"

"I guess. I didn't really think things out very well."

"Just why did you help me then?"

I paused for a moment. Then I switched on the dome light. I needed to see her face. I discovered that she did not look anything like Barbara Stanwyck. "Because deep down I really don't want to believe you would do in anybody. And because . . . ." I paused again. She waited. "Because I'm attracted to you in ways I can't possibly explain. I just don't want to be your next victim, if, in fact, you are a killer."

"Why would I want to kill you?"

"Maybe because I know about the letters."

"Well, hell, if you had read them, you would see that his lover had a lot more reason than I did to kill him."

Just then a campus police car turned into the far end of the parking lot and stopped beside an idling car, no doubt as part of a nightly security check of the whole campus. "Look," she said, "we'll have to continue this discussion somewhere else at another time. I need to get back to my children."

"Why the hurry?"

"I don't trust William to do a good job of babysitting."

"What's the matter?"

"The last two times I left him with the younger kids, he was gone when I got back. We were arguing about it when I was supposed to be meeting you earlier."

"Does he have his own car so he can go and come as he pleases?"

"Yes, Hugh found him a used Nissan Maxima."

"Did anything happen with the other kids while William was gone?"

"No, they were asleep. Now, I really need to go. I'll call you later. When I get home, I'll burn the letters. Thanks for all your help."

Despite my suspicions and apprehensions about her, I was hoping she would give me another thank-you kiss—or a goodnight one—I wasn't choosy.

She didn't.

Probably just as well. I might have been tempted to give her the originals.

After folding up the letters I had given her, she hurried to her van and cranked up, just as the campus cop car began moving toward us. I started up also and left as she did. As I pulled out, I felt under the seat to make sure the original letters were still there. I might have given them to her on my own accord, but I wouldn't want her to intuit that they were there and slip them out while we sat in the dark. That would piss me off.

Chapter 38

As Breda and I left the parking lot, a thought struck me. What if Breda had been seeing someone OTHER than Brad Crawford, or maybe even in ADDITION to him. Was she in fact going home at that moment or was she driving to meet someone else? I did not have a plan right then, so I decided to follow her—at a safe distance, of course, a task made more difficult by the plethora of curves in the road along the river. Fortunately for me, Breda's van had very distinct taillights, three on each side stacked vertically.

I kept expecting her to turn off into a side road somewhere, but she kept going until she reached her own house. I stopped down the road and turned off my lights, then watched as she pulled into her driveway and entered her house. There were no other cars parked there.

I sat in the car for a while, halfway hoping that someone—even William in his Nissan Maxima—would show up, but nothing happened. I broke up the tedium by occasionally checking under my seat to make sure the letters were still there, but after approximately a half an hour I grew bored and decided to go home myself, somewhat disappointed that Breda had not left again or a lover shown up.

As I pulled into my driveway, I glanced at my house. Was there someone in there, moving in the minimal illumination provided by the table lamp I had left on, or had I only seen reflections from my car on the front windows? Was it possible one of the detectives was still there? At that moment, I was not in the mood to confront anyone, including a detective, but especially a killer—though I had to admit there probably would never be a time that I would be in the mood for the latter—so I left.

Where next, I wondered. I headed for Crawford's road, not sure exactly what I wanted to do—cruise by and see if Smockley and his crew were still there, collecting more clues, one or more of which might suggest that I had done in Crawford? Actually go to the door and ask Smockley what was going on? I bet he would love that scenario.

"So, you've returned to the scene of the crime have you, Professor?"

"No, I was just curious what you've found. I've watched lots of those CSI programs on television, and I was wondering if real live investigators did what those people did—you know, with Q-tips, infrared lights, et cetera."

"It's been my experience," Smockley would say, "that killers can't stay away. You must be the guilty party. Cuff him, somebody."

I made a u-turn in the middle of the highway, almost getting hit by a vehicle that suddenly appeared from around a bend in the road before I could completely straighten out, and headed off in the opposite direction of Crawford's house, back toward the University.

As I neared the campus, I felt once more under the seat to make sure that the letters were still there, but then I chastised myself for my own paranoia. What or who the hell could have removed them? Mice hiding in the car? The killer lurking in the backseat floor of my Suburu, in a space that was hardly big enough for me even to keep an extra quart of motor oil?

I began contemplating taking the letters to Smockley, but I again imagined our conversation.

"So you sneaked into Professor Disner's office and stole these letters, knowing that it was a scene we were still investigating."

"Yes, but I had a reason."

"And what was that reason?"

"Breda wanted them."

"Oh, it's Breda to you, is it, not Mrs. Disner?"

"Yes, but . . . ."

"And why did she want them?"

"So she could keep Disner's affair quiet."

"Disner's affair, you say? With whom?"

"I can't say."

"And what would you get out of all this?"

"I'm not sure."

"Seems to me you must have a pretty big stake in all this. Cuff him somebody."

All right then, I would not take them to him, but I could mail them. I smiled to myself as I imagined Smockley tearing open the envelope and hissing out a "What the hell! Who sent these? I bet it was that Professor Davidson. Send someone out to the University and cuff him."

Chapter 39

I was still uncertain about where to go next. Feeling a draining lethargy, as if gremlins had sewn bags of sand into my bodily cavities, I decided to go for a jog, hoping to get my energy back, but I was leery about running on my favorite route out on River Road, not just because it was near Crawford's house, but because it was now quite dark, and I could imagine the killer lurking for me somewhere on the river's edge, maybe poised with a rifle on which was mounted a night vision telescope.

I opted for a more public place that was well lit, in fact the parking lot next to Sloan Gymnasium, where, after changing clothes in my car and folding the Disner letters into the large side pocket of my jacket, I ran laps around the perimeter for approximately forty minutes, maneuvering around parked cars and dodging vehicles driven my students in a hurry to get to late night intramural basketball games. However, when I finished, I realized that running had not solved my problems—providing me with neither a clue as to the killer nor a plan for the rest of the night.

Where the hell should I spend the night? My office? No, that's about three circles too deep into hell. I slept there one night when I was too tired to drive home after working well into the night making up exams, but found myself in one of those no-win dilemmas that often comes to someone sleeping in a strange place. Besides having no bed to sleep on, half reclining in an old corduroy chair that had been left by a former denizen of my office, I had to contend with a crack of light that shone around all the edges of the door, a problem I tried to solve by wearing a sleep mask I kept in my desk drawer, given to me by a flight attendant on a trip I took to England a few years back. It did not aid my sleep in the office since it felt itchy and stifling, augmenting the discomfort I felt from the excessive heat pouring out of the vents, heat that I could not regulate.

Adding to my reluctance to sleep there was the realization that if I could manage to snag the master key from secretary Yvonda, as I did to open Disner's office, who's to say that the killer couldn't do the same thing and enter my office while I slept there, assuming I could actually doze off.

How about sleeping in my car? At least the killer would not know where I was unless he followed me, which I probably could prevent if I drove for a while and kept my eye on the rearview mirror and then found an out-of-the-way spot to park my car. It would be just my luck, however, to get mugged by someone totally unrelated to the murders or spotted by a policeman, who recognized my license number and reported my activity to Smockley. I could imagine the ensuing scene.

A tap would come on my side window, like the one Marion Crane heard in PSYCHO delivered by a state trooper after she spent the night in HER car in the desert. In my case, there would be the added effect of a flashlight shining in my face through the window.

"Wake up, Professor."

"What?" I would say, jerked into consciousness, afraid that I was on the verge of getting a bullet in my brain. And then, "Don't shoot!"

"I'm not going to shoot you, you idiot! Step out of the car." The voice would be unmistakably Smockley's. "What are you doing sleeping out here in the middle of nowhere?"

"I love watching the stars. I must have fallen asleep."

"You weren't trying to hide from me—rather, the law—were you, Professor?"

"Why would I be hiding from you?"

"Because you know that I'm on the verge of arresting you."

"What for?"

"Two murders—Professor Disner's and Mr. Crawford's. Plus, now, I might throw in a charge of loitering."

Given the possibility of a confrontation with Smockley if I did sleep in the car, I weighed the pluses and minuses of going back by my house and checking it out again. After all, I was not positive I had seen anyone there earlier in the evening. Going back was worth a try. I almost would rather face the killer than Smockley. Plus, I did not like the idea that paranoia could create homelessness.

Right after the incident with the hooded figure on the Wakeless trail when I could not park in the parking lot next to my building, I looked up the word <u>paranoia</u>. It supposedly involves delusions of persecution, in some cases accompanied by delusions of grandeur. Well, we could certainly dispense with the delusion business, due to the recent events, though I had to admit that previously, I had thought of death, particularly murder, as a kind of fiction. The only time it took on a semblance of reality was when I watched the movie FACES OF DEATH, but film, even in a quasi-realistic version, has a way of keeping the subject of death in the abstract. Two bodies with holes in their heads turned things around for me, giving a high degree of realism to these abstractions. Knowing I could be next on the killer's list dispelled "delusion" in a hurry.

We could also dispense with that other business too—about feelings of grandeur. I, in no way, felt grandiose, pompous, cavalier, lah-de-dah about death. I was flat out scared, filled with fear. That is what paranoia really boils down to—fear. I wondered if a person could die of paranoia. We have all heard the expression, "It frightened me to death." I think Roderick Usher in Poe's "The Fall of the House of Usher" died of fright or fear or paranoia, or whatever one wants to call it, when Madeline broke out of her tomb, dragged all those chains up the steps, and then stood outside Roderick's reading room. I could imagine myself dying of fright if I woke up with a hooded figure looming over me in the night. He probably would not even have to stab me or shoot me. I would be the last person to boast that "Death be not proud" or take on Death in a game of chess. I would simply try to hide.

Paranoia also usually involves a distrust of others. I can attest to that. I did not trust Breda nor most of the people in the University, especially Glick, Bwanger, and Popson. For a while I did not trust Crawford, but now I did, since he was dead. The only person I really felt I could trust was Sturgeon.

Sturgeon! I wondered if he had any advice. I decided to call him. This time I did use my cell phone. To my amazement, it worked.

He answered on the second ring. "Ben Sturgeon here." I was thankful that he did not answer with his usual line, "This is a live recording. I'm here but you should still leave a message."

"Ben, this is Tyler. I need your advice."

"Sure, as long as it's not about committees, teaching methods, schedules, rosaries, repentance, salvation, or any other topic related to the University or religion."

I relayed to him the events of the night, including my raiding Disner's office, finding the letters, getting caught by Doris and then Glick, including my story to Glick about the Shakespeare textbook, then photocopying the letters before giving the fakes to Breda. I also told him about finding Crawford.

"Did it occur to you that Breda might have been the one who shot her husband and maybe this Crawford fellow too?" he asked.

"Oh, yes, and it's still occurring to me. In fact, I told Breda as much."

"Tyler, Tyler, don't you think that if she were the guilty one, your telling her of your suspicions might give her a fairly strong reason for taking you out also?"

"I thought of that, but there's a big part of me that believes that she had nothing to do with the murders."

"Yeah, Tyler, I can imagine what that 'big' part is."

"No, Ben, you'd have to hear her, see her reactions to understand what I mean."

"She might be on the level, but stealing the letters from Disner's office could get you into all kinds of trouble. I doubt if Glick will keep his mouth shut about seeing you in Disner's office—or Doris for that matter."

"Well, the good thing is that I don't think either Glick or Doris know that I actually took anything."

"What do you plan to do now?"

"I'm thinking I'll try to sneak the originals letters back into Disner's office and let Smockley find them in due course."

"My God, Tyler, you're really pushing it. Glick caught you the first go-around. The police will probably catch you the next time. How's it going to look to that Detective Smockley if he finds you in Disner's office?"

"I know it sounds dumb, but I don't want to simply mail them to the police."

"How about fingerprints? Are yours all over them now?"

"I did take the precaution of handling them by the edges, and I can try wiping each one off just in case."

"Tyler, people like you and me were not cut out for espionage. We're college professors. We always get into trouble when we try to do something sneaky. Ask my wife about my attempts to gamble behind her back some time. Promise me you won't try to get back in there tonight."

"All right, I promise, as if I could anyway without the key, but right now I've got to figure out where to sleep tonight."

"Do you want to come here? I've got extra room."

"I don't think so. I don't want to put you and Kim in trouble, plus I hate being driven out of my own house with fear. Let me at least go check out my place and see how I feel about it. In the meantime, could I leave the letters with you? I'm afraid Detective Smockley might come searching again."

"Sure, you can do that."

It took only a few minutes for me to swing by Sturgeon's house, and then I was headed home.

Chapter 40

When I reached my house, I first drove by without stopping, peering at the front door and adjacent windows, without seeing anything suspicious. After turning around up the street, I again drove by, searching to see even a shred of evidence of danger, but again saw nothing.

This time, instead of turning around, I parked down the street and walked back to the house, using as a shield the hedges growing along the street in front of the house of my elderly neighbors, the Purdeys. This allowed me to get within approximately fifty feet of the front corner of my house, where I crouched behind the Purdeys' two garbage cans, which had been set out that day, in the front corner where our two lots meet the street. The only light came from the Purdeys' front porch lamp, which usually stayed on all night, every night. I studied my own house for several minutes, straining to see movement, shadows, something really obvious like a glowing cigarette, or hear a bump or cough or tell-tale muttering.

Nothing.

I was just about to creep forward so that I could put my ear to the wood siding, when my neighbor's door opened and Mrs. Purdey stepped out on her porch. Mrs. Purdey had been a widow until a year ago, previously married for thirty years to an electrician named Lackey, who got careless one day and provided a link with his own body between a generator and a high tension line. With her take from the insurance company, she bought and managed a salon called the Save the Mane, until, in her words, she was swept off her feet by a widower named Mecabeus Purdey, who made her promise to stay at home and prepare three squares a day for him. She often offered to give me a free haircut, and I actually planned someday to let her.

At this moment she was carrying what I assumed—but could not immediately verify—was her small dog, Johnson, a Pomeranian about the size of a Nerf football. It could have been their cat. From where I squatted, it was hard to tell, but there was no mistaking the sudden yapping that issued forth from Johnson, who must have sensed me out in the semi-dark yard, causing Mrs. Purdey to peer around also. "Why, Mr. Davidson, is that you? What on earth are you doing in our garbage?"

I was torn among my choices—answer her from where I stood, scurry over to her, or run back to my car. I chose the second option, speaking, as I began moving toward her, in as quiet a voice as I could so as not to alert anyone in my house of my presence, but loud enough for Mrs. Purdey to hear me. "Hi, Mrs. Purdey, I was, uh, just checking the size of your cans, I mean garbage receptacles. I was, uh, planning to buy a new one and thought it would be appropriate if we as neighbors had the same sized cans."

Apparently I was not loud enough.

"What did you say, Mr Davidson?" she shouted. "Did I hear it right, that you want to use our trash cans to exercise with?" Johnson matched her in volume with his continued barking.

I hustled the last few yards to her, sure that my cover had been blown. As I neared the porch, Johnson stopped his yapping but began growling in such a way that I was convinced he was actually talking. Mrs. Purdey must have thought so too, for she responded. "Yes, Sweetie, there was something there." She turned to me and said, "He probably thought you were a possum." She began stroking the dog on the head. "You're a good dog. I'll take you for your walk in a minute, but first you must say something nice to Mr. Davidson." Johnson continued "talking" all during the rest of my conversation with Mrs. Purdey, as I repeated my excuse for hovering near her trashcans and offered apologies for alarming her—thankful during all of the discourse that I had not already set out my own almost new trash can. I thought about including Johnson in the conversation, but figured that anything I said would sound like a foreign language to him.

"It's perfectly all right, Mr. Davidson," Mrs. Purdey said. "I'm just glad you weren't a possum. Johnson really gets agitated when there's one around." Patting the dog's head and then clipping on a leash, she said, "Well come on, Sweetie, it's time for your walk." The two of them started in the direction of my house, Johnson tugging eagerly at the leash, giving the impression—judging by the strain on the five-foot Mrs. Purdey—that he was a much larger dog.

I regretted that I had not chosen option three and sprinted for my car.

As Mrs. Purdey and Johnson reached the edge of my property in their stroll up the street, I was faced with a decision of which way to go myself—to my house or down the street to my car. Still reluctant to enter my house, I chose the latter, hoping Mrs. Purdey would not notice the oddity.

She did.

"Where on earth are you going, Mr. Davidson? Your house is this way."

"Yes, I know, but I left my car down the street while I . . . while I checked out other people's trash cans."

"Oh, I see," she said, "You truly are serious about making your receptacle match those in the whole neighborhood—how thoughtful."

"Thank you, Mrs. Purdey. That's awfully kind of you to say."

As Mrs. Purdey and Johnson went on their walk, I drove back to my house. I pulled into the driveway and left the car close to the front porch, feeling that I could better detect someone in the house if I came in through the main room and turned on the bright lights controlled by the switch just inside. The kitchen light was dim by comparison. Plus, I typically came in the back way. I did not want to give the killer an advantage in case he knew my routine.

Mrs. Purdey and Johnson were coming down the street as I stepped out of my car. As soon as he spotted me, Johnson began yapping again. As annoying as the sound was, it gave me an idea.

"Mrs. Purdey, I was wondering if I could get your opinion on something."

"What's that, Mr. Davidson?" Johnson had stopped barking and was growling/talking again.

"I'm about to repaint the inside of my house. In fact, I'm going to get the paint in the morning and was wondering if I could get a woman's opinion on the color. Would you mind stepping inside and looking? It wouldn't take but a second. You could bring Johnson with you." I knew I was being a coward, but I did not want to enter the house alone. Having already used Glick for protection on the elevator, I figured I could use an elderly woman and a diminutive dog as re-enforcements in case the killer was inside. I had no shame at that moment.

"How about that lady who's been visiting you lately? Couldn't she give you an opinion?" she asked.

"What lady?"

"The one who lets herself in. I've seen her come and go three, no, four times in the last week."

As I tried to remember all the times Breda had come by, I floundered for an explanation. "Oh, her. She's a colleague of mine—or rather the wife of a colleague. He died. You might have known him or read about him—a Professor Disner."

"Yes, I did read about his murder, though I did not know him personally." Johnson continued rattling out talking growls, sounding like he was saying "liar" and "horse shit." I thought I even caught "nevermore" in there somewhere.

"Anyway, she wanted me to help her write a eulogy about her husband to distribute to friends and relatives who didn't make it to the funeral. I told her where to find the copies I had worked on. I've gone through several revisions. I didn't think to ask her about the paint, her recently becoming a widow and all."

"As I said before, you're so thoughtful, Mr. Davidson. Yes, I'd be glad to look at your walls."

As I unlocked the front door, I engaged Mrs. Purdey, but not Johnson, in trivial conversation, raising my voice to the level of a Roman orator, while I faced the door. "The weather certainly is mild for November, isn't it, Mrs. Purdey."

"Yes, it is, Mr. Davidson, the mildest I've seen in a decade or so."

I pushed open the door and continued as a stentorian. "The mild weather is one reason I feel I can do some painting."

"I understand," she said, "but I can hear fine in case that's why you're shouting."

"Oh, I'm sorry. I guess I'm just excited about your opinion concerning the paint color. Come on in." I reached in and snapped on the living room lights.

As soon as we all were inside, Johnson began tugging on the leash. I said, "It's fine if Johnson wants to look around. You can unleash him if you want to."

"Oh dear," she said, "I'm afraid he'll get into mischief. He likes to explore."

"No," I blurted, "it's fine with me. Let him have a spin around if he wants. I know dogs love new smells."

"All right then, if you insist. I just hope he doesn't tear up anything or mark his territory."

As soon as she unsnapped the leash, Johnson tore off toward my bedroom, barking in staccato bursts.

"What in the world!" Mrs. Purdey exclaimed. "Johnson, come back here this instant!"

Johnson did not come back, but rather began growling, then obviously tearing into something, judging by the sounds. I wondered if it were the pant leg of the killer. I waited to see if he would let up a bit, half-consciously picking up the only loose object within reach—a potted cactus plant. I wished I still had the pineapple from two nights before, but I had eaten it. How I might transform the cactus or the pot into a tool of real defense was anybody's guess. The cactus was approximately the size of a dill pickle. The pot was only slightly bigger than a coffee cup.

Mrs. Purdey spoke up. "Don't you think you ought to see what Johnson's attacking, Mr. Davidson?"

"It's probably nothing," I answered, "maybe a mouse."

"Well," she said, "I hope it doesn't make its way over to my house."

"I suspect it won't, Mrs. Purdey."

"If you don't mind, Mr. Davidson, I'll go check on Johnson. I hate for him to get so agitated."

To my shame, I let her go. I rationalized that the killer would not harm an old lady nor her dog, but I—I was a different matter.

In a few seconds I could hear Mrs. Purdey gasp. Johnson suddenly went silent. I felt anxious for the two of them, but I felt angst—complete with fear and trembling—for myself. Angst outweighs anxiety any day. I moved to the front door and put my hand on the handle. I waited for what seemed to be minutes. I finally called out, "Mrs. Purdey, is anything wrong?"

A long pause ensued.

I repeated the question.

Mrs. Purdey suddenly broke out in a scolding voice. "You naughty dog, just look at what you've done."

I left my front door and, after setting down the potted cactus, mince-stepped to my bedroom to see what she was talking about. I discovered Johnson, his mouth full of gray and white fur, straddling a squirrel that he must have just killed.

"I'm truly sorry, Mr. Davidson. I had no idea Johnson could be so vicious. Was the squirrel a pet?"

"Oh, no, no. It must have gotten in somehow during the day and couldn't get out. It's all right. I'll clean him up if you want to take Johnson into another room." I was becoming more convinced by the minute that I should put myself in the third circle of my book DAVIDSON'S HELL, with all the cowards, or the fifth circle, with all the deceivers. I might even qualify for Dante's Hell—in the sixth circle with the fraudulent being punished for putting others at risk.

"Yes, maybe that would be best." She snapped the leash back on Johnson and pulled him away from the dead squirrel, something Johnson was not particularly happy about, judging by the fact that he started growling again and stiffened his legs so that he took on the appearance of a ceramic toy dog.

"Don't you want to know what I think?" she asked as she neared the bedroom door.

"Yes, of course. You're probably thinking I'm a pretty shoddy housekeeper, if squirrels are running rampant in my house."

"No, I meant about the colors."

Colors. Images of gray and white fur ran through my head. So did green and yellow and red.

"You know," she said, "the colors of the walls."

"Oh, those colors! Yes, let's look at the walls in all the rooms, including the bathroom and the kitchen, which we haven't checked out, rather, you haven't seen yet. I can come back to this squirrel later. Notice the bland color in this room, which is the same as the one in the living room. You and Johnson lead the way. The bathroom is the next door on the left."

Chapter 41

As the three of us roamed through the house, Mrs. Purdey in the lead, Johnson trailing her on his leash, me in the rear, looking frequently over my shoulder, Mrs. Purdey offered her opinions on colors. Johnson had little more to say. As Mrs. Purdey surveyed my dull white walls, I wondered what you call a search party when the majority of the searchers are not aware of the true object of the search—a red herring search party, maybe?

"Oh, I think a nice lemon yellow would work nicely in the kitchen, Mr. Davidson," Mrs. Purdey said. "It would brighten things up a bit and also complement the green I suggested for the living room."

"You might be right, Mrs. Purdey," I offered, though I was thinking that after following her suggestion all I would have to do is add some red and I would have a daily reminder of Disner dead on the floor of the toilet stall.

"Yes, definitely," she said, "yellow in the kitchen and maybe the bathroom and green in the living room and bedroom. That should do it. Now, if you don't mind, I better be getting home. Mecabeus will probably think Johnson and I got lost."

"Thank you, Mrs. Purdey, for giving me your opinion. I'll certainly think about those colors. They are, in fact, the colors for my university."

"See, we have similar tastes, then, don't we, Mr. Davidson?" She tugged at Johnson's leash. "Come on Johnson." She then said to me, "I'm sorry about the squirrel in your bedroom, Mr. Davidson."

"No problem, Mrs. Purdey, but speaking of Johnson, I've been thinking about getting a dog myself, but I'm not sure what it would be like having one in the house, particularly at night. You wouldn't consider loaning out

Johnson overnight would you, allow me to make a canine test run, so to speak? I'd have him back to you first thing in the morning."

"Oh, dear, I wish I could, but I simply can't sleep unless Johnson is lying across my feet. He's my little heating pad, you know."

I considered offering my electric pad for the night, but gave up the thought. "I understand, Mrs. Purdey. See you soon."

The minute Mrs. Purdey and Johnson were out the door, I locked up, again wishing I had installed more security beyond the keyed lock/door handle combinations that even I could probably open from outside with a credit card or dinner knife. Why the hell didn't I have a deadbolt or a chain? And why had I not taken advantage of an opportunity a few months previously when offered a free puppy outside Blethens Groceries, by a couple of children who were trying to find a home for eight or nine products of an "accident" their Boston terrier had with a male golden retriever.

I took another tour of the house, feeling somewhat bolder, having carried out most of one already with the aid of Mrs. Purdey and Johnson. Only, this time I checked under the couch and beneath my bed, as well as in the closets, places I was reluctant to search in the presence of Mrs. Purdey, fearing she would see through my ruse about paint colors. I stopped short of searching the kitchen cupboards. If a killer had climbed into one of them, well, so be it. I would just have to die. Besides, I was afraid I would discover all the cans and bottles arranged in neat rows, like Julia Roberts discovers in SLEEPING WITH THE ENEMY, signifying that her deranged husband was lurking somewhere close by.

I found nothing to be alarmed about, except I was faced with the problem of what to do with the squirrel Johnson had killed. I wanted to get the remains out of the house, but was apprehensive about unlocking either door and facing whatever or whoever might be outside. I opted to put it in the kitchen trashcan, accepting the fact that it might smell up the house by morning. I also drew together all the drapes, pulled down shades, and closed blinds throughout the house, all of which I usually did to shut out light for better sleeping conditions, but this night for the purpose of keeping me out of a killer's gun sights. I even added a bit of duct tape to hold the drapes together better.

I also went on a search for the squirrel's entry point into the house, irrationally thinking that if a squirrel could get in, a person could also. I finally located a hole in the top of my bedroom closet, a portal that was, to my relief, too small for anything larger than a squirrel to pass through.

195

After carrying out these measures, I tried reading, returning to Poe's "The Fall of the House of Usher," since I was supposed to teach it two days later, perhaps not the wisest choice at that moment. I began to see myself as Roderick Usher, as he was trying to read to his visitor, the narrator, a fictitious piece called "The Mad Trist" by Sir Launcelot Canning, while being interrupted by sounds of wood being ripped apart, the grating of iron hinges, and the "death cry of dragons," whatever the hell that is. I myself was constantly distracted by sounds from without—in my case, dogs barking, owls hooting, bumps in the night. More than once I was tempted to scream out, "Madman, I tell you that she (or he) now stands without the door!" but I did not have a visiting friend to scream to, so I internalized a lot.

Car noises bothered me the most. It was bad enough when I could hear an automobile simply go by my house—maybe containing a potential drive-by shooter. Worse were the sounds of a car slowing down as it approached my house, as if someone were checking to see if I was at home. Worst of all were the sounds of a car starting up from in front of my house, implying some back action—perhaps someone sneaking around the edges of my house, looking in slits I had not successfully blocked, checking for a spare key under one of the mats or on one of the door lintels.

Speaking of which, had I left a key in one of those places? I could not remember. Is that how Breda had gotten in? Did she have it at that moment or maybe given it to someone like Crawford? At least I did not have to worry about him, he being dead. In any event, I was not about to open either door to find out.

Eventually I discovered I was reading the same line from Poe over and over ("But the good champion Ethelred, now entering within the door, was sore enraged and amazed to perceive no signal of the maliceful hermit"), so I decided to go to bed, but first I leaned a pizza pan against the back door and an ice bucket against the front one, figuring that if anyone did try to get in, the noise, though it might not be quite so evident as the clamor Madeline Usher made, would be sufficiently loud to warn me.

I had hoped for some sleep that "knits the raveled sleeve of care," but got instead something more like a sleeve of fear raveling my sleep. Whenever I would doze off, I would be startled awake by what I perceived to be distinct noises—ones that of course grew quieter the more awake I became, to the point that when I sat up in bed they had become inexplicably silent. As I drifted off, I thought I heard the sounds of switchblades flicking open, pistols cocking, choker chains unreeling from little canisters.

The same thing would happen with movements. In a state of stupor, I would see the shapes of a stalker, with a knife in his hand, or a gun, or even a chain saw. Of course the moment I sat up in bed, the images would transform into only the shadows on the wall created by the light from the digital numbers on my alarm clock. Wind currents in my drafty bedroom made me feel as if someone were touching my skin, perhaps locating me precisely so that I could be stabbed or shot. I also had a moment when I was sure I smelled something dead, but on sniffing the air I determined it was merely the odor emanating from a pair of dirty socks draped across my headboard, either that or particles of the dead squirrel. To complete the synaethesic quintet, I even imagined I was tasting death at one point or two, but it was just a foul taste from breathing through my mouth, probably from my hyperventilating.

Getting angry did not exactly help induce sleep either, as I lay there seething over the fact that my own bed was no longer a safe zone. Scenes of bed and bedroom invasions in movies ran through my head—TIME BANDITS, SOMETHING WICKED THIS WAY COMES, or THE GODFATHER, for instance. I thought about animals and people that are bolder, even more ferocious in their own territory, little birds and dogs running off bigger interlopers. Why couldn't I feel that way, become a macho character like one played by John Wayne? I decided if I could get through the night, I would become more aggressive in taking on the potential killer. I just hoped nothing would happen during the night that would make me wet the bed.

Chapter 42

I lay awake for an hour or so, shifting from my right side to the left, next trying a flat-on-my-back position, then repeating the cycle. I was tempted to take a sleeping pill, but I was afraid I might not hear an intruder, even if he knocked over the pizza pan or ice bucket. I finally settled on a Benadryl capsule, figuring it would help me sleep normally and aid my breathing to boot. I was thankful that I did not live close enough to the University to hear the bell tower, which was programmed to clang out the hours of the night, though it did spare everyone its renditions of music after 9 pm.

As I waited for the Benadryl to take effect, I wondered about my vulnerability. Should I have on clothing more protective than a tee shirt and shorts? I came to realize that short of medieval armor, which of course would be less than conducive to sleeping, nothing would really help much if someone were intent on stabbing me, and even the armor probably would not stand up to a .38 slug.

I also thought about making a sleeping dummy out of extra pillows and a couple of cushions off the couch and then lying between the bed and the wall away from the door, but was too weary to carry out the process.

I also thought more about Breda. My trust level for her was at around only fifty percent. So what was it that made me attracted to her? Was it her trim body, her graceful legs, her long, dark hair, her velvety, tanned skin? The song "Pretty Woman" started running through my head—"ruby lips and shapely hips." Maybe it was the way she talked, with an almost Southern genteelness, soft, but with an added assertiveness. And when she did talk, she seemed always to avoid trivia.

Maybe I was attracted to her because of the contrast between her and her many foils—the female faculty members and the wives of the men in the English Department. Take Associate Professor Gertrude Lonzer, for instance, who could never speak on any subject except teaching techniques and who took any meeting—be it for freshman composition or student recruitment—way too seriously. Besides, she was so top heavy, she always seemed to be in danger of tipping over.

She was far more appealing than Jolena Belvin and Holly Dinkins, two assistant professors who would remain at that rank forever, having no desire to publish any scholarly work, choosing instead to meet together as often as possible and discuss their various physical afflictions, including bloating, varicose veins, and sties, particularly if they oozed. I tended to agree with Ben Sturgeon about Jolena, who he believed to be as ugly as a camper top on a pickup truck. Holly looked a tad better, but wore, as a contrast to her three-piece suits, far too much makeup, making her look like an academic version of a pole dancer.

Glick's wife, Martha, was mildly attractive, but she frowned most of the time and quoted scripture a lot. Her eyes were the color of pewter. My contact with her mostly came when I attended performances delivered by the community choir, where I could see her in the alto section, distinguished by the fact that she flicked her head in sync with the notes.

Clark Bisson's wife, Mildred, was perhaps the most attractive woman associated with the Department—but only if you consider a Stepford wife attractive. She seemed to have a plastic face glued on—perhaps from botox injections—and her speech was always peppered with cliches, her most common comments being "I'm having a bad hair day" or "I'm as happy as a lark," depending on her mood.

Disregarding the foils, what was really amazing—and disturbing—to me was that I found Breda to be so attractive despite the fact that she had chosen to marry the biggest clod in the history of the University, had born him five children, and potentially had murdered two men.

I finally drifted off into a fitful sleep, but it did not last very long. I jerked awake and sat up, then felt around me, half expecting to lay my hands on a horse's head—or maybe the head of Johnson's dead squirrel. I needed to pee, but was reluctant to go to the bathroom, fearing I would discover all the towels neatly arranged on the racks, again ala SLEEPING WITH THE ENEMY, so I lay down, eventually falling into a slightly deeper sleep.

Somewhere during the next couple of hours I dreamed of a parade of souls, led by the Grim Reaper in a hooded jacket, who was holding a scythe and the oversized facsimile edition of Shakespeare's First Folio I had seen in Disner's office. In the parade were Disner, President Popson, Glick, Bwanger, Smockley, and Breda, all making their way up a hill, on which stood a fog-shrouded bell tower, which was ominously clanging out "Dies Irae" from Berlioz's SYMPHONIE FANTASTIQUE. Breda was reaching out to me, inviting me to join the danse macabre.

Just as I was about to take her hand, I was aroused by a tapping sound coming from the front part of the house. For several seconds I lay still, wondering if I were actually awake, hoping I would not hear the noise again. I had visions of Dustin Hoffman in MARATHON MAN, sitting in his bathtub with a washcloth over his face, becoming terrified upon hearing noises from the next room.

There! It came again, but I was able to locate the sound better. It seemed to be coming from my front door. I eased out of bed and worked my way from my bedroom to the front of the living room, near the door. Once more the tapping sound came, a noise that made me think of a bird's beak—Poe's raven maybe—or fingernails. My first reaction was to wish I had installed a peephole in the door, but then I realized I would be too afraid to use it, imagining that the person knocking would sense that I was looking out—and put a bullet in my eye. I remembered far too well that character in ANGEL HEART who lay dead, shot in the eye.

I first pulled off the piece of duct tape on the front drapes, being careful not to make any noise. I then looked out through the slit I made to the street to see whose vehicle was parked there, but saw nothing. I next decided to sneak a peak through the Venetian blinds on the window that looked out onto the front porch. I tried to be stealthy, but of course, the second I bent down one of the slats, it produced, not a "ping" as it had once before, but rather a loud "twang." It was dark on the porch, so all I could tell was that it was a woman with long hair, wearing glasses. Could it be Mrs. Purdey, who had let down her hair and donned glasses, coming back this late for something she had forgotten?

Whoever it was must have heard the slat twang, for she stepped toward me and then spoke. "Tyler, let me in!" It was Breda.

Chapter 43

I released the bent blind (which twanged again) and moved to the front door, which I opened, forgetting the ice bucket leaning up against it. "What was that?" Breda asked after the bucket slid across the room and crashed into the kitchen wall, making almost as much noise as cymbals in the hands of a neophyte in an elementary school band.

"Just an ice bucket," I answered, turning on the living room light.

"What was it doing next to the door?" she asked, with a tone of voice that suggested she was less than glad to see me.

"I . . . I wanted to remind myself to take a cold drink with me to school tomorrow."

"Couldn't you just write yourself a note?" She looked at me with her head cocked. She was dressed all in black, including her jeans, which looked as if they had been custom sewn for her slim legs. To me, she appeared to be simultaneously sexy and deadly.

"I guess so, but I often overlook notes." I wanted to change the subject as quickly as possible, so I asked, "By the way, where's your van?"

"I parked it down the street in front of a vacant lot."

"Fine, but what are you doing here?"

"I want to talk about these." She pulled from her pocket a large wad of papers, ones that I quickly recognized as the photocopied letters I had given her earlier.

"Are those the letters to Hugh?" I asked. "I thought you were going to burn them when you got home."

"No, Tyler, as you can see, I didn't burn them."

Trying my best to disregard her hostile use of my name and to avoid talking specifically about the letters, I asked, "All right, but why have you come in the middle of the night? Couldn't this wait until daylight when diurnal people like me are up and about?"

"I'm sure I've been noticed by your neighbors when I've come before. I figured fewer people would see me coming right now. And if some people happened to be up, I figured they would think I'm just another one of your girlfriends who couldn't contain herself."

"That's highly unlikely since I don't have any girlfriends right now."

"If you say so, but about these letters. The reason I didn't burn them was because it would be pointless. Why did you give me copies instead of the originals?"

I tried to put on my best lying face. "Copies? What are you talking about?"

"I'm no fool, Tyler. When I got home with the letters, in better light, I had an opportunity to study them carefully. I can recognize the difference between an original and a photocopy. The ink looks different. It smears more easily on the photocopies."

So much for my antiquing job. I had to come up with an answer quickly, as Breda stood with one hand on her hip, the other holding the letters as if she were confronting me with evidence that I, not Disner, had been the one cheating on her. I said, "Whoever sent them to Hugh must have made photocopies and kept the originals. Those that you're holding are all that I found."

She looked at me for several seconds, then dropped her arm and the letters to her side. She sighed and then said with a softened voice, "I guess that is possible. It just makes me nervous to know that the originals are out there somewhere. I'd kill to get them back."

"Yes, I understand," I added, though her comment made me extremely uneasy. "But I don't have the originals," which was technically true since I had dropped them off at Sturgeon's house. I realized at that moment that I had lied more to Breda in the past couple of days than I had collectively to everyone else in the last several years.

She again stared at me for several seconds, before speaking, now, to my relief, without any sign of anger in her voice. "You know what? I think I'd like to have something to drink. Got any wine left? I'll get it if you'd like." She took a step towards the kitchen.

Remembering the pizza pan against the kitchen door, I blurted out, "NO! I'll get it! Just make yourself comfortable on the couch."

"It's the least I can do," she said, "and besides I'm the one who came barging in here in the middle of the night." She took another step toward the kitchen, but before she could advance any farther, I stepped around in front of her, blocking her progress.

"No, I want to get it!"

"Well, of course, Tyler." She turned and stepped back toward the couch. "I didn't mean to invade your kitchen or anything."

"It's just that . . . that I know where everything is. I'll just be a sec."

"Do you mind if I smoke?" she asked.

"It's all right," I said. "The ashtray is where you left it. Make yourself comfortable." I didn't want to tell her that Smockley had bagged up the butts from her last round of smoking, fearing that it might upset her. "By the way, what's with the glasses? I haven't seen you in them before."

She took a cigarette from her purse and lit it. "I usually wear contacts for my nearsightedness, but I took them out earlier, thinking I was going to sleep. I didn't feel like putting them back in when I decided to come over."

"I know the problem. I wear contacts too, but keep a pair of glasses around somewhere, though I can't find them this week. I'm farsighted, but I can manage without either contacts or glasses, like right now."

After she sat down, I went to the kitchen and poured a glass of merlot for her and one for me, but not before returning the pizza pan to its usual resting place in the bottom of the stove. I then delivered Breda her drink and joined her on the couch. "Cheers," I offered.

"Yes, I could use some happiness right now," she said, clinking her glass against mine.

We sat in silence for a couple of minutes, she smoking her cigarette, both of us sipping the wine. I spoke first. "Breda, did it ever occur to you that YOU might be in danger?"

"What do you mean? I haven't done anything to threaten anyone or make anyone jealous or angry, unless I've upset some population control freak, who's after me for having five children—but that's more Hugh's doing than mine."

"How about the possibility that whoever killed your husband might assume that Hugh told you things that might implicate the killer, information that maybe you yourself don't even recognize as vital, until someone like Smockley asks the right questions?"

"Hugh didn't tell me much at all—except what he wanted for dinner or that I needed to pick up dry cleaning, a service which, by the way, he started using a whole lot more after he became Associate Dean. I doubt if I'm in danger of knowing anything threatening to the killer."

"Then, how about the fact that you're the wife of the man that Hugh's lover wrote all those letters to? If his lover was the one who shot him, isn't it possible that she would have enough passion left over to come after you too? You are, after all—or at least you were—the obstacle that kept them from having total freedom to pursue their . . . ."

"Their 'making the beast with two backs'?"

"All right, their passion."

"To tell you the truth, I haven't given it much thought. I've been too mad at Hugh for having the affair." She reached over and crushed out her cigarette in the ashtray.

"Well, I think you should worry a bit, particularly since Crawford's dead too. Obviously the killer didn't stop with just Hugh, unless coincidentally there have been two similar, but unrelated murders in a very short time around here. Crawford's murder is what really got me to worrying about myself, and I believe you should be thinking about it likewise. In fact, somebody could have been watching you tonight as you drove over here."

"Thanks a lot for telling me all this. Just what I need—more to worry about."

"Sorry, but I'm just being cautious."

"I know you are, but somehow I haven't wanted to accept the possibility I was in danger, but you could be right. This all makes me really, really tired. Can I just sit here for a few minutes?"

"Sure," I said, though I was a bit annoyed that she did not appear to have suffered the degree of apprehension that I had.

She removed her glasses and laid them on the end table next to her. She then slid down a bit so that she was almost facing the ceiling, her legs stretched out, one ankle over the other. Her posture made it possibly for me to view her graceful shape, without seeming to leer. She sat quietly for a while, then suddenly straightened up and said, "I just can't get those letters out of my head."

"Did you reread them all?" I asked.

"Yes, and the second time through them made me realize that, despite the fact that Hugh was a real shit with his lover, the two of them experienced a lot more passion than he and I ever did."

"What do you mean?" I asked.

"They obviously were 'getting it on' right frequently. I'm reluctant to admit it, but Hugh and I didn't have much of a sex life, but that could have been mostly my fault."

"How so?" I asked. "After all, you did have five kids with him."

"Let's just say that I was very fertile and lucky that we didn't need too many tries at reproducing. Plus I did a lot of fantasizing when I was with him."

"About whom, if you don't mind my asking?"

"For a while it was about the UPS delivery guy, who must have worked out a lot in the gym and wore those tight brown shirts and shorts. I had a huge crush on him. There was also a cop for the Sheriff's Department, who gave me only warning tickets a couple of times when I got caught speeding on River Road. I think he liked looking down my blouse while standing beside my car. And there was—is— someone else."

"And who might that be?'

"You, silly."

Maybe there was some truth to the comments about Breda's interest in me cited in one of the letters written by Disner's lover. "Me?"

"Don't act so surprised."

"Why didn't you tell me this the other night when I was talking about how I felt about you?"

"I would have, but I didn't want you to think that I was just saying it to get your help with the letters."

"I have to admit that I probably would've thought that at the time, but thank you for telling me now." I still was not one hundred percent sure that I believed her, since there still was the issue of the original letters, but I was feeling better about her. "At any rate, I'm flattered," I told her. "How long can you stay?"

"I'm in no hurry."

"What's happening with your kids? Who's taking care of them?"

"My, my, Tyler, you actually care about my kids?"

"Well, I wouldn't want anything to . . . ." My voice trailed off as she put her index finger to my lips and emitted a "ssshhh" sound. I came very close to taking her finger in my mouth.

"For your information, my sister is there. I told her that I might have to get some fresh air during the night if I couldn't sleep. She knows I've been in turmoil ever since Hugh's death. I doubt if anything will happen, but if it does, she can handle it for me. I did check on all the kids before I left, and they were all sound asleep. I'm sure they'll stay that way until somebody awakes them in the morning. So I guess I really am in no hurry to get back. Do you mind," she asked, as she put her wine glass on the end table next to her glasses.

"Mind what?" I asked.

"Mind if I put my head down for just a moment?"

"Of course not," I said, not expecting that she would snuggle against me and rest her head on my shoulder, which she did.

I sat still for a few minutes, listening to her breathe, wondering if I should put my arm around her or take one of her hands in mine or do absolutely nothing but enjoy the moment. I looked down at her, admiring the curve of her breasts, which I could see easily due to the fact that her blouse was again unbuttoned one button too many. I could not blame the cop for doing the same thing. She really had an exciting shape, a shape that conditioned me so that I was beginning to trust her, maybe as high as eighty percent.

I began thinking about what it would be like to make love with her, this time trying to exclude any thoughts of Crawford and Disner, though the latter did pop in my head as I went through a stage of wondering if a relationship with Breda constituted a form of adultery. Was she in fact still psychologically married to Disner? What exactly was the statue of limitation on marriage when one of the partners was deceased? I guessed it depended on the libido.

The longer she lay propped against me, the more my mind dwelled on the positive side of the topic. I began picturing her atop me in my bed, her hands on my chest, her head tossed back as she moaned in pleasure, then screamed out in ecstasy, a pack of Trojans still on the nightstand, unopened because neither of us wanted to waste one second before making love.

But then the possibility crept in that I had left myself vulnerable and that the only thing Trojan about this night was the horse that I had let in through the gates. What if she were really my enemy? I had another vision of her sitting atop me, but now she was feeling along the side of the mattress for an ice pick, like Sharon Stone's character does in BASIC INSTINCT. My desire to make love to her suddenly waned, making me realize that one's sex drive can be stifled by worrying, just as the desire to sleep can be. The trust factor dropped to below fifty percent.

My sex drive came back in a rush when suddenly she shifted toward me, stretching one leg across mine and placing a hand on my chest, making me realize what a roller coaster ride my libido could cause. "This feels way too good," she said. "You might not get rid of me too easily if we stay like this."

"What makes you think I want to get rid of you?" I asked, thinking that the trust factor was back up over eighty percent.

"Because you're still not sure about what part I've played in this fiasco."

I pulled away from her enough to leave a couple of feet of space between us. "What do you mean?" I asked, putting on my best face of wonder, which was not entirely faked, since I actually was amazed that she had so accurately assessed my state of being.

"I mean that you need to know I had nothing to do with anybody's death. And you need to know that I want those letters for no other reason than they're an embarrassment. And you need to know that I've wanted to be here next to you for a very long time. And one other thing, I'm confident that you want me here as much as I want to be here. So . . . ?"

"So . . . !"

"So, what are you going to do about it?"

"What are my choices?" I asked, as I moved back toward her, wiping out the space between us.

"Well, you could show me to the front door, maybe even walk me to my van—an option that doesn't sound terribly appealing—or sit with me here and read Shakespeare or Dickens or Stephen King to me the rest of the night—another option that I don't recommend—or make love to me—the option I do recommend."

"That's it, just three options?"

"Yep, that's all they wrote, so what's it going to be?"

I studied her face for a few seconds. She did not look at all like Sharon Stone. "I think the third option is the only option," I said.

"My kind of thinking exactly," she said, "but . . . ." She hesitated for a moment before adding, "I hate to bring this up, but I really can't afford to get pregnant—five already being way too many—so I hope you have some means of . . . ." Her voice trailed off.

"Prevention," I asked?

"Yes, prevention. I'm fresh out."

"I think I have just what we need," I said, realizing the unopened pack of Trojans was about to become more than just an ingredient of wishful thinking.

"And one more thing. Can we start slowly? It's been awhile since I've done this."

"I understand," I answered. "I've had a related problem."

We did begin slowly, but sped things up in a very short time. I did not think of an ice pick even once. I didn't even mind the Trojans participating.

Chapter 44

I lay awake for at least an hour after we made love, still charged with adrenaline and looking for any signs of Breda's desiring an encore. Plus, I had skipped all my usual preparations for ensuring sleep—draping a black sheet over the closed, but slightly light-permeable window blinds, turning on a fan to provide "white" noise, donning a sleeping mask, and adding a pair of socks to keep my feet from getting cold. I did not want Breda to think I was some kind of finicky, sleepless basket case, which, I suppose, I really am.

Breda seemed to have no trouble at all drifting off to sleep, breathing progressively more deeply and slowly, though in my mind, she could have been faking it, waiting for me to fall asleep so she could take an ice pick to me or at least rifle through my house looking for the real Disner letters. Even if I had just experienced the best sex I could remember, I still did not trust her one hundred percent—but the percentage was at least climbing.

I slowly relaxed as I listened to her breathe. When the breathing turned to stage one of snoring, I relaxed even more, despite the low rumble. I finally fell asleep, thinking about a morning reprise of our sexual ecstasy.

Some time in the middle of the night, I was awakened by movement near the bedroom door. "Who's there?" I blurted out.

"Shhhh" came the reply. I could tell it was Breda, since she had made the same sound just a few hours earlier when she put her finger to my lips.

"What's going on?" I asked.

"I don't know, but I thought I heard noises outside the bedroom window and just now at the front door."

I climbed out of bed and, after pulling on the shorts I had earlier draped over the headboard, stepped past her into the living room, which was slightly more illuminated than the bedroom, since my new neighbor across the street from Florida had installed a street light, I guess because he missed all that sunshine back home.

"Stay still," I whispered, "and I'll try to see if anyone is outside." I attempted not to sound like a comic book hero protecting a damsel in distress while he braved a journey into the siege perilous, particularly since I was way too apprehensive that someone was actually outside.

I tiptoed to the front door and stood listening.

No sound came from just outside, but I thought I heard something from the back door leading into the kitchen, a metallic noise as if someone were inserting a key or a tool into the lock. I shuffled that direction, never picking up my bare feet, thankful that I had not broken any glass in the kitchen lately. Along the way, I picked up the first object available, an unopened jar of orange marmalade my aunt had sent me the previous Christmas, which had been gathering dust on the counter.

Again, I listened at the door.

Again, I heard nothing just outside, but then thought I heard the same key insertion noise at the front door. I retraced my steps to the living room, supplementing the marmalade with a bulky pepper mill I kept on the kitchen table, so that I now felt doubly armed.

However, when I reached the front door, I could hear no sound at all. I began to think that the house itself was conspiring with the intruder, plotting to wear me out so that I would go to bed and thereby allow the killer outside to enter at will while I slumbered soundly from exhaustion.

"What's happening?" Breda whispered.

"I'm not sure. I keep hearing noises at the doors. Did you hear them?"

"No," she answered, "but I did hear something outside the bedroom again. Don't you want to go in the back yard and look?"

I paused for several seconds while I considered my answer. If I said no, I would sound like a coward. If I said yes, I likely would get a bullet in my forehead as a reward for my bravery. Her question struck me as being on a par with did I want to climb into the ape's cage at the zoo.

Finally, I compromised and said, "Let's go back to bed, and I'll set something against the doors to warn us if anyone tries to break in."

To my surprise, she agreed. "Why don't you use that ice bucket that reminded you to take a drink to school tomorrow?"

"Good idea," I said.

"And how about a pan for the back door? Do you have a pizza pan stashed away anywhere?"

"Yes, I do—another good idea." I placed the ice bucket and the pizza pan where they had been resting before her arrival. Then, after listening at the window in my bedroom for a minute or two, I invited Breda back into bed.

The only good thing that came from the scare was that she and I made love again. I probably would not have heard the crash of either the ice bucket or the pizza pan. And the trust factor was up to at least ninety percent by the time we finished.

Chapter 45

Early the next morning, after only an hour or so of real sleep, I was dreaming that I was strapped into an electrocution chair, with leather restraints looped over my arms and around my ankles. Smockley was pacing back and forth in front of me, holding in his hands what looked to be surgical tools. Every so often he would pause and study the tools as if deciding which ones to use on me. Somewhere in the background the theme song from the movie BRAZIL was playing.

"So, you thought you could kill the courier and then escape from Casablanca using the letters of transit, didn't you?"

"Exactly what are letters of transit?" I asked, wondering about the mixing of movies.

"They get you out of one place and into another," he said, toying with a pointed device that resembled one of my dental hygienist's instruments. "Where do you think you're going, anyway? There's no where in the world any better than Casablanca."

"I hadn't planned to leave Casablanca."

"Why not?"

"I like the water here. And besides, I have a woman."

"You must get her out of you mind and learn to love only Big Brother!" he shouted, pulling from somewhere behind me a cage of large rats.

"Exactly who is Big Brother?" I asked, wondering how we switched films yet again.

"The University, of course," he said, as he began banging on the back of my chair with a heavy looking tool that resembled a shoe tree—bam, bam, bam.

I tried to get free to reach behind me with my right arm to stop the noise, but couldn't. But then I began to wake up and discovered that I couldn't reach up with that arm because, in reality, someone was on it. And the noise was real too. Someone was knocking loudly at my front door.

My first reaction when I realized this latter fact was to leap out of bed, but I first had to free my arm. When I tried, it was then that I focused upon Breda, stretched out beside me. I pulled my arm out and then reached over and touched her face just to be doubly sure that she was real and that the previous few hours had not been a dream.

As the pounding on the door continued, she began to stir. Finally, she sat up, holding the sheet to her chest. "What the hell is that? Are you expecting someone at . . . .?"—She paused and looked at my alarm clock beside the bed—"at seven in the morning?"

"No, I most definitely am not," I answered, before adding, "All I want right now is to repeat the best moments from last night."

"I'd like that too," she said, with a softened voice and a smile, "but obviously someone is desperate to see you. Do you have any idea who it is?"

I was just about to answer "no" again when a very distinctive voice gave me an unequivocal idea who it was. "Professor Davidson, I know you're in there. Open up. I need to talk with you—now."

"Damn, it's Smockley!" I said. "I was just having a nightmare about him. It's one thing to have a sound from reality show up in a dream; it's another to have a person from a dream suddenly appear in reality."

"He simply cannot find me here!" she said in a frantic voice. She began pulling covers off her and searching for her clothes, most of which were still in the living room, in the process reminding me how beautiful her body was. Fortunately, due to my still duct-taped drapes and closed blinds, Smockley could not share my viewing pleasure. After snatching up the last pieces of her apparel—her socks—she asked in a low tone, "What are we going to do?"

I thought of one possibility—open a rear window and help Breda out of it—but it would be just like Smockley to have one of his cohorts waiting in back, hoping I might try to beat a retreat. I also thought about ignoring the knocking in hopes Smockley would go away, but Smockley had to know I was there (since my car was in the driveway) and, with warrant in hand, would probably eventually break down the door if I didn't open it. "Why don't you hide in the bathroom while I go talk to him. Go ahead and get dressed so that if he does happen to search around and find you here, you can at least claim that you were in the neighborhood and felt the urge to use the toilet."

She shot me a look that screamed "flimsy story!" but she did go into the bathroom and close the door—taking with her the clothes she had gathered.

Once she was hidden, I made a quick survey of the living room, discovering in the process the cigarette stub Breda had left in the ashtray and her wine glass. I quickly dumped the butt in the kitchen and put the wine glass in the sink, then hurried to the front door, which I opened suddenly, as if I were really hacked that anyone would disturb my rest. "What could you possibly want that you would have to get me up this early, DETECTIVE?" I asked with as much force as I could muster, hoping my bluster would put him on the defensive.

It didn't, partly because I had knocked the ice bucket into the kitchen wall when I opened the door, but mainly because I was standing there naked, the result of my flurrying around to help Breda and forgetting my own state of being.

"Calm down, Professor," he said, stepping in, uninvited. "Do you always sleep that way, or are you just glad to see me?"

"Oh," I said, no longer acting tough, "clothes. I'll be right back." I hustled to my bedroom for a pair of gym shorts and a tee-shirt.

When I returned, now partially dressed, I asked, "What do you want to know, Detective?"

"Among other things, what was that clatter when you opened the door?"

"Oh, it was nothing. I forgot that I had put an ice bucket near the door so I would remember to take a drink with me today."

"I see," he said with a slight smirk. "But why did it take you so long to answer the door. Trying to hide something, were you?"

"Of course, Detective," I answered, regaining a bit of my composure. "I was stuffing the freezer with another body I found. It's been almost fifteen hours since I found Crawford dead, so I was a bit overdue for finding another. Want to check it out?"

"Despite what you think," he said, "you're not funny." Morning had softened Breda's appearance and her voice. It had done nothing for Smockley, whose face looked like a bear trap and whose voice sounded like 20 grit sandpaper.

"Is this visit really necessary?" I asked.

"Yes, I want to know what you were doing in Professor Disner's office."

"Who told you I was there?" I asked, though I knew the answer already.

"Professor Glick called me late last night and informed me of your little visit. What were you after in there?"

"Didn't he explain it all to you? He's very precise about most things, including proper grammar—such as the use of "may" and "can.""

"Don't try to shift things toward me. I want to hear what YOU have to say about being in Professor Disner's office."

"Well, as I'm sure Professor Glick—Do you mind if I just call him plain old Glenn?—as Glenn probably told you, I needed to get some notes in a Shakespeare text I thought Hugh had borrowed."

"How'd you get in?"

"I borrowed the master key from the Departmental secretary. I returned it immediately."

"That's not what Professor Glick said. He said that you were in there twice."

"Oh, right, twice. Yes, you see the first time I went in there, I looked in the wrong book, so, after discovering my mistake, I had to go back. I really had to hustle because the secretary was ready to leave for the day."

"Did you find what you were looking for?"

"You know, actually I didn't. I could have sworn that Hugh had my text and notes. I still haven't found them, but at least I've eliminated the possibility that they were in Hugh's office."

Smockley looked at me for a moment as if I had just told him that elves really did make Keebler cookies. "Why didn't you tell me all this when you were getting off the elevator last night?" he asked.

Last night? Was it only last night I had run into Smockley in my building? It seemed like a week had passed, but I guess spending part of the previous night with Breda had distorted time for me.

"Well, Professor, why didn't you?"

"I guess for the same reason Glenn failed to mention it—because it didn't seem important. I hated to bore you with academic details." Remembering my dream, I had a vision of Smockley suddenly calling in a crew of Fahrenheit 451 "firemen" to search my house for books and then setting fire to the whole place.

He reached in his inner coat pocket for his pad of paper and began writing notes. Then he looked at me and said, "There's no such thing as a boring detail when there's a murder investigation going on." He then looked around the living room. "Anybody else here?"

"No, of course not. What makes you think there is?"

"I can detect smoke odor still in the air, and you told me you don't smoke." He made me wonder if his duties included sniffing luggage at airports.

"Actually, you're just smelling the remains of some matches I struck last night."

"What for?" he asked.

"Well, you see, my neighbor, Mrs. Purdey, dropped by last night and brought her dog, who killed a squirrel and I lit the matches—like you do in the bathroom sometime—to get rid of any lingering odor from the dead squirrel and then I bagged up the squirrel and it's still in the kitchen and you can see it if you want to because it's still there." The song from BRAZIL in my dream started running through my head.

"Slow down, Professor. What was she—or rather they—doing here?"

"I asked her to give me her opinion on color schemes for the house. I plan to repaint soon. I didn't ask the dog for his opinion."

"And when did all this happen? Remember, I was here last night searching your house between seven and eight." Smockley's tone sounded like the one my father used when I tried as a teenage to explain why I arrived home three hours after my curfew.

"It was later than that, when she and the dog were out walking, maybe nine or ten. I can't be sure exactly when."

Smockley sat down on the end of my couch and began writing more notes on his pad. As he jotted, I looked to his right at the end table—Breda's glasses were resting there in plain view! In my haste to remove the cigarette butt and wine glass, I had overlooked them.

Smockley wrote and paused, then wrote some more, before pausing again, letting his eyes roam around the living room. I sat down on the far end of the couch away from the end table, hoping that when he did glance up from his writing, he would look my way.

He didn't. Instead, he looked at the table. "I didn't know you wore glasses, Professor."

"Oh, yes, Detective, I do. I put them on after I take my contacts out at night."

"So, why don't you have them on now? You surely didn't have time to put in your contacts this morning, if, as you say, I woke you up. And if they aren't in, why aren't you wearing the glasses?"

"I just hadn't gotten around to it. Here, let me have them."

Smockley picked up the glasses and handed them to me. "They seem awfully small for you."

"I like them that way," I said, pushing them on, though the temple pieces barely reached my ears. "I hate to feel much weight." Smockley was a blur even though he was only three or four feet away.

Smockley remained silent for a few seconds, making me wonder what expression he was wearing. I imagined it to be a cynical sneer. Finally he said, "What I want you to do is take me through the steps of what happened with you yesterday, beginning with you getting the key to Professor Disner's office and ending with me seeing you get off the elevator. Don't leave out anything."

I described my activities, of course leaving out a sizeable number of "anythings"—including searching Disner's office for the letters, finding them, photocopying them, and giving the copies to Breda. I did tell him everything I could about Crawford. I filled in large gaps of time by claiming that I was grading papers.

The whole time I talked, I was looking through Breda's lens, which had been prescribed for her nearsightedness, making everything appear to me, with a case of farsightedness, like scenes in a movie when someone has been conked on the head. The consequence was that I acquired a raging headache, which gradually translated into a sentence structure and tone better suited to a rant. "THEN, I TOOK THE ELEVATOR DOWN WITH GLENN GLICK, AS I HAVE ALREADY TOLD YOU AND MET YOU, ALL RIGHT, DETECTIVE?"

"Fine, Professor," he said. "That should do it for now, but you didn't have to shout." He stood up and moved toward the front door. As it clicked open, he said, "By the way, I happened to notice the van belonging to the Disners parked down the street. You wouldn't know anything about that, would you?"

"Nope," I said. "Maybe one of the Disner kids knows somebody around here, or Mrs. Disner is doing volunteer work visiting shut-in old people, or she's having breakfast with one of her friends. I guess you'll have to ask her—or the kids when you see them."

"Uh-huh," Smockley said, looking toward my bathroom. "I'll just have to do that, and I'll be keeping an eye on you."

I would have responded that I would also keep an eye on him, but at that moment I could barely keep an eye on anything. He must have sensed that fact, because he said, "You might want to reconsider those glasses you wear, Professor. They don't appear to fit very well."

"They're all right temporarily," I responded. "Like I mentioned earlier, I normally wear my contacts."

I followed him out into the yard, just to authenticate my wearing them, prompting him to say, "You don't need to see me to my car, Professor."

"Oh, I'm just going to check for my newspaper. Thanks to you, I'm wide awake, so as long as I'm up, I might as well have coffee and read about what's happening in the world. I may have missed a body or two in the county."

Hearing no response, I walked to the paper box, which was located in the front left corner of my lot, next to the spot where I kept my trash cans. I almost tripped two or three times, being disoriented by Breda's glasses. As I pulled out the newspaper, a voice I had heard the night before called out, "Good morning, Mr. Davidson."

Though I could not see her, I knew from the direction that it had to be Mrs. Purdey. "Oh, hi, Mrs. Purdey. How's Johnson this morning?"

"Why don't you ask him," she replied. "He's right there next to you on the end of his leash."

I looked down and around me, finally spotting something in motion. "Oh, he looks fine. Hi there, Johnson," I said, hoping I was speaking to the dog and not a paper sack being blown by the wind.

"I'm sorry about the mess last night, Mr. Davidson," Mrs. Purdey hollered. "I'll help you clean up this morning if you'd like."

"Oh, that's all right, Mrs. Purdey. It was nothing. Thanks for coming over and offering your advice on the paint color."

"You're certainly welcome."

"Well, see you later," I said, turning back to my house. Though I could not see him, I hoped Smockley had heard the conversation so that he might actually believe my story about the squirrel and smoke from a match. I heard his door shut and then the car start up. Even if he had not heard the conversation, I was glad he was leaving. I desperately wanted to get Breda's glasses off my head.

Chapter 46

The second I entered the house I did remove the glasses, setting them on the table. I then went to the bathroom door and spoke to Breda. "It's all right now; he's gone."

She opened the door and stepped out, fully clothed, to my disappointment.

"Do you think he knew I was here?" she asked.

"I can't be sure, but I got the feeling he did. Could you hear any of the conversation?"

"Some of it."

"How about when he asked about your van?"

"Yes, I heard that part. How did he take your answer?"

"He seemed suspicious, judging by the way he looked at the bathroom door. And, incidentally, you left your glasses out and he spotted them so I had to pretend they were mine."

"Yes, I heard all that too." She laughed and then said, "I wish I'd actually seen that whole scenario. How did you make them stay on?"

"Pure physics. They're small enough that they squeezed my temples."

"Would you put them back on so I can see how you look?"

"Absolutely not. They've already given me a headache."

"All right, I won't force you to. But what happens now? I really need to get home to check on the kids, but I'd prefer not running into Smockley. You don't reckon he's down at my van, do you?"

"He might be, but it wouldn't really matter as long as he doesn't see you coming out of my house. I for sure don't want him to know that you were here, since I told him no one was."

"What do you suggest then?"

"I know, I'll pull my car to the rear and you can get in. Then I'll drive you to your van. If Smockley's there, you can drop down and I'll take you farther away and leave you. You can walk back to your vehicle as if you had been visiting someone farther away on the street. You don't happen to know anyone around here do you?"

"Besides you, no."

"Maybe say then that you were looking for property or you just wanted to go for a walk and happened to choose this street randomly."

She gave me the same "flimsy story" look, as she had the night before. "I'll work on it," she said. "Now let's check outside and see if Detective Smockley or his cohorts are visible."

We looked through the blinds, seeing no activity except for Mrs. Purdey and Johnson walking up the street. "I'll go move the car," I said, "but first I need to put in my contacts. I'd rather not have to wear my glasses, in case I run into Smockley again, and I certainly don't want to go another round with yours on my head."

"Oh, I don't know," she said. "I'd like to see you drive with mine on."

"Forget it," I replied, heading for the bathroom to put in my contacts.

Once I was in the car, I pulled to the rear and then waited as Breda came out of the kitchen door and got in the passenger-side seat. "Is this all right, or do you think I need to get in the trunk?" she asked with a cynical bite in her voice.

"No, stay there, but be ready to scrunch down if we see anybody." After waiting for Mrs. Purdey and Johnson to get out of sight up the street, I backed out of the driveway and headed in the direction of the van, which Breda said she had left about two hundred yards down the street around a curve.

This curve kept me from seeing her van until I was almost to it, but her vehicle was not the first thing I saw. It was Smockley's car, parked in front of the van on the other side of the street to my left. Smockley was standing between the two vehicles, talking on a cell phone, facing my way.

"You better duck down!" I said, as soon as I saw him. She did, putting her head in my lap. It was too late to turn my car around since I was almost upon Smockley already.

As I approached the vehicle, Smockley spotted me and then motioned for me to stop. "Dammit," I said to Breda, "stay motionless!" I steered the car as far as I could to the right side of the road before stopping, so that my

Subaru tilted away from Smockley. I then rolled down my window halfway and hollered to him, "I need to run to school to retrieve some papers to grade. Can I talk to you when I get back?"

He took a couple of steps toward my car, reaching the edge of the pavement, then cupped his hand over the phone and answered. "Just tell me one thing more. What do you know about the relationship between Mrs. Disner and Crawford?" He took another step, this time into the street.

"Nothing, really," I answered. "Why do you ask?" My voice rose an octave on the word ask, prompted by the fact that Breda had her face buried in my running shorts and had chosen that moment to begin stroking the inside of my right thigh.

"No special reason," he answered, "other than the fact that we have evidence that she had been to his house as many as a dozen times in the weeks leading up to the murder of Professor Disner."

"I'm afraid I don't know anything about that. Now, if you'll excuse me, I've got to run. I'll be back soon." I felt as if I were being questioned by Columbo, who, as usual, had saved a zinger for his last inquiry.

"I'm sure we'll be talking again, Professor. And by the way, where are those cute little glasses?" He took a couple more steps toward me, so that now he was standing on the center stripe of the street—on tiptoes, it appeared to me. Another step or two and he would surely be able to see Breda's feet curled up on the passenger seat. It was one of the few times in my life that I wished I had a SUV, preferably one that sat so high that it tipped over easily in safety tests.

"I put in my contacts," I said, as he took yet another step toward me. "Now, I really have to hurry." I sped off so fast that if Smockley had been a traffic cop, he might have chased me and pulled me over. All I could think about was the fact that, despite Breda's hands and face in a couple of my major erogenous zones, the trust factor had just fallen below fifty percent. When she sat back up and put her hands in her own lap, it fell to about twenty-five percent.

"Want to explain what Smockley just said?" I asked, trying my best to keep an even tone, though I think my voice went up an octave again, this time on the word explain.

"I don't know what he's talking about."

I turned and gazed at her, long enough that the car began to drift so that we were suddenly bumping along on the shoulder of the road, narrowly missing a mailbox one of my neighbors had mounted on an old plow. "Watch the road!" Breda shouted.

Realizing that driving a car while looking at the passenger can only occur in movies, I corrected the steering and slowed down. "Come again," I said.

"I said, 'Watch the road!'"

"No, I was referring to what Smockley said."

"Really, Tyler, I don't know why he said that. I've already told you about the only times I went out there—and why."

About a half mile away from my house, I turned onto a dead end dirt road that crosses my street and drove until I was forced to stop at a fenced in pasture, where six or seven cows lifted their heads from feeding on grass and stared at me the way some of my students did when I digressed into a discussion of Kafka. After stopping, I asked, "Why would he say that, if in fact you hadn't gone there?"

"I have no idea, but he's wrong. It makes me wonder if someone else was out there, someone who looks like me or who drove a van like mine or even who took my actual van."

"Did Hugh ever drive it?"

"Yes, frequently. We argued over his doing that since I had all the kids to attend to, errands to run, stuff like that, and he would leave me the two-door Toyota Corolla and take the van off to school with him being the only person in it, unless of course he was using it as a mobile bedroom to meet his lover in. It's certainly big enough, though he and I never fooled around in it."

I did not know whether to believe her or not, and I was not sure what she could say or do that would help matters. I figured short of making love again, this time in my Subaru, with the cows watching, with Smockley still in the vicinity, my trust factor was not likely to go up, and even with the sex, probably not above fifty percent. I needed more time to think.

"Maybe you ought to hop out and walk back to your van from here," I said.

"All right, but is there something wrong? You seem distracted."

"No, it's fine. I'll talk to you later. Just give me a few minutes to clear out before you head back. Have you thought of what you'll say to Smockley?"

"Yes, I'll tell him that I've been looking in this neighborhood for cheaper housing, now that Hugh's gone."

I probably should have been offended by the Marxist implications of what she said, but I let it slide, mainly because her excuse sounded better than any I had come up with. "All right, but he's likely to grill you about being out so early in the morning."

"So what if he does. I'll just feed him a cliché about the early bird/ worm business. He appears to me to be the type who goes for clichés. I think I can handle our Detective Smockley."

"I'm not so sure. He's shrewder than you might think," I said, amazed with myself that I was actually defending Smockley.

"I'll give it my best try. I can be very persuasive when I want to be."

My problem was that I believed she could be—with me being one of the persuadees.

Chapter 47

After I left Breda, I drove to campus, parked in the lot next to the English building, and waited for approximately ten minutes before heading back home. I never left my car, having no intention of going in my building right then, particularly since my class was still a couple of hours away. While I waited, I must have seen three dozen people wearing hooded sweat jackets, three or four that strode rapidly to my car, before veering off, causing me to grip my steering wheel so tightly that I began to fear that it would look like the one John Candy warps in PLANES, TRAINS, AND AUTOMOBILES.

I drove back to my neighborhood without incident. As I passed the vacant lot near my house, I noticed that both Smockley's car and Breda's van were gone. I wondered about what kind of questions Smockley asked and what kind of answers Breda gave and if Smockley actually believed her.

Mrs. Purdey was in her front yard with Johnson. She waved at me, so after pulling into my driveway, I walked to the edge of my yard and spoke to her. "Hello, Mrs. Purdey. Did you and Johnson have a pleasant walk?"

"Oh, yes, we did. He's such good company. It looks like you've had lots of company yourself this morning."

"Yes, I guess I have," I said, wondering if she had seen Breda climbing in my car.

"Well, you missed one of them, while you were gone."

"What do you mean?"

"A few minutes ago a car pulled up, a different one than before, but then immediately left."

"What kind of car was it?"

"A white one."

"I mean what make or model was it?"

"Like I said, a white one."

"I see." Her answer prompted me to recall the last paper I had graded the night before, written by Cletis Derringer. It was a review of the film LIKE WATER FOR CHOCOLATE, containing non-descript observations that Mrs. Purdey could as easily have made, such as: "This film was supposed to illustrate magic realism and stuff like that, but I didn't find any magic or realism. It had a weak plot and weak characters that showed their weaknesses. I don't think the director achieved what he meant to achieve, so the film was less than an achievement. It just didn't do anything for me" and so on.

Mrs. Purdey obviously did not understand the importance—to me— of details about cars pulling up to my house. I tried to think of what cars I remembered to be white. The long list included most of the cars in the county. The short list was not much shorter than the long list and included the cars belonging to most of the people I knew, including Smockley, Breda, her son, the county school superintendent, Bwanger, Glick, the owner of Jack the Dipper Ice Cream Emporium—the list was endless. Crawford's car had been white, when he was alive, and, I supposed, still was. The only cars with color I knew of right off hand were mine—a bright red—and Sturgeon's—a dark blue.

I asked Mrs. Purdey, "Could you tell me how many doors it had?"

"Let me see," she said. "I was looking at it as it pulled in front of your house and then as it drove off in front of my house. I believe it had two doors.

"Two doors?"

"Yes, a front and a back."

"You mean it had four doors, then."

"Well, I could only see the two doors on the side facing me. I would have needed to be on the other side of the street to count those."

"I understand. By chance, could you see who was driving?"

"Oh, no—the windows were coated with something that made them dark."

"They were tinted then?"

"I wouldn't know about that. They were dark, though. Why do you need to know?"

"I was just curious. I've been expecting . . ., expecting for someone to drop off a package for me. Thanks for the information."

I turned to leave, but I was tempted to ask Mrs. Purdey to tour my house again, with Johnson along, but I figured I could manage the trip into the danger zone by myself this time, since it was a bright, sunny morning.

I first went to my front door and unlocked it, then looked in the living room and dining room as I stayed in the doorway. I next strode around the side of the house to the back door and entered there into the kitchen, making as much noise as a group of bush beaters on a safari, trying to flush out a lion. Seeing nothing in the kitchen, I checked out the rest of house, emboldened by the fact that I was carrying two golf clubs I had pulled out of the bag in the trunk of my car—a putter and a fairway wood, which I figured equipped me for striking an intruder at either close or long range.

I finally felt comfortable about being in the house, enough so that I showered and shaved, after, of course, I locked the front and the back doors. I also took time out to sit on the bed and reminisce about Breda and the night we had spent there.

Of course, thinking about the night in bed led to thoughts of Smockley's banging at the door that morning and interrupting the pleasure I felt being with Breda. Smockley—I wondered what he was doing right at that moment. He was not the type to be sitting at his desk with his feet propped up while he ate a donut. Maybe he was out tormenting some other suspect, like he did me. More than likely he was at Disner's office, combing through potential evidence.

This got me to wondering if I had left any clues to my adventure there—and also if I had overlooked any other letters.

Ah, the letters—what was I going to do with the ones I had already taken? I couldn't give them to Breda, now that I had already given her the photocopies, saying, "Oops, I gave you the wrong ones." She would certainly ask, "Why did you make copies?" and I wouldn't have an answer except to say, "I didn't trust you," an answer sure to lessen the chances of our repeating the night-in-bed scene.

Why not just go ahead and give them to Smockley, but of course I couldn't do that. He most certainly would say, "You're under arrest—for trespassing, obstruction of justice, and withholding evidence." He would probably come up with charges I had never heard of.

I decided right then I needed to return to Disner's office and put the letters back in his HARVARD CLASSICS where I had found them—and let Smockley discover them in due course, if he was smart enough, which I felt confident he was.

But first things first. I realized I hadn't eaten and was growing weak from hunger, so I searched my refrigerator. The best I could do was a three-day-old taco I had left wrapped up. I finished it in five bites, hoping it hadn't been poisoned.

Chapter 48

After a shower and a phone call to Sturgeon—to verify that he was still home—I drove to his house and retrieved the letters. I told him all about the activities of the previous night, except the parts about Breda and me in bed, and then informed him of my decision about the letters. "I hope I'm doing the right thing by putting them back," I told him.

"I believe you are. Just don't get caught," he said.

I rushed from Sturgeon's house to campus, arriving just in time to teach Shakespeare's THE TAMING OF THE SHREW. During the discussion, I kept thinking about Breda—about how good she looked and felt, but also about the possibility that she killed people. I began wondering if Shakespeare considered having Kate kill Petruchio for a truly dramatic effect, maybe after Petruchio rudely leaves his own wedding party early and drags Kate off to his country estate. I could envision a scenario with Breda in which I said, some months after our wedding, in the style of Petruchio, "I will not let you visit your friends and parents unless you swear the sun is the moon and your old Uncle Bill is actually a young girl." Breda, in the same vision, wearing a black hooded jacket, pulls out a gun and shoots me in the forehead.

Wedding! With Breda and me? Would I ever marry her? Probably not. Marriage is supposed to be based upon trust and truth. I have already lied to her, and I suspect she's lied to me. The latter, not the former, is the reason I probably wouldn't marry her. Just because I lied to her doesn't make it right for her to lie to me. To lie WITH me is all right, but not to lie TO me.

Laura Allworth was still the one I wanted to marry, certainly more than the woman she had fretted about, Susan Paradit, the one I dated before going out with Laura and the one I definitely could not marry. I never want to marry someone who believes in a required ten-step progression for sex, starting with removing one's shoes, then socks, then belt, then pants, next shirt, one button at a time, and so on, in the right order or else you have to start over. Nor could I marry someone who would require, through the entire marriage, that I wear a condom every time we had sex, and not for the purposes of birth control.

Laura gave meaning to all the clichés about love that I had heard in sappy songs. She did create a hunger and an endless, aching need; she did leave my soul to bleed; she drowned my tender reed.

Breda was like an older version of Laura, but the main problem with marrying Breda was the fact that she had children, lots of them, all of whom had Hugh Disner's genes in them. And one of her kids was almost as old as the students in my freshman English class, old enough to drink black coffee—and probably lots of harder stuff—and to drive a car.

At the end of the Shakespeare class, I worried about what I had actually said during the fifty minutes or so. It would not have surprised me for one of my students to raise a hand and ask, "Where does a character named Breda appear in the play? There's no one by that name in the dramatis personae in my edition." I guess I could have answered, "Remember 'The Kugglemas Episode' by Woody Allen, in which a modern character suddenly appears in the novel MADAME BOVARY? It's sort of like that."

I was glad when the class finally ended, but then I had to figure out how to get in Disner's office to return the letters.

Obviously, I would need a key to get back in, which meant I would have to go either to the secretary, Yvonda Dunkirk, or to the cleaning lady, Doris McGuire. I started with Yvonda, whom I found sitting in her office cleaning her nails with a letter opener.

"Hi, Ms. Dunkirk. Could I interrupt you for a second?" I leaned on the doorjamb, trying to look casual.

She glanced briefly in my direction, before returning her attention to her hands. "If it's about getting the master key again, forget it."

"Why, what do you mean?" I asked

"I know what you did with it the last time you borrowed it."

"Oh, and what was that?" I straightened up, as if erectness might make me appear more honest.

It didn't work.

"Professor Glick told me that you used the key to enter Professor Disner's office and that I shouldn't let you have it anymore."

"He did, did he?" If I had not already disliked Glick sufficiently, this bit of news would have sealed the deal. "Did he also tell you why I needed to get in Disner's office?"

"Yes, he said you were taking one of Professor Disner's books."

"Didn't he tell you I was looking for one of my own books?"

"No, all he said was you took a book. He also said he didn't trust you."

"Well, you tell Professor Glick that he can take that book and stick it. . . . No, never mind. I'll tell him myself. But I need to get in my own office. I left my keys at home, and I'm in a hurry."

"How'd you manage to get to school then?"

"I jogged today."

"In those clothes?" she asked, looking at my usual school wear of black jeans and a dress shirt—unstained with sweat.

"No, I, well, I keep a set of clothes in a locker at the gym for just such an occasion. I guess the reason I left the keys was because I had on running shorts."

"Well, if that's really the case, follow me. I'll go unlock your office myself." She stood and opened her top desk drawer, whereupon she lifted out the key, still on its huge key ring. I had no choice but to follow her and allow her to open my door, making sure not to jingle the keys in my pocket.

After she returned to her own office, I shut my door and shadow boxed, throwing violent air punches at an imaginary Yvonda—and Glick. I eventually calmed down, but I was still left with the problem of getting into Disner's office. Doris was my only other means.

I would have to wait approximately an hour before she reached Disner's office, if she followed her usual trash pickup routine. In the meantime, I pondered the excuses I could give her for needing to get back into Disner's office, hoping, of course, that Glick had not ordered her to keep me out.

I could tell her that I left something there the time before—say some papers I had with me. I could even grab up some of Disner's if necessary, if she did not look too closely at the name written on them.

Maybe I could claim that retrieving one book of mine from his office reminded me that Disner had borrowed another one that I now needed.

Or perhaps I could say that I wanted to make sure I had not disturbed anything when I was there before.

Any of those excuses might get me IN the office, but how was I going to find time to return the letters to their original locations, with Doris standing there, as I was sure she would be? I would have to figure out some way to get her to leave for a few minutes.

I graded a few papers that I promised I would return the next day, but after forty-five minutes, I figured I better go check to see where she was in her rounds. Carrying the set of papers I was grading, I walked down the hall and turned the corner toward Disner's office. To my horror, she was just about to open Disner's door when I saw her. I realized I would have to play it by ear. The only good news was that the door to Glick's office was closed, meaning that he was most likely gone, since he was extremely public when he was present in his office, much more so than I.

"Doris," I said as I jogged down the hall, "just the person I need to see!"

She eyed me as if she thought I was trying to accost her. "What for?" she asked.

"I need to leave some papers for Detective Smockley."

"Why don't you just give them to him directly," she said, pronouncing the last word as if it were spelled "dreckly."

"I won't see him, but I figure he'll come by here soon. I've seen him up here several times," which was another lie. "You probably have too."

"You aren't here to take something like you did the last time you were in Professor Disner's office, are you?"

"Oh, no, no, no," I said, shaping my mouth into a circle so the words came out like a refrain in a song. "As I said, I'm only here to leave something—for Detective Smockley. See, these papers." I patted the stack of essays I was carrying, keeping the back of the last page toward her.

"I guess it's all right, then." She unlocked the door and headed straight to the trash can to check it. I stood watching her, holding onto the essays. Finding no refuse in the can, she turned to me. "Are you going to leave those papers or not?"

Having no alternative, I placed them on Disner's desk, face down. I had a disturbing vision of being unable to retrieve them and having to face Smockley once he discovered them. He would ask, "How comes it that a set of papers with your name and the current date written on the tops happen to be on Professor Disner's desk?"

"That's a good question, Detective Smockley. I've been wondering what happened to them. I guess I left them somewhere and the person who found them thought they belonged to Professor Disner."

"Why would they think that? He's dead and the papers have your name on them."

"Well, maybe it's because both our last names begin with a 'D.'"

"No, I think it's because you were in here and got careless. You professors are famous for being forgetful. But now it's caught up with you. One of you deputies cuff him and read him his rights."

That all might not happen, but if I couldn't retrieve them, I would still have to face my students the next day, who were expecting me to return their papers.

"Where are our papers you promised?" they would ask.

"I don't have them."

"Why?"

"They got locked up, and I can't get to them."

"Where?"

"In a very private place."

"You didn't grade them, did you? You lied to us. We're going to give you a bad student evaluation at the end of the course."

"I'm leaving now, Professor. Are you finished?" Doris's voice brought me back to the moment.

"Yes, yes, of course. After you," I said, as I bowed and made an exaggerated sweep of my arm, as if I were one of Castiglione's courtiers.

"Doris eyed me as she had when I had first called out to her in the hall, but did actually step into the hall, leaving me to close the door, which I did—after I had turned the center locking mechanism to the unlocked position.

"Here," she said, I need to make sure the door's locked." She reached toward the door.

"Allow me, madam," I said, blocking her. I grabbed the door handle and pretended to twist it as I pushed inward, stopping short of actually turning the handle. "Yep, it's locked all right. We certainly wouldn't want anyone to get in there, would we?" I added another fake twist for good measure.

At that point I figured it would be a good idea to get Doris away from the scene, so I said to her, "Doris, while I've got you, I was wondering if you keep a vacuum on this floor. I really need to clean up some debris in my office."

"Yes, we have one in the utility closet out by the restrooms."

"Could I get it now by chance?"

"I need to finish my rounds, and, besides, I could do the job for you."

"Oh, no, I couldn't make you do that. I'd like to do it myself."

"All right, if you insist. I'll get it in a few minutes."

"It would be a great help if I could get it now. I need to leave soon for a meeting, but if I got the vacuum, I could finish the cleaning before I left."

She stared at me—hard—as if I had just told her that I planned to marry her. "Come on then. You professors are so impatient." She led me to the closet and produced the vacuum. "Just leave it in your office when you're finished," she said.

I rolled it to my office and then left it while I headed back to Disner's office, making sure that I carried the letters with me. I peeked around the corner of his hall, spotting Doris who was about to enter Glick's office just beyond Disner's. Hoping she had not tested Disner's door, I waited until she had finished checking the rest of offices on the hall and was out of sight around the far corner, then hurried to Disner's office.

To my relief the door was still unlocked, and I was able to slip inside without being spotted by Doris.

Chapter 49

I made sure the door was locked and then turned my attention to the shelves. Since I had been in such a rush the last time I was in Disner's office, the first thing I did was to make sure I had not overlooked any volumes that might contain letters, signified by being set out from the rest by a quarter of an inch or so. All I could find were the ones I had previously inspected, which I had left slightly protruding.

My biggest problem was deciding which letters went in which volumes, having been prevented—thanks to Doris and Glick—from writing down that information in my flurry of activity when first removing—i.e., stealing—the letters.

The match between the letters about saving reputations and Volume XVIII containing Sheridan's "The School for Scandal" was easy. So was the match-up of the letters about guilt and going to Hell with the volume including Marlowe's "Dr. Faustus."

I ran into a snag with the letter complaining about Disner's being an overly rational conservative. Did it go in the Descartes volume or the one containing the works of ancient medical practitioners? I finally realized that the latter was the hiding place for the letter in which the writer voiced a concern about transmittable diseases so I inserted the business about Disner's personality in with Descartes.

I also had a problem deciding where to put the letter about Disner's attempts to end the relationship. Did it belong in the pages of Byron's "Youth and Age" or those of Shakespeare's "The Tempest"? I suddenly remembered that it had been housed in the section of "The Odyssey" where Odysseus dumps Calypso.

I did the best I could, working feverishly, finishing just as the bell tower chimed six times and then began to play a truncated version of Beethoven's "Fifth"—the part in which Death comes knocking at the door. "Da-da-da-dum" doesn't sound so formidable when played in slow motion, but the piece still seemed to fit the occasion.

I stepped to the door, but not before giving the office a last, quick once-over, checking to see if I had inadvertently left any evidence of my having been there—student papers, grade book, keys, shoes, all of which were items I had misplaced on recent occasions.

After retrieving the essays I had laid on Disner's desk to fool Doris, I replaced them with some I found on one of Disner's shelves, setting aside for the moment my concern that Smockley would wonder how they got there. I was just on the verge of a fantasy about another confrontation with him when I heard the door handle being turned—three or four times in quick succession, as if someone were testing to see if were locked. My first reaction was to slide to the door hinge side in hopes that if someone did come in suddenly, I would at least be hidden by the door.

Whoever it was did not go farther—maybe because he or she didn't have the key.

Was it Doris, making a final check on the offices she had cleaned up, paying particular attention to Disner's door since I had been the one who supposedly locked it? I felt slightly offended that she would not trust me, but then, again, she was perfectly within her rights not to. I could not exactly fling open the door and shout at her—if indeed she were the one outside—"What do you want, Doris? Can't you see that I'm busy messing with police evidence!" But the thought did cross my mind.

Was it Smockley? No, he would have a key and would come right on in, unless he lost the one the University supplied him for his investigation, something I highly doubted. Smockley never misplaced anything.

I stood behind the door, listening, hoping whoever was out there would leave, but I could tell that someone was still out there, clothes rustling, snortled breathing, a couple of bumps against the door. I wondered if the person were listening on the other side for sounds from my side—the two of us forming a mirror image separated only by the door. I tried to be as quiet as possible, hoping I would not sneeze, burp, develop a hole in my pockets, allowing my keys to crash to the floor, or make any other detectable noise.

I was beginning to think the person had left when suddenly there was another attempt to turn the door handle. Did the person think that repeated tries would make the door give in and say in effect, "All right, you win. I'm going to unlock myself now? Come on in."

I waited some more—at least half an hour, the passing of time revealed to me by the bell tower, which, after clanging one note for the half hour, began playing "Old Man River."

After the last dying notes, I listened even more intently at the door, but heard nothing. I risked making some noise and got down on the floor, trying not to move so quickly that my joints popped. I then peered out under the door to see if I could spot the bottom of a pair of shoes or detect any movement.

I didn't.

After another fifteen minutes or so, I finally got up the nerve to open the door—trying hard to keep clicks and cracking noises to a minimum, the whole time thinking I might be better off if I held a weapon—something like the pineapple I had picked up at home the night Breda showed up.

No one was outside the door, so I stepped out and quickly pulled the locked door behind me. I still had my hand on the door handle when Doris stepped around the corner, almost as if she had been lurking just out of sight until I appeared.

"Professor Davidson, what do you think you're doing?"

I briefly contemplated telling her I was doing isometric exercises and had randomly chosen Disner's door as my immovable force, but instead said, "Oh, I was just testing the door to make sure I had locked it earlier. One can never be too careful, I always say. It's sort of like going back to check on the stove even though you know you turned it off."

She stared at me as if I had used a simile involving checking on the lit fuse of a bomb, cocking her head to the side, raising her eyebrows, opening her mouth as if she were going to speak, but didn't. Her actions made me wonder how many times you could lie to someone without that person balking and calling you a liar. I suspected I was at or near the limit with Doris. I drew comfort from the fact that Disner had lied more than I ever could—at least before he was murdered. I guessed that he had given up the practice since then. Dead men tell no lies.

Hoping to distract her, I asked, "Did you also test it?"

"No, I took your word for it that it was locked."

"It was indeed locked. See, it still is." I twisted the knob again, not having to fake my actions this time.

"Uh huh," was all she said.

Ignoring her continued glare, I started down the hall toward my own office, but I was brought to a halt by her voice. "Aren't you forgetting something, Professor?"

I came way too close to answering, "No, I put all the letters back into the HARVARD CLASSICS," but I recovered quickly enough to say, "Forget something? I don't think so."

"The vacuum cleaner, you forgot the vacuum cleaner that you used in your office," she said with a touch of impatience.

"Of course, the vacuum cleaner, I'll get it right now."

"I'll come with you. I need it right away to clean the faculty lounge. You professors are so messy with your snacks."

"No, I'll meet you there with it. That's the least I can do." I definitely did not want her to come by office and see that I had not used it. "See, I'm on my way." I half ran to my office, retrieving the vacuum in a matter of seconds. I thought about going ahead and using it, but I knew Doris would hear it all the way down the hall, so I simply rolled it to the faculty lounge, where, to my relief, Doris was waiting for it.

Chapter 50

My work was not done once I returned to my office, since I still had to make it look as if I had vacuumed my carpet, in case Doris came by again. I spent the next twenty minutes or so picking up by hand tiny particles of lint, dirt, and paper (much of which looked like confetti, but which actually consisted of the fuzzies that had been stuck to the edges of notebook paper students had torn out of their spiral notebooks and left hanging for me to contend with). The whole time I worked I was cursing Breda for directly or indirectly causing me so much trouble.

While I was finishing the task, still on all fours, the phone rang. It was Smockley calling. "Professor Davidson, I'm glad I caught you."

Caught me! Did he know I had been in Disner's office again, returning the letters? Had he been spying on me? Had he deputized Doris, who had reported my activities to him immediately?

I tried to act dense. "Caught me, what on earth do you mean?"

"All I meant was I'm glad I caught you in your office." There was a pause, as if he was trying to figure me out, but then he went on. "There have been some new developments in the two murder cases that you've played a part in. I want you to stay in your office, with the door locked until I can get there."

"What's going on?" I asked in alarm. "Why do I need to stay here?"

"I'll explain it when I get there. Just sit tight."

Unsure exactly how one "sits tight"— buns squeezed together, maybe—I said, "All right, but make it fast because I've got appointments for a pedicure and a manicure." Again he paused before eventually signing off. I guess he didn't think I was funny.

As soon as I hung up, I began speculating on why it was so urgent for him to meet me. Had he discovered evidence that incriminated me? Was it possible Smockley knew more about my activities than even I knew? Why did he want me to keep the door locked? Did he think I was in danger?

I decided to fill the minutes of waiting by picking clean more of the detritus on my carpet. I began to identify with monkeys searching for parasites on each other.

Still on the floor I suddenly heard a key being inserted into my door. Sure that it must be Doris, I tried to spring up so that she would not catch me in the act of carpet cleaning.

But it wasn't Doris. It was Glick. He was as surprised as I was. "What are you doing here?" he asked.

"Shouldn't the question be what are YOU doing here. It's my office. And how did you get a key for it?"

"You're not the only one that can borrow keys, you know. I got this one from the clean-up lady, who's vacuuming the faculty lounge as we speak."

"But what are you doing in my office?"

"I've come to look again for those letters you took from Hugh Disner's office."

"What letters?"

"Let's don't waste time, Tyler. You know which ones I'm talking about, and I know you've got them. Remember, I was there with the cleaning lady when you broke into his office. Your excuse about searching for a textbook was pretty flimsy."

"How did you know about the letters?"

"The person who wrote them told me about them—and their contents. But I couldn't find them in here. I looked last night after you left. I also searched your house and your car today. I've now concluded that you've been carrying them around with you. I decided to look in your office again in case you left them here today. If I didn't find them, I was going to your house to confront you head on. But, you're here, so let's have them."

"I'll consider it, if you tell me who wrote them."

Glick stood in the doorway for a moment. I thought about trying to knock him out of the way and bolting from my office. He must have read my mind, because he came on in and shut the door.

Finally, he spoke. "My daughter, Deidre, wrote them. She was Hugh's lover. He told her he kept them in the office when she expressed concern about them showing up in public. He was trying to reassure her that no one would see them."

"When did you find out all of this?"

"Just recently. For a long while she kept everything a secret, but after Hugh was killed, I noticed she was acting very strangely. She seemed to be a lot sadder than she should have been over the death of one of my colleagues. I tried to get her to talk about it, but she wouldn't, at least not until this week."

"Why this week?"

"She saw Hugh's widow in the grocery store with one of Hugh's children. It really bothered her, set her to thinking how Mrs. Disner would feel if she discovered the letters. She finally told me all about it—said that the letters were very explicit about her feelings, but you probably already know that. I didn't like what had happened between her and Hugh, but I told her I'd get the letters."

Knowing how conservative Glick was, I figured all of this must really be difficult for him. I tried to be sensitive. "Did your daughter kill Disner?"

"Absolutely not."

"Did you?"

"No, of course not. I just want to keep our family out of this sordid business as much as I can."

"It seems like you're not the only one who thinks that way," I said, as I thought about Breda and Bwanger. "All right, so I took them. What now?

"So now you give them to me." He reached in his pocket and pulled out a gun. It would not have surprised me if he had aimed it at my feet and said, "Let's see you dance, Mister." I'm no expert on weaponry, but it didn't look like a .38, which Smockley had said was used on Disner and Crawford. This one looked more like a cigarette lighter than a gun, but I was not about to take a chance. Images of holes in heads came to me. "I'll do whatever is necessary to get them back for Deidre," he said.

"I don't have them anymore," I answered. "I returned them to Disner's office. They're in several volumes of the HARVARD CLASSICS. I didn't figure I needed to tell him about the photocopies.

"How about photocopies?" he asked. "I bet that's why you were in the copier room."

"Photocopies! Why would I want photocopies? No, I really did have to copy my students' papers. I would have no use for photocopies of the letters." To change the subject, I added, "And by the way, if you thought

I had the letters, why didn't you try to get them directly from me last night?"

"I did try, but I first had to make sure they weren't in Hugh's office. After I got off the elevator with you—and ran into that detective—I circled around the building and returned to the top floor, where I found the clean-up lady and got her key. She obviously trusts me. After I checked Hugh's office and found the letters missing, I checked your office, using the same key, then I drove out to your house, but there was a swarm of policemen out there. So I waited until they were all gone and your car was there, actually during the middle of the night, but then you obviously had a guest. Sounded like the two of you were having quite a time—Mrs. Disner, if I'm not mistaken. Did you show them to her?"

"No," I lied. "Hugh had told her about them. She wanted them for the same reason your daughter and you did—to keep them out of the public eye. In fact, she wanted to get them and burn 'em. I told her I couldn't find them."

"Why?"

"I don't know, cold feet, guilty conscience, whatever. I hated the thought of destroying evidence that might lead Detective Smockley to the killer."

"Well, there's no point our talking about it any longer. I'm going to take the clean-up lady's key and pay another visit to Hugh's office. The letters better be there or you'll be in big trouble, buster."

That's about what I would expect Glick to say. He and Disner must have taken the same course in college, "Cliches and Other Repetitions."

"And don't try to tell that detective about me and the letters. If you do, I'll have to tell him about your own little visits to Hugh's office also and about you and Mrs. Disner. I'm sure he'd love to hear about that." I half expected him to lay his index finger alongside his nose and give a flip signifying hush-hush, like the British do. At least he didn't make more of an issue about the photocopies.

He opened the door and left. I wondered if he would run into someone in the hall before he pocketed the gun. I also wondered if Smockley would show up while Glick was still in Disner's office. I shut the door and tried to sort out my thoughts.

I was just coming to the realization that it was not a good thing to be cooped up in my office while Glick was in the building carrying Doris's keys. Despite Smockley's order for me to "sit tight," I wanted out of there. But before I could leave, a strange thing happened. Someone was trying to turn the locked door handle—without using a key. "Glick, is that you again?" I asked.

No one answered, but the sound of a twisting door handle repeated itself. "Doris, is that you?"

Again, no one answered.

I looked around for something to arm myself with, but discovered I had even fewer items in my office than in my house, which would serve for defense—no pineapple, no ashtrays, no ice buckets, pizza pans. All I had was a bust of Shakespeare and some cumbersome text books. I picked up the bust and held it by its legs. The end with the head and cavalier hat looked heavier. I then waited, wishing I were somewhere else.

Fifteen minutes went by with no reoccurrence of the twisting sound. But then someone inserted a key. I figured it was Glick coming back, so I cocked Shakespeare to deliver a blow—if indeed it was Glick and he still had his gun out.

But it wasn't Glick. It was Doris, who yelped when she saw me poised as if I were going to drive her into the linoleum outside the doorway. "Don't hit me," she screeched.

"Oh, Doris, it's you. I . . . I was just . . . I was just putting away this statue. What can I do for you?" It was obvious that Glick had given back her keys.

"I came to pick up your papers for recycling. Do you have any?" Her voice quaked and she gazed at me as if she thought I had gone completely mad. But I also caught her glancing at my carpet, as if she were checking to see if I had actually vacuumed it.

"No, I don't have any today," I answered with a harsh tone. I started to close the door, but then an idea struck me. "Doris," I said, "I need to point out a problem down on the first floor, which you need to tend to."

"What is it?" she asked.

"Someone spilled something. People coming in might slip on it and get hurt. Here, come with me and I'll show you. We can take the elevator down. I'll just close up my office."

As we walked to the elevator, I chastised myself for again using a woman to skirt around a potentially dangerous situation, but I didn't chastise too forcefully. I just wished that Doris also had a dog.

My immediate problem upon reaching the first floor was to find a spot where it looked like someone had spilled something. I finally settled on a faded stain about three inches square that looked like dried coffee. It was in no way a slippery threat. "I guess the person who spilled it partially cleaned it up," I said. "Better to be safe than sorry, don't you agree?"

She looked at me as if she would never agree with anything I said again. I started to thank her for being a temporary escort service, but I didn't think she would understand. I left as quickly as I could, figuring Glick must have found the letters in Disner's office.

Chapter 51

Compared to the odor of threat in my building, the night air outside smelled good, though in reality it had problems of its own—mainly the pollution caused by the glut of cars on the move around campus. Did college students still cruise at night like they did in high school, making the lot next to my building and Campus Drive versions of Main Street, Home Town, USA? I half expected to see Ron Howard and Richard Dreyfus in a Chevy Impala and hear Wolfman Jack on a car radio.

But then I actually welcomed the traffic, seeing it as another kind of escort service, taking up where Mrs. Purdey and Doris left off. I felt safe enough to head for my car, parked at the far end of the lot.

Halfway across I came upon Glick's Buick. It's hard not to identify it, with an oversized decal in the rear window announcing membership in the Big Panther Club and the clincher, his license plate with the letters NGUGLICK.

I started to cut through beside it but was blocked by the wide-open driver's side door. Glick's left leg was still outside the car, his shoe resting on the pavement, canted a bit toward the inside. I wondered if he were reading Disner's letters.

Should I say "Excuse me, Glick" and force him to shut the door? He might pull out that ridiculous pistol and point it at me.

Should I simply back up and try a different route to my car? He might have already seen me since I was no more than three feet from him.

I decided to speak to him. "Glenn, did you get the letters?"

His lack of a response suggested that he had not spotted me. I started backing up, but something was not right. Glenn was a blockhead, but he wasn't deaf, plus I couldn't see a silhouette of his upper body through the side window. I moved forward and spoke again. "Glenn, did you find the letters?"

Still no answer, so I looked inside. Glick was slumped to his right against the center console, his head nearly resting on the passenger seat.

In his left temple was a hole—roughly the same as those I saw in Disner and Crawford. I reached in and tried to feel for a pulse on the side of his neck and then on his wrist. I've never been good at finding a pulse, even my own, so I was not immediately sure Glick was dead.

However, one look at his eyes—wide open and staring at nothing—like Disner's had been—convinced me he was a goner.

I don't know if the familiarity of the scene influenced me or if some other perversion set in, but my first thought was that there now was a tie between the number of lovers I had enjoyed while employed at NGU and the number of murder victims I had discovered.

Did this mean that if I took another lover, I would find yet another body? I guess it wouldn't be all that bad if the lover were that new beauty who recently joined the History Department and the dead person were Bwanger or President Popson.

But back to the problem at hand. I suddenly felt that I had to get out of there— quickly. But where to go?

I didn't want to go back into the building. Disner was murdered in that place.

I didn't want to get in my car. Glick had just been murdered in a car—his Buick.

And I didn't want to go home—for two major reasons. Crawford had been killed in his home, and, besides, I would have to get in my car to get there. And how was I to know the killer wasn't waiting there for me?

Where was there a safe zone, a place where no one had been murdered lately?

I didn't think anybody had been killed in the girls' dorm, but how would I explain my lurking in the halls?

I thought about the gym, where the worst thing that had happened was a scuffle or two between rival fraternity members playing against each other in pick-up basketball games.

I also thought about the University Center, where the only negative was loud noises from arcade games and wannabe musicians, hoping for an audience from passers-by, like aspirants in New York City or London.

There were fewer people in the UC. I opted for the gym.

Chapter 52

As soon as I entered the hall outside the gym, I used the free phone, hanging on the wall ("Local calls only"), to dial 911. I thought about calling the sheriff's office directly, since I had the number memorized, but I figured they would patch me through directly to Smockley.

"What now?" he would say.

"I think Professor Glick has been murdered."

"Where?"

"In the parking lot outside our building."

"What were you doing out there?"

"Leaving."

"I thought I told you to stay put in your office until I got there."

"I got nervous."

"Of course you did. You knew I was coming."

"No—that's not it. I . . . ."

"You what?"

"I just needed to get out of there."

"So you could go outside and kill Professor Glick?"

"No, like I said, I only found him. I didn't kill him."

"At this point, it doesn't matter if you killed him or not. Ben Franklin said that three moves equal your house catching fire. In my book, finding three bodies equals killing at least one person. Three strikes and you're out. You're going down, Davidson."

In reality I got the 911 operator, the only trouble being that she sounded like someone belonging in an ad for breakfast cereal, the puffy kind that kids like—cheerful and upbeat. "What do you need to report?"

she asked in a singsong voice that made me half expect her to follow up her question with a jingle.

"A potential murder."

"Do you mean that someone is about to be murdered, or do you think someone is dead and might have been murdered?"

"The latter."

"Please give me your name, sir, and the location of this occurrence, as well as details about the victim."

I hesitated telling her my name, but I realized that Smockley would probably listen to the recording of my call and recognize my voice anyway. "Tyler Davidson and the victim is a Professor Glenn Glick. He's in his car in the parking lot next to the bell tower in the center of the campus at NGU. It looks like he's been shot." I would have added a couple of specifics about the size of the hole and the location of the wound, but relaying gory information to the person on the other end of the line would be, in my mind, roughly equivalent to showing a George Romeros film to my six-year-old niece.

"We're sending an ambulance."

"I don't think that's going to help Professor Glick, but fire away . . . , I mean, go ahead and do that."

I hung up and entered the main part of the gym. My expectation of a crowd there proved to be well-founded. There were two full-court pick-up games in progress (played side to side in the gym), with lots of by-standers waiting to play the winners.

I sat down on the floor against a concrete wall and watched the games for a while. Despite having my back against the wall, which rose some forty feet and extended approximately fifty feet to each side of me, I kept looking over my shoulder, as if the triple killer might suddenly emerge from the wall, bulging out momentarily before breaking through, like Freddy Kreuger. The smell of sweat should have comforted me, but it combined with the smell of fear that had returned to me the moment I discovered Glick lopped over sideways in his car. I could taste the taco I had eaten much earlier, bubbling up as if I had a bad case of acid reflux.

I slowly calmed myself by watching the players in the games and observing how they served as microcosms of the students I had come to know in classes—some constantly on the move, some lagging behind on each exchange, hoping they wouldn't have to play defense, some showing off, hot-dogging with flamboyant but mostly ineffective shots or passes, some clumsy, some quite proficient.

But these thoughts led me back to the cast of characters in my murder-filled reality, and I began to wonder how Disner, Glick, Smockley, Crawford, and Breda would fit into the scene before me. Disner would be the dopey player I watched, who chattered the whole game, repeating "I'm open, I'm open." Glick would be the guy I saw playing in a designer knit shirt over a t-shirt, who seemed to run up and down the sideline, never really mixing it up in the center lane. Smockley would definitely be the guard that took charge, directing the offense and playing solid defense, blocking a couple of shots and stealing the ball from inept neophytes. I didn't know enough about Crawford to put him in the game—maybe the player with big hands, who looked adept, but did very little to further the cause of his team. Breda was the lone female in the gym, who was shooting on a side basket by herself.

At that moment, I was probably the player watching from the sideline, waiting for a future game.

As I sat, I also wondered what was taking place in the parking lot near my building. Had the emergency team arrived and tried to revive Glick? Was he in fact actually dead? Was Smockley sniffing around Glick's car, searching for clues that would implicate me? Was he looking for me at that very moment? Should I have gone back out there as soon as I had hung up after the 911 call?

And what did Glick have in common with Disner and Crawford? Who would kill all three of them—other than a eugenist with good taste?

The longer I sat, the more nervous I became, prompting digestive and urinary problems. I developed a very strong urge to go to the toilet, but I kept fighting the need as I thought about finding Disner dead in the one in my building. But then I figured that the one in the gym would be a lot safer, since it was in the locker room, which was usually filled with sweaty players preparing to shower. So I crossed the hall and pushed open the heavy door leading into the locker room.

The place itself seemed almost subterranean with mist in the air and a clamminess which had settled on all exposed surfaces, including the benches and, as I discovered, the toilet seats. But the place also reminded me of the boiler room of an old high school, the site of half the scenes in horror movies, with lots of overhead pipes, suspended by wires from the ceiling, valves, and a cacophony of hisses and clangs from expansion of metal. The sounds were complemented by an array of macabre visuals, including hanging towels and gym clothes—wet t-shirts, shorts, jock straps—reminding me of another gothic element in horror movies, old chandeliers.

What was missing from the scene was the crowd of fatigued students I had counted on. The room was deserted, except for one kid who had just stepped out of the shower, but even he was gone almost immediately, miraculously drying off and dressing in less than a minute.

Also missing were any sounds coming from the gym where all the action was taking place, prevented from reaching my ears by the heavy door I had just come through. I realized that if I could not hear those noises, any noise I might make would not be heard on the gym side of the door.

Still, I needed badly to use the toilet, so I entered the first stall, being a bit superstitious about stall number three, the one Disner had chosen in my building.

I immediately discovered that there was no toilet paper in stall number one, so I moved to the second one, which I discovered to have a clogged toilet.

I then moved to number four, not even checking number three. The first thing I had to do there was dry the seat, a task made slightly difficult by the fact that the paper itself was damp.

Chapter 53

After drying the seat, I latched the door and sat down on the toilet, only to discover that the seat was loose, making my visit roughly akin to sledding down a hill on a garbage can top, but I wasn't about to move to another stall.

I hadn't been there more than a half a minute when I heard footsteps, which came, stopped, and then retreated, with what sounded to be hard-soled street shoes. These sounds were followed within another minute by the softer noises made by basketball or running shoes. Whoever was wearing these shoes paused for fully thirty seconds outside the stalls, as if choosing carefully which one to enter. Did people actually select toilets by the strength of their bodily urges, picking stall number one when needing to really go, or number four on a light day?

Or was this person trying to figure out how best to get at me? I was beginning to feel betrayed by my own body, which demanded that I be in the toilet in the first place.

Finally, the unknown visitor entered the stall next to me, the third one, prompting me to think back to Disner's murder and speculate that Disner's killer might have sat for a few moments in the adjacent stall before killing Disner. I was further disturbed by the fact that I didn't hear the latch on the stall door click shut. But I did hear another kind of click, which in my state of alarm became the sound of a gun being cocked.

I nervously finished my business, repeatedly looking up to see if the occupant next door was peering over the top of the wall at me. I wondered if Disner's killer had peeked over the wall at him and popped him in the forehead the moment old Hugh looked up.

But I was reluctant to leave, envisioning the door still open in the adjoining stall, as if the occupant were just waiting for me to exit. I waiting and listened, finally becoming so exasperated—and curious—that I ventured to see who was there. As carefully as I could—given the looseness—I stepped up on the toilet seat and slowly rose, my head, I'm sure, appearing as if it were the sun climbing above the eastern horizon.

When my eyes finally cleared the top edge, I looked down—only to see the top of a shaven head of a young man I didn't recognize, dressed in gym clothes, the shorts of which were around his ankles. He was holding a cell phone, on which he was texting some kind of message. My gasp of surprise caught his attention, and he jerked his head up at me. "What the hell are ya doin' you pervert!" he screeched.

I was left with the impossible task of justifying my actions. I really didn't believe "I thought you were someone else" would be appropriate, or even, "I ran out of toilet paper and was checking to see if you had any." I certainly didn't want to say "I thought you were out to kill me."

All I could come up with was "Sorry!" which I uttered as I stumbled off the loose seat and bolted from the stall, hoping like hell he had not recognized me.

From there I ran back to the gym and reclaimed my spot on the floor against the wall, where I sat trembling for several minutes. Eventually I calmed myself enough to mull over what had just happened—which was essentially nothing, unless one counts risking a charge of voyeurism, which could be added to several other potential charges against me, including trespass, theft, lying to the law, and semi-adultery with Breda. I was beginning to believe I could end up in several circles I describe in DAVIDSON'S HELL, not to mention Dante's "Inferno."

Why hadn't that guy shut his door? And why had Disner's door been open on the day he was murdered? Had Disner opened it for someone familiar to him? Who would have qualified to be that familiar? Breda? But why would she have ventured into the men's room, unless of course her sole purpose had been to plug her husband.

I doubted if Disner would have opened the door for Glick or Crawford, and besides, they were dead now and probably no longer could be considered suspects in Disner's murder.

How about Bwanger? Nope, he's too weak to hold a gun, much less fire it with a steady hand.

I was just beginning to consider Smockley when my thoughts were interrupted by a kid wearing gym shorts and a tee-shirt, holding a bottle of an orange sports drink. It was William Disner, Hugh and Breda's oldest son. He took a long swig before speaking, slopping it over his chin and down onto his shirt like the celebrities do in ads. "Hello, Doctor Davidson," he said. "What are you doing here in the gym?"

"Just watching some of the pick-up games," I answered, surprised that he would know my name. "How about you?"

"Oh just playing some b-ball, you, know, shooting some hoops."

"How'd you do?"

"I was hitting pretty well, but I'm really worn out. I've been here for a couple of hours, okay."

"I see," I answered, recognizing that William truly was a product of his old man.

But I really did not see, since there were a couple things not quite right. For one, he was not sweating in the least, and something else—he was wearing a pair of street shoes, leather looking loafers, with hard soles.

"How much longer do you plan to stick around?" he asked.

"Oh, I don't know, a few more minutes maybe. Why do you want to know?"

"I need a ride home and thought maybe you could give me a lift."

"Don't you have a car?"

"Yes, but it's at home. I got a ride here with a friend."

"Gee, I don't know. I'm . . . . "

"It's not too far out of your way."

"I realize that, but . . . . How about your mom, couldn't she pick you up?"

"No, I called her, and she said she couldn't leave my brothers and sisters. I told her that I saw you here and she told me to ask if you'd do it."

"Well, you see, I was planning to . . . planning to . . . ."

Before I could finish, he interjected, "If you take me, you could see my mother if you wanted to."

"What, what do you . . . do you mean?" I stammered.

"Aren't you friends with my mom?'

"Well, yes, in a way, I guess."

"Well, then, it's settled. Just let me know when you're ready. I'll be sitting right over there." He pointed to a spot approximately fifty feet from where I sat and then, before I could object, made his way to it, high stepping as if he were in a marching band—or in one of Hitler's youth groups.

I was left wondering just how much he knew about the relationship between Breda and me. Did he know that we had slept together? Did he know about the letters?

I pretended to watch the games for several minutes, being in no hurry to get to my car and risk running into Smockley, who no doubt was still examining the crime scene at Glick's car. I was half hoping William would grow tired of waiting and seek another means of transportation home, but a couple of glances his way proved otherwise. He remained seated, staring at me, a half grin on his face.

Finally I knew I had to make some kind of decision. I had three options, it appeared. I could stay seated and watch basketball games until the custodians told everyone to leave and then turned off the lights, at which point I would still have to deal with William but possibly NOT Smockley. I could tell William I had to do some work in my office and suggest he find another ride, a move that would probably upset Breda if William had in fact talked to her and a move that would carry me back to a place that was second only to the parking lot where Glick lay dead on my list of undesirable locations. Or I could go ahead and drive William to his house right then, but such a move would entail finding a way to avoid Smockley.

I finally hit upon a solution that would cover a couple of problems at once. I signaled to William to join me, which he did immediately. "William," I said, "I need to use the men's room before we leave. Since you drive, why don't you go get my car and bring it over here to the gym."

"You mean actually drive your car? You've got to be kidding."

"Nope, never been more serious." I handed him my car key. "It's a red Subaru parked near the exit to the lot next to the English building."

"Okay, then. I'll be right back with it." He seemed overjoyed, a reaction I attributed to the fact that he was still in his first year of driving.

Chapter 54

As soon as he was gone, I stationed myself in what I considered to be a safe spot just inside the front doors of the gym, where a steady stream of fatigued players was exiting and where I could see William when he pulled up with my car. I figured he would need five minutes at the most.

Five minutes crept by, then ten, then twenty with no sign of William or my Subaru. Did the little creep steal my car? Was he out joy-riding at that very moment?

A glance at the printed schedule taped to the door informed me that the gym would close at 9 pm. It was five of. As if to confirm the time, the bell tower began playing a version of "Don't Fear the Reaper." It needed more cow bell. I needed to make a decision.

I could slip into the locker room and hide in a toilet stall, standing on the seat so I would go undetected, but what if William showed up with my car and he couldn't get in the gym to find me? Plus the clean-up crew would probably discover me and report me to the police. What would they report—that I was planning to steal toilets, sinks, shower heads?

I could go back to my building and hide in my office, but I knew I'd probably have a heart attack sitting there wondering if someone had a master key and was coming for me. After all, both Glick and I had gotten hold of one.

I could go to the parking lot and check on my car, but of course I'd most likely run into Smockley. Verbally sparring with him would be about as desirable as attending a retreat for improving pedagogy. I started to imagine our conversation, but right then I wasn't up to even a hypothetical dialogue.

Which would be the safest choice? Despite my dread, I elected to take my chances with Smockley. If William had taken my car, I probably could get a ride home with the detective. I was sure he would enjoy grilling me, while I was trapped in his car. I ventured out of the gym and, after failing to see William or my car in the lot outside, headed for the spot where I had parked earlier.

The second I arrived, Smockley spotted me and trotted in my direction. I expected him to draw a gun and tell a deputy to cuff me, but he simply asked, "Where the hell have you been? You called in about Glick an hour ago."

"I've been hiding in the gym."

"From the law?"

"No, from whoever killed Glick—and for all I know Disner and Crawford too. The gym seemed to be the safest spot for the time being."

"Can you tell me why William Disner was trying to get in your car?"

"I was going to give him a ride home."

"But he was opening the driver's side door."

"Oh, that's because I told him to get the car while I used the men's room in the gym."

"Let me get this straight. You found Professor Glick dead in his car, and you called it into the dispatcher. You went to the gym, met this Disner kid, and then sent him to get your car?"

"Right."

"All the while knowing that a colleague lay dead in the parking lot?"

"I guess so."

"You certainly must not have much feeling for your co-workers."

"Well, I was a bit scared."

"Scared or not, you seem to have a knack for making yourself look guilty."

"Sorry. By the way, did anyone else report Glick's body?"

"Nope."

"Why not, you suppose? Surely someone saw him slumped over."

"It's been my experience that most people block out anything unpleasant, like dead bodies, except you, of course. You seem to have made a career of finding them."

"Is Glick still in his car?"

"Yes, we're not finished investigating the scene. Maybe we'll find a link tying you to his murder."

"I'm confident you won't."

"Speaking of finding things, before I forget, here's the key to your car."

"How did you get it?"

"It was in your car door. The Disner kid left it."

"Where is he now?"

"I don't know. He took off running."

"From you, the LAW?"

"Yes, when I saw him opening your car, I hollered to him, and he ran. I chased him around your building but lost him. He's pretty fast. We've got an APB out on him right now."

"Why did you do that? I gave him the key to my car. He wasn't stealing it."

"We suspect that he has obstructed the investigation of his father's murder and may be involved even more deeply."

"What evidence do you have?"

"I can't disclose that right now, but we know that he ransacked his father's office. We think he was looking for some letters that were sent to Professor Disner. We're convinced they are the key to all three murders. You don't happen to know anything about them, do you?"

"'Fraid not." I was surprised by my own continued loyalty to Breda.

"It seems that those letters are really important to someone, most likely the murderer. Anybody who knows about them is in danger. On the chance that you might know something about them, I called you to make you stay put until I could warn you."

"Thanks, I wish I could help you."

"Me too. At any rate, you're probably lucky you didn't end up in your car alone with William Disner. Now give me the details about finding Professor Glick in his car and all the events leading up to, including why you didn't do what I told you about staying in your office."

Over the next several minutes I did mostly as he asked, telling him about Glick's visit to my office, with a gun, but I changed the story a bit and said that I didn't have the letters that Glick wanted, so that he left, I assumed, to go find them in Disner's office. How he got in the office and if he retrieved the letters, I claimed I didn't know.

Smockley listened intently, writing an occasional note in his pad. Finally, he said, "We didn't find any letters on Professor Glick. Are you sure you've told me everything?"

"Why would I lie?"

"I can name several reasons, one being that you're trying to protect Mrs. Disner."

"Oh, come on. Why would I be protecting her?"

"I know more than you think I do. And I know that you're in danger from messing with that family. You've probably gotten in over your head without even realizing it. And it wouldn't surprise me to discover that, even though you were innocent at the beginning of all this, you're not so innocent now."

I wondered if Smockley belonged in DAVIDSON'S HELL. If I had known him when I was writing it, maybe I would have put a version of him in with other overly persistent punishables, like aggressive salesmen and fund raisers. "Am I free to leave?" I asked.

"Yes, you can go. But keep on your toes." He almost sounded as if he cared.

Chapter 55

As I sat in my car, I considered my next set of options—go back to my office, go home, swing by Breda's house, drop in on Sturgeon, or drive around the county all night. I realized that my life had become a series of options. Do only people in trouble consider options? Does a normal life provide its own flow so that a course of action simply falls into place? Does a person sitting down at the dinner table at home with his family ponder choices—to dig first into the mashed potatoes or rather the meatloaf; to take a drink of tea before eating a bite of salad or after? Or does it all happen naturally?

I seriously considered driving to Sturgeon's house, but I really did not want to put him and Kim into danger. After all, whoever was out there could follow me to the Sturgeons' and take me out, as well as them.

I was afraid to go home, but I was also curious about who or what might be there.

Curiosity—tempered with caution—won out, and I headed home, resolved to make a reconnaissance drive-by only.

As I approached my house, I saw a figure walking in the dark, a figure that soon became two—a person and a dog. Of course, it was Mrs. Purdey and Johnson! I rolled down my window and pulled up beside the two.

"Mrs. Purdey, how are you?"

"Oh, Mr. Davidson, you startled me. I thought you were that person that was snooping around outside your house earlier."

"Excuse me?"

"Yes, about an hour ago."

"What did he look like? Was he a kid?"

"He was average height, sort of rounded. It was hard to really tell how old he was, but he walked sort of clumsily."

Her description made me think of Bwanger. Whom did I know that looked like Bwanger? "Couldn't you see his face?" I asked.

"No, he was wearing one of those hooded jackets that hid his face. Plus, it was getting near dark."

A hooded jacket would definitely rule out Bwanger. He'd show up in a three-piece suit. "What did he do?"

"Well, first he stood on your front porch and peeked in your window. Then he went around the side of your house. Of course I couldn't see him then, your house blocking my view and all. But then in a minute, he came back around to the front and looked in one more time. Then he left."

"What was he driving?" I asked, even though I recalled her previous lack of detail when I asked about a white car.

"I don't know. He walked on up the road. I didn't see a car, and I didn't see him again. Do you know what he wanted?"

"Probably just wanted to sell me something."

"This late in the evening?"

"Yeah, some salesmen are really persistent."

"Do you think he was trying to sell you some paint?"

"Paint? I seriously doubt it. What makes you think that?"

"You said that night when Johnson and I came in that you were going to paint the inside of your house, and I was thinking maybe that person's visit might have something to do with the job."

"Oh, the paint! No, I haven't had time to pursue that lately. He must have come by for some other reason."

"I see. Well, it was nice talking with you. I better walk Johnson for a few more minutes."

I was tempted to invite her and the dog back in while I checked the house, but I opted for Plan B—to enter the house while the two of them were still in the street out front. I gunned the Subaru into my driveway, narrowly missing them and rushed to my front door, which I opened immediately. I turned on the living room lights and then checked through the house, discovering nothing unusual. As soon as my search was completed, I locked the front door and set the ice bucket against it. Then I set the pizza pan against the back door. Finally, I picked up my home phone and dialed a number that I had neglected for way too long. It was Laura's in California. I figured she wouldn't answer.

I was wrong. The best voice in the universe came over the line. "This is Laura."

"Hi, you probably don't remember me, but I used to . . . ."

"Tyler, is that really you?"

"Yes, such as I am."

"I've been hoping you would call."

"You have? Why?"

"I don't know exactly, but I've been thinking a lot about you. I wanted to call you, but was afraid you wouldn't want to talk with me, after the way I've acted. I'm sorry about a lot of crap, but I needed time to prove a few things to myself, particularly about my intellectual abilities."

"I understand, and I want to . . . . "

"I want to see you too." *She could read my mind.* "Lately, I've been getting some weird vibes about you. Tell me, are you all right?"

"As well as could be expected, not getting to see you or even talk with you, and then there's the matter of finding three people dead."

"What? Say that again."

"I've missed seeing you and talking with you."

"I've missed you too. But back up and tell me about the dead people."

Over the next thirty minutes, I told her about Disner, Crawford, William, and Bwanger, but not about Breda. *Would anybody?* After reacting to my news about the murders and cautioning me about being careful, she told me about her work, the comfort she got from playing with Clovis, how much she thought about me, and how she kept expecting me to make a surprise visit to see her.

When we had finished talking, with the door left open for us to meet in the near future, I headed to the kitchen. Fear, coupled with exhilaration from talking with Laura, had made me famished.

I was working my way through a turkey sandwich, reassessing the day's events, when the phone rang. Figuring it was Laura calling me back, I picked up immediately. "Hi, I was hoping you would call back."

No one spoke on the other end.

"Laura?"

Still no voice.

"William, is that you?"

No answer. After listening to nothing for several seconds, I hung up. Silence on the other end of the phone line is the worst kind of negative space. It made me lose my appetite, mainly because I had the feeling someone was checking to see if I was home.

I was just putting the uneaten half of my sandwich in the refrigerator when the phone rang again. This time when I answered it, I demanded, "Who is this?"

"Tyler, it's Breda."

"Did you just call?"

"I tried, but your line was busy, but listen, I need your help."

"Breda, I don't want to sound rude, but I've got problems of my own right now. I just discovered Glenn Glick dead in the parking lot near my building, and I'm just a tad nervous."

"I know about Glenn, but I can't worry about him right now. My problem concerns William. The police have been here looking for him. They claim that he's mixed up in his father's death, though they didn't make it completely clear how. They did mention Hugh's letters. I have no idea where he is right now. Can you meet me somewhere?

"What for?"

"I want to give the letters back to you. I don't want the police to find them here, particularly if William is connected to them."

"Why don't you just destroy them?" I didn't dare reveal at this late date the fact that they were only copies.

"I just don't feel right about doing that. They probably contain proof of who murdered Hugh. But over and beyond all that, I really have to see you. I need you."

Damn, I wish she hadn't said that. It meant that, despite my conversation with Laura, I would have to go. I owed Breda that much.

"Where and when."

Meet me in fifteen minutes at the turn off where you park for jogging on River Road."

"How about your kids?"

"My neighbor's here. She'll take care of them."

"All right, I'll be there, and, Breda, please don't bring a gun. They make me nervous."

"Don't worry. That's not my style."

Chapter 56

I was surprised that Breda had beaten me to our meeting point, but there her van sat, the motor running, the lights off. I pulled in behind her. I wondered why she didn't get out to greet me as I approached the driver-side door. After I tapped on the window, she rolled it down. She sat rigidly with both hands on the steering wheel, staring straight ahead.

"Breda, what's going on? Why'd you want to meet out here? Did William ever show up?"

"There . . . are . . . some . . . issues . . . we . . . need . . . to . . . discuss," she said in a wooden voice with no inflections. I wondered if there were a body-snatching seed pod in the back of the van.

If there were, it was one that spoke.

"I'm one of those issues, Professor." It was the voice of William Disner. When I leaned in to look, I discovered that he was snug up behind Breda, holding a knife to the side of her neck.

"Tyler, I'm sorry, he suddenly showed up from out of nowhere and . . . ."

"Shut up, Mother!" William screamed. "And you," meaning me, "get in the other side of the van."

Now, with no knife jammed against MY neck, it would have been easy for me to simply run back to my car and leave the Disners to work out their own domestic squabbles. But the same power that compelled me to lie to Smockley about the letters led me to walk around and get in the van.

"William, where did you go back at the gym?" I asked in as jovial a tone as I could muster. "I was counting on you to get my car."

"Nice try, Professor. You knew that I'd run into that detective. You wanted me to get trapped, didn't you? DIDN'T YOU?" People who rapidly repeat a question have always disturbed me.

"Calm down, William. I simply didn't want to run into that particular detective—and by the way his name is Smockley."

"Please tell me, no, tell us all, why that was."

Were there other people in the van besides William, Breda, and me? I myself rarely use the word "all" for an audience of two, but I answered him. "He seems to think I might be involved in one or more murders, starting with your father's."

"That's really funny isn't it? I'm the one that wanted him dead. And now I want you dead, and my mother too." He shifted forward so that he could hold the knife on the front of Breda's throat.

"Why, William, why would you want the three of us dead?" I asked, weighing my chances of grabbing his arm and knife before he could slash Breda's throat.

"Let's start with my dear old dad. He was screwing some twit."

"And that was enough to merit getting killed?" I asked.

"Yes, of course. Don't you understand how much pain he was causing Mother?"

"Yes, and that must have bothered you a lot. So why do you have a knife to her throat?"

"Because of you, you asshole!" His voice could have doubled for an air raid siren.

"Me, how do you figure that?"

"She slept with you. She slept with you!" Double answers are as scary as double questions, in my book.

I kept hoping Breda would chime in, but I figured the edge of a knife muted her conversing capabilities. "What makes you think that?"

"Don't treat me like a child. I was there. I was there! I followed her, and I could hear the two of you during the night."

I was tempted to reprove him about beginning too many clauses with "I," but the timing seemed wrong. "All right, then. Was that so terrible that it would lead to murder?"

"Yes! Yes! Yes!"

"Tell me why."

"Because you took her away from ME! I'm the oldest son! I wanted to be the one to comfort her." I could see how Gravel Road Brad would fit into this scheme, but I was perplexed about Glick. *My god, I hoped Breda hadn't slept with Glick!*

Regretting that I hadn't boned up more on OEDIPUS REX, I tried to reason with him. "I'm sure that if you took away that knife, she'd tell you that you were her comfort. She told me as much. At least let her speak."

"She's a slut. She's a slut! I don't want to hear what she has to say."

"But don't you see, William, that she was hurt by what your father did. You said so yourself. It doesn't make sense to hurt her even more."

Breda made a gurgling noise that caused me to think William had actually cut her. However, it must have been just a reaction to pressure on her esophagus, but it was also enough of a prompt to make William relax for a couple of seconds—long enough for me to grab his arm and force it upward, such that the blade drove into the ceiling liner and his hand slid up onto the cutting edge, causing him to drop the knife altogether. I tried to put a headlock on him, but I was in an awkward position, sitting in the front passenger seat with him being behind Breda. He spun away, opened the sliding side door and was out before I could stop him. I started to give chase, but figured I needed to check on Breda first. Besides, if Smockley couldn't catch him, I doubted if I could—though it would have been nice to gloat to Smockley that I had.

"Breda, are you hurt?" I asked.

"No, he didn't cut me. I'll be fine."

"I'm going to call Smockley. He needs to know about this."

"Please don't."

"Are you kidding? William just had a knife at your throat."

"He's still my son. He was just trying to get my attention."

"I'd say he was doing a pretty good job of it—three murders."

"Oh come on, Tyler. All of those victims were shot. If William were the killer, wouldn't he have held a gun on us?"

"You've got a good point, but I'm not going to rest particularly well knowing he's loose, gun or no gun."

"He's most likely heading to either the house or to a secret place he always went to when he was younger and afraid of Hugh punishing him. I'm pretty sure I can find him."

"How did he get out here?" I had visions of him hitching a ride under the van, *a la* Robert DeNiro in CAPE FEAR.

"He had his car, even when you were at the gym. He followed me out here and parked back a ways so I couldn't see him. He's probably there by now."

"I still think we need to call Smockley."

"All right, but not just yet. Give me a chance to find him before you talk to the detective."

"But you're putting yourself in all kinds of danger. I should go with you."

"I don't think so. He's just a bit confused right now, so it probably would be best if you didn't show up with me. I insist, as a matter of fact." *Why is that when certain people say "I insist" (for example, when offering to pick up the tab at dinner), they don't sound convincing at all, while others sound as if they absolutely mean it. Breda was one of the latter.*

"Let's compromise. I'll give you some extra time—maybe thirty minutes—and then I'm finding Smockley."

"All right. I'll go along with that. And, Tyler, there's one more thing. I'm thinking that much of William's problem is my seeing you, not just tonight, but before too. Maybe we should cool it for a while. I can see that I'm going to have to spend a lot of time with him. I hope you understand."

"I do." *Could she possibly know what relief I was feeling at that moment?*

"In the meantime, take these letters. I don't care what you do with them now."

She drove away, leaving me to idle away the lead time I had promised her. I spent some of the time rereading the letters. The rest of my time I spent thinking about Laura.

And I was thankful that I hadn't died in an ugly van.

Chapter 57

After the requisite thirty minutes, I tried dialing Smockley on my cell phone, but all I got was a message, "Service not available." *Why now?* I had included people who stayed on their cell phones in DAVIDSON'S HELL, describing their punishment as being trapped between giant, megawatt speakers that broadcast continual conversations involving personal ailments and favorite ball teams. Now I wished I had included the manufacturers of the cell phones.

I figured by the time I would be in range for a call, I could drive to the parking lot where Smockley was likely to be finishing up his investigation of Glick's murder, so I sped off.

When I arrived there, I was disappointed to find that Smockley was gone, along with the rest of the police force. The only remaining item from the murder scene was Glick's white Buick, or at least what I took, looking from the side, to be his Buick. It was in a different location. I pulled up next to it and got out to look inside. Of course, there was no body. Instead there was a hooded jacket lying on the seat with a cell phone resting on it and a briefcase that looked like the one Bwanger carried. I had just stepped back to ponder the anomaly when I heard the unmistakable voice of Bwanger. "Tyler, why are looking in my car?"

"Oh, Dr. Bwanger, I thought this was Glenn Glick's car. I found him dead in it just a while ago."

"Yes, I heard. What an awful thing to happen, particularly so soon after those other tragedies. But this happens to be my car, though it's exactly like Glenn's, except for the decals and such that he has on his. In fact, we bought them from the same dealer at the same time. The dealer, which, by the way, was Cloffers Buick/Pontiac over in Raysville, gave us a better deal by our buying two at once. I think the police took Glenn's car away."

Now why did he supply all that extra info? "Yes, I understand, but have you seen Detective Smockley? I need to report some information to him."

"I guess he took off. I overheard him say something about going to find Hugh Disner's oldest son. What was it you needed to tell him?"

"Oh, just a few details about the case."

"What did you see when you found Glenn dead?'

"The usual—a slumped body, some blood, a hole where there shouldn't have been one."

"Did you happen to see anyone near Glenn's car before you found him dead?"

"No, I had just come out of the building and was on my way to my own car when I came on the scene."

"Had you seen Glenn earlier, up in the building, talked to him?"

"Why do you ask?"

"I just thought maybe he gave some clue to what happened to him, or what was going to happen to him."

I figured the less I talked about Glick, the better. "Well, I don't know anything other than I found him dead."

"Poor Tyler. You've really had it rough lately, haven't you, what with all the dead people you keep discovering."

"Well, I'm hoping this will all come to an end soon. Which reminds me, I need to call Detective Smockley." I pulled out my cell phone and tried to dial his number. Again I got the message "Service Not Available."

"Damn this phone. I can't get through," I said.

"Can't you use the one in your office?" Bwanger asked. "I'd loan you my cell phone, if I had it with me."

Strange, wasn't that a cell phone I just saw in his car? "Uh, no, I'm a bit apprehensive about going to my office right now."

"Well, then, come with me to my office and use mine."

I wasn't exactly eager to go into the building at all, but at least I would have someone with me. Bwanger could be my new Mrs. Purdey and Johnson. "That might work."

"Let's go. We can take the elevator."

The whole time we were riding up, Bwanger stared at me, a slight smile on his face. I believed that he was relishing the role as a protective father, helping one of his departmental sons in a moment of crisis.

After exiting the elevator, we walked to his office, where he unlocked the door and showed me to the phone. I started to dial Smockley, but hesitated. "Er, Dr. Bwanger, maybe it would be best if I talk to the detective privately. I'm not sure if he would want me to broadcast any of the details I need to relate to him."

"I understand perfectly. Take your time. I need to get something from my car anyway."

I didn't want to be critical of Bwanger at a time like this, with him letting me use his phone and all, but his cloying was almost more than I could take. I was glad he was out of sight for a few moments.

Smockley answered on the second ring. "Mr. Davidson, where have you been? I've been concerned for your safety."

"You need to get out to Disners' house. William pulled a knife on his mother and me. His mother is convinced that he hasn't killed anybody, but I still think he's dangerous."

"I'm there as we speak, and we've already got William in custody. Where are you right now? I hope for your sake you aren't in your office."

"Don't worry. I'm not there. I'm in Dr. Bwanger's office. He let me use his . . . ."

"You're WHERE?"

"Dr. Bwanger's office. You know, my department . . . ."

"Is he in the room with you right now?"

"No, he went to his car for something and . . . ."

"Professor, get out of there right now! Bwanger is the one we're after now."

"Out of here? Dr. Bwanger? But why?"

"Don't ask questions. Just do as I say, NOW! I'll be there as fast as I can."

What the hell. Why is Smockley after Bwanger?

Chapter 58

I figured I better do as Smockley said—fast—but I wasn't too keen on boarding the elevator nor on entering the staircase. Jumping out the window didn't seem like much of an option either.

I scrambled to the office door and was just heading for the seeming lesser-of-three evils, the staircase, when Bwanger suddenly appeared right in front of me. It took a couple of seconds to recognize him. He was now wearing a hooded jacket, the top pulled up over his head, but I could still see his mouth, which was twisted into a sneer. Most importantly, he was pointing a gun at me, a .38.

"Going somewhere, Tyler?"

"Dr. Bwanger, what are you doing?"

"I'm continuing a crime spree; can't you tell? Now get back into my office!"

I backed through the door I had just run out of. "Does this mean you're the one who killed Glick tonight and . . . ."

"Yes, and Hugh Disner and that stupid clod Crawford and now you." He pulled the hood back so I could see his whole head. *I was totally unprepared for Bwanger to appear as the malificum ex machina.*

"But why?" I knew that this was the standard question the victim always asked just before getting a hole in his head, but I had to ask it anyway. Besides, knowing how verbose Bwanger was, I figured he'd actually explain it all to me, buying me some time.

"You're so smart. Couldn't you figure it out? After all, you're the son of the famous Dr. Walter Davidson, whose reputation helped secure you a job here." He punctuated his remarks by jabbing my chest with the barrel of the gun. I wondered if he was acquainted with the guy in Atlanta at my book signing.

"What did you have against Disner? Was it the fact that he was made assistant dean? Surely that wouldn't have mattered to you. You're the department head."

"Don't you see? Assistant dean is one step away from being THE dean. I tried to get them [and by 'them' I assumed he meant the selection committee] to make me both assistant dean and department head, but they wouldn't go for it. Instead, they made that fool Disner assistant dean."

"So these murders all started over titles?"

"That's not the only reason I wanted him dead."

"Don't tell me. You lusted after his wife!"

"No, you idiot!" *Did he just put me into a class with Disner? I was offended.* "He was having an affair with Deidre Glick." He waved the gun in the air as if were flying a model airplane.

"And you were morally outraged by that?"

"Yes! Of course! And as chairman of the English Department, I had a responsibility to keep things tidy. How would I ever advance in the University if I commanded an infected ship? It behooved me to ferret out the diseases. Disner was a cancer."

Behooved? Ferret? Killers aren't supposed to use words like that.

"I get the idea that you were particularly disturbed by the fact that it was Deidre Glick that Disner was spreading his disease to."

"Yes, I watched her transform from a sweet and beautiful young girl into an alluring queen." *Alluring? That's a word I don't often hear.* "I loved her, and I wanted what was best for her. I wanted to take her under my wing and provide for her."

I got the feeling he had wanted to take her under more than just his wing, whatever that was.

"How did you find out she was having an affair with Hugh?"

"Glenn could hear them in Hugh's office, making gross, grunting, sexual sounds, and he notified me. He didn't know it was his own daughter. We would listen together in Glenn's office to those disgusting noises. I didn't know who the girl in there was either until one day I took the master key to Hugh's office after I saw him leave. On his desk was a letter from her and a photograph she had given Hugh. I eventually had to tell Glenn. It almost broke his heart."

I bet it didn't hurt as much as a bullet in the head. "So you killed Disner because he was . . . ."

270

"Because he spoiled one of the few beautiful flowers I've ever known." *At least he didn't use the word "deflowered."* "And on two or three occasions when I was listening outside his door with her in there, I could hear them joking about me. She even told him that I had made a pass or two at her."

"I can certainly understand your antipathy toward Disner. What about Glick? Why'd you have to kill him?"

"It wouldn't have taken him too much longer to figure out my role in Hugh's death. And tonight, he raided Hugh's office. I came up to visit him in his own office, to feel him out about his suspicions, and I heard him next door."

"How'd you know it was Glick in there?"

"He couldn't be quiet. Turns out he was stealing the letters Deidre had written Disner, the ones you yourself stole and then replaced. Your returning them helped me more than you know. I could hear Glenn reading some out loud and moaning about the contents. I went outside and waited near his car for him. He finally showed up with a folder full of the letters. When I confronted him about them, he claimed he was going to destroy them. I couldn't let him do that. They're too valuable."

"Why's that?"

"They give someone other than me a motive for killing Disner, someone who would be jealous or revengeful."

"So where are the letters now?"

"I put them back in Disner's office."

"Where, if I might ask?"

"Why, right in the top of the file drawers, so that detective can find them."

I didn't bother to explain to Bwanger that Smockley had already searched those files and would know that someone had tampered with them. I hoped like hell that Bwanger had left his fingerprints on them. "That leaves Crawford. Why him?"

"He was an indirect participant in the sordid affair. He rented his house to Disner so the two lovers could shack up there. Knowing what Disner was doing behind Breda's back made him bold enough to come on to Breda. I couldn't allow that to continue."

"Did you have feelings for Breda, too?"

"Enough that I didn't want some lowlife like Crawford to have her. And even though Crawford wasn't a member of the English Department, his actions helped besmirch its integrity. He simply had to go."

271

"All of which brings us to me. Why do you feel it necessary to kill me?"

"Because you've meddled in things from the beginning. You've discovered all three bodies of the people I had to kill; you're chummy with that Detective Smockley; and now you know all the details about me."

"You realize of course that Smockley knows about you. I just talked to him on your phone."

"You're lying just to save yourself. He couldn't possibly know about me."

"He's on the way here right now."

"He won't get here in time to save you, and even when he does arrive, he won't be able to connect me to your murder. He'll still be looking for someone who wears a hooded jacket. I made sure that people saw me come in with it on, only they couldn't see my face. One of the perks of being as conservative as I appear to be is that no one would picture me in that kind of jacket. If the police question me, I'll tell them I let you use my phone and then I left after you rushed out. Now move!"

He fanned the gun back and forth and stepped aside, motioning for me to walk down the hall.

"Where are we going?"

"To the men's room on your floor."

Dear God, not the men's room. "Why there?"

"Let's just say I like the metaphor of cleaning up the Department, flushing away undesirable waste. It would be fitting for you to die in the same spot as Disner. Take the staircase, if you would, please."

Where were all those damned music majors who usually lay about on the floor of the hall and staircases?

After we climbed the stairs, I entered the men's room, calculating a plan to turn on Bwanger. All my fantasies about disarming my assailant with a karate chop did not translate into reality easily—particularly when a .38 was involved.

"Get in the third stall," he commanded in a voice that carried more authority than I had heard before.

Where were all the students who frequented the men's room? I wouldn't even care if they didn't flush.

I opened the stall door and stepped in, but I kept my hand on the top of the door. "What now, TORRANCE?"

"Why don't you loosen your trousers and sit down? I'd like for you to be in Disner's predicament."

Where was the clean-up crew? Where was Doris? I turned to look at the toilet and then faced Bwanger again. "Well, give me a bit of space then."

He stepped back so that his body was fully outside the stall with his arm and gun just inside the door line. Now was my only chance. I pulled the door closed as hard as I could while spinning to the side of the stall, hoping I would be out of the line of fire.

I almost achieved what I wanted as the gun went off. The good news was that the gun fell to the floor, clattering on the tile, accompanied by a scream from Bwanger. The bad news was that I had a searing pain in my left side. I had been shot!

But I was still conscious and Bwanger's hand was trapped between the door and the jamb, flipping in all directions like a fish on a dock. My next move was to swing the door outward with as much force as I could exert, catching Bwanger in the face, knocking him backward against the far wall. I reached down to grab the gun, but it was gone. It must have been knocked into the next stall.

My only recourse was to get the hell out of there, but Bwanger had other ideas. As I rushed out of the stall, he tackled me and then crawled on top of me. I wasn't surprised by his bulk, but I was amazed by his agility. *Wouldn't it be ironic if he had been a college wrestler.*

We struggled for several seconds, both of us pawing and groping for an advantageous handhold. Somehow, we worked our way up to our feet, whereupon he encircled my torso with his arms and began squeezing, simultaneously hoisting me off the floor and then jamming me down, as if he were trying to knock me off balance—or test my resilience. I felt like a golf ball in a vertical washer, being sloshed up and down through the cleaning bristles.

I remembered similar tussles I had as a child, when it was unfair to do more than simply pin the opponent. *What the hell, this isn't a child's game. This asshole is trying to kill me.* I jammed my fingers in his eyes, causing him to release me and claw at his face.

In the second or two that he did this, I headed toward the exit door. Out of range of Bwanger, I looked back at him, just to make sure he wasn't about to tackle me. He was scurrying to the second stall where the gun rested on the tiles. I took one brief moment trying to decide if I should go for the gun or go for the exit. I opted for the exit, figuring I could outrun him down the main staircase.

I was wrong.

Two or three strides outside the men's room demonstrated I wouldn't be able to negotiate a staircase with any speed at all. The wound in my side was creating a strange lethargy. I felt I was running in soft sand at the beach. I could picture myself tripping on the top step and tumbling to the first landing, lying there as Bwanger stood over me and then popped me between the eyes. My only chance was to make it to my office, and that chance depended in large measure on Bwanger's hesitating once he came out of the men's room, unsure which direction I had run.

I took off down the hall as fast as my wounded body would allow, making it to the first corner before Bwanger exited the men's room. As I turned the last corner near by office, I frantically searched in my pocket for my keys, finding them just as I reached my door. I fumbled momentarily trying to insert the right key, recalling childhood nightmares (and scenes in lots of horror movies) in which one has to open a door before the boogieman catches up to him. I could hear Bwanger's pounding steps as he ran down the long hall.

There! I had the door open. I shut it just as Bwanger rounded the corner. I felt elated, as if I had just defeated the former county champ in a hundred-yard dash.

But my victory celebration was short lived. I could hear something being inserted in the door. Bwanger had a master key!

I grabbed the locking mechanism in the center of the door handle with my thumb and index finger. It became a contest of strength—Bwanger and his key versus my two fingers. This went on for almost a minute, but then suddenly there was no strain on the mechanism, as if he had quit. I held on in case it was just a ploy. *Where the hell was Smockley?*

Without warning, a shot exploded from outside my office and a hole appeared right beside my hand. The bullet must have passed through, even though the door was metal, and then hit a pile of exams sitting on a chair. There was a brief flutter as papers rained to the floor. If the moment hadn't been so critical, I might have smiled at the excuse Bwanger had just afforded me for delaying grading them. "Sorry students, but several of your tests had a bullet hole in them, and I'll need an extra week to finish them."

I jerked my hand away from the handle, but immediately I could hear the key turning in the lock. Again I grabbed the center locking tab and held on as Bwanger tried to rotate it.

This time the shot came while we were still wrestling with the lock. And this time the bullet grazed the top of my hand, causing me to flinch away. The bullet must have lodged in the wall, since no more papers rained down.

I reached for the door handle with my other hand, but it was too late. The door was opening.

Bwanger stood framed in the doorway, pointing the gun at me. The hood on his jacket was still pulled down so I could clearly see his fat face. "Nice try, Tyler. But the game's over. Time to join the other diseases."

From the bell tower, I could hear the first notes of Berlioz's "Dies Irae," this time NOT in a dream.

Bwanger stepped in and aimed the gun at my forehead. I instinctively raised my unwounded hand as if I could ward off the bullet. At least my office was a more dignified place to die in than the toilet or an ugly van.

"I wouldn't do that, Professor!" At first I thought Bwanger had said it, wanting a clear shot into my brain.

But the voice wasn't Bwanger's. It came again. "Put the gun down and step back from Professor Davidson!"

It was Smockley's voice. And for the second time it sounded good to me. Bwanger hesitated before doing as Smockley commanded, but then Smockley spoke again. "PUT THE GUN DOWN!" There was so much intensity in Smockley's voice that I myself mimed putting down a weapon, though of course I didn't have one.

This time Bwanger did as he was told, carefully laying the gun on the floor as if it were a fragile antique. He suddenly looked as old and feckless as I had always envisioned him.

"Cuff him and take him to the car," Smockley ordered to two men I had not even noticed until that moment.

After they had left, Smockley called for the Emergency Medical team. While we waited for them in my office, he asked me if I would answer some questions. I said, "Could we do this somewhere else?"

He answered, "Would you prefer the men's room?" *Who would have ever guessed Smockley had a sense of humor?*

Chapter 59

The next afternoon, after spending the night in the hospital, where I had received stitches and dressing for the wounds on my hand and side, I sat in Smockley's office, relaxing for the first time in weeks, realizing I would be able to sleep in my own house that night without leaning a pizza pan or an ice bucket against my doors and arming myself with a pineapple or a statue of Shakespeare.

"Would you like a cigarette?" he now asked, as he tilted back in his chair, appearing far more casual than he had ever with me before.

"I don't smoke, but if I did, this would the best time imaginable to light one up," I said.

"Better than right after having sex with Breda Disner?"

"Careful, Detective."

"Just joking, Professor. I can see the attraction."

"Well, I believe the attraction is going to have to stay in neutral for awhile. She told me she was going to need more time with William."

"Too bad. I think you two would make a cute couple. But I can understand her concern. What are you going to do to fill the void, write more professional articles, assign more papers, or the like?"

"No, as a matter of fact I think I'm going to make a surprise visit to a friend in California, get away from here for a few days, maybe avoid answering a lot of questions in my department." *And avoid hearing that damn bell tower.* "And when I get back, I think I'm going to get a dog."

"A pet takes a lot of attention. I know because I have a cat."

"You do? What's its name?"

"Pitty Sing."

"But, that's the name of a cat in a story by . . . ."

"Flannery O'Connor. I know."

My God. He's read one of my favorite authors. "Well, I'm willing to expend a bit of effort, and besides, if I ever need a pet sitter, I have a neighbor who would probably help out."

"Sounds like a plan to me. Now, are there any questions you want to ask me?"

"Yes, how did you figure out it was Bwanger?"

"I've got to thank William Disner for that."

"How so?"

"After we picked him up—and he didn't put up any resistance, due to his mother's being there—we asked him lots of questions. He was quite cooperative. Among other things he told us that he had suspected his father of having an affair early on. Seems that he showed up at his father's office and heard some telling and disturbing noises coming from inside."

"He's not the only one, but I'll tell you about that later. Go on."

"Anyway, he started hanging around the building and one day followed his father out to Crawford's place. He was on his bike, but he could keep up with his father, who was driving a car. Seems that Disner drove pretty slowly."

"I can attest to that."

"He saw his father go in the house, and he waited until Disner and Glick's daughter came out later. The way they parted company confirmed what William had heard inside the office. He somehow managed to get a duplicate made of Disner's office key and foraged around when Disner wasn't there until he discovered a couple of letters from Deidre Glick that were fairly explicit about what was going on, but you know that already, don't you, having read most or all of them."

"How'd you know that?"

"I've known about the letters from the day after the murder. I found them in the top desk drawer. Disner wasn't too careful about hiding them."

"But I found them in the HARVARD CLASSICS."

"Of course, I put them there."

"You? But they were filed so carefully. You'd have to know the contents of those pieces of literature!"

"Do you think it's possible I'm not an illiterate rube?"

How many ways had I misjudged him? I felt like a dope. "Of course it is, but you have to admit that you led me on. I bet you were even familiar with HMS PINAFORE the day Disner was murdered, when you made me sing some of it."

"Yep, it's one of my favorites. Like I said back then, you sang it well."

"Thanks a lot. But why did you put the letters in the CLASSICS?"

"I had to make it appear possible that I hadn't discovered them previously. I needed to find out who was interested in finding them. Like I said before, you have an unusual talent for making yourself look guilty."

"Speaking of being guilty, remind me to give you the photocopies I made of them. They're in my car."

"I know. I figured you had them the night you rode the elevator down with Glick. I expected you to give them to me a lot sooner than tonight."

"Sorry. But tell me more about how William fits into all this."

"The letters drove him into a rage."

"Why?"

"Because he's a true mama's boy. I think he wanted to be an only child. He was jealous of his siblings, and he was protective of his mother."

"Yes, I gathered as much."

"In William's mind it wasn't so much that Disner was hurting his wife as much as he was hurting William's mother. He wanted to kill his father for what he had done."

"Did he make any comments about Crawford?"

"Yes, he thought his mother was interested in him. Given time, he might have taken out Crawford because of jealousy."

"And taken me too. At least that's what he indicated in the van while holding a knife to his mother's throat. This all sounds as if you're making a good case for William's being the killer."

"He might have been if Bwanger hadn't gotten there first. You probably were in as much danger from William as you were from Bwanger. As it stands, William is a disturbed minor. Bwanger's a responsible killer."

I felt as if I were listening to the psychiatrist at the end of PSYCHO explaining the twisted mind of Norman Bates. "But I still don't see how you made the connection to Bwanger."

"William mentioned that on several occasions he went out to Crawford's house on his bike or in his car and hid waiting to see if his father might show up. He mentioned that a white Buick cruised back and forth in front of the house, driven by a hooded figure. I assumed it was Glick, checking up on his daughter. I asked William if he had noticed the license plate, and he said he had. He remembered it because it had the same numbers as Hank Aaron's homerun total, 755. I immediately called my nighttime contact at the DMV and found out that Glick's license is . . . ."

"I know, it's a vanity plate with NGUGLICK on it."

"Then I remembered that Bwanger had a Buick similar to Glick's, so I checked on his number and guess what was on it?"

"Hank Aaron's 755?"

"Yep. That surprised me, but I first rationalized that Bwanger might have heard about Disner's affair and was on some kind of moral patrol."

"Actually, that's not far from the truth."

"Anyway, William said that during one of his surveillances at Crawford's, he also discovered that someone else in his family came visiting there, his mother. In fact, the evening that you found Crawford dead, William was out there. His mother wasn't home, so he suspected she might be out seeing Crawford. He drove out there and parked down the road, then hid in the bushes. He never saw his mother, but he did see you come and go. But before that, he saw the Hank Aaron Buick pull up and a hooded figure get out, go in the house, and then coming running out. When I heard that piece of information, I immediately moved Bwanger to the top of the list of suspects. Right after I found out all this, you called from Bwanger's office. That's why I told you to get out."

"I'm glad William is a baseball fan, and I'm glad you made it in time."

"Me too."

Chapter 60

As Smockley made some final entries in his notebook, I thought about what I still needed to do. I should let Sturgeon know about the adventures that night. And I would have to give Doris a gift to change the perception she must surely have of me, flowers maybe, anything other than new vacuum bags. And I probably could take something over to the Purdey household, maybe a pizza for her and her husband and a dog bone—or the remains of the squirrel—for Johnson.

But all these tasks could wait until later in the day. What I wanted to do as soon as possible was book a flight. I probably could milk the fact that I was wounded to get a week off from classes. Who was going to object? Bwanger? Disner? I doubted it, unless they could speak from their graves. Popson might raise a fuss, if he actually kept up with faculty minutiae, something I also doubted.

Smockley stood up. "I guess you're free to go. I think I have all the pieces fitting together." He still looked like the cartoon Dick Tracy, but he sounded like Warren Beatty's screen version.

"Thank you for all your help. I really didn't want to die in my office, any more than I wanted to die in the men's room."

"I can imagine. At any rate, I'm sorry that it turned out to be your boss."

"Well, to tell you the truth, I'm glad it was Bwanger instead of William. Killing three people might have messed up the kid's life—at least until he got old enough to start dating girls seriously." I paused while Smockley laughed. "Besides, I wasn't exactly fond of Bwanger."

"Me neither, if we're on a kick to reveal our secrets. He always acted as if he were morally better than everyone else. Catching him with a gun in his hand about to shoot you certainly destroyed that pretension and made my job easier. If he hadn't wanted so much to take you out, he would've been harder to nail. Got any ideas why he'd risk blowing his cover to get you?"

"I think it was because I didn't live up to the reputation of Walter Davidson."

"Who?"

"My father. Plus, he wasn't too keen on the woman I dated in my first couple of years here—well before Breda Disner entered the picture. She's the one in California. It all adds up to a long story. Remind me to tell it to you some time, over a beer maybe."

"Sounds good to me. Maybe we can also discuss Flannery."

"Yeah, I'd like to hear what you have to say."

"And, Tyler, good luck in California."

"Thanks, John. I'll let you know how it goes."

About the Author

Joseph Meigs was born in Atlanta, Georgia, and raised in Berkeley, California, and Jacksonville, Florida. He holds a B.A (1964) in English with minors in chemistry and biology, having attended the University of Florida on a basketball scholarship. He received his PhD in English there in 1970 and went on to teach literature and film studies at Western Carolina University until retiring in 2005. He has been a photographer and watercolor painter for approximately thirty years, currently serving as the resident artist for the Jackson County (North Carolina) Arts Association. He is the author of the novel TENURE TRACK (published in 2002). He enjoys skiing, golf, and restoring Datsun 240Z's.